Also by Victoria Wilder

The Bourbon Boys
Bourbon & Lies
Bourbon & Secrets
Bourbon & Proof

BOURBON & PROOF

VICTORIA WILDER

Bloom books

Copyright © 2025, 2026 by Victoria Wilder
Cover and internal design © 2026 by Sourcebooks
Cover art © Whiskey Ginger Studios
Cover design © Echo Grayce at Wildheart Graphics

Sourcebooks, Bloom Books, and the colophon are
registered trademarks of Sourcebooks.

All rights reserved. No part of this book may be reproduced in any form or by
any electronic or mechanical means including information storage and retrieval
systems—except in the case of brief quotations embodied in critical articles
or reviews—without permission in writing from its publisher, Sourcebooks.

No part of this book may be used or reproduced in any manner for the
purpose of training artificial intelligence technologies or systems.

The characters and events portrayed in this book are fictitious
or are used fictitiously. Any similarity to real persons, living or
dead, is purely coincidental and not intended by the author.

All brand names and product names used in this book are trademarks,
registered trademarks, or trade names of their respective holders.
Sourcebooks is not associated with any product or vendor in this book.

Published by Bloom Books, an imprint of Sourcebooks
1935 Brookdale RD, Naperville, IL 60563-2773
(630) 961-3900
sourcebooks.com

Originally self-published in 2025 by Victoria Wilder.

Cataloging-in-Publication data is on file with the Library of Congress.

Printed and bound in the United States of America.
LSC 10 9 8 7 6 5 4 3 2 1

This is for the women who put on a brave face. The ones who stand taller, shove those shoulders back, and smile, even when you would rather roundhouse kick all the bullshit in the face and then cry over it.

There's something beautiful about embracing that balance. Lean into the strength and the softness, being the hero and the rescued, the reader and the main character.

And I think you deserve a little extra for being so fabulously fierce AND such a good girl.

Daddy Foxx is waiting…

A note about *Bourbon & Proof*

While this story is a work of fiction, there are some heavy subject matters that you should be aware of before diving in.

The following is a list of potential triggers that are not meant to be spoilers or tropes, but rather a warning of what's inside if you need it:

Violence and death on page, descriptive gore, violence toward women, discussion of deceased parents and family, scenes inside of a hospital, "daddy" kink, vulgar language, spit-play, use of sex toys, D/s play, and multiple descriptive open-door sex scenes.

Playlist

The Rules of Bourbon

Every bourbon is whiskey, but not every whiskey is bourbon. There are rules for bourbon to be called bourbon.

1. It must be made in the United States
2. The mash must be at least 51% corn
3. It must be aged for at least two years in a new, charred, oak barrel
4. The whiskey cannot enter the barrel higher than 125 proof
5. Nothing can be added but water, and only to lessen the proof when necessary

In Fiasco, Kentucky, there's one more rule that loosely relates to the bourbon that's made there: **Never fall for a Foxx brother.**

Chapter 1

Ace

THE SCREEN DOOR SLAMS SHUT behind me as I drag my fingers through my hair slicked in sweat and river water. Unbuttoning my shirt, I toss it into the trash. I can burn it later. The caked dirt and blood along the collar and cuffs are hard to see on a black shirt, but they won't go unnoticed at the dry cleaners. I wear a suit to the distillery every day, but killing someone is few and far between. If it had been planned, I would have changed and called in the necessary support. I don't fucking like surprises.

All I have going in my favor is that it's the Fourth of July, and in Fiasco, that's the perfect time for someone to disappear. Everyone is in town celebrating and enjoying the distractions of dancing and fireworks. I prefer to avoid both. And truthfully, tonight, that worked out for the best.

I pull on a pair of Wranglers I typically wear to the stables and tuck my wallet in my back pocket. Not wanting to go upstairs, I dig out a pair of socks from the dryer. My black undershirt is still damp, but I need to get out of here. Right now, I want to disappear for a while, take one of the horses out for a long ride, and clear my head.

"Where are you goin'?" Griz asks when I turn the corner into the kitchen.

Swallowing down my frustration, I pour a heavy-handed splash of bourbon into the first glass I see sitting on the counter, ignoring the question that I don't have an answer to.

"Things get out of hand?" he presses as he gives me a once-over. I'm good at masking emotions, but I just put a man down, and I'm still pissed about it.

I drain what's left in my glass. "Why aren't you in town?" As I pull on my boots, I add under my breath, "Usually can't drag you off that stage."

"Atticus," he says in a more biting tone, eyeing the way I'm trying to get the hell out of here. "Not gonna ask for the details…"

He never does. My grandfather knows there are things that need to be handled sometimes, and asking questions only makes those things linger when they'd be better off forgotten.

When I still don't respond, then push out of the screen door, his voice carries through it. "Find something that'll ground you, Atticus. If it's those horses or a woman, I don't care. But the only way I'll stop hovering is if you can figure out a way to balance all of this without letting it consume you. You'll only be able to do it if you have something more—something to care about."

I love him, but sometimes I could do without him telling me what's best. I've taken on enough of the family legacy. I like the ease of being on my own, caring for the family I already have, and getting lost in the details of making good bourbon. He just needs to let me do life my own way.

Picking up my pace, I move past the garage and toward the stables. I grab a saddle, pads, bit, bridle, and reins to suit up my fastest horse. An old black stallion that's pretty as hell, but he's an asshole of a horse when he's not running, and he's always trying to bite me. I don't care. He's fast. And that's all I want. To feel the wind on my face and my heart pounding so loud the beat drowns out everything else.

The sticky air hits my skin, and I tilt my head up toward the purple-tinted sky—a storm's coming. When the road bends and forks, I slow down and realize something's off. It should smell like damp earth and the sugared air that Fiasco inherits from our distillery, but instead, exhaust and burning rubber have my instincts flaring. *Fuck this day.* Every part of me urges me to ignore it and keep riding. There are no headlights in sight, but as I move to the left of the fork, I hear music. An angry anthem jacked up loudly but muffled through speakers. Pulling on the reins to bring my stallion to a stop, I squint to make sure I'm seeing what I think I am. The outline of a classic muscle car. It's too dark to be sure, but I have a gut feeling that it's a 1969 Ford Mustang. And it's idling too close to the riverbank for my liking. There shouldn't be any cars this far out, not to mention perched along a muddy edge on the side of the river that's running angrier from the heavy rainfall this summer.

Nearly blinding me, headlights flip on, the music cresting louder and clearer as the driver's door swings open. A riff of an electric guitar and aggressive bass has my horse stepping back, just as AC/DC screams out about being back in black.

What the hell is she doing out here?

I try to see if there's someone in the passenger seat. Maybe she was fucking around with someone. It isn't uncommon for people to park on the trails. But the dim interior light only proves that there isn't anyone else in the car.

"What are you doing out here?" I shout over the music, trying to keep the horse at a distance, but despite pulling the reins, he moves us closer.

She mumbles something to herself and looks up at the night sky. "Playing with myself," she yells back sarcastically. And then follows it with a raspy and unconvincing, "I'm fine."

I know she isn't fine. She wouldn't have said that if she truly was.

My horse skirts to the side of the car to be out of the glare of the headlights, allowing me to see her better. It's dark outside, but the reflection of the dashboard light catches her just right. I give her a once-over. She isn't drunk; she's smarter than that to drive out here wasted. That isn't it. But the way her dark, wild curls are messier than usual, how her tank top hangs too loose around the neckline, and smears of blood color her eyebrow and collarbone have me down and off the horse before I even notice her feet. No shoes.

It's like an alarm has been set off.

Bloodshot eyes find mine as I rush toward her. She holds her hands up, warding me back from touching her or coming any closer. My gut sinks at thinking about what the fuck happened. Who would have done something to make her hands shake and voice sound like she's been screaming.

"Where are they?" The words come out gruffer than I want, but it's taking a helluva lot of willpower to tamp down my rage.

Her blue eyes snap to mine, knowing what I'm asking. *You're not dealing with this on your own.* I've witnessed Hadley Finch in a lot of moods over the years—pissed off, playful, prim and proper—but not shaken or on edge like this. This is panic and anger, and those two things never go well together.

It's clear someone was pawing at her and got rough. As much as I've found her annoyingly optimistic, gradually appealing in the past handful of years, and slightly unhinged beneath her surface, she's as close to family as one can get without having our last name. Hurting her will never be acceptable or even remotely tolerated. This isn't going to end well for anyone involved.

Blinking back tears, she lifts her chin. "I took care of it. Knocked him out with a cinderblock." *Good girl.* Her face breaks for just a moment, squinting to cry, but she composes herself almost as fast. "I don't know… He may be more than knocked out."

I stay quiet, studying how she's working really fucking hard to keep it together. When she finally meets my eyes, I tilt my head to the side and say, "Don't make me ask again, Hadley. Tell me where."

She exhales, swallowing roughly. "The stables. At my father's stables."

A part of me wants to hold her and tell her I'll fix this, but it's clear she doesn't want a hand anywhere near her. *Fuck.* "Do you need to see a doctor?" I bite out.

Tears finally fall as her eyebrows knit together, but she shakes her head. "Didn't get that far," she mumbles.

I can feel my adrenaline spiking as I watch her let out another trembling breath. This will *not* happen again. Clenching my fist, I twitch my jaw at the thought of her being hurt in a place where she should be safe. Without another word, I'm striding back to my horse and turning us back the way we came.

"Where are you going? Ace, I don't need you—"

"Don't finish that sentence, Hadley. You go to the main house, and you stay there, shower, do what you need to do. But do not come looking for me. I'll come find you."

She slams her foot against the side of her car. "I've had enough of men telling me what to do tonight!" she seethes through gritted teeth. Eyes watering and fists clenched, she shoots daggers my way.

I've always told myself that I tolerate her in my life because she loves my brother the same way I do—without an ulterior motive. Just because. I've never needed to ask Griz what he thought of her; he considered her one of us the first time she smiled as she destroyed him in a chess game. It's a long list of moments that would be categorized as mundane and unimportant, but they mean something to my family—to me. Hurting her isn't going to go unpunished.

"Then I'm asking," I say back in a calmer tone. I mount my horse and wait for her to acknowledge what I've asked.

She's so goddamn stubborn that she stares at me, battling with herself. Her chin wobbles and watery eyes start spilling again, but she doesn't say anything. On an exhale, she simply nods.

I ride fast, head down, and pray that nobody sees me. I don't slow until I reach the stables at Finch Stables, passing her father's estate on the way. I ignore the logic that keeps ringing through me to stay out of it. To call my brother Grant instead and have him come out with a patrol car. But I'm not going to be satisfied until my knuckles are bloody from giving someone a reason to never touch her again. It's a part of me that's been cracking for a long time: morals that linger on the edge of acceptable, sanity that's been waning—hell, even a twinge of sadism teetering along my skin. I'm expecting to find a douchebag knocked out or, at the worst, nursing a bruised ego and maybe a broken dick, but instead, I find a man smiling with a handkerchief pressed against his lip.

"Who the fuck are you?" he asks with a careless glance.

Shit. This isn't just any fucking guy who works for Wheeler. The youngest Switcher brother is a real son of a bitch. Coming from one of the largest cattle ranch families in the West that tends to have money and pull, means this isn't going to be a simple fix. This can't be the last place he's been before he goes missing. Rumor is, his father's on death's doorstep. Switcher's set up to take over the business, and if I had to guess, that's what led him to Fiasco in the first place. A calculating Wheeler Finch. A man who makes deals with shitty people as long as it pads pockets or gains him some kind of clout.

I move my right hand to my belt buckle. I'm not going to bust open my hand on this one. My knuckles are already bruised from earlier. Glancing around him, I can't see a holster of any kind, so he's not carrying, but I wouldn't put it past him if he has some kind of weapon nearby. He's a cattle rancher, and they're rarely unarmed.

He takes me in, smirking as he stands. "You're Ace Foxx."

"And you're in some trouble," I toss back.

"How's that?" His eyes narrow as he sizes me up.

"You put your hands on someone who doesn't belong to you," I say, walking closer as my blood heats. I wrap my belt around my fist and, without stopping, throw two quick jabs to his nose before he even knows what's coming. The second one cracks and busts open the bridge on contact.

One hand flies to the streaming blood, and the other moves to his back, pulling out a small pocketknife. *Pathetic.* "You're misinformed. She very much belongs to me—just made a nice little deal for her."

Her fucking father. I knock his wrist with my fist, and the knife goes flying. As I rush forward this time, my forearm meets the front of his neck just as his back hits the wooden pillar in the center of the space. "We don't put our hands on women here unless they ask."

His voice comes out strained as he seethes, "This ain't your business."

The fuck it isn't. Any other night and this might be different, but my nerves are already shot. And seeing her like that... I swallow the smart choices and good sense and instead give in to the anger that's climbing. As I throw my weight against him, he yells out the second the metal pierces his skin. The nails that had been protruding from the center wood beam are there to hang reins and rope, but right now, they dig into this piece of shit. They hold him up perfectly, like a partner in a fight, and I rear back for a left hook to make sure he feels it. Three more, and the weight of his body is too much for the rusted nails nestled deep into his skin. His body hits the cement and hay with a nauseating thud. Blood slowly pools around the crown of his head like he hit something hard and sharp the moment he hit the floor. *That was too easy.* I would have preferred a little more of a fight with this fucker.

Chest heaving, I focus on the blood and hair caked along the protruding nails. My throat burns as I try to calm myself.

I pull out my phone and fire off a text like I've done countless times before when I need an assist.

ACE:
Need to schedule a cleaning.

The bubbles beneath the text pulse immediately.

THE JEWELER:
A specific piece?

I drop a pin with my location.

ACE:
Full set. Brand new.

THE JEWELER:
Timeline?

ACE:
By sunrise. Between us only. I'll owe you a favor.

THE JEWELER:
My favorite form of payment.

It's just past midnight, but my colleague will work fast. I know the travel distance and exactly what needs to be done to erase this.

I don't check for a pulse. If he isn't dead yet, he will be shortly. There's too much blood for it to coagulate and clot. One of those nails nicked an artery, pulsing red out in time with his heartbeat that looks like it's already slowing.

Fuck him for dying so quickly.

I send another text to make sure all loose ends will be tied up if worse comes to worst with witnesses.

ACE:
I'm going to need a list of everyone who was at this house tonight.

I pin the address to the Finch estate.

THE ARCHITECT:
> Easy enough. Any trash to sort?

ACE:
> Already handled.

As I glance at his slumped-over body, the silver glint of an obnoxious, oversize belt buckle catches my eye. I bend down, flip it open, and take it off him in one quick pull. He doesn't look like any kind of bull or bronc rider. His lanky body barely looks like he's worked a day at the ranch, never mind riding pissed-off animals for a living.

I step outside, needing to breathe and think through the kind of repercussions this might bring my way. The ripple effect of someone's life coming to an end. Someone who has people who'll look for him. It isn't regret I'm feeling, but rather the weight of inconvenience. I have people for this. But tonight turned into a clusterfuck I wasn't prepared for.

Small flashes of lightning illuminate my surroundings, but not a single light shines anywhere amongst the property. The trainers, farrier, and whoever else Finch employs are in their housing on the far side of the property, likely sleeping or still out for the night. I'm pissed that not a soul was here to help Hadley when she needed it. Lincoln mentioned she had her father's obligatory Independence Day dinner party, and yet nobody's here.

Just as I pocket my phone, I take a step out onto the dirt road and glance down the main drag, catching on the lights still on at Finch's estate. I shouldn't provoke this situation, but there's a part of me that knows, even with Switcher dead, this won't be the end of Wheeler Finch pimping his daughter out to the highest bidder. The thought of her being used as a bargaining piece makes my stomach sour.

Bourbon is in my blood—how to make it, age it, sell it, drink it. A Foxx knows bourbon better than anything else. An art form and business that began in backyards and basements. It survived being outlawed, oversold, and under delivered. The point is, it survived. It came back stronger. Better. For just about anyone, it should have been enough. Luck and hard work aren't the forces that allow our brand to succeed. It's that we're willing to color outside of the lines that built its longevity. There's more to being a Foxx that lingers under the surface. Gray lines and moral compasses that never really pointed due north. Hadley lives among the gray as Wheeler Finch's daughter. The most important difference is that my family doesn't use each other. We support, fight for, and protect each other. No matter the cost. Hadley's been treated as if she's an expendable commodity. And that makes me want to hurt someone.

The businessman persona is levelheaded and strategic. But I have a wicked temper if provoked. And I am fucking provoked.

I turn over the silver buckle in my hands as my cleaner pulls up and gives me a nod. He takes in the situation in front of him and starts to process what will wipe this clean.

"Ace, does that need to disappear?" he asks, looking at what I'm holding.

I give my friend a tight-lipped smile. "Probably." But I'm walking away before I can think any better of it. I ignore the last bit of cleanup that needs to happen in order to erase James Switcher's existence from ever being in this stable.

"You look like you're about to make a bad choice, Foxx," Julian calls out.

I ignore him. He knows me as well as, if not better than,

my brothers sometimes. My brother Lincoln had an inkling, but not the level at which I'm willing to cross lines. And right now, I'm fueled by more than anger or even adrenaline—it's the need to protect someone who means something to my family. To me. Too many people would ignore this and chalk it up to it somehow being Hadley's fault—saying the wrong thing, wearing the wrong thing, being in the wrong place at the wrong time. No fucking way is this going to be a preamble to what lies ahead for her. It'll be easier to plant this mess on Hadley's father, to create a situation that looks like he killed a man in cold blood, but even more than that, I want his daughter out of his business dealings. There has never been a chance for Griz to step in and demand it, but now there's enough here to threaten him.

Most homes are left unlocked in this part of Kentucky. It's a bad habit and one that I imagine Wheeler won't make again. I throw open the front door, not caring that my entry is loud and aggressive. Quiet threats aren't in my repertoire. At least not tonight.

"Isn't this an interestin' turn of events," Wheeler Finch says in his low Kentucky drawl.

I stop at the threshold between the foyer and the study as he sits at his too-large desk and puffs on a cigar in a pair of blue plaid pajamas.

He looks me over. "Maybe I should call the Fiasco PD and see what they think of you just walkin' into my home at this time of night."

"They might start asking other questions if you do that." I pause, tossing the heavy silver buckle on his desk. "Like why a wealthy cattle rancher would come here for dinner but never leave? Or how there would be his blood or DNA found on your clothing or property? Or why your daughter looks like she's been roughed up and god knows what the fuck else."

He hums to himself, puffing away on his cigar. His lack of a reaction is enough of an answer for me. I know Hadley doesn't love spending time with her father, but now I understand that, at the core of it, he doesn't care about much other than himself.

"You realize she's not one of your horses? That you can't just groom her and sell her to the highest bidder?" I let the disgust of it escape in my tone, and he hears it. That's my mistake.

Wheeler tilts his head to the side, looking too curious for my liking. "You realize she's not *yours* either?"

I bite down, holding back from giving him any more of a reason to elaborate on that. My fingers curl into my palms as I clench my fists at my sides.

He's right, and I fucking *hate* it. She isn't mine. She doesn't belong to my family in any way other than us wanting her around. My jaw tightens to the point that I can feel the muscles straining along my neck. I know the games Wheeler Finch plays because I'm familiar with the board. I make up the same rules, pick the same players. Wheeler Finch takes vulnerabilities and wields them. And so do I. But it's the goal that's different.

"What was the payout?" I ask, trying to erase any emotion in my voice.

His eyebrow quirks higher. "You know the influence that comes with a name like Switcher. Beyond that, it was an investment in my newest trainers and business partners, the King brothers—"

I cut him off. "How much?"

Looking down at my boots first, he pauses before he says, "A breeding facility. Padding of the coffers." He laughs to himself. "And it would have been a nice opportunity for some good grass-fed, free-range beef always in my freezer."

When I don't say anything, he searches my face, and it's

clear he knows why I asked. He sits back in his chair, sizing me up before adding more. "And a share of Switcher Cattle."

There it is.

He clears his throat, picking up the silver buckle. "It would have been a significant quarterly payout for siring a prize like my Hadley."

I have to hold in the rumble forming in my chest. I want to fucking deck him for that statement.

Wheeler's from Kentucky. Born and raised in Fiasco. He knows Foxx Bourbon. He's made plenty of plays over the years to invest and carve out his own piece, but neither Griz nor I would ever allow it. He came at us for the land that we kept buying. All of it, from our farmhouse to what's butted up against his property line. He's tried to find ways to partner Foxx Bourbon with his horse business for years.

"There is nothing that I'll ever want enough to work with that man," Griz said to me not long after my brothers and I went to live with him. *"You'd be smart to keep away from anything he touches."* It's never made sense why his daughter is the exception.

Standing from his desk, he stalks toward me as if he's in charge of this conversation. A tactic that takes practice, but I'm good at allowing people to believe they have leverage over me.

"But..." He tilts his head to the side, releasing a sigh. "There will be others." He eyes the silver buckle and smiles. "I'm rather exceptional at my job, Ace. Racing and training can be learned and hired out, but reading people, understanding the stakes, and knowing the odds is always what sets apart luck from strategy."

The truth in that has me swallowing my brimming annoyance. I cross my arms as unease takes over my senses, not liking where he's going with this.

"I wouldn't put all my money on one pony. There are plenty of others who would be an excellent match for my daughter—*and* my business. Hadley knows what's expected of her. She understands her role in this family. The same way she spends my money on whatever her frivolous heart desires. I don't question her lack of motivation or income. And whatever it is she's doing with that brother of yours."

I grit my teeth and hold back from yelling in his face that they're fucking friends. I hate the insinuation that there's more between them. People have been making that assumption for a few years now.

"I love Hadley. But not how the gossips in this town would want," Lincoln said after she'd fallen asleep in his room. Griz looked at me to push him on it, but I know my brother. If he wanted Hadley Finch in any way beyond friendship, I would know. He likes to roll up his sleeves and throw punches, but he's the softest one of us. If he cared about her in that way, it wouldn't have been a secret for long. He's shit at keeping those.

I keep listening, letting Wheeler carry on his bullshit justification for treating his daughter with so much disrespect it disgusts me. "She doesn't question my stipulations. My daughter is groomed to be loyal," he finishes. *That isn't the woman I know, or maybe I just don't want that for her.*

The moment I walked into this house, I knew I was going to regret it. There was no strategy in coming here, only an emotional reaction. But I'm not going to allow a night like tonight to happen again.

"She'll make her own choice. Who she marries, what she does with her life," I tell him.

His chin tips up. "Why?" he asks.

The logical part of me knows this is an unnecessary risk and that I should stay out of his family affairs. But he doesn't know that she's become more our family than his.

"I wonder…" he starts to say, just as a realization of some kind washes over his face, leaving a weaselly smile in its wake. "Am I wrong about which Foxx my baby girl is fucking then?" His eyes light up, as if he just discovered something. "She's been playing you all." He tuts. "That's my girl."

"Watch your mouth," I bite back, pointing my finger at him. Hadley isn't *his* girl. *That* much I know. She's held on to her father out of loyalty, or too many years of abuse, but she spends so much time at my family's home because she can breathe there.

Like he can read my mind, his smirk wipes clean from his face, and in its stead, the ruthless businessman streaked in greed rears forward. He knows I wouldn't have barged in here unless I had planned to do to him what I'd done to Switcher. Or to make a deal. While killing him sounds enticing, a deal between devils has more guarantees.

Wheeler rubs his thumb over the gaudy silver buckle when he asks, "What are you offering, Foxx? It's a steep request."

It will be the only deal I ever make with him.

I casually cross my arms over my chest. "I don't make requests." He'll see this as a Queen's Gambit—sacrificing his pawn to gain control. But to me, it's the only way. And she isn't a piece to be played. "A deal for a demand."

The asshole tilts his head. "I'm listening."

10 Years Later...

Chapter 2

Hadley

I sneak a glance at the clock—6:40 a.m. I still have thirty minutes. The dark blond between my thighs licks me a little too far to the right, humming as if he's delighted with his work. I stare at the wooden beams that splinter sporadically above me. *I'm not into this.* The moan that rattles and lingers in his throat is all wrong. The tone off. It almost sounds like a repeating chorus. Cringing, I squeeze my eyes shut. This was impulsive because I wanted a distraction, which has been the case for many nights lately. I texted him for an early morning orgasm, but it's becoming awkwardly clear that isn't happening. As I look over his broad shoulders, his hair color is a little too light to apply a particular fantasy I like to imagine. The one that could make me orgasm the fastest—within minutes, usually.

A small vibration thrums on my nightstand. And as much as it's an asshole move, I slowly flip over my phone to read the awaiting text. I shouldn't have looked.

Hawk's eyes bulge wide when he sees what's in my hand, and he moves up quickly to a kneeling position. "You're hurting my ego a bit here, Hadley, if you're texting someone right now," he says, even-tempered, rubbing his hand across his bare shoulder.

I close one eye and try to ease being caught out. Giving him a flirty smile, I tell him the truth. "I'm stressed out about the weekend. It isn't you."

He tries to play hurt or annoyed, but a small smile quirks his lips. "This type of thing is supposed to be fun. Ease your stress, not add to it."

He's right. So what am I doing? I sit up, dropping my phone on the bed and pulling my legs away from him, knees toward my chest. "My mind got away from me, and then I didn't want to fake it."

As he stands from the bed, his charming expression peeks out just as he pulls his navy-blue T-shirt back on. When it covers his broad chest, *Fiasco* in bold white letters reminds me of where we are, the letters *FD* just below it. This started as easy and fun. I never planned for much beyond that. I didn't want more. Still don't. It's one of the more mature things that happened in my thirties—recognizing sex for what it is and what it isn't.

"Do I need to call for some backup?" he asks, caging his arms around me.

I scrunch my nose. "I don't think that's it, handsome."

Having a threesome with the fire chief and the new recruit was initially a joke. I said it out loud, and like some kind of sexual manifestation, it happened. In no way, shape, or form am I complaining. Sex is never anything more than fun for me—a natural need. An exchange between two people, and in that case, three. It's the best kind of distraction. But like most of the things that've been good in my life, it's run its course. This time, probably for longer than it should have.

I flirt with a lot of people, and I've known Nicholas Hawkins for years. He's older, which is like catnip for me. And he's a bit of a hero, running into fire-filled buildings and rescuing people. Fiasco gossips had a field day over the young fire chief when he'd been officially appointed to his role just under a decade ago. Hawk's brother kept being re-elected as governor, which meant he was usually invited to events and parties that my father threw over the years. One hot afternoon, he got fed up with me pushing the bell on my roof deck that connected to the fire station, and I suggested that we fuck around and find out.

The way that stunned him felt good. I needed to shift my attention to something attainable. And then, by some miracle from the goddesses, he and another intensely attractive fireman were taking turns making me orgasm after a fire alarm malfunctioned at Midnight Proof.

And I got greedy. And a little selfish. The chaos of the past year had me barely sleeping, even with the late-night hours from Midnight Proof. Calling Hawk has been an easy distraction.

My phone buzzes again, and I glance at the name on the screen and the curt message below it. One of the reasons why a distraction was necessary.

DADDY FOXX:
The best man's speech is mine.

Hawk laces up his boot and says, "How about we pick this up later tonight?"

I focus on typing back my message and mumble, "Okay."

> **HADLEY:**
> I'm the best friend. It's mine.

> **DADDY FOXX:**
> I'm not doing this with you.

> **HADLEY:**
> You're going to have to be more specific. "THIS" can mean a lot of things.

> **DADDY FOXX:**
> Stop it.

> **HADLEY:**
> Make me.

If anyone were to ask me, I don't believe in the stupidity of love at first sight. That's a patriarchal practice that allows women to accept that attraction can be mistaken for love. Love should take time. Learning and longing. Maybe even a pinch of sacrifice and discovery. Or maybe my jaded perspective only exists because of my lack of experience on the subject matter. *Lust* and *like* are L-words I understand. *Fucking* and *fantasy* are F-words that deliver. I believe in fantasy at first glance and lust at first sight. And both of those, for me, come in the form of my best friend's brother. The six-foot-something pissed-off bourbon boy. His pretentious suits and rugged boots. His intensely dark brown hair laced with gray and silver that seeps into his sideburns and along each temple. A strong brow and gray-blue eyes that never look wistful or light, only stoic and layered with too much responsibility, strategy, and perhaps a bit of danger. Broad shoulders, an arrogant nature, and all the vibes of a man who does whatever the fuck he wants. Atticus Foxx, the ultimate fantasy. And because some days I think that karma must really have it out for me, he just keeps getting better with age.

In the background of texting said fantasy, Hawk cuts in. "You know what? I forgot I'm on an overnight shift tonight."

I bite at my thumb and smile at the reality in front of me. "How convenient. That's just across the street."

It was annoying at first, the fire station being directly across from my townhouse. This old three-level building that has been home for a while now. At first, the station bell and the engines were a bit of a nightmare considering I worked late hours. But when I discovered the bell that connected my roof deck to the fire station, it became a perk.

He clears his throat and kneels back onto the bed, moving closer. "I wasn't going to say anything, but…I'm good enough for some night games, but not to go with you to the wedding?"

Oomph. I give him a tight-lipped smile. "Night games are more fun than a wedding."

Nodding, he shoots me a look of understanding, but I can sense some hurt there.

I let out a breath and overthink why I wouldn't just bring him to my best friend's wedding. It's easy to picture him in a tux, but a part of me doesn't want to make this more than what it was meant to be. "Can we just keep things where they are right now?" Biting my lip, I look around the room.

"And what happens when I want more?" he asks as he buckles his belt.

"Then we call it." There's no sense in beating around the

bush. Maybe it's time to call it. That isn't the kind of question I expected from someone wanting simply to fuck around.

He crooks his finger for me to come closer, and I scoot myself toward the end of the bed. As I look at him, he tilts my chin up. He has a crooked smile and a little scar cutting through where his lip bows; it's something I've always found attractive. Mysterious and a charming imperfection. "You're too much fun to say no to…"

"Then don't." I smile, but then I force myself to add, "But Hawk, if this is more for you, then we should stop. No sad feelings or bad blood, just a high five and some good memories, yeah?"

He gives me a tight smile and checks his phone. He's one of the good guys—even-tempered and never pushy. He's easy to be around. Maybe that's the appeal, especially lately. He leans into having fun despite being in charge of a full station of guys and is responsible for multiple towns across Montgomery County. And even though he's folded into similar circles that I had been born into, he never kisses my father's ass or looks for handouts from his brother. That's his brother's play, not his.

My phone buzzes in my hand again, only this time, it keeps buzzing. There aren't more texts from my best friend's older brother. Instead, a new unknown number displays across my screen. My throat dries and my heart rate kicks up enough that I feel slightly lightheaded. The anxiety is instant.

I rub along my wrist and pinch my eyes closed for a second. I've been blocking new numbers regularly. It started with media outlets wanting statements about my father's arrest. It's since graduated to people looking for what my father owes. Angry people who, in some way, have been slighted or mistreated and feel it's okay to come after me in the most passive-aggressive way possible—social media, emails, and then texts. Avoiding it is annoying but rather simple. No more online social platforms, email could be easily changed, and my phone number too. Until it's somehow found again. And the messages are becoming more specific.

I breathe in through my nose, purse my lips, and push the air back out. Doing that again, I slowly count to ten.

The name Wheeler Finch is no longer associated with Triple Crown winners, unmatched training, and wealth. Instead, it's tied to headlines that read: "Kentucky Horse Murderer," "The Largest Con in Horse Racing History," and my favorite, "The Devil of The Derby." He made millions of dollars for himself and his partners by fixing races, threatening and blackmailing trainers and jockeys, and drugging horses with performance enhancers and snake venom. I couldn't even wrap my head around some of those when I'd heard them. Then, as the sweetest cherry on top, the whole disaster of Finch & King Racing was left in my name while he faces a roster of charges. For me, it doesn't need to be proven in court; I know he did it all. And I hate him for it. I can't understand the fact that he's on house arrest pending trial. His waiting feels too much like a luxury—police guarding entrances on an expansive estate, an ankle monitor, and constant approval for outside communication. His assets, however, are under my control.

I've known my father isn't a good man for a long time. But even that is a gross understatement considering the charges awaiting him. It's been almost a year since he was arrested, and every day since, I've felt the aftershocks. Arresting the proverbial bad guy was only the beginning.

Nobody tells you what you're supposed to do when the life you've built starts to fray around the edges. Things that I've felt in my gut since I was young have been true all along. Being proven right comes at a cost, and it's a much higher currency than ideas and affirmations.

My mother's gone. And my father is the only family I have left. For most of my life, I've mistaken obligations for care. And I learned too late about love and its exchange rate. I stupidly allowed blood and loyalty to win out. And because of that, most of my hometown assumes I'm a loving daughter. But if anyone really paid attention, they would have seen how often I avoided being where I was expected. And now I get side-eyes and snarky comments since everyone's accepted the bullshit my father doled out. It disgusts me. And that disgust is the reminder I need for anger to replace my anxious thoughts.

I press the side button on my phone, pushing the call to voicemail.

Today's going to be a good day. A great one, even.

My black leather-bound notebook has my favorite pen tucked into the last page that I wrote on.

April: Late-night favors of the skin-and-licking kind right after having the most perfect combination of potato chips topped with charcuterie—brie, gouda, camembert, and prosciutto. Warmed for 5 min at 350 degrees. Salty perfection.

I turn the page and take a quick second to jot down a thought that would make a perfect end to tomorrow night's speech, just as an aggressive pounding on my front door has me looking up. Tossing the book aside, I slip on a fresh white tank.

"You expectin' company?" Hawk asks with a quick flick of

his eyes down my body as he starts moving toward the door. "I'm a little more decent than you are…"

"You sure about that, Chief?" I say in a flirty tone.

"Want me to answer it?" he asks with a smirk and a shake of his head.

There's another loud rap of knuckles on the door before he reaches it. I pluck out my newest pair of panties from the black-and-pink striped bag and yank off the tag, slipping into the bright pink silk slowly, being mindful of the delicate lace that encircles each leg and the waist. Glancing at the clock, I realize whatever extra time I thought I had is now long gone. *Shit.* The sunrise should have tipped me off; they always want to be on the river before dawn.

The heavy fists on the front door echo out again.

When the door swings open, I expect it to be my best friend, with his dark-rimmed glasses and goofy smile. He's more than ready to kick off his wedding weekend. But instead, it's an unapproving glare and deafeningly silent exchange from Ace. He leans against the doorway and crosses his arms, his face reprimanding me with an *I don't like waiting* look.

It's so much fun to push him whenever possible, mostly because nobody ever does, but this morning, I'm not even doing it on purpose.

I sarcastically smile at the man wearing slutty Wranglers instead of his typical suit. It's impossible to ignore how much I appreciate the build and stature of the man I'm *not* bedding and never have. Internally, the attraction bells are sounding off like race-day trumpets. Externally, I try my damndest to appear casual about the current situation: the man I'm hooking up with, the man I fantasize about during those hookups, and then me, who's in only a tank top and underwear. *Fuckity fuck.*

I clear my throat and then nonchalantly ask, "You boys have met before, right?"

Neither needs to answer, because they have. Plenty of times, just never like this.

Ace barely glances at Hawk, instead walking past a waiting handshake and into my apartment with an exasperated exhale.

"Not interested in your morning bullshit, Hadley. You're going to make us late."

I wave at the air in front of me as I hustle by him, looking for my favorite fishing hat. "Being late only matters for parties and periods, Atticus."

I hear him swear under his breath just before he says, "You have no pants on."

It's so satisfying that he noticed. Sucking in a gasping breath, I brush by him again, my hand slapping my chest. "Did you see my panties?!" I smirk as I walk past him. "Or was it a little lip slip?"

I saunter up to the waiting fire chief, who's witnessing the back-and-forth between Ace and me. He can read exactly why I haven't slowed. When I reach the threshold of the front door, I drape my arms around his neck and kiss his cheek.

He smiles against my neck and whispers, "You okay here if I leave?"

But instead of bristling at the innuendo, I lean into him, catching the campfire smell that always lingers on his skin as I say, "More than capable of taking care of myself, Chief. But thanks for asking."

He kisses along my shoulder, and if I was a betting woman, I'd be pretty confident that he looks right at Ace as he grabs a handful of my ass and squeezes me in his bear hug.

When I pull back, he looks over my shoulder briefly, and then back at me. "Stay out of trouble, Hadley."

"Unlikely," I hear Ace mumble from my kitchen, like the looming presence he is, as Hawk leaves me with one last quick kiss.

With Ace watching me move around my apartment searching for my lucky hat, it's hard not to add an extra sway to my hips. It is *his* attention I've always craved, after all.

"What are you looking for?" he asks as he, too, takes a look around my apartment. This place is filled with soft pinks and purples, and sleek, modern lines, and it's decorated with anything and everything I love. A bohemian vibe with a lot of bold colors and local artwork. My pink ostrich feather floor lamp doesn't give off much light, but it reminds me of old Hollywood. The same way the movie posters of *A League of Their Own*, *Mannequin*, and *The Money Pit* hang along the hallway leading into my living room. Favorites because I like them and not because some critics told me I should. I have no idea if any of the paintings or photography peppering the rest of my walls are worth anything. I didn't buy them for that reason. I simply like what I like. There's a black cat clock that's eyes swipe left and right on every tick and tock, pictures of my life scattered along the walls, and a closet that has far too many sports jerseys mixed with dresses and colorful accessories. It's cozy and maybe a little cluttered, but this space is all me.

"Ah! Found it," I say, holding it up like a prize.

But he simply glances at the clock, and then pours himself a glass of water. "Hawk coming this weekend?"

I search for my shoes that are meant to go with my dress for tonight and my tux for tomorrow. "He's on call!" I yell from my closet. It's not a complete lie, but I won't go into the flawed reasoning as to why I didn't invite him as my date.

When I come out with my rose gold pumps in one hand

and curling iron in the other, Ace looks at me with his brow furrowed.

Today, he's all bluegrass Kentucky. A horseman and not a bourbon boy. The Wranglers that hug his thick thighs are their own version of an assault weapon. His black T-shirt has the Foxx Bourbon logo stitched along the sleeve in black embroidery, making the gray that runs along the sides of his otherwise dark, almost black hair stand out a little more. I teased him often about being old, but the truth is, Ace Foxx is just like his bourbon: better with some age. And damn, do I drink him in every once in a while. *If only I literally could.*

"Where's your bag?" he asks, moving toward the door.

I lean back, peeking from the doorway of my bedroom. With a smile, I tease, "This your way of telling me you want to have a sleepover, Ace?"

He looks at me with narrowed eyes, stopping all movement. I *may* have pushed him too far with that one. His jaw is clenched, like he's holding back from saying something like, "Cut that shit out, Hadley." But instead, he stares at me, meeting my eyes first, and then looks up to my hair. The quiet that's settled around us is nothing short of uncomfortable now. Maybe he's not in the mood to dish it back today.

"My gear is in my trunk already," I say, lifting my chin toward the door. When he still doesn't say anything, my cheeks flush hot.

This is one of those times when something feels different. Like I'm not the only one wondering if the attraction and pull is mutual, if it would ever tip over between us. There are times when he looks at me like this, and I want to physically push him and scream, to beg him to tell me what the hell he wants.

"Ace—"

But he cuts me off. "I'll be downstairs. You have five minutes or I'm leaving."

I swallow the feeling of rejection, telling myself again to get over it when it comes to him, and then hustle to wash my face and brush my teeth.

When I waltz outside ten minutes later, sure enough, the asshole left without me.

"You must've really pissed him off today." The low Kentucky drawl of Griz Foxx rings out to my left. His thick white mustache matches his full head of hair, sideburns cut tight against his weathered skin. It isn't surprising that the Foxx brothers are so damn good looking. Not when they had genes like this. Most couldn't guess Griz's age; the man still moves, jokes, and drinks as if he's the same age as his oldest grandson.

"And it's not even seven a.m. yet," I say with a laugh as I walk closer. "Did he leave you here too?"

He nods. "Did his charming mood have anything to do with Chief Hawkins coming out your front door?" he asks, leaning against my car with his arms crossed over his chest.

I give him a kiss on the cheek as he takes my shoes and makeup bag from my hands. "Griz, I have no idea what you're talking about."

He gives me a *Yeah, right* lift of his eyebrows. "Said he'd meet us at the river. Figured he either had something happen at the distillery or you got under his skin again." He raises his hand, waving at Skip from the bait and tackle truck. Griz is never too busy to say hello to people. The two old timers exchange a few niceties about where the fish are biting lately, and then he and I make our way out to the river.

Griz smiles with his eyes closed as he casually leans back

into the plush leather seats of my 1969 Mustang. "Can I tell you something without you speeding up any higher?"

"That doesn't really feel like the start of a good conversation, Griz," I tell him with a chuckle.

"I'm going to say the thing that everyone says you're not supposed to say." He looks ahead at the familiar road leading to one of the few secret places still left in this town. "I thought I'd be dancing at your wedding long before I was ever going to dance again at one for Lincoln or Grant. I'm happy seeing them happy, don't get me wrong, but I thought you would have sorted things out by now."

My throat is suddenly dry. His disappointment at the fact that I'm not married hits my chest in a way I wouldn't have expected. Griz is the only person—well, maybe not the only person, but one of the most important—whose opinions matter to me. He's been the voice of reason for most of my adult life. The patriarch to a family I wanted to be a part of and who folded me in without batting an eye.

"Griz, you, of all people, should know that getting married is just an agreement to love someone. Feels like paperwork for promises that can be made without it. I don't know if I want to make a business deal out of my feelings." But even as I say it, I hate it. I've been leaning into this single and powerful persona for so long that it's started to feel like a lie. I hate that women are painted into these corners, that you have to be one versus the other. A part of me craves to prove it all wrong.

"That's not how I meant it, kiddo," he says more quietly as we pull down the dirt and gravel road. "I just thought that you—" He cuts himself off, making my eyebrows pinch. Redirecting the conversation, he says, "You are as much mine as the rest of my boys. Maybe not by blood, but by everything else that matters.

Loving someone isn't a weakness. You can be exactly the woman you are—strong, smart, sassy as all get-out—and still give in to it."

I glance over at him as he stares out the window at said boys, seemingly unfazed by the words that just affected me deeply. Lincoln's smiling and yelling something to Grant, who simply nods with a twitch of his lip. In the distance stands Ace. The oldest who always seems to be a little bit farther away than the rest—watchful and protective. I sit taller in my seat, pushing my shoulders back and readying to mask the affection I can't seem to shake for that man.

"Maybe I just haven't met the right person yet," I add with some attitude.

Griz lets out a soft grunt, like he heard the punch line to an unspoken joke. "Maybe so. But I see plenty of what goes on around here—more than most. Have for a long time."

The truth is, I want to be loved out loud. Choosing to marry a person is just about as loud as it got. That seems like something I could only witness, not participate in. I watched Lincoln find it with Faye. I witnessed Laney arrive as a stranger and pull Grant out of despair.

Love has transpired around me in intensely epic ways, which means I have to believe in it. I just stomped it out of my own reality. For years, my father ingrained in my mind that marriage for our family was a business deal. Then one day, he quit pushing it. I somehow earned the freedom to find it and chose myself instead of looking for happiness with anyone else. The world tells you to be kind, then to be selfish, then to share it with someone. To have mind-blowing sex, then to find your best friend. To depend on yourself, but to lean on others. Truthfully, it's exhausting—all the convoluted hypocritical messages that, in my mid-thirties, are altogether paralyzing.

"Griz," I exhale, giving him a lazy smile. "Life is complicated right now. I can't think about folding someone into my mess." It's an excuse, but a good one at that.

He nods to himself, knowing those words quite simply mean to back off.

I cut the engine and look out at the three Foxx brothers wading out in waist and thigh-high waters, casting their lines. From this angle, they all look like the boys I knew growing up. The bourbon boys who fueled gossip the same way these flies and feathers lured fish.

There's something poetic about watching them in the morning light. Affection for people who only cared to see the best in you can quickly turn a person into something entirely new. I would always be grateful to them for that.

Griz interrupts my reminiscing with a pat on my leg. "You practically raised yourself, Hadley Jean, but the little part I played in that, I never once told you it's okay to not go after what you want in this life. It's too damn short to sit here and watch."

As he stands out of the car, I hear Lincoln shout, "Griz, did you white-knuckle it the whole way over?"

Grant's next. "You're lucky there's not a patrol ticketing this early."

I flip him off just as my phone buzzes again.

"I drive like the goddesses intended!" I shout back to them both.

"How's that, Hadley? Like there are no rules?" Linc laughs.

I smile, pulling on my galoshes. "Fast, flawlessly, and instilling fear in overly confident men." I look out to the center of the river. "You too scared to hitch a ride this morning, Ace?"

He doesn't answer. His wide stance and strong arms move effortlessly, casting the way Griz taught all of us years ago.

I inhale the morning smells and brush off being ignored. "River's high today," I say to Griz.

He adjusts his hat, crossing his arms and looking out at the view. The side we're on is much calmer than the other. But today, they both look high and ready for a good showing.

"You know the routine." He nods toward where Ace is standing. "If it gets too rough or you lose your footing, find the center—the limestone plates that cut the river are shallow enough to keep you from moving to that far side and under. Find the center."

As I get into my flow of fly-fishing, laughing along with the boys, my phone buzzes, instantly sobering me all over again.

> UNKNOWN:
> Miss Finch, my patience is wearing thin. I expect payment and penance. Do not push me.

It's a new number but with a similar tone of threat. And there isn't a single thing I want to do about it. If people my father had worked with are looking for payouts, I'm not going to be the one to do it. Everything he was involved in makes me sick to my stomach.

Over the past year, I've been dodging one problem after the next. There were side-eyes and snarky comments simply for being my father's daughter. There've been plenty of threatening messages, property damage, letters, and social media canceling that came with it. Today isn't going to be the day to deal with the barrage of bullshit. Swallowing my nerves, I pocket my phone.

When I look up, Ace is watching me. The tendons in his neck flex and his jawline tightens, like he's pissed that I caught him looking. I give him a taunting smile and wiggle my fingers at him.

This weekend, my best friend in the entire world is marrying the love of his life, and despite the texts and nudging of marriage, or the brooding oldest Foxx brother, I'm ready to celebrate.

Chapter 3

Ace

IF YOU WANT TO DETERMINE the strength of a bourbon, most people look at its proof. The higher the proof, the higher the alcohol in that batch. It doesn't make it better; it just makes it stronger. But when it comes to business, especially in Fiasco, after the bullshit this town has had to deal with over the past year, stronger is better.

"Roughly nine billion dollars," I interrupt. I've had enough of the discussion. The last thing I wanted was to have this meeting this weekend, but time hasn't been on my side lately.

It's been just over a year since the headlines. A nightmare for a state whose reputation was tarnished by greed and strong-arming. It was almost catastrophic for the small town at the epicenter of it all. The head of the largest and most respected brand in horse racing, Finch & King, was charged with things from fixing races and illegal drug distribution and administration to animal endangerment, animal cruelty, grand larceny, and there's still an ongoing investigation into the deaths of a trainer and jockey. Wheeler Finch ran the business in Fiasco, which meant it hit us the hardest. The scandal has affected small businesses because of affiliation, media scrutiny, and public embarrassment. Midsize businesses impacted because of wrongfully invested funds and plain old theft. Kentucky horse racing as a whole took it the hardest—it shook all parts and we're still feeling the vibrating aftershocks. Cleaning it up meant there would need to be a lot of players, but each one has a purpose.

The governor and Fiasco's mayor both came out unscathed by all the chaos, which has made me more than curious as to how that's fucking possible. But as they look at me with surprise, realizing I said *billion*, I know I have their rapt attention. "That's right around three hundred forty million in taxes that the great state of Kentucky benefitted from the bourbon industry last year alone. Perhaps it's worth considering my suggestions."

"While that's very true, Ace, you're forgetting that the horse industry has the same kind of impact. And this past year has been nothing short of threatening to all of it," the governor says as he looks over my shoulder for a waitress. He won't find one. In fact, he's already managed to piss off Marla by calling her "ma'am" when we first walked in here. I wouldn't be surprised if she spit in his meatloaf.

He's a piss-poor excuse for a civil servant, but plenty of people get off on his rhetoric and appreciate that he goes to church every Sunday. Somehow genuflecting to an altar and talking about "the good ol' days" is enough to earn him more clout than the man deserves. It helps that he was born and raised in Kentucky—he's liberal enough and old school enough that most couldn't tell you which party he favors, only that he's been governor for coming up on twenty years. His family owns a pharmacy in the next county, his brother's the fire chief, which is rather convenient, and somehow, people like him. But his backbone is as sturdy as the licorice my sister-in-law is always gnawing on. And I don't trust him. I exhale my frustration, because their lack of planning and problem-solving are impacting small businesses in my town. Eventually, it'll impact my business—and my family.

"Ace," Marla says, coming up with a pot of coffee in one hand and a glass of bourbon in the other. "You wanted the chocolate soufflés for dessert. They'll take about twenty to set. Should I start that for you now?"

I smile at the way she only keeps eye contact with me. It's the reason I suggested an early dinner here instead of something private elsewhere. There's a cocktail party in place of a rehearsal dinner tonight for Linc and Faye, and there isn't a chance in hell I'm going to miss any part of it. But this meeting is necessary while the governor's in town. He needs the reminder that there are still a helluva lot of good things happening here, despite the media circus that's been so heavily focused on the horse racing scandal. I also need Foxx Bourbon to remain in his favor, and keeping him fed, happy, and feeling like my investments and proposals for growth are positively impacting him will do just that. Griz has always been clear exactly who should stay on a short list of "friends." The governor is right at the top of it.

"Might I trouble you for a coffee with the dessert?" he asks Marla.

But instead of answering him, she gives me a tight-lipped smile. *Ah, fuck, she's winding up for an insult.* It's a fifty-fifty shot when bringing out-of-towners to Hooch's if it'll show off the charm of Fiasco or, in this case, a pissed-off Southern woman who gives less than zero shits about ruffling feathers. His brother might be the fire chief, but the governor isn't a local.

"Are you up for a tasting tonight, Governor?" the mayor asks.

I turn my head slowly, watching the mayor offer something too comfortably that isn't his to offer.

"The distillery is closed for the evening," I cut in. "My brother, Lincoln, is getting married tomorrow." Looking at my watch, I rub along the leather band. "I'm hosting an evening tonight for him at my home."

The governor sits back in his chair and nods. "That's right. Griz mentioned when I saw him, asked if I'd like to stay for it."

Fucking Griz. It's a constant point of contention. It has been for more than two decades now. My grandfather refuses to take his foot off the pedal and allow me to drive. I stifle the twinge of disappointment I always feel when he steps in and on my toes. I'm long past being a kid or finding my footing.

I hum in response and allow my annoyance to play out as information I already know. "If I show up at the distillery with guests tonight, my sister-in-law, Laney, will tear off my head."

That makes them chuckle, and the discussion turns to the sheriff who just got married this past spring. It gives me a reprieve to fish out my phone.

ACE:
Is the private room open right now?

LUCIFER:
It can be... What are you giving me for it?

ACE:
Business. Is there any entertainment?

LUCIFER:

> I'm always entertaining, you should know that by now.

I mask the small smile that comment just pulled from me. Above all else, Hadley is certainly entertaining. There aren't many people that can change my mood as quickly as she's mastered.

LUCIFER:

> And I'm closing at 9 for your brother's bachelor thing that you're hosting, remember?

"What about you, Ace?" the governor asks, bringing his attention back to me. "Ever planning on getting married?"

It isn't a question many people outside of my family ever have the balls to ask me to my face. The answer is simple. But it's the reasons behind it that are multiple levels of complicated.

I keep my answer truthful and to the point, as usual. "No plans." I smile, even though the idea of being married isn't something I want—at all. My brothers felt that need, and when they met their people, they were eager to fulfill it. I don't feel the same. There isn't some mystery around it; I don't let much linger with women I fuck. It's better for everyone that way.

My pocket buzzes again, only this time when my eyes catch who it's from, I'm more than acutely aware that there are eyes on me beyond the men at the table.

The mayor holds up his hand like it's respectable to beckon someone over that way. Marla's going to get violent. But instead of a coffee carafe-wielding woman approaching, it's my brother's former partner at the police department, Delaney.

"Detective, how are you?" the mayor asks.

He nods, looking at each person at the table as his hand falls to my shoulder. "Very well. How are y'all doing this evening?"

Del and I have danced in plenty of the same circles over the years. Aside from being my brother's old partner and friend, he has a connection to many U.S. government agencies who have, in some way or another, passed through Fiasco. Often, Del keeps me in the loop with what's happening below the line here. A mutual respect for each other and the town we proudly call home.

"Del, I was just reading all about the new mess that Fiasco found itself tangled up in." The mayor looks at the governor, making sure he hears whatever the knucklehead is planning to say next. "It's been about ten years since a missing persons case was connected to Fiasco."

That particular missing person was *not* missing. "Ah," Governor Hawkins says over a mouthful of ground beef. "Hard to forget a big name like that just disappearing."

I try not to tense or react, knowing exactly what happened to James Switcher.

Del glances at me briefly before he says, "There are always missing persons cases that come across our desk. That particular one wasn't connected to anything here in Fiasco."

The governor glances my way before he says, "Plenty of negative press here to last a lifetime. Bodies and missing persons? I'd hate to see anything other than bourbon making Kentucky someplace to talk about."

Giving him a nod, I reiterate what I want, the whole reason I'm here tonight. "If you help clear the approvals needed, drum up excitement around some of the plans for building up Fiasco, then that would be a way to garner some good press." I look at the mayor when I add, "There are plenty of people here wanting to look like they're making a positive difference, and then there are those of us who are actually doing it." My phone vibrates in my pocket. There are a few people that, when they contact me, I do not, under any circumstances, keep them waiting.

> **THE ARCHITECT:**
> Touching base. Had a slight change in plans that we need to discuss. Your order is quite...aggressive.

I swallow, knowing exactly how to handle the fallout for an "order" like this one. The aggressive nature had a purpose, but I anticipated this text. She prefers in-person meetings when this type of *business* is being discussed. But I don't have time for that.

The mayor interrupts and asks another rhetorical question. "And you think moving the budget away from infrastructure and into things like parks and recreation is the way to do that, Foxx?" It's like he doesn't want this town to move forward. Either that, or he really is an idiot.

Finding my patience, I look at the governor when answering. It's his cooperation I need and his signature on the dotted lines. "We're moving into the spring and summer months, and we have the luxury of underwater caves and caverns. Places for people to explore, climb, dive, create memories they'll share on social media. It's an attraction. We just need people hired to keep those places clean, safe, and monitored. It seems like exactly the right time to move the budget into something that'll be visible and positive to Kentucky. As far as new attractions and businesses, I have plenty of ideas we can explore."

Bourbon is my occupation, and I run it well. But there's

more I care about beyond it. Keeping my family safe and strong is the biggest one, but there are also plenty of people who don't have the same luxury. I'm not a hero by any stretch; I have no problem with violence if it's necessary, but not with people who don't deserve it. The good people of Fiasco deserve some life breathed back into them and their livelihoods after the past year.

"I like your thought process. You have any estimates of the numbers that might bring in?" The governor looks at the mayor as if he should have these details, but he doesn't. That's what I was doing here. Governor Hawkins wants to treat our state like a business, so he's getting the businessman. And one of the best tactics in my line of business is warming them up, getting them comfortable, and then getting what I want. Ignoring the mayor, I give the governor a nod and tell him the only thing that'll sway a long-standing politician with his level of attention. "There's also quite a bit of tourism possibilities I'm considering investing more in. How about we discuss that over one of my specialty bottles?"

Thirty minutes later, the low lighting mixed with the cool air inside Midnight Proof changes the mood entirely. It's the best spot in Fiasco, hands down. The vibes are unmatched. The drinks are well done. And there's entertainment worthy of being a destination. Hadley knew what she was doing when she built this place. I'm not quite sure how considering she's always been a bit of a princess about life and hard work. But she turned an old bar and a run-down building into one of the sexiest speakeasies on the map.

"Governor," Hadley says smoothly, a warmth in her expression that would draw anyone in. But that welcome is all for show since nobody noticed the brief glare she gave me as I came in. "What a pleasant surprise." Her eyes flit to mine again as she says, "Ace hadn't mentioned exactly who he was bringing with him."

He extends his hand across the bar. "Pleasure, as always, Hadley. My brother was just talking about you."

I grit my teeth and flex my hand at my side, recalling watching Hawk's hand squeezing her ass this morning. It isn't my business that the men she flirts and sleeps with are rather pathetic choices.

She smiles, ignoring the way the governor blatantly stares at her chest. Plucking a couple of bottles from below the bar, she starts making a drink as she asks, "Are you planning to be back in town again for Derby weekend? You very much enjoyed the after-party at Foxx Bourbon last year, if I recall."

He had until he lost a decent amount of money to Laney. My brother's wife cleaned the floor with him in a nice game of Texas Hold'em. Grant had to step in when everyone realized he wanted to raise the stakes and play for one of his horses. Laney had been a hand away from taking one home, but she folded and called it a night before he embarrassed himself much further.

Hadley, on the other hand, is unpredictable. Disturbingly beautiful, easily the smartest person in most rooms, and she carries herself with more confidence than she knows what to do with. Right now, however, I need her to chill the fuck out.

"Hadley *Finch*," the mayor says, making his way toward us. I thought we had shrugged him off after dinner at Hooch's. No such luck.

My eyes narrow on him. The spineless wonder wants to make everyone in this group aware of the social threat she poses by being a Finch, but the governor knows who she is, as he's been to many gatherings at her father's home over the years. *Asshole.*

He sips his drink out of a cocktail straw and then adds, "You'll need to remind me which horse of yours ended up in the winner's circle last year. Can't recall if I'm rememberin' correctly or if it was another one of Finch & King's fillies."

The backhanded question has my nostrils flaring. I want to slap the stupidity right off his face. But Hadley simply wipes her hand on the towel slung over her shoulder and smiles. She isn't going to exchange niceties though. Nah. She's taking inventory. Planning all the ways she'll make her words linger long after they've been said. She's the kind of woman who will start a bar fight and watch men fall over themselves like idiots to finish it. Because she can—her charm is so damn sweet sometimes that it'll make your teeth hurt. That's only around the people she liked. Then there were moments, like this one, when she recognized a gauntlet being thrown and she showed up like a fucking gladiator.

Smiling at the mayor, she says, "That would be my girl, Fergie. But it's been a long time. That was years ago now." Then she shrugs. "And yes, we're all aware of who my father is—my last name matches his. Isn't that right, Governor?" She pours out three shots along the bar. "Daughter to the deplorable Wheeler Finch." Cupping her hand around her mouth, she whispers loudly, "I'm not a fan either, just share some DNA. Less intentional of a connection than some, I'd imagine."

I swipe my hand along the back of my neck and suggest, "Gentlemen, I'm going to head up. Hadley, I'll take the bottle I've requested when you have a moment."

She looks over her shoulder and nods to one of her waitresses before looking my way. "Of course, Mr. Foxx," she says too sweetly.

Mr. Foxx? Jesus Christ. I clear my throat and nod, knowing the kicker is coming when I see her back straightening ever so slightly as she glances at the mayor.

"Oh, and Mayor," she says, holding up her finger, "the next

time you walk into my bar ready to insult me, you'd be wise to remember my last name you so quickly pointed out. It may still be splashing the tabloids, but your friends"—she glances at Governor Hawkins—"have enjoyed a few cocktails in my father's home over the years. Interesting that little tidbit was left out of all those articles about the fall of Kentucky racing, don't you think?"

Neither the governor nor the mayor has the gall to respond, only nodding dumbly. And with that, she winks. "Have a nice evenin', gentlemen." She salutes us with two fingers at her brow. Her middle finger lingers in the air a second longer, like she couldn't help herself from flipping him off.

I wipe my hand across my mouth, trying to hide my smile, and then move up the stairs.

The private balcony room at Midnight Proof is vaulted above the main floor and looks out among the dark velvet curtains draped along the walls and the chandeliers placed in various spots throughout. It provides an excellent bird's-eye view of the entire speakeasy for prime people-watching. The warm glow around the room gives off just enough light to squint at menus and find drinks but allows for enough shadowed space for couples to slip hands under tables or skirts. Midnight Proof is just the right mixture of a vintage-style speakeasy brushed with the modern appeal of a forward-thinking cocktail menu and nostalgically sexy entertainment.

"My brother got the better deal with that one," the governor says as he looks out. "Pretty little thing." His attention stays focused on Hadley. With a smirk on his face that I have the sudden urge to slap off, he adds, "Lucky bastard."

The insinuation makes my stomach sink. I hate knowing as much as I do about Chief Hawkins and Hadley's rather cliché situation. *She's* never been tight-lipped about her sex life. I've narcissistically always thought it's because she wanted me to know. And I stupidly listen too closely to her conversations with Lincoln about it. I study the governor as he watches her. It pisses me off that he's even looking. I need to pivot his focus. "Still pulling the same funding for your upcoming campaign?" I ask, taking a sip of my bourbon. It's a loaded question.

If I had blinked, I would've missed the way his shoulders tense and he pauses mid-sip. But he plays it off when he tilts his head to the side with a sly smile. "Why, Foxx? You interested in donating to my campaign?" Sipping *my* bourbon, he continues to leer at Hadley. "Your support is always welcome. But I still have the funding I need for getting elected another term."

I doubt that. The details I have on Governor Hawkins's background are mostly predictable. On-again, off-again women, never married. But his brother is his only family. He has investments that prove lucrative but have been shuffled with curious timing to the current events in my small town. Add that to the fact that his campaign donations are mostly private and anonymous. Anyone who paid attention knows the governor and Wheeler Finch rubbed elbows for a long time. There have been plenty of events where both were present.

I watch the mayor out of my periphery lean forward to take in the burlesque performance that was just beginning. My soon-to-be sister-in-law, Faye, puts on one helluva show. She's also an incredibly talented private investigator, a certain skill that not too many know about. A little detail that I, as well as the local PD and FBI field offices, have found valuable recently.

My phone vibrates, allowing me a brief escape from watching these men embarrass themselves with how oblivious they are to their own lack of power and influence.

LUCIFER:
A heads-up about the company you're keeping today would have been nice.

ACE:
Heads up, the governor is going to make a pass at you.

LUCIFER:
You say that like it's anything new.

ACE:
You're seeing his brother.

LUCIFER:
Sounds like a challenge.

ACE:
Please tell me you're joking.

LUCIFER:
Why? You worried about me, Daddy?

I puff out my cheeks and blow out an exhale. *Jesus Christ, that nickname.* Pushing my buttons is her favorite hobby. I'm going to learn my fucking lesson one of these days. I don't know why I engage. When I do, it's like fuel for her. And then I end up in a bad mood, slightly dizzy, and with a fucking hard-on.

I can't recall exactly when she turned into a fixture in our lives, only that it happened overnight. I hadn't been paying attention, and all of a sudden, she was there. Dinners turned into fishing trips and Saturday morning card games. Lazy moments and long days before the years seemed short and our lives became too hectic. She's been here, and it's been an incessant hurdle to avoid looking like I care.

Smiling at whatever the governor's rattling on about now, I pocket my phone and glance at the bar to find her attention up here and on me. I've become exceptional at masking feelings and schooling reactions to every sideways bullshit that crosses my path. Except when it comes to her.

Her mouth tips up a fraction of an inch. She knows she got to me.

Chapter 4

Hadley

I remember hearing once that nothing good ever happens after midnight. Old, patronizing theories about being a lady and not looking for trouble or some bullshit. I hate the insinuation so much that I named my speakeasy Midnight Proof. I wanted a place where people could escape. A forbidden location where music and cocktails were sexy again. Somewhere someone could walk in and be completely consumed by the experience. It's the one thing I've done that I'm proud of. From the chandeliers to the coupe glasses to the entertainment and everything in between. Midnight Proof is mine. It defines me.

"You're killing me in that dress, Hadley," Faye says as she digs in her bag. The low-cut, billowing neckline isn't my usual game, but I'm leaning into the flair of the bride being a burlesque dancer. Sequins and sparkles are necessary. It's a complete juxtaposition to what I wore this morning, wading in a river with galoshes and a trucker hat that read, *Reel Master Baiter*.

I opened the speakeasy today with limited service and closed up about an hour ago. Faye decided she wanted to fit in a performance to work off some nervous energy before the festivities.

Lincoln and Faye had requested late-night cocktails hosted at Ace and Griz's house instead of a typical bachelor or bachelorette party. The wedding ceremony and reception are tomorrow night, but they wanted to celebrate as much as possible while friends are here from out of town.

I glance at Faye when I feel her looking at me. Her blond hair is pinned to the side, and while she always looks impeccable, tonight, in a tight white cocktail dress, she's goddess-level gorgeous. The cool-toned blues and purples from the dashboard lights show off a smile dancing on her lips when she asks, "Is Hawk coming tonight?"

With a casual side-eye, I pause, trying to play off my answer as nonchalant instead of cold. "It's not like that with us. It's nothing serious."

She lowers the visor and taps her finger along her lipstick-painted lips. "It's been going on for a little while. I wasn't sure if it started becoming more."

I smile, loving the fact that I have someone like her to even ask. "It's been easy."

"Which means…" she leads with a quirked eyebrow.

"It means, I'm not planning to bring my fling as my date to things that are important to me, like your wedding."

Giving me a curt nod, she smiles. "You'll have more fun without him." She looks out the window and toward the property. "He is, however, missing a helluva look on you right now. You belong on stage, Hadley. Damn, girl." She exhales and changes the topic just as quickly as she brought it up. "Every time I drive up this road, I'm reminded of how beautiful it is."

Canopy trees hang over the narrow road that leads into the part of Fiasco that's owned by Foxx Bourbon. The distillery, along with offices and tasting bar inside, sits at the center of the vast landscape. Around it are more than a dozen rickhouses that hold countless aged barrels of bourbon. The Foxx family has properties all throughout Kentucky with more rickhouses. There are cornfields as far as the eye can see that grow the corn in their mash, and fields of rye and barley in neighboring states that were purchased and leased to guarantee the baseline of what made up their blends. But here, along this stretch of road in Fiasco, there are stables, a cute farmhouse where Grant and Laney live, a smaller studio that now's vacant again after Laney married Grant, and a few miles away, along the flat land, are horse paddocks leading to the beautifully architected main house.

I smile as the stunning two-story home comes into view. A modern farmhouse that's more of a sprawling estate than simply a larger home. It's one of the most beautiful places I've ever been inside, which says a lot considering I'm not new to money.

We come to a quick stop, parking just along the edge of the driveway that's already lined with cars. Low bass music filters through the speakers peppered throughout the patio as we move across the well-manicured grass and around the side of the house. Faye squeezes my arm when she sees Lincoln, and I keep walking to give them a few minutes. I can't help but watch them hold each other, speaking in hushed voices and smiling like they're the only two here. Happiness looks good on him after all he's been through, and I feel lucky to witness it. I look around, taking everything in; it's like the Foxx estate fucked around with old Hollywood glamour to show out for this wedding weekend. Flowing fabrics, flickering candles, metallic accents, soft lighting; it's as dreamy as can be.

As I walk toward the double doors that lead inside, I give Jimmy from the distillery a wave. He pours a few glasses of bourbon for the men sitting along the outdoor bar. "Jimmy, looking good as a bartender," I tease.

He smiles, his face turning a familiar shade of pink, like it does any time I talk to him. "Nah, I'll leave that up to you and Laney. Just helping Ace. I start on the Fiasco PD next week."

It's been a bit of a running joke for a while now that Jimmy Dugan Jr. has had just about every job Fiasco has to offer. His father owns Dugan Hardware, and unlike so many family businesses in small towns, his father told him—after enough injury-induced accidents—that he could do what makes him happy. After a few fumbles, he started at the cooperage, shaping and hauling barrels for Foxx Bourbon. Most of the town gossips thought that might be it for him, but he went ahead and decided to enroll in the academy. Somewhere along the way, someone passed him and approved of him wielding a badge and gun.

"I'll make sure to stop in and check out the uniform," I say with a wink as I canvass the rest of the space. There are a couple of faces I don't recognize—one at the long counter in the kitchen talking with some of Faye's friends from Nashville. I hold my small clutch in one hand while I pull out my lipstick and walk toward the butler's pantry—off of it is a guest suite that I like to consider mine. But I stop short and do a double take into Ace's office. A woman with cropped platinum hair is perched on his desk in a black cocktail dress with her back to me, looking through papers that I'd guarantee do not belong to her.

I know he wouldn't want just anyone in there. Most people who come to the main house for a party or event are never so bold as to wander without permission.

"Excuse me," I say, stepping into the room. She stills but doesn't turn around right away.

As I move closer and with a different vantage point, I realize she's not alone.

"There's a list," his deep voice says quietly to her, not having heard me.

But it's her stiletto heel that's perched just above Ace's belt that has me freezing in place. "Multiples will take some time."

I suck in a breath. Ace's typically unaffected, stoic gaze has hints of amusement, his head resting against the back of his high-back leather chair. His hands are occupied, one with an almost empty rocks glass of bourbon and the other fisted and propped under his chin.

But then, he glances my way.

Shit.

The amusement drops from his face immediately. "Get out," he says gruffly, sounding nearly emotionless.

My cheeks heat instantly. Lips parting, I can't find anything to say back. I'm stunned by his tone. The woman turns her head to the side, looking at me only out of her periphery. It's enough to shake me.

I was just verbally slapped. My embarrassment morphs rather quickly into anger as I turn back down the hall, walking toward the loud buzz of more people peppered around the kitchen and bleeding out the doors to the backyard.

With my blood boiling, I breeze past Laney and Grant draped over each other on a chaise longue, then watch as Faye shows off her engagement ring to a small group of strangers I don't know and glare as Lincoln laughs with one of the guys from his team. My fake smile stays plastered on my face, shoulders back, and jaw tight as I make my way to the bar.

I can unpack why Ace's few words and the condescending tone hit me as hard as they did after I've had a shot. I'm not nearly drunk enough yet.

"Jimmy, I'd like either an impeccable Manhattan or a full motherfucking fist worth of bourbon."

Jimmy looks my way just as I adjust my tits in my dress, frozen in place by how to respond. He glances down to the end of the bar at Griz, who I notice at the same time. Most people look to him for direction when Ace isn't around.

Griz knows that something is wrong right away; it's one of his superpowers—knowing how people are feeling just by body language alone. "Give the lady the bottle, Jimmy." Then he glances at me again. "And a water," he adds, just before he turns back to his small huddle of ladies from book club. I don't miss the side-eyes they give each other at my very apparent state of exasperation. I'm so tired of getting those looks from people who watched me grow up. The assumptions they're making about me because of my father make my stomach roil.

I inhale a deep breath and lift my chin, trying to mask how I'm feeling. My pulse kicks too high for simply standing in place and stewing over what just happened.

"You're a mighty good time, I bet," a deep voice says to my left. The stranger sucks in a long pull of air from his vape pen and lets out a puff of smoke that smells sweeter than the Fiasco breeze, more like cotton candy. He chases it with a sip of his bourbon—two fingers, neat.

I uncork the bottle of unlabeled bourbon. For Jimmy's sake, I hope it's not one of the important years. Giving myself a luxury-level pour so it'll last me a little while, I then ask in a serious tone, "Is that what you think?"

Flirting is one of my favorite pastimes. Charming people

feels like the easiest way to connect with someone, and in my line of work, I do it often. It's far easier to find distraction in the handsome Viking-like man sitting next to me than to spiral.

But when my phone buzzes in my hands and another unknown number flashes across the top of my screen, the message is like a gut punch.

> **UNKNOWN:**
> You can expect a visit, little birdie, if you can't settle the debts. Ignoring us will only make it hurt more.

"You look awfully serious," the stranger says playfully.

"I don't know you," I say, sizing him up as I swallow down the nerves that just engulfed me. "But you look familiar." I pause, thinking about how I recognize him. "A couple of years ago, at the distillery, in Ace's office." Tonight, he's wearing dark jeans and a Henley, a leather holster-style harness that has no purpose other than to just add to the sex appeal that leaks from his pores. It isn't exactly cocktail party attire, but I wonder if he isn't here to celebrate Lincoln or Faye. Maybe he's here for someone else.

He leans on the bar, crossing his arms in front of him. "You're Hadley, right?" he asks, circling his finger around the rim of his glass. "Ace has told me about you. And I pay attention to the details." Without offering more, he sips his bourbon.

I mimic him and take a sip of my drink, letting it warm my chest and calm my jittering senses. "And what details might those be?" Tilting my head, I lock my eyes with his and lift my eyebrows.

He leans in so close that his chest brushes my exposed

shoulders. "I think you know exactly which details I mean." A smile quirks his lips. "The kind that'll garner me a slap across the face if I say them out loud."

This man flirts his way through just about whatever he wants, I imagine. But my curiosity is piqued, and I wonder what the hell Ace would be saying about me to this man. I look at his hands, covered in more rings than most men here would normally wear, as he fidgets with a coin. There's something different about him. I can't see him being friends with Ace. He's closer to my age, far more casual than the typical businessmen that Ace calls acquaintances. Men like him are noticeable, and they don't fade into backgrounds. I turn my body toward him and give him a teasing grin, one that speaks for my interest. He seems like someone I could get lost with for a little while. "I promise, I won't slap you. Unless you ask me to."

But our private conversation is interrupted by a clearing throat. And I'd be lying if I said I didn't know by smell alone who it is—oak and oranges. I hate how my body recognizes it with only a breath. Sighing my annoyance, I turn slightly to find Ace standing behind me with an almost angry look painted across his face. *What the hell does he have to be pissed about?* His jaw is tight, as if he was biting down on something—or biting back whatever it is he's just dying to say. I feel his gaze along every inch of my skin, abrasive like flint and ready to catch fire. And it's instant, like some kind of perimenopausal hot flash or just my severe lack of sexual gratification.

His attention zeroes in on me first, and then flicks to the man sitting next to me. Ace shifts his body, crowding closer as he speaks into my ear. "I need to have a word with you."

I nearly laugh. "Pass. I'm having a very nice conversation with my new friend…" I respond easily, keeping my eyes on my stranger and leaving it open-ended for him to insert his name. But instead, the curious stranger keeps quiet, seemingly holding back a smirk as he keeps his eyes on Ace.

"You're not," Ace clips out. "Let's go. I need to talk to you. Privately."

I spin fully on the bar stool, uncrossing my legs and standing to face him. The stilettos give me a bit more height to meet his glare. My chest grazes his, the gold sequins of my dress dragging along his suit jacket. Stepping closer to the bar, I wiggle my fingers at Jimmy to signal for him to come back over.

"There's not a single thing I want to do with you right now, Atticus." I turn my head to the side when I say, "Publicly or privately."

I'm not interested in hearing a damn word out of his mouth. I need to get away from him before I say something I'll regret. Kicking back what's left in my glass, I completely ignore my plan to nurse it. It burns the whole way down.

A rumble sounds from Ace's throat as he steps closer, leaning into me, his chest against my back. "Hadley, I'm not fucking around." Warm fingers brush the exposed skin of my back, making me shiver. It isn't the first time he's ever touched me casually, acting like it's nothing, but it's the first time I want to ignore it.

Catching only the outline of his white dress shirt with his untied bow tie hanging beside the collar in my peripheral, I note he's changed from earlier when he was at Midnight Proof. And *Jesus*, he looks even better.

"Too bad," I say with a smile.

I left like he so rudely demanded, and now he wants to talk? *Fuck that.* I'm a smart woman. My mind is always moving. I can think of at least a handful of things at once, balance about a dozen more, and then plan all the little details in between. The devil's always in the details. Or maybe my devil is in crisp black suit pants and a white shirt with the top two buttons forgotten, with a square jawline that always looks like it's a bite away from cracking molars. *My* devil is a Kentucky bourbon boy, but goddesses, he's always looked like a man. The kind of man that isn't simply handsome. No, he's downright beautiful. My devil makes bourbon, rides horses, and makes sure his family comes first. There have been moments when I feel included in that, but tonight isn't one of them.

"You're pushing it, and this isn't something—" His words cut off from the arm I snake behind me. I turn my wrist, my fingers finding the outline of his dick. I've had quite enough of him today.

He doesn't pull away or jump back. *Of course he doesn't.* I've been pushing his buttons for many years now, and only lately have I been able to get a rise out of him. But I've overestimated and I've forgotten who I'm playing with. I forget the reason why I've been slightly obsessed with him for most of my life: the dangerous confidence that lingers around him like an aura. The assertive energy that isn't learned or earned; it just exists. He moves closer, his fingertips at my back gliding along my waist as his arm gathers me closer.

I swallow past a lump in my throat, trying to wade through the haze of my heavy pour, his body pressed against mine, and my decision to touch him in a way I never have. The taste of bourbon still lingers on my tongue, and with it, a wave of boldness rolls through me again. I flex my fingers, and I'm rewarded, or maybe punished, with the knowledge that Atticus Foxx is instantly hard. Large and thick, just as I imagined. And that confirmation sends a wave of panic and excitement through me, warring for priority. This move wasn't meant to be seductive. I wanted him to submit, to stop speaking, to surprise him into silence. I've wildly missed the mark.

With as much confidence as I can wrangle, I say quietly, "You don't have the privilege of telling me what to do, Ace."

His mouth hovers lower, so close that his lips brush ever so slightly along the curve of my ear. "You sure about that, sugar?" His hips press forward, trapping the arm I have between our bodies. The grip of my hand is unwavering as he lets out an audible exhale, speaking so softly that it sounds like words dragging slowly along dirt and gravel. "I've been deciding what you get to do for a long time now."

A breath falls from my mouth, along with a small and traitorous sound.

Laughter from the other end of the bar snaps me back to reality. I blink and refocus on the outdoor space—the cool night air, the low music, the crowd. People are occupied with their own conversations, but the stranger at the bar is still there, smirking to himself. He witnessed this.

Somewhere in this exchange, everything else fell away. And like he's made the same realization as me, the warmth of Ace's body disappears as quickly as it came. When I turn to see where he went, feeling dizzy and wound tight, it's like he was never here at all.

Just a fantasy.

Chapter 5

Ace

Lincoln isn't a crier. He wears his emotions more proudly than any other Foxx, but rarely have I witnessed him cry. Which is why I'm almost slack-jawed as he rubs beneath his glasses with his pointer finger and thumb just as Hadley cracks a joke about not earning the title "best man" because it was already taken by the groom.

"I've had the coveted role of best friend for a long time now." She glances at me. "Ace is still salty over it." The crowd lets out a laugh at my expense. The kicker is, she isn't totally wrong. "And I had hoped, for a long time, that I might get ousted too." She smiles at Faye, who shouts, "NEVER!"

Hadley laughs softly, but her eyes are glassy, getting ready to probably hit everyone's heartstrings. "For all the hopeful romantics in the room, and I know there are quite a few of you, Faye and Linc have the kind of love that makes us hopeful. Aside from being sexy as hell"—hoots and hollers ring out—"you're relationship goals. You push each other to do better." She looks at Lark and Lily. "Earmuffs, loves." They both cover their ears, their mouths stuffed with cake. "You support each other, whether it's wielding weapons or swinging titty tassels. And fuck, you make love look like an adventure and not a boring destination. I love you both. I wish you timeless energy to spend together, endless time to grow together, and an ever-growing roster of delicious, fun, sweet, and kind moments for as long as you both shall live!"

A round of applause and cheers, accompanied by silverware tinging against glasses, vibrates around the room.

Dammit, that was a good speech.

Faye and Lincoln both get up to hug her, and I don't miss the way she glances at me when they do. *Pain in the ass.* I can tell by the smirk on her lips that there's more.

And sure enough, she's not done. She kicks back the full glass of champagne and claps her hands in front of her before the music can pick back up. I've been lying to myself all day long, playing off that her hands on me last night were so easily forgotten. I've spent years keeping my distance, but for a while now, she's been pushing closer.

"Now that the sweetness has been delivered, let's bring on the salty. I'm going to need you and you," Hadley shouts, pointing to Lincoln and Grant, and then she hops up onto the bar and perches her ass there as if it's her throne. Both of my brothers are well past their usual limits, but they look obnoxiously happy with their wives draped in their arms while laughing at the brunette jester holding court. Beautiful and drunk.

"Where's the other one?" Hadley rasps out, her finger tapping her painted red lip as she dramatically crosses her legs and flashes a pair of gold stilettos with red bottoms.

Fucking hell, it's impossible to look away.

Taking another sip from the newest batch of bourbon we bottled, I enjoy the way this particular blend hits my palate—an underlying smokiness mixed with hints of cinnamon and sweetened caramels. We've had some favorably warm winters over the past few years, which had the barrel wood expanding more than contracting, depositing even more of the sugar from the toast and char that bathed the inside of the wood. It isn't the kind of flavors that hit right away. That's what people always misunderstand about bourbon. It evolves along your tongue, and the details are found only when you savor it. I like the discipline it takes to enjoy it.

I glance down at the length of chairs and tables spread throughout the distillery. My sister-in-law, Laney, is in charge of larger scale events we host here, and she's outdone herself.

They had their lavish ceremony on the large lawn behind the distillery. It was a little more over-the-top than Grant and Laney's wedding a year ago, but that isn't a stretch considering the bride and groom. Faye is a natural in the spotlight and Lincoln is a showman. My nieces managed to steal the show, walking down the aisle as Faye's bridesmaids. And even I needed to look away when they each gave her a ring for her right hand, calling it their promise to her. My brother was the happiest I've ever seen him as he watched that exchange. It felt good to witness so much good after too many years of loss. I might be older, but I look up to both of my brothers for falling in love so bravely. I'm not built the same way.

This place truly looks like the perfect mixture of a distillery and a speakeasy—it has Lincoln and Faye written all over it.

Lincoln is brilliant at what he does. There isn't a single person I trust more to make the perfect mash bill than him—even Griz.

He surpassed just about anyone in this industry a long time ago, with creativity and understanding the complex combination of science and agriculture that it takes to make bourbon. This distillery is a part of him, just like performing on stage is a part of Faye.

"I see you back there, trying your hardest to ignore me, Ace." The low thrum of the band keeps time with whatever song they had lined up, emphasizing Hadley's interruption. She rests her hand on her hip, and then holds out her drink for the bartender. "I don't think many people know this, but Atticus Foxx is the reason my beloved Midnight Proof even exists," she says with a more drawn-out blink of her eyes. *Yeah, she's three sheets to the wind.*

I stand up, and with it come a few whistles and hollers from the back of the room, Lincoln's being the most recognizable.

"See..." Hadley holds up her hand, cupping her cheek as she whisper-shouts. "The only thing you need to do to get that man moving is threaten him with a good time. Or an old story."

Jesus Christ. The idea of her on top of a bar, telling old stories, has my adrenaline pumping and nerves ticking higher than usual. There are a few stories that need to remain quiet, and she's a wild card. It's the part of her that I try not to encourage, even though there's a part of me that's drawn to it. I'd never admit it, but she's one of the few people who could actually get me to do something I don't want to do.

Laney moves behind the bar and pulls out a few bottles, moving them next to where Hadley stands. They were instant friends, cackling together from the moment Laney was dropped in Fiasco. I wasn't all that surprised. Hadley has a way of making people feel comfortable and welcomed. And she's fun. Chaos with a quick tongue and sharp bite, but fun nonetheless.

With two bottles snatched up and held between her fingers on one hand and a shaker in the other, Hadley makes a long, dramatic pour. She glances at me first, almost like she's asking permission to keep going, and I don't give her much of a nod before she's doing just that. "The first time I ever tried to make a real drink, I completely messed it up."

Some scoffs, and then a "Doubt that!" sounds from the back, and it starts a round of laughs.

Hadley smiles and picks up two more bottles and gives them another long pour as she speaks over the chatter. "But it was for my best friend, and wow, did he do a good job at pretending it wasn't awful." Her eyes shift to mine. "Ace, however, was brutally honest with me."

The memory is an easy one to recall.

"Are you going to put anything else in that?" I asked as I watched her pour what seemed like a full glass of gin. I must have startled her, because she jumped at the sound of my voice. It had been weeks since I was in the same room as her.

She stood a little taller as I walked closer. It was a habit I'd always noticed—like she was trying to ready herself for whatever was coming. Giving me a side-eye before she moved back to her curious choice for a mixer, she said, "As a matter of fact, I am." She raised her chin, and then looked across the counter of the kitchen.

"What are you trying to make?" I asked as I glanced at the backyard. It was crowded with coworkers from the distillery. Nights like tonight made Griz's small farmhouse seem even smaller than it already was. I had plans to build something much bigger; I just needed him to agree to it.

"One of the girls asked for a French 75, and then Lincoln said he could go for one too. So I figured, how hard could it be?"

I raised my eyebrows at her. "You know how to make a French 75? I thought you were more of a vodka Red Bull or premade cosmopolitan in a can type."

I instantly regretted making fun of her as she sent me a glare. I knew she didn't have many friends. Lincoln was her closest, Olivia too, but beyond that, there weren't many.

"So you just need lemon juice, simple syrup, and champagne?" I told her, trying to erase my asshole comment.

She looked around the counter to see if any of that was accessible. "Um, yeah. Exactly."

She concentrated so hard, biting her lip, and I couldn't help but notice how pouty and pretty they were. Or the freckle just to the left of her nose and more scattered along her shoulder where her oversize T-shirt hung off. The way she didn't hesitate to take my direction, even though I knew she wanted to tell me to fuck off. It made my neck and face heat as I canvassed her curved waist and rounded hips.

She pulled out an elderflower liqueur, and then some Grand Marnier, which had no business in a French 75, but she added them anyway.

I cleared my throat, knocking away the too-detailed observation of a girl I shouldn't be looking at this way, and one who was far too young for me. "That's going to taste awful."

Topping the mess inside the glass with ice, she covered it and started shaking it up. "Sorry," she said, speaking louder. "Can't hear you over the shaker."

When the shaker was frosted and she stopped, I said, "Since you're technically a guest here and my brother sent you inside to do this, I'll let it slide, but we don't offer people anything other than bourbon under this roof. Especially to people working at our distillery. We'll stock it and people can help themselves, but we'll never offer it."

She laughed out, "Really leaning into the bourbon boys thing, huh?"

I rubbed my thumb along my bottom lip and watched as she poured out two glasses and topped them with mint. "Leaning into exactly who I am and what defines me hardly feels like a bad thing, Hadley."

Clearing her throat, she licked her bottom lip. "Taste it," she said, pushing the glass across the counter.

I took a sip of it, the tinted purple drink looking more like a floor cleaner than anything I wanted to taste, but I did it anyway.

"Fuck, that's awful."

With her big blue eyes, she watched me put the glass back down, and something shifted in her expression that had nothing to do with her poor rendition of a classic cocktail. I knew she was going to take this as an opportunity to ask what happened after I left her that night nearly a month ago. I could see it plain as day in her stare. There wasn't an easy way to tell someone what I found, finished, and cleaned up.

"I have questions," she said, uncharacteristically quiet.

I didn't have any trouble looking people in the eye while I lied to them. It was an asset I'd learned a long time ago. "I don't have answers for you." I looked across the mess she made on the counter as laughter echoed from the backyard. "You're an awful bartender, Hadley. Stick to being whatever it is you're planning to do with your life," I said flippantly, then strolled out of the kitchen. But the look in her eyes followed me all night.

A small tray of coupe glasses appearing to her right draws my attention back to the present as she finishes the story—without the details we still hold as a secret. More gracefully than I would have expected, she hops down from the bar. Her fitted tuxedo jacket was shed seconds after the ceremony, leaving her creamy skin and curves, from her shoulders to her waist, impossible not to follow like a damn treasure map. Her suit wasn't like mine, the haltered cutout of a white tuxedo shirt and black satin bow tie precisely tailored to be tight around the neck, running down the sides of her breasts to the material that's gathered and clasped at the small of her back. It's the sexiest fucking thing I've ever seen her in, and that's saying something considering how many times I've looked.

When I glance back at her face, she's staring right at me with a smirk that clearly reads, *I caught you looking*. She pours out the light purple-tinted cocktail into five glasses. "I made my toast to the bride and groom already tonight, but it's only natural to toast to the family that loves its people." She holds up her glass. "To the bourbon boys who became damn fine Foxx men." That gets me a wink. "Cheers, and thank you for fiercely loving, teaching, and accepting…even a Finch among you."

I swallow and stand a little taller. The way she likes to poke usually pisses me off, but right now, that swell of emotion feels less like annoyance and more like pride. This woman has been pouring drinks for a while now, but I haven't let her mix anything for me other than a rock among hefty splashes of bourbon. Griz smiles and takes the first glass. Grant plucks his next, then Lincoln.

With her blue eyes glassy, she smiles wide with admiration. When I take mine and sip, I'm immediately hit with the tart lemon that balances the earthy flavor of the gin. On my second sip, I appreciate the rest of the well-done traditional ingredients of simple syrup and a champagne topper. It's easily the best version of this drink I've ever had. I keep my smile stifled. Lincoln is doing enough of that, beaming at her for a well-delivered speech and a non-bourbon cocktail to boot. I still should have been the best man.

A few snickers from behind me pull my attention. It's Griz's book club ladies—gossips who never turn down a chance to spread rumors over a glass of something strong. "It's like she doesn't even care…" Another whisper rings out of choppy words. "Finch… Not ashamed of it…"

Lincoln has mentioned some of the shit she's been dealing with lately regarding her father. I already knew about it, but I let my brother think he was telling me new information.

I turn and glare at the two older women. Romey, who likes to run her mouth whenever possible, and her sister, who owns the hair salon in town. They're loud enough that Hadley heard them. I don't miss how those few words steal the moment away from her. As soon as I catch their attention, both lean into the other, eyeing what I'm wordlessly conveying: *Shut your fucking mouths, ladies.*

The evening taxes on as if it isn't well past midnight. Laney and Faye have sandwiched Hadley in the middle of the dance floor, while Griz just keeps whistling every few songs from different spots in the room as he chats the night away with the guests.

My phone vibrates in my pocket. With everyone here tonight, I can guess it's something that'll need my attention.

> **THE JEWELER:**
> Heard an interesting story today about a bird.

What the hell is he getting at?

> **ACE:**
> Sounds nice. Hadn't realized you'd taken to bird-watching in your old age.

> **THE JEWELER:**
> You're older than me.

> **ACE:**
> You sure about that?

While we aren't friends, there's been a camaraderie built over the years. A sense of trust between two people in similar roles: handling what's needed and keeping the judgment and feelings far enough at bay to sleep at night. His text has my attention because there's plenty of underlying context in that one sentence. *A bird.* It bothers me instantly, knowing Hadley's name is being mentioned in any circles he's involved in.

> **THE JEWELER:**
> A lot of people looking to collect, and she's not paying.

"You look like someone pissed in your bourbon," Lincoln says as he approaches, taking a seat at our table.

Clapping and laughter grow louder as Faye, in her typical form, starts peeling off pieces of her wedding reception attire.

Ignoring him, I nod to the dance floor. "Your wife is about to give us a performance."

He smiles, letting out a sigh. "She's fucking beautiful." Leaning forward, he shouts through a laugh, "Rosie Gold Foxx, you better save some of those moves for later!"

Grant, somewhere in all of this, slipped into the chair to my left. I don't have to look at him to know where his attention is. Seconds later, Laney perches herself on his lap, out of breath. "Dance with me, cowboy. Then we can get out of here."

I don't hear the rest of their exchange, but I can't help smiling. My brother had a rough go of it before she showed up here, and while he has worked himself out of it, she makes him smile just about every time I see him.

"Faye, those stay—Ah, fuck," Lincoln says, standing up and moving quickly to the dance floor just as Faye holds up a pair of fishnets and a fairly drunk Hadley cackles at her side.

Hadley hugs my brother as he reaches her. He glances at me when she says something to him, but he shakes his head. Now *that* has my attention. They sway together and laugh, her head kicking back and a big smile tilting toward the low-hanging chandeliers.

"Careful, Atticus…" Griz mutters to my right.

"Where did you come from?" I ask with a chuckle. He's got a glass of bourbon in one hand and a cigar unlit in the other.

"I never understood it," he says, watching the dance floor and likely eyeing the same woman I just was.

If I don't ask, he's going to keep delivering cryptic phrases until I do. "What have you never understood?"

He takes a slow sip, draining the bourbon that remained. His leg crosses over the other as his arms drape along each side of the worn brown leather.

I eye the empty glass. "You might want to consider slowing down tonight. How many is that?"

He gives me a side-eye. "Most of my body is made up of bourbon and grit, Atticus. I'm just fueling up."

As much as I give him shit for always being in my business and having a way of interjecting when I least want him to, I still want him around as long as possible. I don't seek out his approval any longer, but that doesn't mean his opinion doesn't matter. Not many know about the dual life he maintains. He's respected and sometimes mistaken for being a charming old man, but that's only the surface. The man's in his eighties but he treats life like he still has plenty to live. Most people make the assumption he's in his mid-sixties, not too far after retirement. But like a lot of the details of Griz's life, that would be a lie. There have been small things about his age that I have started to take note of over the last couple of years: He's a bit slower to get up and move around, more reliant on his golf cart to navigate our expansive property. Late nights still happen, but they're peppered throughout the weeks with more naps and caffeine. His mind is sharp and memory even clearer, but he's ready to move away from the stress that lingers from what takes place behind closed doors and in back rooms. And that reminds me…

"Do me a favor and keep visitors to a minimum over the next few days." I don't want to give him information or the details of what I need to get done. I have a plan, and if he knows too much, too soon, then he'll fuck it up somehow.

"Yeah, yeah." A gravelly laugh sounds from his throat.

After another minute, I can still feel him staring at my profile, so I turn to meet his stare. The serious look on his face isn't one many see, or ever see, too often, but right now in the dim light, I catch a glimpse of the Griswald Foxx who's dangerous. The man who has far too many friends, the man who has been a conduit and connector between politicians and drug cartels for decades. I've learned everything from him—that shaking hands and greasing palms are just as valuable and risky as some of the favors we've been promised or have asked for. A man who blurs lines about the rights and wrongs of killing someone who needs to be removed, a situation that requires cleaning without questions. A man who has loved and lost plenty. An older mirror image, if I'm not careful.

"How did your meeting with Jim Dugan Sr. go?" He changes the subject effortlessly, probably sensing where my mind is. I try not to get worked up about him asking. He knows when the meeting's scheduled.

"It's next week. And I imagine it'll go just fine."

"The governor goin' to be a problem? You know if he approves the big box store coming into Montgomery County—"

"Griz, I told you, I'm handling this. So *let me* handle it," I say firmly.

Foxx Bourbon has always been the metronome that kept time and tempo in Fiasco. Fiasco turned into a destination instead of another statistic or sad story from economic downturn or mishandled property. Small businesses thrived here. Handshakes bound agreements. And gossip ran wild about how that was all made possible. I've always felt a responsibility for the place I grew up, even if that means getting blood on my hands because of it. Griz instilled those values in me.

"You know, you're a damn idiot. You keep staring at her and she might finally notice," he says, shaking his head. I should have known he wouldn't let it go. "I don't understand for the life of me why—" He cuts himself off. If he really thought about why, he'd have his answer. The reason why I would never act on the vibrating impulse to take exactly who I want, the way I want her.

I sip my bourbon and try to ignore him. Glancing around the room toward the bar, I'm careful not to let my attention flicker back to the wildly drunken brunette rolling her hips in the middle of the room. He's right; I have been staring, and I didn't even realize it.

"Being married and in love looks good on your brothers." He glances back to the dance floor just as Lincoln lifts Faye into his arms and Grant twirls Laney before pulling her close. "You're up next."

He hasn't said anything like that in years.

"Find something to ground you." They should have been forgotten words Griz said on an unforgettable night ten years ago. A few years later, my brothers started losing the people they loved. Griz had loved and lost again as well. I know a part of him believes in the bullshit curse that any woman who falls for a Foxx ends up dying. I don't believe in curses, but the reality of loving someone and losing them seems more like a punishment than something beautiful.

Brow pinched, I watch him closely as he gets up from his chair. He starts laughing as he hits the edge of the dance floor, like his statement won't needle and burrow under my skin. There have been plenty of people, especially in Fiasco, who are vocal about the oldest Foxx brother still being a bachelor. I never saw the negative. Let them talk. People are unpredictable, and that makes things complicated.

The most unpredictable of them all sways her hips in the center of that dance floor. I can't help but lick my lips and swallow at how, despite not wanting it to be the case, she makes my mouth water. Her long dark hair flows wildly behind her as her smile lights up the whole damn room. She wears a tux better than any man has, the way it grips every feminine part of her.

Last night, with her hands on me… I stifle the memory for probably the hundredth time today and rub my hand over my mouth. The willpower it took to walk away from her only existed because people were watching.

It can't happen again. I'm not up next; I'm doing just fine without.

Chapter 6

Hadley

Still on the dance floor, I look to my right and find Linc with his arms wrapped around his beautiful wife. The smile that's been plastered across his face today is one I'll never forget. He's always been one of the best people I've ever known, hence the best friend status. The kicker is, seeing him fall in love with Faye over the last year has made me feel grateful. I don't know if I'll ever experience a love like that, but if anyone could have a shot at seeing it through, then it would be Linc.

I glance toward the crowd, my eyes finding a set of light gray whirling with hues of blue staring back at me. I can't help but make sure he knows that I caught him looking once again. Crooking my finger in a *come hither* motion, I whisper, "Come here, *Daddy*."

I've been trying for the better part of the past decade to get under his skin. And somehow, I finally unlocked it. One word that I'd merely stumbled into saying for some reason was what had done it: *Daddy*.

Clearly not entertained by me, he blushes and pulls his lips into a straight line, even though he keeps watching. He's always so good at that—being unreadable. Ace is so often an impenetrable force that I can't help myself from wanting to crack open.

But then he stands, draining his drink with his eyes still locked on me. *Well, fuck me, is he going to actually come out here?*

A vibration of excitement sweeps across my skin, leaving the briefest tingle of nervous energy in its wake. My hips continue moving to the sounds of Hozier crooning through the speakers as I let my eyes blink languidly, appreciating the build and stature of Ace *motherfucking* Foxx.

I'm not a tiny person, but Ace takes up space. His broad shoulders and height are just a part of it. Beyond his eloquently masculine posture, the thighs that fill his pants, along with a nicely rounded ass, it's the spark of authority. There's power in the uncertainty of what he's capable of doing. Danger licks his skin the way I'm always itching to.

The man doles out big dick energy like he's dealing cards. And every person who comes close to him knows it. Ace draws people's attention. It isn't just me. He's magnetic. There's never a room he enters where at least half a dozen eyes don't stop what they were doing to watch.

I smirk as I study him. Oh, how I love to see him bite back whatever emotion I'm able to stir.

And like almost every other time, when I poke or prod, he moves. Just never in the direction that I crave. And that's what Ace was to me: a craving. Instead of coming to join me and his brothers on the dance floor, he heads toward the double doors.

"Hadley Jean, get your ass over here and dance with me," Lincoln shouts over the music, dancing over to me as Faye takes a dessert break with Lark and Lily. My smile takes over, leaving any inkling of feelings for his older brother to float away in the breeze.

"You alright?" he asks as he swings me around to some cover of "Addicted to Love."

"Linc, I'm always alright," I say with dramatic flair.

When he spins me, and I come back toward him, he prods again. "You didn't bring Hawk. I take it that's over then?"

I sigh. "We're only ever going to be a bit of fun."

He leaves it alone at that, and after just a couple more songs, Faye's being brought out onto the dance floor by Griz. As they come closer, Linc leans over to kiss his bride. "You want to swap?"

Faye laughs out, "No way! I've been waiting for my turn with Griz all night." And like he's been waiting to show off, he twirls her around. She leans over, puckering her lips at me. "I need one from you too."

I give her a kiss back and they dance away, still laughing. "She might be my favorite now," I tell Lincoln as we watch the patriarch of the family dance with their newest member.

"You said that about Laney too," he says while still smiling at his wife.

"They're fucking fabulous, what can I say?" I glance back toward the bar, silently berating myself for always looking. When I find Ace talking to the bartender, it seems like a good time for water. "I'm parched," I say as I spin under Linc's arm and toward trouble.

"Go get him, Hads!" he calls out after me. I do *not* need the encouragement, but it makes me smile nonetheless. Linc is my best friend for a roster of reasons, one of them being that he knows exactly what to say when I need it most. The Foxx men are good at that—Lincoln provides encouragement, Griz has wisdom, Grant's the good conscience, and Ace is my rook. Protector, instigator, and yet somehow, it always feels like more. A driving force to do better and prove him wrong.

The room crawls with busybodies and watchful eyes. People love weddings almost as much as they love the rumors that come out of them—who got too drunk and who went home with whom.

"Hello, bartender, I would love a water," I singsong with a charming smile. I instantly feel Ace's attention on me. Brushing up against his arm, I look right at him when I add, "And a bourbon. The 1910. Neat." I hold up my hand. "Three fingers."

"She'll just have the water," he says as he glides one hand into the pocket of his pants, angling his body toward me.

I lift my eyebrows. "You do not have a say about what I'm swallowing tonight, Daddy—" I can barely finish, gasping as his arm wraps around my waist, moving us down the hall toward the restrooms. "What are you—"

"Keep moving," he bites out. "I'm not having this conversation in front of one of my employees or the rest of this fucking town."

My senses are on fire, lit up from the inside out, as I push his hand from my hip and stride ahead of him. Once I reach the edge of the distillery hallway, right where the light ends, I turn to look at him again.

But he doesn't stop, eyes darkening on me as he walks me backward, just a few feet farther, into the shadowed space.

"That's enough," he says, voice low, his body so close and distracting that I don't register what he's saying.

I can't begin to unpack why making him mad has me feeling so triumphant. Enough to have me saying something I've wanted to for a long time.

I aim for unaffected as I rest my head back against the wall where he has me caged. "You know what's tiring?" I ask as I look down the front of him and then back up to his stupidly sexy face. "Finding you staring at me, and knowing what it looks like when someone wants something—"

He steps closer. "Is that what you think? That I want *something* from you?"

I drag my bottom lip through my teeth. If there was ever going to be a time to be blunt with him, it would be now. Why add a filter when I'm already this deep into it? "I don't think you know exactly what you want from me. But it's driving you wild, trying to figure it out. That much is obvious."

His body inches even closer, and my heart beats so damn fast that I feel out of breath.

"You're a pain in my ass, Hadley." His eyes search mine before glancing down at my lips again. But he quickly realizes how close he is and takes a step back.

Not so fast, Daddy.

I take a step closer, head tilting back so he has no choice but to keep his eyes on mine. "What did you want to tell me so urgently that you needed to pull me into a dark corner? Or was talking not on your mind?"

"To knock it off." Taking another step back, his hands move to his pockets. "You're working awfully hard lately, trying to get under my skin."

Without a thought, I blurt, "I felt exactly what I was working on making hard last night." And I don't regret it when I see his jaw tic, just as I expected it to. Looking at the perfectly manicured scruff along his chin leading toward his full bottom lip, I add for good measure, "Or was the blond with her feet on you responsible for getting you all worked up?" I sarcastically open my mouth, mocking surprise. "Is that your little kink, Ace? Stilettos and femdom?" Erasing the space he's building between us, I watch as his throat bobs.

As I run my fingers along the center of his shirt, my thumbs graze the buttons, and I can feel how quickly I've turned the tables on him as his breath catches.

When I look up at him, though, I realize the mistake I've made. Pushing his buttons is one thing, but this close, with his blue-gray eyes locked on me, I almost forget my own name. With a narrowing gaze, he brushes a curl out of my face and behind my ear. His thumb traces the line of my jaw so softly that it feels like I'm practically imagining it. My whole body heats, and words, thoughts, the world outside completely disintegrate at the simplest touch.

The low rumble of his voice raises goose bumps along my skin when he says, "I think if you knew my 'little kinks,' you wouldn't push me with that bratty mouth so often."

Oh, fuck.

Heart racing, I'm overheated and out of my depth. Dirty talk and submissive behavior are nothing new, but the suggestiveness coming from him has me ready to shove away thoughts of feminism and simply adopt a needy dialect of phrase combinations like "yes, sir" and "please, Daddy."

His hand falls down my arm, grazing my skin until he reaches my elbow, and instead of pulling his hands away or retreating to his pocket, he follows the same line, along my waist and down my hip. The light touch has me holding my breath, my panties warm and wet as my thighs clench. Taking the smallest step closer, he breathes me in, perhaps gathering his wits.

So I do what I do best when it comes to Ace: I push it. "I think if you really were paying attention, you'd catch on that my bratty mouth would like you to finally do something with it."

Huffing a laugh lacking humor, he leans forward, his lips so close that they brush my cheek as he moves toward my ear. "Knock. It. Off."

And without another glance at me, he walks away like I'm not standing here. Wide-eyed, out of breath, and dizzy from whatever the hell that just was, I yell out after him, "Make me!"

Chapter 7

Ace

I THROW THE STABLE DOOR closed behind me and take the stairs up two at a time. I need to cool the fuck down. She pushed it, alright. *"Make me."* I had no business pushing back, showing my hand, and getting so close to touching her, kissing her. Breathing roughly, I pause with my hands on my hips. As I look down at the worn wooden floor, I can't help but smile and shake my head. I already fucking regret getting that close to her.

Laughing to myself, I glance up and then pull the whiskey thief from the corner. She's gotten too close. I've been doing fine, ignoring the way she burrows into me more and more with every fucking year that moves on. But the way I catch her looking at me in the same way she just called me out for looking at her…

I lean on the workbench and suck in a deep breath. I want to be distracted for a few minutes, work her out of my head, get my dick to calm down before I go in that house and do something stupid, like fuck that bratty mouth.

I rushed out of there so fucking fast and tried not to look at anyone on my way out. I wasn't in any position to carry on a conversation as if that moment didn't just shake me in a way that I didn't fucking plan for.

She'll stay at the house tonight and won't trek back to her place. The guest suite has been her spot in the house for a long time. Mostly it's a test of sheer willpower not to knock on that door. There's a roster of reasons why I can't, but it never makes it any easier. Tonight won't be any different despite the way she's testing limits. I'll push down the way I want her, like usual. I'll remember the agreements I made to stay away from her and the unspoken promise I made to myself to never hurt her.

I dip the long copper pipe of the whiskey thief into the lowest of the eight barrels stashed up here. This isn't like what Grant did, making batches of bourbon as a form of therapy. This is an appreciation for a classic mash bill—the perfect combination of corn, barley, and rye. And it aged right here. In a space that feels like my reprieve from the rest of my world. Above horses I love and outside of the person I need to be when I'm making bourbon for our business. This, right here, is for me. A space where I don't have to be the oldest brother, the smartest in the room, schooling my emotions and masking my physical responses to whatever bullshit comes at me. I'm the bourbon boy and the lead of my family's company. Everything in this room is only here because I want it to be. I glance at the drawer to my left, where there's one of the few things I should feel guilty about but don't. It's the only thing I allow myself to have when it comes to *her*.

Filling a glass with my bourbon, I take all of it in one shot. *Fuck it.*

I throw open the drawer and lift out the black envelope with cursive handwriting in white to a PO box in Colorado that's always auto forwarded to the house. The return address is always the same, even after realizing how careless it was.

This was never some kind of undiscovered or perverted kink that had one day been revealed. It's much simpler than that.

"Why do you have two bags of underwear? Lincoln asked as he peered into a pink-and-black striped bag. "Actually, you know what? I don't want to know."

I had the afternoon to relax before I'd be at the distillery nonstop for our newest release, but the two of them were so loud it was impossible not to listen.

"I have goals, Linc, and some of those goals are financial," she said from behind the trunk of her car as they looked in the back. "There are plenty of beautiful people in this world who have fetishes. Who am I to judge?" They shut the trunk and walked toward the porch, lingering just outside my window.

"Hadley, we can loan you the money. What the hell is the difference if you're paying us back or the bank?"

"I want this to be mine. Nobody else's. So I'm going to sell my panties and make some extra money."

I sat up, my spine growing rigid. She couldn't be serious.

"I've been sending pairs out once a month. Ask me how much I've made."

"I really don't want to—"

She cut him off, "Two grand. That's a part-time job—a good one. And a girl needs to eat."

I couldn't stop thinking about that fucking conversation. It didn't take too long to find her listings, with some help from a friend. It was simple after that. I didn't want anyone else to have that kind of access to her. I didn't overthink it. I couldn't have a say in who she fucked or dated, but I could control this.

Since then, I've been an anonymous, well-paying client who offers her double if she only sends them to me. Five years' worth of panties, and I helped her get Midnight Proof off the ground without needing to ask her father for a fucking dime.

The white lace of this pair is barely a scrap of material, but fuck, does it smell good. I drag it under my nose—notes of something sweet and salty, like I imagine her skin would taste like if I dragged my tongue where I wanted. I move the scalloped material across my lips, making my mouth water. As I take another sip of bourbon, the spice and caramel notes on my tongue combine with the lingering smell of her pussy. It's the way I prefer to drink my bourbon. A classic single barrel that continued to age. And the fantasy of her.

The feeling of her hair brushing against my thighs as she braces her hands along my waist, nails dragging and digging into my thighs. I throw open my pants, shove my boxers down, and take out my dick. Wrapping the soft lace around it, with a loose grip so I can feel the material against my skin, I give myself a slow tug. My mouth drops open and the breath I had been holding rushes out as I grip tighter and do it again.

Fuck. I tip my head back and get lost in the idea of her wanting me. Of pleasing me, ready to take the directions I give her and eager to savor every drop that leaks from the slit of my dick. I rock my wrist back and forth, feeling the material graze the tip as I think about the way she would look up at me through those pretty dark lashes. It's a filthy dreamed-up image I tuck away to replay over and over as I grip myself hard and stroke my dick from base to head. I'm dripping all over my knuckles. And all of it would look so pretty painted on her lips. I'd tap the head against her slick tongue and drag the underside up and down as she gets me nice and wet.

My dick swells at the idea of her doing exactly as I say, watching me as I move my cock along her tongue, in charge of my own pleasure. I push in farther just to see her gag on it. But she doesn't. Her eyes simply water as she keeps them trained on me.

I give her a nod, letting her know she can close those lips around me.

And, oh, she fucking does. The groan that her tongue and lips pull from my throat should be embarrassing, but I don't give one single fuck. She plays with me for a little while before taking me deeper. Swallowing around me, she enjoys how I fill her throat. I drag my fingers into her hair and let them tangle into the wild, curly mess of it. She moans, wanting more, lost in this moment. *Fuck*, I want more too. I moan, realizing I've edged myself too long, because I come without any warning. Every muscle in my body tenses, and then my legs practically give out as I fill the white lace. With sweat on my lip, my pulse races. I try to drag out whatever is left of my orgasm and rock my wrist more slowly. The slicked, messy panties feel so fucking good. What I wouldn't give for it to be her skin, her mouth, her pussy. My body shudders. I'm so damn sensitive now, but a part of me isn't ready to come down from this high completely.

There have been women over the years, plenty of beautiful women to satisfy and substitute. But that's all it's ever been. The attraction is always surface level. No sleepovers and no repeats. Easy to erase, move on from, and forget. The whispers to "never fall for a Foxx" piss me off, but it works in my favor. It's kept my control intact and her safe.

An agreement that I've regretted the moment I made it. It's been a decade of growing lust and longing for what I can't have, but I've always thrived off control. Though, the way she's been pushing... It's relentless. That smart mouth and seeing her with someone else in the way I want her, it's fucking fraying every edge I've got left.

Wiping away the evidence of my weakness, I toss it to burn later and hope this unyielding desire for her will turn to ash along with it.

Chapter 8

Hadley

> *April: Grabbing a man by the balls is wildly effective.*

THE RINGING IN MY EARS won't stop. An ongoing, muted chime that's obnoxious enough to force one eye open. A nice little wave of nausea hits, like I need the reminder of how many cocktails I enjoyed last night. Every damn thing that happened and everything I said come rushing back to me like a wave pulling me under. *Oh fuck.*

My head feels like it might explode when I roll over too fast. Searching for my phone on the nightstand, I feel my fingers graze an unopened water bottle. I sit up and find two ibuprofen pills next to it, along with a clementine. I smile. I've stayed here too many times to keep track, and every time there's something thoughtful waiting when I wake up. Griz always thinks ahead like that.

A wall of texts lights up my phone, and as I pick it up to

swipe and read, I accidentally answer the call that flashes across my screen. *Shit*.

"Miss Finch?" a voice says loudly, and then moments later, I'm met with my father and his attorney, both looking at me through FaceTime. "I'm here with your father."

I wipe the makeup from under my eyes, rubbing away any sleep that still lingers, my hangover gnawing at my senses as I attempt to keep my emotions in check. "What part of 'stop trying to speak with me' aren't you understanding?"

"Miss Finch, as your father's attorney, I'm begging you to please consider transferring the money that has been outlined. There are rather aggressive people who have not been paid." He exhales heavily, then adds, "Not to mention, those upset about all they've lost."

"Who do you think is getting those angry phone calls, hm?"

My father's fist pounds on his desk as he sits beside his attorney. "For Christ's sake, Hadley. It doesn't matter if you're angry with me; there are people who will get what they're owed, regardless of if you're having a temper tantrum about it. For once in your life, start acting like a Finch." If he had said something like that to me a decade ago, it would have hit harder. Now it's a compliment. I haven't been acting like a Finch or doing what he wants for a long time. What makes him think I'll start now?

I blink, trying not to react to his threat. My father is very good at causing chaos. He's been doing it my entire life. I was simply an inconvenience. Until I wasn't. He is the ultimate narcissist, above all the other things in his repertoire. Anxiety ripples through me, my stomach twisting and the headache feeling more like lightheadedness. I want to ignore all of this. I don't want to go near a single part of the mess he's made of his life.

"Be careful, pumpkin, you wouldn't want the things you've

worked so hard for to end up more of a mess than they already are." His attorney tries to cut him off by holding up his hand.

A reaction will only feed the monster. I bite down on the anger that surfaces at his threat to my business and don't respond. But he takes that as an opportunity to keep talking.

"Heard Lincoln Foxx got married last night—"

He doesn't have a chance to say anything more. I hang up and toss my phone to the bottom of the bed, turning over and screaming into the pillow until I expel every ounce of breath from my lungs. *Fuck him.*

I've heard more from my father since his house arrest than I have for the majority of my adult life. He wants something, or rather, all of what I currently have control over. It's the one thing he never planned—if anything were to happen to him, all of it, from the money to the land, businesses, and properties, would go to me to handle. He'd left the power to the one puppet he never really controlled—and he was finally realizing that. I throw my feet over the side of the bed and wince at the idea of putting my heels on, but that's what I get for not bringing a change of clothes.

I peer out of the double doors and down the hall. It's too early for the sun, but it's bright enough in here to quietly navigate to the front door and outside.

"You're my favorite, you know that, right?" Griz asks as he sits on his rocker on the front porch, with a mug in each hand, both steaming. His mustache kicks up. "Why are you sneaking out of here? You finally end up in my grandson's bed?"

I bark out a laugh. "Griz!"

"I don't know what the hell you two are waitin' on. Even with a nice nudge, that man is so damn stubborn."

I swallow at his words as I peel the clementine he left for

me. What am I supposed to say to that? I can't keep chasing someone who doesn't want to be caught. Maybe I've never been as forward as I was last night, but he just left me standing there, turned on and in the dark. That seems like all the answer I need.

Griz chuckles to himself, sipping his coffee.

"He seems like he's got it all figured out. But Ace tries to be too many things for too many people. He has his own way of doing it, but that man's single goal in life is to protect people. Especially the ones he cares about most. And Hadley Jean, that man has tried most of his life to ignore how much he cares about you."

I look out toward the stables. "I know he does. It's just not the way I want."

He taps my hand and gives it a squeeze. But it's what he says next that I don't know if I'll ever be able to forget. "He would only ever be able to choose you. That man won't love anyone else. Believe me, I know. Because when you find it"—he shakes his head—"it's impossible to think about anything else."

"Griz…" I trail off, smiling to shield myself from the fantasy instead of the reality.

"I'm pretty sure the same goes for you." He takes a few chugs of his coffee and places his hand over mine. "They might say to never fall for a Foxx, but nobody ever said what could happen if a Foxx fell for you. There isn't a damn thing more real than the way you look at my grandson."

He's not wrong.

He reaches into his back pocket and fishes out a picture. I know it's Shelby Calloway right away. I knew her first as one of the top trainers for Finch & King. My father was never shy about telling people how she could train the hell out of horses. But I got to know her when she became an unexpected person in

Griz's life. Faye's mom started coming for family dinners about a year or so after Faye left town. I remember Griz and Shelby sitting out on this porch, laughing together. It always made me smile, seeing him with her. He deserves to find someone like that again. She passed away unexpectedly a few years before Faye came back to Fiasco. I know how it feels to miss someone. It's something that all of us have in common.

"Is that Shelby?" I ask anyway.

He nods, handing me the photo. "Some people just hit different—for no reason other than that." Resting his chin on his fist, he says, "Shelby had been in a bad place for a long while before she looked my way, but once she did"—he makes an explosion sound—"that was it. Made me feel more like myself than any other person on this planet. And that's saying something." He clears his throat, taking the picture back from me and returning it to his pocket. "You remember Ace's nana?"

I nod, vaguely remembering her and the way she always had cinnamon buns baking.

"She was a wonderful woman," he says. "Miss her too. But I don't think we're meant to just love once. It's too good not to feel it as many times as we can." He glances at me with a pointed look. "Stop being an idiot."

I raise my eyebrows as a laugh bubbles from my chest.

"The both of you," he says, shaking his head like I've been truly reprimanded.

I let the conversation settle. It's been a long time since I spent a morning with Griz and just let him talk. I think a lot of people see the easy smile and older charm but forget that he's been the heart of more than the Foxx family. He keeps a pulse on Fiasco, much like Ace does.

"You know the one thing nobody ever tells you about getting older?" Griz asks just as I sip the extra cup he had out here for me. "The copious amounts of bird-watching."

I smile as he gets up and leans against the porch banister, grabbing a pair of binoculars perched there. "You sure it's bird-watching, or are you spying?"

He laughs at that, but his thick mustache barely moves. "Here, take a look," he says, holding them out to me.

"Alright, what am I looking at?"

I look out to the large white building with a prominent Foxx logo painted along its side in black—opposite colors than the rickhouses that line the expansive property. Those are all black, from roof to foundation, with a simple white logo that shows off it's theirs. The black is meant to absorb as much heat from the sun as possible. Griz said it's just a little part of their secret sauce, letting the natural elements of Kentucky shape the way their bourbon's made.

"The oak tree. To your left, just before the path down to Grant and Laney's place."

I move the lens around according to his direction.

"There's a nest of these tiny little things—loud when they're awake, but it sounds sweet. I've never minded loud. Preferred most things that way—music, women, life, you name it."

I smile, because it's such a Griz thing to say.

"There's one that's always bringing something back to the nest. At first glance, it looks like there's just one. But every day, I watch, and I see the other one stop in, check up on the other, and then fly off. I bet she doesn't even know it—how much that one pays attention to her, stops in, making sure she's okay."

I lower the binoculars and look down at the leather strap.

It's pretty obvious he isn't talking about the empty nest in that tree anymore.

"You're pushy by nature, Griswald Foxx. But why so much today?"

He leans against the porch pillar and looks out at his expansive land. I take in the way the years have chipped at some of his stature. He's still strong and solid but slower in his movements now. The bit of dark hair that lingered in his eyebrows and peppered his hairline when I first met him is long gone. He's all white and silver now.

"I want my family set. I need you to be okay." He swallows whatever else he was going to say and instead clears his throat. "I'm just trying to add fuel to the gossip I started. I heard about you disappearing in a dark hallway with Atticus."

Smacking his arm playfully, my head shakes as sarcasm laces my words. "Those damn gossips."

"You hungry, Finch?" Griz nudges my elbow. "I'm hungry as hell. You're drivin'."

Fiasco mornings aren't typical for me. Midnight Proof isn't cleaned up and cleared out until at least 3 a.m., which means I'm sleeping the moment my head hits the pillow. Lately it's been earlier than that. Business stopped booming when Fiasco made headlines. A night off wasn't going to hurt much, and Lincoln and Faye getting married was a great reason to close the speakeasy and enjoy myself. It feels like forever since I've had a night or day off from everything.

"As I live and breathe, Hadley Finch gracing us with her presence, all before noon," Romey says from the end of the counter.

"Knock it off," Marla clips back at her, giving me a tight-lipped smile as she nods to the last open seat.

A few heads turn to follow me, and it's not hard to hear the less-than-quiet whispers as Griz and I make our way through the place. Hooch's isn't pretty, but Marla makes great food, and I need caffeine and something greasy to ease the hangover.

"You look rough today," Marla says as she pours us cups of coffee once we're seated. "You were a helluva best man at that weddin', though." She smiles, looking down as I take out my black journal, phone, and a pen from my bag. There are plenty of days I spend scribbling away at this counter.

Prue pops her head up from her book and answers instead. "Speaking of best man—Hadley Jean, there's only one left… You going to snag him?"

Romey bats her sister's arm. "Stop that right now. Ace is not the marrying kind. And look at her—"

Griz leans into me and says, "See, I'm not the only one noticing."

Jesus Christ, it's too early for this. I fold my arms on the countertop and blow out an exasperated breath.

"I am looking…" Prue says. "She looks better hungover and annoyed than most of us ever look on our best day."

Marla waves them off as she stands in front of us, waiting for our order.

Griz asks for cakes and eggs as I stare off at the specials board. Why is everyone so hard up to marry me off? I hate that, for this crowd, being married is a solution for happiness. I am happy. Mostly. I think.

"I'm going to bring you what I want if you don't tell me in the next few seconds," Marla barks out. She's such a grumpy bitch. I love her.

My smile cracks as I say, "Bring me whatever you want, Marla."

Jimmy Dugan talks with Griz about some of the rumors that have been swirling around. I overhear him say, "I'll be on patrol, third shift to start, but it's better than issuing parking tickets on Main." He releases a nervous exhale and adds, "I don't envy Del lately either. He and the FBI team are dealing with another body surfacing down by Fiasco Falls. The PD softball team likes to talk a lot, and then they say to be quiet, so I'm not really sure what the hell I'm supposed to do." Shrugging, he takes another sip of his coffee. "Probably not yammering on with you. Honestly if I could steer clear of any of that, I'd be happy. Blood and bad guys aren't in my wheelhouse."

"Jimmy," Griz says. "You do realize you're on the police force, right? Bad guys and some violence are in the description."

He shoves a piece of buttermilk pie in his mouth and says, "Yeah, I know, but Ace said…"

That's all I hear before a very loud sob rings out from the far end of the counter. Vinny from Fiasco Flowers chokes back a cry while he's talking with his partner.

Marla brings out her "nesting egg" dish—over medium eggs on top of arugula and wilted spinach surrounded by crispy hash browns and strips of bacon.

"This is perfect," I beam.

She gives me a tight-lipped smile and pours a refill of coffee. "What's going on over there?" I ask.

"Vinny has to close up shop. Not enough foot traffic to keep the storefront anymore." I've known the tourists have been sparse, but Vinny's run that flower shop since I was a kid. It makes my chest ache to think this might be the reality for more than just Vinny if things don't change soon.

My phone buzzes, and this time when I see an unknown number, my stomach doesn't churn. For some reason, the words coming through feel more like kindling.

> UNKNOWN:
> Pumpkin, you will pay out what has been requested. I will not ask again. DO NOT make me remind you that while you may control the finances of Finch & King, I do not need your permission to utilize what is mine. Do not ignore me. You will regret it.

My father. He is the only person who calls me that: *pumpkin*. How he's still able to access burner phones is a massive flaw in our system. I've never hit delete and added to junk so fast. Permission is something I sought out when I was younger. The approval of doing something I was supposed to do, and the nod from authority when I did, felt right. Maybe I'm a good girl at heart. Masking the vulnerability of what that truly means, as society would define it—a weak constitution submissive, and uptight. I'm not even a fraction of any of those things. I've made sure of it.

As a kid, I would've told you I was a daddy's girl. The only good thing my mother left was an empty black notebook and a sweet, albeit morbid, note on the first page: *My darling girl, you are so much stronger than you'll ever know. I'll love you even when I'm gone.* She swallowed a lot of pills, and then took a bath. My father said it was the weak way out of hard things. I always thought he was right, until I realized maybe he was the reason she felt like she had no other choice.

Regardless of how my mother left us, it meant it was just me and him from then on. A child and an aggressively eager businessman who measures success in money and influence. I didn't realize that until I was older. If I looked back in my black book, it would be crystal clear, but while you're living it, toxic people don't seem hazardous.

Most of the time, from as far back as I can remember, I was left to figure out my own meals. Hooch's for a bite when the fridge wasn't stocked. Donuts for breakfast on Sundays. I tucked myself into bed. Made my own doctor appointments. I figured out the simple things, like having to keep a bedtime if I didn't want to be exhausted for school. And the closest thing to approval was only when I was riding horses or playing the part of the loving daughter. On the occasion we spent time together, it was always in the company of horse trainers and jockeys or someone who could be considered influential to my father's career. The last name Finch has always been associated with horses and money. As I grew up, respect from others for my last name did too.

The authority figure I looked up to was never interested in my well-being. My father has only ever been interested in being obeyed and the visuals of being a loving father, not the actual role of it.

My phone buzzes again and a twinge of nerves works down my arms and settles in my stomach as I look at a picture of me. Sitting in this spot from mere moments ago when I was looking down at my phone.

I glance around the space and behind me. Everyone who's here right now I recognize. The angle is from the side windows, but when I look up, nobody is there. This time, the image is from a different number. It's not from my father or from any of the other host of texts that have been flooding in. No words or threats, just the confirmation that I'm being watched. I sit taller and push my shoulders back. Suppressing a shiver of unease, I turn off my phone and stuff it into my pocket.

For the last decade of my life, I looked at permission as the antithesis of everything I chose to do. In my father's eyes, opening a speakeasy, gallivanting as a single woman throughout town, living on my own—hell, even having family dinners with the Foxxes—was a direct *fuck you* to the narcissist who barely raised me. There's something wildly addictive about finding out exactly what you're made of when blood is nothing more than an unfortunate scientific connection.

I let out a sarcastic laugh because the joke is on me. As much as I want to yell a giant "fuck you" at my father and all of the text messages and threats that keep coming, middle fingers and loud words are simply reactions. It won't stop or stall any of it. I don't have any upper hand here other than to ignore what they all want. And despite the way my skin goes taut or my heart rate picks up when my phone vibrates or someone I don't recognize spends too long looking at me, ignoring them and not paying a damn cent is the least helpless thing I can think of doing.

Picking up my fork, I pepper my food with hot sauce, sitting taller and smiling at the people around me. I'm pissing off plenty, but no matter how much uneasiness flares in my gut, not touching that money and ignoring the threats is the only power I hold.

Chapter 9

Ace

"You need to start taking more risks," Griz says as he steeples his fingers in front of his mustache.

Risks aren't something I like taking, unless it's a gambit and there's a purpose. I haven't shared with my grandfather what I've been planning and how it all encompasses Foxx Bourbon and Fiasco. He certainly doesn't have a clue about the agreements I was forced to make years ago because of risks that didn't have any strategy behind them.

"Like you've been doing?" I clap back.

"What the hell is that supposed to mean, Atticus?" he says low and slow.

Foxx Bourbon is a well-oiled machine simply because I won't have it any other way. And its success—through Prohibition, the Depression, and when Kentucky elected overeager politicians and our country appointed questionably capable leaders—continues because of the relationships built and favors earned over the years.

I've never had any moral dilemmas about the things I'm required to do to keep my business thriving and family safe. Favors are a currency I value, which is why when Hadley walked into my office the night of Faye and Lincoln's joint bachelor party, she saw a woman with her hands on me and not the plans being negotiated. Plans I wasn't expecting to have to make moves on just yet, but Griz forced my hand by inviting those friends.

There's a small group I trust. Friends of the Foxx family who go back generations, but then also some new ones who are smart and tactical. The Architect, much like The Jeweler, is someone with her own agendas. She has thriving businesses and a very specialized, rare talent. We each have our own titles for the other as a way to keep a less detailed paper trail if anyone looks too closely. The Architect, specifically, has a knack for removing problems. She runs one of the most prominent architectural firms in the country. She sees the macro-equation, the bigger picture, and what needs to happen in order to get there.

I've been taking *too* many risks. And no matter what I do lately, those risks seem to be involving Hadley. It's a challenge most of the time trying to ignore her, but now that I've felt her hands on me? I blow out a breath and shake my head, trying to ignore it again. *Fuck.* Tilting my head back, I look up at the wood beams that run the length of our kitchen.

"What are you doing? Why are you looking up like that?" He stirs his coffee and flips open the top of the pillbox labeled "Sunday." I stare at the palmful of pills that I know ranges from a multivitamin to an alphabet of other things that he swears are keeping him alive. "Your brothers want to see our company not only make great money, but evolve."

This bullshit again.

"They want to shake things up around here, and I can't understand why you're giving them such a hard time."

It always comes back to this. I don't understand why he's so eager to push me on it. I shouldn't have to tell him that we thrive on tradition. He's the one who muttered those words first. Our brand can make small adjustments and moves in this industry, but if it's too much, then we'll lose our footing.

"Because I fucking love bourbon," I rush out with frustration.

The process, the taste, the variety of how it can hit someone's palate differently every time. But I've been pushed to my limits here. "I've said yes. To everything they've asked, the fucking barrels aging in a cave, the peach flavor bullshit—which I still can't fucking handle, by the way. What else do you want from me?"

"I want you to be happy. I want you to make your own blend that you're excited about the same way that they've been. I want you to bend more easily on things that are good for you." He leans back and folds his arms in front of him. "You're going through the motions. I want you to find more than just bourbon to be passionate about." Clearing his throat, he adds, "You're not taking any chances. You're being too careful."

I hate how the word "careful" lingers with his disapproval. Out of all of us, I've done everything he's ever asked of me, and here I am, still feeling like a goddamn kid and not good enough. Being careful is the only way all of this is going to work.

"You say 'careful' like that isn't exactly what you told me to be all those years ago…"

"Do I want to know?" Griz asked, just as I hit the top step of the porch. The darkness hid the blood and sweat that blended into the

hair on my arms. I was distracted by what had just been negotiated. And still buzzing from the piece of shit I'd killed before that.

I cleared my throat and stopped my momentum to focus on him. "You don't. So don't ask," I said as I continued my path inside. The sun was going to start peeking over the horizon line any minute now, and I needed to clean up, figure out exactly how I was going to keep this agreement with Wheeler off the books, and make sure Hadley kept away from me for a while.

"Just be careful, Atticus," he called out from behind the swinging door. "When it comes to her, be very careful."

Griz waves at the air in front of him, like he's heard enough. And dismissing the memory that I seem to have no problem recollecting. I never knew if he assumed something had happened or if he just knew somehow that there was trouble. Griz had a sixth sense about these things. And yet I was never going to offer up any details. He had always been adamant about not doing business with Finch.

"You know Hadley walked in," I say, pulling the carton of eggs from the refrigerator.

He puts down his coffee mug as I carve out the center of each slice of bread. "When?" he asks.

"I was trying to figure out why, of all nights, we had uninvited visitors," I say while cracking open an egg, then tossing the shells into the sink behind me. "And come to find out, you had invited them." I crack and toss three more times, trying not to get angry about being left out of whatever loop Griz had made. "Why would you do that and not tell me first?"

"What did Hadley walk in on?" he asks, ignoring my question.

"The Architect was perched on my desk. She had some interesting information to share about a Pacific Northwest winery and a horse sanctuary out in Montana." I pause to see if he gives me any kind of reaction to that. But he simply sips his coffee and watches as I move around the room. "That, and Julian was fucking flirting with her at the bar."

"Ah," he says like that's the most important piece of information. "So this is about Julian flirting with Hadley."

"I couldn't give a shit who she flirts with," I say sarcastically. "Don't make this about something else when I'm asking you what they were doing here. I couldn't find you or either of them after that, which means you're keeping something from me. The last time that happened, our fucking rickhouse burned down."

"You know exactly what burned it down. Don't go blaming it on me. You're the one who was so eager to collect a favor." He's quiet for a few beats before he says, "I've been in Fiasco most of my life. Been thinking about that a lot lately." Getting up from the counter, he moves slowly. The next decade's coming closer, and I can tell he feels it in his bones. "One of those eggs-in-a-hole for me?" He points at the six I've got cooking.

I nod, but stay quiet, letting him take his time to finish that statement. Griz is always more forthcoming when you give him space to run his mouth. I flip the bread just as the egg white turns opaque and leave it for just a moment without breaking or overcooking the yolk.

"You and your brothers are doing what needs to be done. Have been for a while now. I thought it was time I start letting our *friends* know that."

I plate the eggs, sprinkle the salt and pepper, dole out three shakes of hot sauce on top of each, and then slide his plate in front of him.

He looks at me pointedly. "Favors I might owe, our book of contacts, all of that will fall to you."

Trying to work through his reasoning, I dive into my breakfast. I cut into the center with my fork, allowing the deep golden yolk to run into the bread. It's our weekend morning breakfast. Every week for as long as I can remember.

Everything he's saying is true. I've been the lead on most things here, and I'm taking the lead on getting Fiasco out of the hole that was dug for it. But Griz always likes to have his hands in things. He can never turn away from knowing everything about everyone. "Why?" I ask before I even realize it.

"It's time. That's all. It was only right to tell them in person. I knew her father and Julian's long before you ever came into the picture." He takes the last bite of his breakfast. "Plenty of people—media, law enforcement, locals—are paying attention to the comings and goings since the Finch & King scandal. But during wedding festivities"—he smirks with a shrug of his shoulders—"there are plenty of out-of-towners who come to events like that. No one would bat an eye at who's coming through."

He waits for my acknowledgment, and I give him a nod. It makes me uneasy, how cavalier he's being, but it wasn't a bad call; it was strategic having them there that night. Griz might be the easygoing flirt to the rest of the world—the patriarch who plans female-dominated book clubs and can carry on an easy conversation with a stranger—but he's methodical. Smart. And intentional with everything he does.

The front door opens, and a loud argument about the Boston Rebels hockey team filters down the hall.

"McCabe isn't getting any younger," Lincoln says just as they come into view.

"It's a bullshit move. They shouldn't have even considered trading him," Grant says.

I shift a glance at Griz, who looks barely bothered by the two of them dropping in. I don't care if they come over, but they rarely show up without texting our group chat first.

"So nice of you to join us," Griz says, wiping the yolk with what was left of his toast.

"What are you guys doing here?" I ask, pouring more beans into the espresso machine. Apparently I'm making more coffee. We often have chats about marketing and distillery happenings or argue about blends and barrels, but I hadn't planned on that today.

"Griz said he wanted to talk about the Ditch the Derby event that Laney has been planning," Lincoln says, opening the fridge. "I think it's the most promising way to snag two waves of people during Derby weekend and bring them down to Fiasco. We've got locals who want something else to do that day. They've enjoyed The Oaks—"

Griz holds up his hand, signaling for Lincoln to take a breath. I glance at Grant, both of us knowing that Griz isn't interested in talking about Ditch the Derby. There's something else, and in my gut, I knew it was coming.

I watch the way our grandfather takes his time before he chooses his next words, and it has my pulse jumping higher. I never know what the old man is going to say, but right now, it feels like something big.

"You three boys…" He clears his throat and glances at each of us. "*Men*. You haven't been boys for a long time."

Lincoln looks my way, sensing the same tone that I am, I'm sure.

I stand up taller, almost bracing for what he's about to say. "I've decided I'm going to officially retire."

What?! I'm instantly relieved, and then immediately skeptical.

I almost laugh out an exhale. I was holding my breath, waiting to hear he was fucking dying. It would've made sense with some of these arrangements he's been making. Even though I'm not delusional to the reality that he's getting up there in age, retirement is a word that's almost perplexing when it comes to my grandfather.

Lincoln puffs out his cheeks, blowing out air. "Griz, how is that different from what you are now?" The relief in his tone is obvious too. I think we were all bracing for impact.

Griz looks down at his hands that are doing a helluva job at wringing the napkin in front of him. He's nervous. *Oh shit.* When he raises his attention, he looks me in the eye, inhales, and then says, "Foxx Bourbon will be evenly split between my married grandsons."

It's like I've been thrown into an ice bath, yet my body is instantly running hot. Nostrils flaring, I keep my focus on my grandfather. "What *the fuck* are you doing, old man?" I ask, my tone eerily quiet.

Grant smiles out of the corner of my eye. He heard it. There isn't a single funny thing about those words.

"You're planning to keep quiet about decisions regarding bourbon." Lincoln barks a laugh. "I'll believe it when I see it." He clearly didn't hear the part about "married" grandsons.

"Don't do this, Griz," I say, shaking my head. "I'm not sure what point you're making."

Lincoln opens his mouth, trying to keep up with what I'm saying.

Grant tilts his head toward our middle brother and says, "Griz said *married* grandsons."

Lincoln chuckles nervously, adjusting his glasses as he shakes his head. "He's not serious." Linc then turns to Griz. "You're not serious…are you?"

Griz stands from his chair, chin tilted up just slightly, and doesn't say a word. The bastard just threw down an ultimatum. *Son of a bitch.*

Through gritted teeth and without breaking eye contact with him, I say, "You've been grooming me to take the lead on this business. There are...*things* that I've taken on directly from you, and you're telling me that I'm *out* unless I'm married? What the fuck, Griz?"

"Watch your mouth," he says, pointing at me.

He has some nerve telling me to watch my mouth right now.

There's no disguising the way his words both hurt and piss me off. If I unfolded my arms, my hands would be shaking. I can hear my pulse in my ears, and my neck is warm the same way it gets when I'm rearing for a fight. If he thinks this is going to push me to do something I don't want, he's sorely mistaken.

"Change it," I demand. I bite down on my molars so hard my jaw cracks. Getting married just isn't happening for me. I don't understand why he's doing this.

Griz looks down at his hands, maybe mulling over the choice, or maybe just drumming up the courage to say, "No."

I want to shout that I've done enough. This feels like a punch to the gut. Everything he's ever requested of me has been executed flawlessly—bending rules, breaking laws, fighting, taking the lead, knowing when to follow. All of it, my entire life, and it's like he's forgotten. He has no fucking idea about the things I've been working on. The way that I've worked my ass off to build our family name. And now he throws in this bullshit stipulation masked as an ultimatum—no fucking way.

Chapter 10

Hadley

I lay on the horn outside of Lincoln's house. The door flies open, and Lark and Lily Foxx come pouring out. On their heels is Faye looking like she just rolled out of bed as she leans against the porch pillar and waves in her colorful kaftan robe—even at the crack of dawn, that woman is stunning.

"Are you our surprise today, Auntie Hadley?" Lily shouts in my face, excited and laughing. Honestly, her energy instantly erases the messes I need to figure out. I get to just live in the present and have fun with these two rascals.

Unlocking the doors, I open and step out so Lily can hustle into the back seat. I look over the hood of my car at Lark, who I know is going to ask…

"Hadley, please let me sit in the front." She smiles and mouths, *please, please, please* on repeat.

I point at her. "You need to convince your dad. I'm on strict orders that you two are only to be in the back seat and I need to stick to the speed limit. Otherwise I don't get to do surprise mornings."

Lark rolls her eyes as she folds the front seat back and huddles into the back seat with her sister.

"Your dad, however, never gave me any rules 'bout what we could do this morning." I wiggle my eyebrows in the rearview. "Where we going, girls?"

They both look at each other and smile. I know exactly where they're going to say before they shout, "*Church!*"

Lincoln called me and asked if I'd hang out with the girls for a while this morning. He usually lets Faye sleep in on weekends, and he got called to Griz and Ace's house for an impromptu meeting. It was the perfect excuse to spend some time with my favorite littles and then bring Griz a sweet treat. We roll down the windows, and I lay on the horn again as I back out of the driveway, "Time for *CHURCH*!!!"

It's just a house on the edge of town perched alongside the Fiasco River. Its sliding glass window faces the main road, with white blinking holiday lights strung around it. The flower boxes at every window of the farmhouse are filled with a happy mix of colors, from gold daisies and purple coneflowers to the white and pale-yellow plethora of chamomile and aster huddling in the spaces between. It's the most unassuming spot in Fiasco, where fields of flowers are harvested in late summer for bouquets that sell for far less than they should along the most aggressive side of the Fiasco River. Tourists who sought out the best donuts in the Southeast call it by its name, The Holey Donut. Blasphemous locals, like myself, call it Church.

"We need to bring Griz his favorites," Lily says. "But what about everyone else—Dad and Uncle Ace? Is Uncle Grant there too? How many can we get, Hadley?"

I shrug my shoulders. "However many you want."

The truth is, I'm anxious to run into Ace. It's been enough time since the wedding for us to pretend like my hands on him never happened. But I'm angry, and a little hurt too. My ego took a massive nosedive when he walked away from me. A part of me hoped he'd knock on my door, slip into my room, and finish that too-close conversation between my legs, but no such luck. I need to stop thinking something's going to happen, because as much as I want him, I don't want someone who doesn't want me. I don't know why I can't just let that sink in. I should be feeling confident and just tell myself, *Fuck it, I met him toe to toe, grabbed his dick, and pushed him for a reaction. I got one—no big deal.* Except, all of it was big. *Jesus*. Expelling a breath and letting out a laugh with it, my cheeks feel heated just thinking about it. Then, as some kind of abhorrent payback, he soaked my panties with a few words and a new curiosity about the kinds of things that wind him up and get him off. Yeah, all of this is a big deal. And pulling me into a dark corner of the wedding to, what? Make me stop pushing him? Okay, Ace, let's see how many mixed signals you can fire off in a matter of hours.

"Presh, please tell me you still have glazed," I say as we make our way to the window. If there's a person who embodies a small-town, upbeat sprite of a woman, it's Prestley Timkins. Her French accent isn't one people find often in Kentucky, but it's one of the many things that makes her truly original. Tack onto that her impeccable use of scarves woven or wrapped in her hair and the way her donuts taste like beignets, and she's a treasure. She's one of my favorite people, not much older than my mom would have been. Presh makes me feel like she cares—always listens to me carry on about mundane things, like boys and makeup, when the Foxxes aren't interested. She has that streak of misbehavior too that a part of me connects with. It isn't a secret that Presh inherited her former husband's business of forgery and fake IDs. It isn't a serious hustle; if I had to guess, it's mostly underage college kids looking to finally get into bars and clubs. It's how I got mine. But everyone in Fiasco seems to have some kind of hustle; it doesn't matter if it's above or below lines. People do what they have to do to make life work for them.

"Hadley, my love. I know to always save extra for you." She smiles, leaning over the window ledge. It isn't a formal storefront, just a specialty window that she had installed in her kitchen for easier access to take orders and keep tabs on her ovens.

"Hi, Presh, what's special today?" Lily asks as she tries to see inside and past where Presh had been leaning. "Lark says it's something chocolate, but I'm guessing it's something with raspberries since they're just in season."

"Lily, my goodness. You look more mature every time I see you. Lark, you as well. Absolutely beautiful." She looks at me with a smile. "You always, Hadley." Her eyebrows raise as she asks, "You doing alright these days?"

She, along with the rest of the world, knows about my father's arrest and his charges. But only a few people have taken the time to ask how I'm doing. The anger I hold for him is eating away at me, and even though I'm trying my hardest not to show it, I'm getting awfully tired of the weight of it all.

"I'm thriving. Obviously," I say with sarcasm and a smile. I have no interest in tearful truths while I'm responsible for Lincoln's girls. They're two of my favorite people, and I believe they need to be kids for as long as life allows. They don't need to overhear, let alone sense, the burdens I'm carrying. So I do what I'm exceptional at: I push it aside. Focus on the things that make me feel good and normal. And right now, that's donuts. A lot of them.

She gives me a nod and a smile, hearing loud and clear that I'm only willing to show my surface today. Then she brings her attention back to Lily with a wink. "Lily, you're smart to think about what's in season. But you and Lark are both right. My special is a dark chocolate with a raspberry ganache filling."

Lark looks at me with a smirk, because she already knows what I'm going to say.

"Presh, we're going to need a dozen of those and a dozen glazed. Plus three for our drive," I say with a smile. "I'm bringing the girls to the distillery, and I know as soon as people see the mint-green boxes, everyone's going to be begging for one of these."

"Absolutely. I'll put a powdered jelly in there for Griz too, then," she says. "You mind telling Griz that I had a question about an order he placed? I don't have a phone number for him, only Ace." Lowering her voice, she whispers, "I got the impression he didn't want Ace knowing about what he was doing, so…"

Now I'm intrigued.

The girls move around the patio and try picking up the ducklings waddling around the little pond. The small inlet is calm and quiet compared to the river at the edge of her property.

She moves around the kitchen, pulling out trays from the oven and turning off timers.

"Are you thinking you might stop by the distillery for Ditch the Derby day?" I ask.

"Maybe," she says. But I know, like most of her "maybes," that she won't.

"Laney, Faye, and I are going to do some cocktail experiments tonight. I bet the girls would love to have you join us."

She smiles as she folds up the mint-green boxes for our donuts. "I like being here. I have everything I need. But you and your girlfriends are always welcome to come visit me." The gossip in this town has buzzed for years about Prestley. After her husband disappeared, she became a bit of a recluse, never leaving her home. Bold rumors ran rampant around the time that happened—whispers about her being a black widow and giving a man who was too rough what he had coming. I'd met men like him, got too close, and they conveniently disappeared too. It isn't something that makes me think negatively of her.

Lark lays on my horn and yells out, "Auntie Hadley, can I ride in the front seat? Please, please?"

Presh passes me the small stack of too many donuts and smiles. "Thanks for coming to see me. It always brightens things around here."

"How long have you and Dad been friends, Hadley?" Lily asks with donut glaze shimmering from cheek to cheek. She just turned ten, and while her attitude doubled, along with a newfound interest in skincare thanks to plenty of YouTubers, moments like this are nice reminders that she's still a kid.

"Your mom thought your dad was the cutest guy in the world." I smile as I picture a young Linc. They both know this story, but I think they like to be reminded every once in a while. Their mother, Olivia, passed away just over six years ago now. "And he tried to be sooo cool and pretend like he didn't notice her, but we were persistent," I say, thinking back to all of those years ago. "Your mom and I followed him home after school for almost two months before he asked if we wanted to see the tire swing down by the river. It didn't take long for them to fall in love after that." I'm still not too sure how it happened, but we ended up being fast friends too. And it's a friendship I treasure. People would always make assumptions before Faye came around—that one of us felt more than friendship or that men and women couldn't be "just friends." We were the exception to all of it. Or it was simply that he had fallen for the girls' mom, and I had taken one look at the oldest Foxx brother, and my brain chemistry had been altered. I, of course, keep that information to myself.

I pull up to the main house—that's what mostly everyone calls it, but it's Ace and Griz's place. Holding the door open for the girls, I tilt my head back and enjoy the sweet smell that carries all the way over here from the distillery. Fiasco always holds a sweetness like sugar and cinnamon. My mom said once that it's because Fiasco is sweeter than anywhere else. But it's Foxx Bourbon that makes the air almost taste like freshly baked croissants and pecan pie. There was a cocktail-infused night recently with Laney and Faye when we licked the air between bites of charcuterie. Lincoln explained to me a long time ago that it was the yeast breaking down the sugars in the massive vats of their mash bills. Toss in thousands of oak barrels aging at all temperatures and that smell is what's left until the bourbon is ready.

"Hey, Uncle Ace," Lily says as she shimmies her body out of the back seat, smiling as she holds up the boxes from The Holey Donut.

Without stopping, he says, "Save me one for later, Lily," and keeps walking straight past us, no eye contact and seemingly all sorts of angry. His hair is a mess, like he's been running his fingers through it, and the scowl on his face is murderous. He glances briefly at me as he passes, but there's no trace of the man who, regardless of his mood, always nods at me or, at the very least, gives his nieces some attention. Something's wildly wrong.

"Did my little flowers bring me donuts?" Grant calls out, pulling our attention and effectively distracting the girls from the ire that just billowed off Ace. An easy smile takes over Grant's face as he focuses on the girls and the donuts, while Lincoln blows past him, stopping next to me. He looks defeated for not catching up with his older brother. *What the hell just happened? It's not even noon!*

Glancing toward Ace's back getting farther away, my gaze swings back up at Lincoln, then over to Grant. I raise my eyebrows, silently asking them what's going on.

Grant just gives a small shake of his head, signaling, *don't ask. Fat chance of that.*

Lincoln's hands are slung into his pockets, watching his brother walk away with nothing but anger wafting from him.

"What's going on?" I ask, shifting my weight. Whatever this is, it isn't just a disagreement about a blend.

"Griz decided to tell us he's officially retiring," Linc says in a less than enthused tone.

I crack a smile. I figured that would happen eventually—none of us are getting any younger. "And that's bad?" I ask, trying to unpack the reality that Griz won't be in charge any longer. Ace had taken most of the control years ago, but Griz is Foxx Bourbon. He'd built that brand with his boys.

"Yeah, it's bad. Griz decided to add a stipulation."

Of course he did. Griz always had something cooking under every surface. I've been around here long enough to know that.

Lincoln meets my gaze. "It'll be split evenly between his *married* grandsons."

My breath catches. As I open my mouth to speak, I can't help the laugh that bursts from it.

Lincoln nudges my arm. "Yeah, I had the exact same reaction. I don't know what Griz is getting at. All I know is, there are only a couple of times in my life that I've seen my brother that angry or upset about something." He exhales and answers my next question before I ask. "Griz won't change it. I don't know what the old man is thinking, other than he's in for a helluva fight. From the three of us, not just Ace. The stipulation is ridiculous."

I stare out at the stables, where Ace just disappeared, and think that getting married is the easy part. It's finding someone, falling in love, and then making that all happen before… The idea is ridiculous, but viable. Maybe it was cooked up from too many of Griz's book clubs, but if he just needs to get married…

"Don't laugh," Lincoln says, noticing my jaw's still practically hanging open. "I think Ace is more hurt than even mad."

I cover my mouth. I'm not smiling at Ace's current predicament. Suddenly I'm warring with myself about how I can come to his rescue. A man who didn't bat an eye to rescue me.

Crossing my arms, I stare at the massive Foxx logo painted across the stable roof, nerves thrumming with an idea.

Maybe I've finally reached the lowest depths of loneliness and I'm having an existential crisis. Even shifting aside the fact that I want him on a biblical, yet pathetic, level, I could be his most convenient solution…

It's about time I pay him back for taking care of me all those years ago.

Chapter 11

Ace

"Marry me."

I whip my head to the side, looking over my shoulder. Is she fucking kidding right now?

As I stare at her with narrowed eyes, Hadley slides down the side of her white horse and stalks toward me.

"I'm not in the mood for this," I grit out and look back at the water.

With a huff, she says, "I said marry me, Ace."

I don't have the energy for her. I take a breath and watch this side of the river—calm and slow, while across the way, it ripples faster, plunges deeper, and swells beneath the caverns. It eventually turns into a loud waterfall about three miles away. I feel like that water right now—no turning back, hurtling toward something big and unmoving, fueled by rage and momentum. I'll need to figure this out, above everything else I've been trying to handle on my own. Fuck, this blindsided me, and I hate that even more.

A part of me is relieved that it's her. My brothers are going to try to either fire me up more or push for a solution. I'd been riding for well over three hours before settling here. The sun was starting to cut the horizon line, and I was lost in every emotion I could muster from what Griz said today. *"Foxx Bourbon will be left to my married grandsons…"*

What the actual fuck?

I've done everything he's ever asked of me, and beyond just the bourbon business. This was never part of any plan. And I had too many plans in the works to even consider marrying someone.

I glance back, taking in her expression as she waits for my response. Breathing hard, she puts her hands on her hips, squaring off like she's a damn superhero.

Squatting down, I drag my fingers through the cold clear water, washing off the dirt and sweat from gripping onto my horse's reins. It's careless to be this lost in my own head. I squint my eyes, standing and turning toward her.

"You're proposing, huh? To me?" I scoff out a sarcastic laugh.

"You heard me." Then she fucking smirks and crosses her arms, propping her tits as she takes another deep breath and repeats herself for the third time. "Marry me." Her blue eyes search mine for a reaction.

I'm already shaking my head. "That's not an option, sugar. Or a solution."

She shows no signs of rejection, just her pretty lips quirked up at the corners at hearing what I carelessly just called her. But then I let myself get lost in the idea of it for the briefest of seconds. The way it felt to be close to her the other night. The years of wanting her and never allowing myself to even consider it. And lately...

No. No, I can't even think about it.

Her chin holds high, shoulders back, like she's the most confident thing in the world and not asking the most vulnerable question a person could ask. As I try to move past her, she grabs my arm, stopping me. "That is *exactly* what that is, Ace. A solution. And it might be the closest I'll ever come to paying you back for what you did for me."

It's a situation we never talked about. She didn't need any details, only that Switcher wasn't a problem for her any longer. And she'd never know what I agreed to in keeping it that way.

She shrugs a shoulder. "I've been a part of your family for most of my life." Her voice stays steady as she lays out her truth. "I never thought I would *ever* have a chance to truly help." Those blue eyes seared into me without relenting as I stared into the quickly transforming stormy sky. "Put aside whatever happened at Lincoln's wedding or the bachelor party and just stop trying to figure everything out on your own for a minute, and *look at me.*"

That's the last thing I need. Closing my eyes, I suck in a deep breath for as long as my lungs will allow. The heaviness in my chest and the numbness in my limbs are unrelenting.

"You're not even going to consider it?"

I make the mistake of finally looking at her when I say, "No."

With cheeks pinkened from the wind and heat, she searches my eyes for an answer I'm not equipped to address. Her hair is wild from the ride she took to get to me, and I have to hold back a sigh at how beautiful she is. It's almost comical, this fiery woman with her white horse, trying to save me. I don't need anyone to do that for me. I'm the one to do the saving, not the other way around. Top that off with the fact that she's the one person I promised never to touch.

But when she licks at her pretty lips and takes a step closer, that promise seems like the dumbest fucking thing I've ever made. I can't look away from the way her shirt falls from her shoulder, or how her newly sun-kissed skin is peppered with freckles, how easy it would be to forget every single reason I shouldn't and just kiss her. *Fuck!*

I swipe my thumb along my lip and grit my teeth. I've cracked three molars because of Hadley over the course of my adult life, so what's a few more? If I keep looking at her like this, I know whatever's left of my resolve will crack too.

"You were never a very good liar, Ace," she says, squinting her eyes like she can see right through me. Her self-assured, casual attitude pisses me off more. She smiles to herself and moves to her white horse, running her hand down its neck and along its mane. "You forget that I've known you for a long time. And I pay attention."

It would be better for her to stop talking. "Hadley," I breathe out quietly, almost as if it's a plea. But she doesn't hear it that way. If anything, she takes it as permission to keep going.

"You have this thing you do with your thumb when you're about to lie to one of us—you rest it on your lower lip, like you're giving yourself a moment to make sure the lie is digestible." *How the fuck has she noticed a detail like that?*

But it's my lack of response and the lingering quiet that has her lips tilting up just as a small dimple peeks out. When I take notice of the small things about her, I know I am teetering on a line. One that I shouldn't be going anywhere near again.

"Each of you Foxx boys have a tell—Griz's 'stache twitches

just as he clears his throat. Lincoln is the worst." She follows the obvious statement with a laugh. "It's written all over his face. I love him so much, but that man *cannot* keep much to himself." With a sigh, she continues. "And Grant is the hardest; maybe because he lies the least out of all of you. He'll rub at the back of his neck." She points to the air. "Laney spotted that one. But you…" Her mouth pulls down as she shakes her head. "You're the easiest, Ace. Maybe it's because you lie too much, or just that I pay too close attention." She runs her hand along the horse's saddle, tilting her head back. With her eyes closed, chin tipped up toward the mist that's started to break from the sky, she says, "But I asked you to marry me because maybe I'm selfish—" She cuts herself off and shifts her body to look right at me. "But at least I'm brave enough to admit that. You're not considering it, because I think you're scared," she says with a sturdy resolve. As if she's figured it out.

"Is that so?" I ask, trying to find my footing here, my body coiled tight. I don't even know why I'm engaging in this discussion. This isn't how I do things—I always have an idea of what's coming; I'm always prepared. Except for today. *And except when it comes to her.*

She laughs out, "Holy shit." Her voice softens when she adds, "That's it, isn't it?"

"Knock it off, Hadley," I say in a defeated tone. "I've got enough to figure out on my own. I don't need this." I wave my hand at her. "Go home."

Only that has her laughing more, like that's the funniest fucking thing. But she doesn't budge; in fact, she doubles down and takes a step closer. "I'm right, aren't I?"

I shake my head, swallowing the urge to prove her wrong.

Tilting her head up to look at me, she asks, "Too scared to go after what you want, Daddy?"

My eyes flick up to hers as my breath catches in my chest.

That's all it takes.

The last push.

It's enough to rip away a decade of self-discipline to keep away from her. Years of filling my time with women who would never stack up to the fucking fantasy with big blue eyes and a smart mouth.

It takes less than twenty feet to reach her.

She doesn't scurry back or cower when I yank her body flush against mine. No, not Hadley. She holds me just as fiercely, her hands gripping onto my shirt as if she needs to hold on to whatever I plan to do with her.

My fingers tangle into her hair as I angle her exactly how I need. I'm not just going to take; I need to see that she wants this, to know that her words are more than just a bratty attitude or to prove a point. Her eyes look up into mine as her lips tip up, waiting. But when her fists tighten in my shirt, it's enough to know that she wants this. Wants me.

"Fuck," I gasp just as I kiss her. Her mouth meets mine like it's the first clash on a battlefield. War declared. Hard and dominating, matching me breath for breath. Like it's always been between us—push and pull. A fight with no winner, and in its wake, only pleasure. There's no learning or fumbling movements. Her lips part for my tongue, and she welcomes it with hers. Teasingly, it coaxes a groan from my throat without warning and a hum from her chest. She nips at my lips as I pull back for a new breath, like she isn't ready to stop, the fucking brat. The scrape and twinge of pain makes me want more. My pulse thuds in my neck and echoes in my ears, blood heating. I want every piece of her, as if she's my last meal.

I don't think ahead or linger on what comes after as I kiss a woman I've been wanting for longer than I can even remember. With her body melting into mine, her hands that gripped my shirt move up around my neck and her fingers sink into my hair. It feels so fucking good to feel her touch like this.

When I drag my lips from hers, I can't pull back entirely. It's like my body won't allow it. Being this close, with her wrapped around me and submitting to exactly what I want, feels too right. I rest my forehead against hers, her chest heaving like I've stolen every breath from her, when she's pulled every sane decision from me. The smell of her has always been sweet—sugary. But this close, it's better than anything I've ever tasted. The way her lips are so soft and sure… I'm already craving more. Leaning in, I lick at her bottom lip, and she answers the invitation by tilting toward me and giving me another taste of her mouth. *Good fucking girl.*

My phone vibrates in my back pocket, slamming me back to my senses with a jolt. Clearing the haze and knocking me back into the reality of what we've just done, what *I've* just done. I flinch. This is reckless. Proof that I can't control myself when it comes to her. And now I've done something I can't undo, rewind, or fucking forget.

Her eyes search for what changed so quickly, why I've pulled away.

I close my eyes for the briefest moment, knowing I'm about to hurt her. "This was a mistake." On a shaky breath, I rush to add, "This can't happen again." Taking a full step back, I let go of her and pull from her grasp. Her arms unhook from around my neck, her hands gliding down my shoulders and forearms like she's not ready to let go.

It's been years of being careful, and it all dissolved in a careless moment. That heavy weight from just minutes ago is back, the one I've been carrying for ten years.

"There are plenty of ways I can make my daughter's world a helluva lot more complicated. And don't think I won't find a way to do it." He paused for a moment before letting out a short laugh. *"And just like that,"* Wheeler said, snapping his fingers. *"I've found the one thing a Foxx wants most."*

I take another step back so that there isn't a single part of me touching any part of her.

The easy smile and warmth that emanate from her are sucked away and replaced by a rigid stance. Her shoulders push back, hands shifting into fists and anchoring onto the curve of her hips. But there isn't hurt or impatience resting on her face—or even regret. Instead, her puffy, smudged lips hold a knowing smirk. She licks at her bottom lip and, fuck, I liked it so much more when it was my tongue licking there instead.

There are plenty of things to say. Meaningless filler words that she's already reading loud and clear with my body language alone. This isn't about her ridiculous question anymore. This is about us. The teasing and jokes she's made, the glimpses of her I tried to make sure went unnoticed. Flirty promises from her bratty mouth and my dominating urge to see a woman as strong and charismatic as her submit to me. My quiet obsession. *Us* isn't an option.

She scoffs and shakes her head. On an eye roll, she says, "Okay, Ace. Whatever you say, Daddy. You know what's best."

Ah, fuck.

I shift my stance, instantly feeling like there's no right way to play this. I watch as she moves in quick steps toward her horse, grabbing the reins and mounting the all-white Thoroughbred mare. The horse's coloring is as unique as her.

She's the only other person I know who rides as hard and fast as I do. My brothers take it easy on their horses, but

Hadley and I like to push. She likes to see what these beauties can do when given the chance. It's the part of her I've always seen—power and radiance that simply needs to know what it feels like to run. Standing in silence, I watch her ride away. The thrum of the river barely registers against the blood rushing in my ears and the sound of hooves moving at speed away from the river's edge.

I have no strategy, no move or gambit. Bending forward, I brace my hands on my knees, half out of breath and dizzy, while my other half is ready for a fight. "Fuck!"

Chapter 12

Ace

THERE ARE ALWAYS FIRSTS. I'm the first son, first grandson. The first to know bad news. The first to deliver it. The first time I watched a man bleed from his stomach and die on the bathroom floor, all I could think of was that being another first. Part of me knew that it wasn't going to be the last and only, not with the way my father rushed past me, shouting for Griz to get his ass in there. Firsts had value and meaning more tangible than the rest. Lines are as gray as the morals deciding what's inherently good or bad. It took me a long time to understand the role I would play in all of it.

This is the first time someone asked me to marry them.

I blow out a breath, letting a smile escape while thinking about it. She fucking asked me to marry her. Like that would be a perfect solution and not the source of an even bigger mess.

"I suppose you're not making me breakfast anymore," Griz interrupts, sidling up to the long kitchen counter. I pluck a clementine from the fruit drawer and roll it to him.

His shoulders jump with a laugh that never surfaces from his mouth.

I cross my arms over my chest, head tilted his way. "Change the fucking stipulation."

"Look at that. It's Wednesday. Hooch's does a mean stuffed French toast on Wednesdays," he says as he meanders out of the kitchen, whistling a Bob Dylan song instead of answering my demand. People don't make stipulations on inheritances or businesses based on marriage—it feels like a bad '90s movie that my sisters-in-law would watch.

"Fuck!" I whisper-shout, dragging my fingers from the front of my hair to the nape of my neck. I've gone nearly forty-three years without wanting to be married. It wasn't a part of my story—I didn't want to settle for someone I didn't want.

"You will not go near her." Wheeler's threat has replayed in my mind over the last ten years, and every time, it's chipped away at the idea of wanting someone for keeps.

Shaking my head, I run my thumb along my lower lip, where she nipped and kissed. There isn't going to be another first like that one—and I've been at war with what I do next. The smart, logical part of me knows I made the right call. As fucked as it was, pulling away from her was the only thing keeping me from ripping her clothes off and fucking her right out in the open, in that spot.

"We need to talk about what happened," Lincoln interrupts as he walks into the kitchen.

"We don't," I clap back. "You just show up now?"

"What's for breakfast?" he asks, looking at my cup of coffee and jar of overnight oats.

"Not making you breakfast," I mumble over a bite.

"In a great mood this morning, I see…" he mumbles as he

grabs one of the jars out of the fridge. He takes a seat, lounges back, and then stares at me like it's my turn to talk. Truthfully, I'm not ready to talk to either of my brothers about it because I don't have a solid plan or a response that's not completely reckless—like marrying his best friend.

"What?" I bark out.

"You just had a whole conversation in there, didn't you?" Smiling, he points to his temple. He pulls off his glasses and rubs along the bridge of his nose. "We're not going to push you out or try to run this place without you, Ace. You don't honestly think Grant and I want to box you out of what is basically your show."

Releasing a heavy breath, I lean on the counter. "That's not the point. He wants to tie things up, but for what reason? And yeah, I want my piece of this place, but that part I can handle." It's a confident response wrapped in a lie.

Lincoln steeples his fingers in front of him, looking at me as if that'll get me to say more.

A thought dawns on me, my mouth going dry, knowing that my brother and Hadley rarely have secrets between them. "Have you talked to Hadley?"

His brow furrows at the out-of-left-field question. "I talk to her just about every day. Why?"

If she told him about what transpired, he wouldn't keep it to himself. I stare back and think through how I'm going to navigate everything.

"Why are you asking?" Lincoln asks again. *Great.*

My phone lights up on its charging station across the room. It's a good distraction, but when I swipe it, I notice the wall of unanswered text messages.

THE JEWELER:
> There's an interesting development with a New York-based group.

THE JEWELER:
> Alright, no problem. I'll be more direct. There are some pissed-off Russians making heart eyes at some investments with your little bird's last name connected to it.

THE: JEWELER:
> Still not interested?

I'm fucking interested. I look up at my brother, who's still waiting for an answer. Maybe she mentioned this to him, because she sure as hell hadn't mentioned it to me.

"She seems off, that's all. Heard a rumor about angry acquaintances of her father's who are looking for payment," I say, trying to play this off as a casual conversation.

THE JEWELER:
> Fine. I'll be at Midnight Proof tonight. If you don't show, I might have to shoot my shot.

Julian knows exactly what to say for me to respond, and I hate that he's aware of my weakness. We're on the same side of things, a history of knowing how to clean a crime scene and erase people from existence. A forced friendship, if you could call it that, simply because we bend the same rules and connect the right and wrong people. Griz knew his father, who taught his son both trades as well. Jewelry making and "cleaning." A family business a lot like ours—secrets, lies, and erasing the proof that either of those things existed.

> **ACE:**
> What do you want?

> **THE JEWELER:**
> Showing your hand, old man. I didn't think you were that easy.

> **ACE:**
> Fuck off.

> **THE JEWELER:**
> See you tonight at 10 p.m.

There have been a number of organized crime families sniffing around in the past couple of years. Shortly after Laney's arrival was the first time, but that was deflected with a few favors I had collected. Any organized crime that came close to Fiasco anymore had more to do with buying some extra cases of bourbon or getting prepared for some big betting with the Derby fast approaching. Liquor, horses, and money bring all levels of trouble. But it isn't anything new. And it rarely warrants my attention, but *this* has it.

Lincoln gets up from the chair after it's obvious I'm distracted by my phone. He stops in the doorway and turns fast. "She asked me if I had talked to you too."

I look up, my eyes meeting his immediately. *Shit*.

He rubs at the back of his neck. "What happened?"

"None of your business," I answer flatly.

"If something happened," he says, watching me curiously as I try to get the hell out of the kitchen, "it wouldn't be the worst thing—"

"Don't," I cut him off. I don't want him to finish the statement. My brother caring about me hooking up with his best friend is laughable. Honestly, he'd probably coldcock me if he knew how I left her. If he knew what she asked me and how I flat out said no…

I shake my head and take a breath. Yeah, Lincoln would throw a pile driver without thinking twice.

"Don't ask me questions about things that you're not going to like the answers to, Linc," I say in a measured, stoic tone. "I know she's been getting hassled about her affiliation with Finch & King Racing. Just wanted to know if she's gotten any more threats regarding her father."

It's a half-truth, but the only half he's going to get today.

Chapter 13

HADLEY

> *April: Grape Pop Rocks might be wildly underwhelming. But if you add them with cherry, it's a damn mouth party. Maybe not as big of a party as kissing Atticus Foxx, but a close second.*

THE QUIET CRACKLE OF THE grape and cherry candy fire off in my mouth as the moody bluegrass band plays a new set. I smile and close my eyes for a moment as my senses overload with the sweet and sour taste mixed with music that's always felt like a part of who we are in Kentucky. Bluegrass is nothing new to Fiasco, but it's something different for Midnight Proof. A talented singer who came looking for a gig during last year's Bourbon & Blues Festival was the perfect addition to Faye's burlesque nights. I glance around, pocket my little black journal, and appreciate that the bar is full tonight. It's a welcome change. Fiasco has been feeling the aftermath of what Finch & King had tarnished.

But people still love to drink. It's been slower as a whole, so I don't bother holding back a smile as I watch my bartenders shake up long lines of shots and specialty cocktails. My whole waitstaff is busy hustling. Since we're a cocktails-only establishment, everyone on my team can mix their own orders, which means the bartenders handle the busiest section of the place: the bar. Each seat is taken, and tonight, it's standing room only. It's always been meant to feel like Midnight Proof is versatile—social and a place to meet a stranger in a packed bar, while my tables and lounging spaces can be intimate and quiet for couples.

It leaves little time to get lost in thoughts about Ace's lips and the way it felt so effortlessly toe-curling as they moved with mine. I would've done anything he wanted in that moment, and I wouldn't have regretted it. A woman knows when a man wants her. There's a look that can't be put into words, but we know when someone wants nothing more than to devour as much of us as we'll allow. And all I can think about is how much I'd allow.

There have been years of drawn lines and feigned disinterest. But then the tiny scar on his upper lip tipped up just a little bit. He looked at my lips as if they were his favorite batch of bourbon. And that was it. Every carefully constructed wall crumbled. It's impossible to decide who made the first move, but our limbs and bodies, mouths and tongues collided like they'd finally been returned to where they should have been all along. It hurt the second he pulled away.

"Hadley," one of my regulars says with a smile. "Any chance you can make me that cherry bombshell drink?"

"Absolutely, darlin'," I say as I make my way down the bar to grab what I need.

My phone buzzes in my back pocket, and the name that's waiting has me stopping short.

HAWK:
> Feel like company later?

I'm going to need to do more than drop a "no thanks" text. It's been weeks since I've spent time with him, and I can't find it in me to be close with another man—not after touching and kissing Ace. It just feels…wrong. Hawk deserves a conversation, not a text message. The man's been inside me, so that demands at least a coffee and a hug. But my phone buzzes again before I can pocket it, and the text that comes through has my stomach souring. It's the consistency of these that's starting to make me more uneasy.

UNKNOWN:
> You need to make some deposits.
> I'm done with asking, pumpkin.
> Do not make me angry.

Pumpkin. The threats from my father and whomever else has been texting me are turning into an anxiety I can't keep brushing away. At some point, I'll need to deal with it. This one, however, pisses me right the fuck off. I have no interest in touching any part of his estate. All of it may be in my name, but it can burn, for all I care.

I take a few deep breaths and try to calm the way messages from him burrow underneath my skin. There's a part of me that still hates disappointing him. I'm sure it's a part of me that's been conditioned over the years. So I do exactly what I should when it comes to narcissistic people: I ignore him. I pocket my phone and leave it on read.

"You own this place?" a man with a deep scowl and a bald

head asks as I get my bearings behind the bar. I recognize him—he's a bloodstock agent. Worked exclusively for my father in finding the right Thoroughbreds and developing the breeding program for Finch & King. His body language is all wrong—his face is reddened, lip curling with the question, and he isn't here with anyone that I can see as I glance behind him.

"Yes. This is my place." I smile tightly as I swipe beneath the bar for the cherry liqueur. Replacing the cap with a pourer, I ask, "What can I get you?"

He laughs to himself. "So you're the Finch bitch."

"Creative," I counter. "Haven't heard that one before."

Resting his forearms on the bar, he leans in between two customers. "Fucking figures that you look like that." His eyes move down the front of me.

"I know, it's distracting." I take a breath in and scoop ice into my shaker, then pour in the house-made gin. As I give it a few furious shakes, I look him in the eyes and say, "You going to order a drink there, big guy, or are you planning just to give me rapey eyes and insult me? Because if it's the latter, I'm going to have to ask you to leave."

He doesn't like that. His eyes bulge, mumbling something I can't hear over the crowd and music as I top the cocktail with a sprig of thyme wrapped around a bourbon-soaked cherry.

I glance at the far end of the bar and catch a pair of stormy blue-gray eyes watching me. *Ace.* Usually it's a swirling stomach feeling when I catch that gaze resting on me, but right now, with big-mouth, little-dick getting next level pissed in front of me, I feel a sense of relief knowing he's here.

"For starters, darlin', you can quit fucking smiling and tell me exactly how you plan on paying me back for the money and horses your fucking father owes me," he says, quiet enough that his words only carry to those sitting on either side of him. It isn't the first time someone who's been screwed over by my father has found their way in here. Most of the time, they never make it too far, but this is the third time now that a horse breeder, trainer, or rancher has approached me and demanded I pay them. One of the more frustrating parts is, I don't know who the good guys are who just got fucked over by my father versus who knew and participated in all of it.

I look over the angry man's shoulder toward the door, but Brady is busy with a loud group of bachelors. When all this started, I didn't want to hire the extra security that I probably should have, since business has been surviving and not thriving. The cost hasn't seemed justifiable, but now I'm regretting it.

"You going to answer me, princess, or do I need to be louder and start breaking things?" he prods.

I swallow the dryness in my throat and raise my chin. But as soon as I look up at the angry bald man's face this time, I notice it's pinched, like he's in pain. He stands taller now, back arching, making his chest bow forward awkwardly. Behind him, the man from Lincoln and Faye's bachelor party stands, gritting his teeth and speaking quietly into the bald man's ear. His tall, solid frame dwarfs the bald man's stature. I glance at Ace, who's watching me, not the least bit interested in the commotion this is starting to cause. The long-haired hero guides the bald man to the door, and Brady meets them halfway, ready to do his job and get this asshole out of my speakeasy.

Moments later, Faye rushes toward me. "What the hell was that about?" she asks, her hand on the garter of her costume. If I had to guess, she's ready with some kind of obscure weapon. She's a badass like that.

"An angry customer looking for payment for my father's sins," I say as we both watch the three men leave up the stairs.

"Okay, better question: Who was the sexy Viking warrior escorting him out of here?" She wiggles her eyebrows.

Before I can even begin to answer her, we're interrupted by a deep, gruff voice, one that always has my body reacting. "You alright?" Ace asks as he moves next to Faye.

"A little late to the rescue." Glancing up, I give him a sarcastic smile. "But yes, I'm always alright."

I step around both of them and down the side of the bar. "Faye, you're on in a couple of minutes," I say as I close the bar top behind me. I need a minute, because as much as I'd like to have thick skin and not be rattled by all of this, I am. Plastering a smile on my face to keep from crying, I squeeze my shaky fists at my sides. *Fucking emotions.*

When I get to my small office at the end of the hall, I shut the door behind me, but it doesn't close. Instead, a hand shoots out, stopping it from meeting the jamb. My breath catches in my throat, and I step back, making space for Ace to shove in behind me.

"Jesus Christ," I breathe out, my hand over my chest. "What are you doing? I need a minute here."

"How long?" he asks in a curt tone.

The fact that he's asking a question I have no interest in thinking about has words sticking in my throat. The thing is, he only needed to ask, and I would be honest with him. Taking a few steps away, I lean against my small desk as I sniff out an annoyed laugh. "Since everything happened. A year maybe. Since the moment my father was arrested, people have been coming after me for some version of a penance. Apologies, money, you name it."

He bites down, jaw flexing. "Hadley, for fuck's sake. How am I supposed to protect you if I don't know what's going on?"

My head rears back at that. "Protect me? When did I become your problem?" I ask rhetorically. I want to be the smart and savvy businesswoman, the strong bitch who can hold her own, a woman he could respect and not have to fucking *rescue*. He's already done that once before.

He only stares at me like he's thinking the same thing. Shoving down the nerves, I press my shoulders back. "I can handle it," I lie.

"Didn't look like you were handling it."

Hopping onto my desk, I cross my legs. "You're right. Tall guy with the great hair manhandled baldy." I raise my eyebrows, trying to play off how much that whole situation rattled me. "Who is that, anyway? He was at your place the night I grabbed a handful of your…" I look down at exactly what I grabbed onto before trailing my eyes back up to his.

"Careful," he warns, his gaze searing.

I tilt my head to the side and ask, "Did you send him over, or did he valiantly come to my rescue all on his own?"

He closes his mouth and says nothing. There's no flare of anger or a quip to tell me to knock it off. He looks at me in that way he sometimes does: curiously. A look that has questions or professions hovering just below the surface. I'm usually very good at filling the quiet, adding something to pull a laugh or a smile, but not this time. I let the silence linger. I swallow and glance at his lips, the scruff along his cheeks and chin, the way his "eleven" lines between his eyebrows are so much more noticeable when he's looking at me. It's been years of this push and pull, and even now, after a marriage proposal and the world's sexiest kiss, he still keeps me at arm's length.

"Hadley," he finally says like he's already fed up with me.

"So we're really back to Hadley, huh?" I say with a sigh, uncrossing my legs and keeping them open.

He licks his bottom lip and looks down at his crossed arms, nostrils flaring slightly with his heavy exhale.

"What happened to calling me sugar?" I tease.

It only takes him two long strides to stand in front of me, my pulse quickening when his arms brace on either side of me as he leans on the desk, his mouth grazing the side of my cheek. "You don't get to be called sugar when you're keeping things from me." His words drag from his throat, low and slow, like they ran over gravel before reaching me.

"And if I tell you every single secret?" I breathe out. "What do I get then?" I stare at his mouth, mere inches from mine, and remember the way his lips felt. The intense dance of his tongue and how it stole the breath from me. The sides of his arms, from his biceps to his forearms, all the way down to his wrists, graze my sides. It sends a small tremor through me, different from the unease of what happened at the bar, and more like a jump-start of heat. It fuels me. So instead of leaning back or meeting his stare, I look down his body, widening my knees just enough to extend them and wrap my legs around his.

As I pull him closer, he stays quiet and breathes me in. I can feel him looking at me, chest moving faster as he tries his hardest not to lose whatever upper hand he thinks he may have.

"You want a reward for honesty? Praise for being a good girl?" he practically growls, sending a shiver all the way to my toes.

"You told him to step in, didn't you?" I whisper. "Why do you care?" When my legs tighten around him even more, his body becomes flush with mine. With his hips pressing into me,

I can feel how affected he is right now. I have to suppress a moan at how satisfying that is.

Instead of answering my question, he continues talking as if I never asked. "I don't want you to be a good girl. I would much rather you tell me the truth and then tell me to go fuck myself. That way, I can think about stuffing this pretty mouth—"

But the slamming of a fist against the office door echoes loudly and has him pulling back and straightening to stand. My legs fall away from him as Laney calls my name from the other side of the door, breaking the moment. "Hadley, I've got someone out here asking for you. Are you here, or am I telling them you're not in tonight?"

"I'll be right there!" I call out.

Ace takes another step back, and then another as I stand from the desk and adjust my skirt. I brush by him and turn the doorknob to leave, but something has me stopping to look back at him. With a rough swallow, I say what's been on my mind since our kiss. "I think I made it seem like my offer to marry you also meant it needed to be tied to whatever *that* just was. It doesn't. If you need my help, then my offer still stands." I turn my body fully to face him, letting out the truth I've been stubborn about. "Because…you're right, I don't have things handled. Maybe marrying you is also a way for me to get out of this constant state of being my father's daughter. It would benefit me just as much as you." Tilting my chin higher, I pull as much strength as I can. I feel safe when I'm with him—so many other things too, but those can be stifled, if it means this could help us both. I could never say it out loud, but I didn't want to be a Finch anymore. I didn't want to deal with the money, the threats, the outcomes—almost as much as I *wanted* to be a Foxx. "Friends with the benefit of a marriage certificate. Nothing more."

He shoves his hands into his suit pants pockets and watches me, letting what I've said linger for the briefest moment before he says, "We both know it's not that simple."

I smile with a shrug and open the door. "Maybe not. But I'm still your best option."

Closing the door behind me, I walk down the hall toward the crowded bar and laughter. With every step, I shake off the vulnerability that always escapes when I'm alone with him. And as the live music and applause for Faye grows louder, it drowns out the fact that I just suggested that Ace Foxx marry me… again.

Chapter 14

Ace

"That one will knock you back a bit." I nod to the Glencairn glass that Julian's sipping from. I tip mine on its side—the beauty of these types of glasses meant to sip, taste, and move the whiskey—showing off the coppery color as I let it roll slightly. "My brother is the one who'll talk chemistry with you all day long about how the alcohol in this bottle increased, but it'll hit the back of your throat with some muscle, so sip it."

He closes his fist over his lips after he swallows. "Damn." As he winces, I can't help but smile. It seems like a good time to lighten the situation. I hadn't planned on sending him in to break up a fight tonight, but it made the most sense.

"I could have done a nice tasting at the distillery, but you were the asshole who picked this place." I look down at the packed main floor of Midnight Proof from where I'm sitting. The private space that Hadley reserves is open, and the commotion needs to die down before either of us leaves. Finishing off my glass, I sit back, waiting for him to get to the reason why he needed an in-person visit.

There are only ever two reasons for an in-person visit from one of us. It's either a request for an audience—like Griz did during Lincoln's bachelor party—or there's a job that doesn't feel quite right, and someone needs support. We each respect the lives and careers outside of this additional obligation, so attention beyond texts or phone calls is rare.

While Julian doesn't look out of place here in Fiasco, *we* don't look like people who would be colleagues. We're polar opposites in the way we present ourselves. I prefer suits and bourbon, and he showed up looking like he couldn't decide between being an artist or a cowboy. But I've seen plenty of his work—and he's damn talented. Handmade pieces, from rings and necklaces to headpieces and art installations. Many of which have been celebrated in auctioned collections and on red carpets. But outside of his affinity for titanium and gemstones, Julian also knows how to easily erase a person's existence. From their digital footprint to their skin and teeth. His particular skill set would be a threat to just about every government agency. Except, oftentimes, those are exactly who call in favors and requests.

Leaning back in his leather club chair, he pulls out a black velvet pouch from the front interior pocket of his leather vest and tosses it to me.

"What's this?" I ask, opening it.

He looks down at my hand as I turn it over to drop out the contents.

A thick silver belt buckle. "Aw, honey, you shouldn't have," I joke.

With a smirk, he shakes his head. "No, asshole. That's not

one of mine." He crosses his arms. "That was waiting for me in a PO box under an alias that I haven't used in more than a decade. Look at the initials."

I turn it over in my fingers, drawing over the letters depicting one of the country's most acclaimed rodeo circuits.

The hoots and hollers from the crowd downstairs get louder, along with a drawn-out trumpet and drumbeat. I glance up, and my gaze slides over to Hadley like it's second nature.

"Does she know what you did for her?" he asks, his eyes pinned to her slinging drinks behind the bar.

Turning the buckle over in my hand, I ignore the question. Apparently my lack of response says enough.

"You're in love with her," he says. Air blows past his lips in a low laugh. "I would have thought after all this time…"

I clear my throat and rub my thumb along my lip, taking one last look at the way Hadley moves so effortlessly. I couldn't put into words what the hell I'm doing when it comes to Hadley, even if I wanted to share.

"What am I looking at here?" I ask, bringing my attention back to the buckle. Nothing about the year or championship seems all that important…until it clicks.

"Well, I'm looking at a brunette who I've witnessed you make some *interesting* moves around." He pauses with a pointed look before he continues. "You call me in to clean up a body, and I'm still not sure how he ended up dead on her family's property. And then you ask me to step in tonight with that bald prick. I know her name and that she's close to your brother, but who is she to you, Ace?" he asks with a curious tone. "If you're not interested—"

"Not an option," I cut him off.

He tips his head to the side and smiles. "For me or for you?"

"For both," I say with a finality that tells him to back off.

He smirks to himself and then leans forward, taking the buckle from my hand. "It's been driving me nuts why a rodeo buckle would end up in that PO box. There are plenty of rodeo boys in Montana, but there's no reason for this to end up with me. Unless it was to send a message." *Fuck.* He points to the center of it. "You messed up."

My gut sinks, knowing all the errors I made that night. Ones that cost me more than just money. I glance at Faye as she works her way around the room. There's a reason why I asked for her help. And she's capable. She's already pulled plenty of details about the people affiliated with and burned by Wheeler Finch. People who could be considered a threat. But this right here isn't something she needs to know about.

He tilts his head toward my hand. "That right there was attached to a dead man before he ended up fertilizing some cornfields. And now we need to figure out exactly why it didn't get destroyed, and who would be so bold as to send it to me and not you."

Unfortunately, I already know.

It takes twenty-four hours to gain the access I need. House arrest consists of patrols at the front and back of the house, but only local PD, not FBI. It's rookies and guys pulling the short straw, along with a monitored security system.

"Ace," Jimmy says, looking up from his post in a double take. "Wh-what are you doing here? We haven't been allowing any visitors unless they're mandated by the court." More quietly, he whispers, "You can't be here."

I stop walking and stare at him. "Then don't tell anyone." While I'm not pleased about having to be here, there's satisfaction in knowing that he'll be behind bars soon enough. The charges pending have plenty of witness testimonies and surveillance to prove the mess he created. Wheeler Finch had upset a multi-billion-dollar industry and, in its wake, made large enough waves to affect almost every person in my small town. People are angry. And that isn't including the people closest to me—my sister-in-law, Faye, felt the impact. Her mother was silenced for years before she died, and Faye's sister, Maggie, tried to make it right and still ended up gone. And now Hadley and this threat. It isn't going to go unanswered any longer.

"I've been waiting for you, Atticus," he says in his thick Kentucky accent.

I grit my teeth, watching a satisfied grin take over his face. Holding back the anger that vibrates through my veins, I flex my hand at my side. He was smart to send it to Julian. Doing so was a message; he knows who helped me that night. He knows my secrets. And far too many of them. Wheeler sits casually in his wingback chair, in an office that I've only ever been inside once before.

I glance at the more senior officer, whose father had worked the bottling line at Foxx Bourbon for most of his life. He gives me a nod, and the cameras in each corner of the room stop blinking red. Inserting an earbud in each ear, he crosses his arms, leaning against the wall more casually now. There are a handful of officers who knew either my brother Grant when he was on the Fiasco PD, or his partner, Del, who still serves as a semiretired detective. Today's visit won't be recorded or witnessed. It won't be mentioned to my brother. It will be like it never happened at all.

Wheeler looks past my shoulder, seemingly more tense, realizing we're practically alone now.

The sound of metal hitting the weathered wood of his desk makes him settle his attention on the belt buckle. "Ah, your associate got my little gift, I see."

I look down at my wrist to focus on something other than the severe need I'm feeling to punch him in his smug face. "We had an agreement, Wheeler. The fact that you've gone ahead and gotten caught for all the bullshit you've been wielding these years doesn't change that."

He tuts. "Atticus, of course, circumstances have changed. Most importantly, my daughter is not cooperating."

I try not to visibly tense hearing Wheeler refer to Hadley. Sending another glance to the officer in the corner, I make sure he's not listening to this.

"She refuses most of my calls. My lawyers aren't able to access the funds they need, not to mention that I have some upset associates who are starting to call in some aggressive favors for my lack of delivering what they're owed."

I noticed the limp he's adopted when he walked in here and took his seat. And when I look closer, a bruise along the right side of his face is on the end of healing. Apparently house arrest kept him inside, but it's proving to be a little harder to keep other monsters out. I smirk, appreciating the fact that his daughter wants nothing to do with him and thinking back to her standing up to the bald man at the bar. "Not my problem, Wheeler. But this isn't going to get you on my good side," I threaten as I glance at the gaudy rodeo buckle.

"You know, I always thought it was interesting how your family business just kept getting bigger. Even during the Prohibition, your brand turned bourbon into a medicinal practice. The only bourbon brand to actually grow during a time when liquor was outlawed. Some people might think it was just smart business, but well…" He smiles to himself. "It doesn't matter the political climate or the state of the economy, Foxx Bourbon just keeps growing. I'm guessing your net worth is even more than what an internet search might show."

He isn't wrong, but I want to know what he's getting at.

"Griz, your father, and maybe even further back than that, made some concessions. Interesting company you've all kept over the years…" He pauses to read my reaction.

I squeeze my hand at my side again, pulsing my fingers into a fist.

"A jeweler, an architect, a U.S. Marshall." Brow furrowing, he feigns forgetfulness. "I wonder what kinds of favors you've all done for each other over the years. I doubt much of what Griz had to do or what you've done is all that different from what's landed me here."

It doesn't matter to me if he views it that way. Wheeler Finch only ever looks out for himself. And greed finally caught up with him. "I doubt anyone whose horse was drugged and killed, or whose livelihood you fucked with, would agree." I cross my arms and grit out, "Get to your point."

He smiles to himself, clearly pleased that he's riled me up. The truth is that information is dangerous. And he suddenly has a lot of time on his hands. It's an opportunity to be paying too close attention.

"There's a lot I'm learning these days. People in Fiasco over the years finding themselves in a watery grave or disappearing altogether. It's quite compelling, really. Switcher disappearing the same night as Prestley Timkins's husband—" He tilts his head to the side. "Was that a bender for you, or just an average Friday night?"

I've underestimated him. Again. But I stand quietly and let him spout off what he knows.

He waves at the air in front of him, sarcasm lacing his body language and tone. "You know my associates...they have all kinds of things they've found on you and your friends. That jeweler and his old man go way back with your family." He pauses before he adds, "And a pretty blond architect with worldwide businesses that rank higher on the Fortune 500 than any other in that field."

I grind my jaw, suppressing the gut punch I feel at hearing this. He shouldn't know or recognize Julian or Seraphine, never mind have any awareness of their connection to my family.

"What does any of this have to do with what you want? I'm about done with listening to you now."

"I need you to get my daughter to cooperate. I need access to my funds, and I need people paid off until I'm out of here." He leans his elbows on the table, coming close enough for me to grab him and slam his face into the metal beneath him if I loosen the reins on my control. "If you can do that, then proof that you're more than just a Kentucky bourbon boy will stay between us. And your associates won't have to worry about me selling their information and locations to a variety of whom I can assume might be interested parties."

The threat is enough to swallow the urge to tell him to go fuck himself. As much as I'd like to hear the cartilage of his nose crunch and inflict a small amount of pain in this moment, he needs to believe he has the upper hand.

"Ah, and there's one more thing..." He cups his hand below his chin, making a show of trying to remember. "Yes, that's right. It seems as though a little town not on any maps exists in Montana—beautiful state, I hear. Apparently people come back from the dead there."

"Fuck," I breathe out and rub my hand behind my neck. This motherfucker. I grit my teeth to keep from saying anything that'll tip my hand.

It's enough to push me over the edge, my chest tightening and rage igniting within me. I'm not going to play games, and in fact, the only thing his veiled threats are doing is reinforcing what I've already set into motion.

There's one thing Wheeler hasn't factored into all of this. It's the one flaw to his somewhat desperate attempt to come out of this in one piece and not locked away behind bars. I may have underestimated him, but he's wildly underestimated his daughter.

Hadley is going to do the one thing that I bargained for her to have autonomy over all those years ago. It'll be a gamble. Castling, if this were a chess game. And regardless of the deal I made with him, if we play this smart, then the fallout will be minimal. A shift in the plan, but with the same players.

Wheeler hasn't considered that his greatest mistake isn't appointing her as executor of his estate and business, but how her assets could become shared assets with her spouse. Because until now, Hadley hasn't had a spouse for him to consider.

Turning on my heel, I wave off Jimmy as I hustle down the front stairs, my mind made up.

I'm going to marry Hadley Finch.

Chapter 15

Hadley

May: Trough water is my new favorite cocktail.

*2 oz rye bourbon *lime juice (whole lime) *coconut water *lots of ice.

Also, women asking men to marry them is highly underrated. I've done it twice now.

Answer still pending, but feels hella empowering...

"What are you calling this again?" Faye asks from the farthest galvanized tub.

I toss my black book onto the pile of towels a few feet away, thinking about it and taking in the setup we're submerged in. "Trough water. Our version of ranch water."

"Brilliant," she says with a sigh. "I like it better than the mint julep."

Julep barks out, hearing her name from the back porch. Laney shouts back, "Not you, sweet girl!"

I smile, enjoying the company of two of my favorite people. *How am I supposed to keep the proposal from them?* What did I possibly see coming out of any of this? I'm not the kind of girl who gets the guy. I'm an independent woman in my mid-thirties who doesn't *need* the guy... And yet, I'm *still* thinking about his mouth on mine. The way my thoughts stutter every single time I see him in a room or catch his attention on me.

Water splashes on the side of my face, and Laney says, "You're thinking awfully hard over there, Hadley." She turns her head in the other direction toward the horse trough that Faye's sitting in. "She has that serious look on today, and it's worrying me. She hasn't said the word 'vibrator' or insinuated anything sexual in"—she looks at her wrist, where there's no trace of a watch, smiling back at me—"far too long."

"I'm wearing a very short, cropped T-shirt that says, *Ask Me About My Panties*, while submerged in a tub, drinking a cocktail, and it's two in the afternoon. I feel like I'm very on-brand today," I joke as I sip my cocktail.

Tilting my head back, I bask in the warmth of the sun. I'm ready for a Kentucky summer and all of the sweet and slow details that the season brings with it—festivals and fireworks, river dips and cavern dives, and the simple things like late-night rides and watching Lark and Lily catch fireflies.

I can almost hear them looking at each other, trying to decide what to say next. "You've just had a lot of things—"

I cut off the pity that'll come as a follow-up to that

statement. "Do you remember the time that guy tried to mansplain what a speakeasy was?"

Laney laughs. "Inside a speakeasy…to a speakeasy owner."

Faye smiles into her glass. "I would say I'm surprised, but…"

I draw my pruney fingers along the edge of the trough. "The audacity of people will never surprise me, but sometimes, I truly wish I could see the moment in life when they realize how egregiously they've overstepped. And then just give a slow and awkward golf clap."

"That would be too poetic, Hadley."

I exhale. "A girl can dream."

"So you're good then?" Laney presses, looking at me more seriously.

"I'm fine. Promise." It feels nice to have people who notice even the slightest shift in my behavior. She's not wrong. I've been off since Lincoln's wedding. But I'm not even a little bit ready to share all the reasons why. I turn my head toward Laney and try to shift the subject away from me. "I'm currently loving that you decided to think of us when Grant asked about what you wanted for your birthday."

"I got my hammock over there," she says, tipping her head toward the two oaks holding a massive hammock between the trunks. "And there's something very therapeutic about sitting in these things with junk food and good company," Laney says with a wide, lazy smile as her long copper-colored hair drapes over the back of the galvanized tub.

What each of us are submerged in are really intended to be horse troughs—a spot for horses to drink or feed—but my darling friend made herself at home in one of them when she first came to Fiasco and decided it was better than a hot tub. She brought one in for me, and then when Faye decided to make herself a permanent part of the Foxx family, Laney added a third.

Reaching over, Laney plucks a small handful of sour gummy worms from a candy dish and says, "I just felt like we could extend use of these if we added heaters, and the sound system outside was an easy upgrade."

"I will never complain about your taste, Laney Foxx. It's impeccable," Faye says with a content sigh as she types something on her phone.

When my phone buzzes for the fifth or sixth time, I reach over and see the wall of texts from Faye.

> **FAYE:**
> Are you seeing what I'm seeing?

> **FAYE:**
> Oh my gosh, pick up your phone.

> **FAYE:**
> I'm going to keep texting until the buzzing actually makes you look.

> **FAYE:**
> HADLEY!!!

> **FAYE:**
> Please tell me I'm not the only one noticing that Laney is ignoring her afternoon cocktail...

My eyes go wide as soon as I read the last text. "LANEY!" I shout and turn to her, splashing water all over the place.

Faye gives me a knowing glare, but I ignore it. I've never been one for subtleties.

Laney closes one eye and looks at me. "You noticed."

"Actually, Faye noticed. You're not drinking."

Faye laughs as she sips her light-pink drink that I whipped up for our impromptu afternoon dip. "I was also the one who didn't shout it out."

I splash water at her while splashing Laney again in the process.

"I'm just taking a little hiatus. I'm not pregnant… yet," she says with a smile.

"But you want to be?"

She lifts her shoulder in a small shrug. "I haven't wanted anything more lately. We practice." That has her smiling wide. "I mean, look at the man I married. And we both want to start a little family. So we're being horny and careless." Popping another gummy worm in her mouth, she adds, "And I keep track of when I'm ovulating…so…"

I hop up and out of my trough and into hers, giving her the biggest squeeze the tight space will allow.

She laughs, her eyes watering as she pulls back. "I just don't want to be excited about something that might not happen, you know?"

I know what she means. I've been schooling my own excitement for things, like a happily ever after, for a long time. It always seemed safer to harden my edges a bit than to get lost in the idea of something. I think that's what made us so close so quickly. She isn't a starry-eyed idiot. I like the realist attitudes of both of these women. They went ahead and fell in love, but they did it with both eyes open and fearlessly. I might be older than them, but I'm in awe of them. And their strength.

My phone continues to buzz from where I dropped it before practically tackling my friend. I spare a glance at Faye to see if it's her again, but the only thing she's holding is her cocktail in one hand and a slice of pizza in the other. But when I pick up my phone this time, the name waiting for me makes my stomach swoop and chest feel lighter.

> **DADDY FOXX:**
> Come to the house.

> **HADLEY:**
> I'm busy right now.

> **DADDY FOXX:**
> Come. To. The. House.

Has he actually lost it? He's known me long enough by now to realize that text is going to get him nowhere.

> **HADLEY:**
> Is that any way to speak to a lady?

> **DADDY FOXX:**
> Get your ass up here now.

> **HADLEY:**
> Are we talking about a mustache ride situation?

> **HADLEY:**
> You should have led with that.

> **DADDY FOXX:**
> Knock it off.

> **HADLEY:**
> Wanna make me?

"Fuck," I say under my breath as I look at the alert from the stables at Finch & King, taking my attention away from getting to push Ace's buttons more. I swipe to the security feed and notice the paddocks are empty, which means either my farrier didn't show up today or something's wrong. It's a gorgeous day and my girls love to run, especially on warm days.

"Hey," Laney laughs when I jump to my feet. "Where are you going?"

"Lady Brittany Christina Pink isn't in the south paddocks like she should be. Just want to be sure my farrier isn't skipping his shifts."

I lift my phone to my ear to call him, but on the second ring, it goes right to voicemail.

Faye shouts from behind me, "You need me to come with you?"

I wave her off as I swipe my shoes from the grass and hoist my bag over my shoulder. "I'm good!"

The stables aren't too far. Finch & King butted right up against the farthest strip of Foxx Bourbon property a few miles down from my father's estate and current prison.

I have a stable hand and farrier on rotating schedules to

check in on my horses, feed, and muck the stalls when I can't get there. One of them should be there today.

Most of my father's stables were cleared out last year—boarded mares and foals were quickly moved to new locations after my father had been arrested. The stallion that had been standing stud was auctioned, and any others that were boarding were taken back to wherever they had called home, leaving just the horses I call mine. Less than ten minutes later, my body finally air-drying, and I'm driving along the dirt and gravel that leads right into the breeding stables. They're the nicest, so that's where my girls are staying until I can figure out my own version of housing for them.

I open the center console and snag the Christmas present Faye bought for me this year—a small, handheld pepper spray since there have been plenty of media and trespassers over the past year. Gripping it tightly in my palm, I walk through the double sliding doors, the cool air set at a perfect temperature to keep my horses comfortable. My father loves horses, but only because of the fortune they made him. He loves what they provide. He loves them more than my mother, more than me. And he spent plenty of money making sure his investments had the best. Now knowing how he'd allowed horses under his care to be abused, the investments he made here weren't for them, they were for him.

I stop short when I hear a man's voice carrying out of the front of the building. "There's nothing in the north building—and she's not living at the townhouse address. We've been staking it out for well over a week now."

Holy shit.

Another person speaks more loudly. "The bar is always busy. She's never alone. It's not an easy snatch and grab."

My stomach drops as I listen. Their accents are ones I can't place—they sure as hell aren't from Kentucky. This isn't going to end with me introducing myself and asking them to politely leave. I'm also not going to run away and see whether or not they're going to take or hurt my horses. *No fucking way.*

I don't waste any more time listening. I parked down by the farthest paddock gate, which can't be seen from here, thank goodness. The sight and sound of my car would have tipped them off. I know these stables better than any other place—there are a total of ten stalls in each stable, and the three buildings were usually packed with young fillies. During any other year, it would be rowdy. The weekend prior to the Oaks and the Derby meant a packed house. Every other year, until now, because people no longer associated with Finch & King Racing. My two girls, however, aren't in here. And I don't see them outside. *Shit. Shit.*

I kick off my sandals, not wanting to make any noise, and move quietly down the main stretch of this building. The motion sensor doors connecting to the next building open quietly, and I hustle.

When I make it halfway through the next grouping of stalls, I'm greeted with Duchess Fergie Flossy Glamorous's typical posturing and hoof hitting the stable floor, like a hand tapping in excitement or foot stomping now that her person is here. "Fergie, you beautiful girl, I need you to shush the snorting and ride as fast as Lady."

At the sound of her name, my usually quiet Thoroughbred lifts her head past an open stall, finally curious. Lady takes her bit quickly, and I decide I don't want to take the time to saddle her. I've barebacked plenty of times over the years, so while my thighs and ass are going to pay for it, I need to get them out of here. It takes a peppermint and a good grip to get Lady to stop moving long enough to mount. The doors to the back are wide enough for both horses to get through side by side, and I take Fergie's lead rope to attach it to Lady's bit ring.

Even connected to Lady, Fergie is being stubborn and holding her ground in her stall. I move to her side and give her a shove. "Now's not the time to be pissed off at me for not being here," I whisper to her.

She snorts at me. I swear they know what I'm saying, but I don't have time to say much else or negotiate any further with her, because the connecting motion sensor slider whooshes open, and I tense. The way the breeding stables are set up, the stalls are in the back. It won't take long for whoever is out there to move through the space and find us.

"I'm telling you, there were horses here. They were in the field when I pulled in. I saw a white one and a tan one with a black mane," the louder one says, his voice getting closer.

As if my girls are going to understand what it means, I put my finger over my mouth. I grab a bucket, turning it over to get a boost onto Lady's back. Without the saddle and stirrups, it's nearly impossible without a boost of some kind. But my foot tips it just enough to slide along the concrete, making enough noise to alert the strangers of my presence.

"Hey! Stop!"

I don't look back or take a second longer to move. I tightly squeeze my thighs, tap my heels twice, and say, "Let's see you run." They've never needed vocal prompts; they're trained to move with the pressure of the body riding them, but we need to *move*.

It's not clear if those men are armed, so I don't look back. I keep my body low and push to get to the edge of the tree line.

Fergie whinnies, picking up the pace, and runs along in time with Lady and me. I twist my wrists to hold on to the reins tighter. I haven't ridden without a saddle in a long-ass time. We don't stop or slow. Instead, I have them go faster. I'll ease up when I hit the flat landscape and can see the peppering of black rickhouses with their white Foxx logos.

I'm squinting and out of breath when we finally hit shorter grass. The farthest rickhouse from the main property swipes by my right, and we reach the well-manicured landscaping of the only place that's ever felt like home. With a still-pounding heart, I exhale the breath I'd been holding, seeing a familiar tall and broad body just getting into his sports car. But I don't let myself feel relief just yet. I need to get to him. It makes no sense that even as he sees me, gets out of his car, and starts walking toward me that it's not enough. I haven't slowed; I just need to get there.

He stops and doesn't flinch as I ride right for him. The second I pull to a stop and slide down Lady's side, hitting the ground with both feet, he rushes to me, grabbing Lady's reins. "What happened?"

I'm out of breath, practically shaking with adrenaline as I say, "There were men."

He walks closer, slowly approaching like I'm a wild animal. I put my hands on my hips, and inhale, counting to three to lower my racing heart. I do it again as I turn around and try to coax back the tears that have started to pool. I'm not going to break over being spooked like this. I wait for another handful of counts before I turn back to see him pulling out his phone.

In a stern tone, he asks, "What men, Hadley?"

I just shake my head. "I don't know." Even though I'm here, I'm not asking him to fix this. I simply needed someplace safe, someone safe.

"Del, thanks for taking this," he says with a smile into his phone, eyes on mine. "There were some unwanted visitors over at Finch & King stables. Can I have you or one of the guys go check it out for me?"

As he talks to Del, I lead the horses to the filled water troughs, unhooking them from each other and giving Lady a rub along her neck. I look down at my trembling hands; they're burning and bright red from gripping onto her reins so tightly.

I hear Ace say more quietly, "She's spooked, Del. I don't know who they were, just that they didn't belong there."

As I'm rinsing off my hands in the utility sink along the exterior of his stables, he approaches my side, grabbing a towel for me.

"Tell me you're alright," he demands. I realize he must've hung up because the only other sounds are the late afternoon bugs echoing and my horses drinking vigorously.

"I'd rather not lie to you," I say honestly. But my anxiety peaks, and I start to ramble. "Nothing is alright. For an entire year, shit hasn't been alright. Honestly, I'll take subpar. Even mediocre. Plenty of people live happily in mediocrity. I might have to be okay with that if Midnight Proof keeps tanking. Can't quite call it a success if I'm getting lucky with any busy nights now." I swallow past the lump in my throat, full-on spiraling. "My mental health lately feels like I'm playing Marco Polo in the Atlantic or the Pacific, whichever one is bigger and more ominous. So, yeah…" I release a heavy breath. "I'm the furthest thing from alright."

He doesn't say anything. He simply nods, turns away from me, and starts walking toward the house. Something about watching him walk away has my anxiety morphing into frustration. I take in his crisp white shirt tucked into those black suit pants with the faintest pinstripe as he plucks the jacket he dropped from the ground and tosses it over his shoulder like he has no cares in the world. I don't know why that fires me up so much, or why I'm starting to seethe. What the hell was I expecting? He called the cops for me; what else do I want? Maybe it's the aftereffect of being scared and running. Or maybe I've just had enough of this chaotic excuse for a relationship that I've been so quick to accept in any way he'll offer it to me.

"You know what?" I say to myself and the damn horses because his long legs are now far out of earshot. "Fuck this." Marching after him, I shout, "I don't know what they wanted, but they were looking for me! It's not just random drop-ins at my bar, Ace. Someone's been watching me too; maybe the same guys, who knows, but they sent a fucking picture message of *me* eating at Hooch's the other day to spook me." I raise my arms, defeated. "And, it's working." I try to make up the distance with long strides, and then pick up my pace so I can cut in front of him. As soon as I do, he stops. The look on his face isn't one that I expect—he's angry. "What? Are you mad at me that I came here—"

But he cuts me off, dropping his jacket again, his hands moving to my waist as he guides me back so that I'm pinned to the large oak tree behind me. Any words I planned to say escape me on a gasp as he looks at my mouth.

"You're going to say yes," he says in his deep, low voice—the sound of it feeling like a front-row seat to pure masculinity and self-confidence at its very finest. "You're going to say yes, Hadley. But then we're going to play it my way."

I can't help the laugh that pulls out of me, but his face doesn't break into a smile. His grip along my waist pulses as I search the grays and blues in his eyes, the smell of oak and orange easing some part of me. His mouth—oh hell, I've fantasized about all the things this man could say and do to me with his mouth. All of it tamps the fire that was churning in my gut, and instead, it's being replaced with a warm and eager tension. The palpable energy that always seems to surface between us.

"Okay," I breathe out. "What am I saying yes to?"

He glances down at my mouth again, before his eyes move back to mine, and he releases a small hum, like I've pleased him. "Marrying me."

Chapter 16

Ace

"You're serious?" she asks, trying to digest what's changed.

As she takes a stuttered breath, her chest heaves, drawing my attention lower. Her damp T-shirt molds to her curves, the words written across it making me glance down to her cutoff jean shorts, wondering if she, in fact, isn't wearing any panties right now.

"Nice shirt. And yes, I'm serious," I say, taking a step back and dragging my fingers from the front of my hair to the back, resting my palms on my neck.

Her tongue dips out, wetting her lower lip—the move hitting me square in the dick. Kissing her replays during every quiet moment I have. And even when I'm engaged in something that requires my full attention, it's a challenge not to let my mind wander back to one of the few moments that quite simply knocked me sideways.

The smile pulling at her mouth now is a helluva lot better than when she came riding up here. Grabbing her hand, I lead her toward the house. I'm making this up as I go along. There hasn't been enough time to think through any of it properly, but we're going to need to define clear lines that each of us will have to stay behind if this is going to work. Her hand pulses in mine, holding tighter as we walk up the porch stairs. I lead us to the kitchen, looking down the hallway toward Griz's wing as we pass. The doors are open, which usually means he isn't here.

Marrying her wasn't a consideration for me until my visit with her father. I never planned to move forward with marrying; my predicament of gaining my share of Foxx Bourbon could be figured out eventually.

But the game has changed, and I'm really fucking tired of Wheeler Finch turning the tables on me. When she offered to marry me, she did it because it was about what *I* needed, a misplaced feeling of repayment. But now… a marriage between us has other benefits. It'll be about her too. I need to keep her safe.

I pull out a loaf of French bread, grab what's left of the cheeses from the last event we hosted and the strawberries from this morning's breakfast. She watches what I'm pulling together and, without missing a beat, moves around me, selecting two rocks glasses and reaching for the bottle of unmarked bourbon on the upper shelf. I look over my shoulder, seeing her shirt lift higher as she reaches, her shorts skimming the backs of her thighs just below that mouthwatering crease below her ass cheeks. My dick flexes like a reminder to quit looking. *Jesus*.

"What are you doing? Just pick one."

She turns with a bottle. "This is your good bourbon, and I only know that because I've been here for forever, and I've seen you yell at Linc twice and Griz maybe just as many times for trying to open it when they wanted to celebrate a special occasion."

"Put it back," I tell her, taking in which one she managed to find. *That* one is off-limits.

She rolls her eyes at me but listens. "Then tell me what I can have," she says suggestively. If I shared my rough plans with her, then this move could be more than just trying to keep her safe or about my family business. It could be a way to get Fiasco out of the pile of shit it's landed in and fuck over her father in the process.

All of it demands more time and a strategy that takes every possible player into account. Beyond that, we'll need to convince Griz enough so that he won't ask questions. Truthfully his fucking stipulation made it so he wouldn't try to dig for the source of why I would be marrying her so suddenly. It also means that I'll need to make sure her fucking father gets the news of our nuptials at the exact moment I want him to receive it.

As I slice up the bread, I point to the shelf below. "The tallest bottle." I nod to it as her hand hovers over the right spot. "Pull that one." I think about how much I pushed back putting that exact bottle into production and how sharing it with her might just be the most romantic thing I'll ever do for a woman. Because there's something on that bottle that will seal our deal.

With the right one in her grip, she sits up on the counter next to me, looking over the ornate bottle. I know she's still shaken up from what happened earlier; she's never quiet for this long unless something's bothering her.

I glance at her as she starts to build a piece of bread with a double crème brie.

She reaches along the counter for the jar of Luxardo cherries, opens it, digs into it with her fingers, and pulls one out. With her fingers coated in the dark, rich syrup, she smashes the cherry onto the cheese, and then holds it up to my mouth.

"Go ahead." She smirks. "You're even more of a bear when

you're *hangry*, so take a bite and then you can tell me all about the *rules* I'm going to break."

I open and take the entire piece into my mouth. The tips of her fingers along with it. "Such an overachiever," she says, staring at my mouth as I chew. I raise my eyebrows and hum at the mix of sweet and salty. It's a better bite than I was expecting.

"I know I may not be the best cook, but I can make a mean charcuterie mashup." Plucking a piece of cheese, she goes back into the jar. I don't bother passing her a spoon or skewer to dig out another cherry; there's a part of me enjoying her doing it exactly as she is—fingers messy and distracted. It also allows me a minute to take her in. Her cheeks are still pink, and her hair is wild and messy. It's a feature that was charmingly identifiable when she started spending more time here years ago. I never thought too much of it, but now, it just makes her look really fucking sexy without even trying. She has a small dimple just to the right of her lips. And at this angle, this close, the small scar above her eyebrow is easier to notice.

"You left me there," she said, her eyes blurring with tears as she stood underneath the fireworks on the Fourth of July.

Nearly eight years later, and she wanted to bring it up now.

"I chalked all of it up to the fact that maybe I didn't want to know what happened, or that you thought it was in my best interest, but you just left me." She crossed her arms over her chest like she was protecting herself. We'd gone so long since that Fourth of July, and not once did either one of us push to talk about it. It was the unspoken thing that we both knew would stay between us. She didn't need to know how much more had happened that night, only that it was cleaned up. There were no repercussions for her or an aftermath of any kind. I protected her in the best and only ways I knew how: negotiated, made a deal, and handled it.

Reaching up, I touched her eyebrow, brushing my thumb over the long white line that cut through it—it was the exact spot she had bled from when I found her.

"I left you there so I could fix it," I said as her fingers moved to graze my chest. It felt like she was pushing me away as much as she maybe wanted me closer. I couldn't tell.

"Don't," she whispered, and I cleared my throat and stepped back. She raised her chin and looked me in the eye, just as Laney and Grant came whizzing by from an aisle of empty tents. They looked like they'd just fooled around, and truthfully, I hoped they were good and distracted because I didn't want either of them overhearing this conversation.

"You left me there, and then everything changed. At least for me. And now I'm watching people find second chances and stolen moments with someone they care about, and the only thing I can think is that you make me feel safe. But I have no idea what you did or why you would even want to..."

I did what I did best. I stayed quiet. Even if the truth of how I felt for her lingered at the tip of my tongue.

"You're just going to ignore me then?"

She walked away when I didn't give her more.

What she never realized is that I couldn't ignore that woman, no matter how hard I tried.

The first time I noticed her scar was that Fourth of July, the same one when Grant was falling hard for Laney. I had worked so hard to stay away from her, and in that moment, that night, I hated myself for not knowing about that fucking scar.

I put the knife down, wipe my hands on the dishcloth next to me, and turn just slightly. My arm grazes her leg as I move to stand in front of her. And without even asking, her legs widen just enough to make space for me to stand between them. It isn't entirely necessary, but I do it anyway, reaching around to the other side of her to grab the bottle of bourbon she took down.

She watches the move, her mouth full, chewing a massive strawberry. Swallowing roughly, I think better of it and take a small step back. Space always does me favors in moments that I can't properly manage. And staring at her mouth, this close, for any longer, isn't manageable.

"This was the only bottle that Griz spent time making and perfecting with the design team." I glance at her as she watches me. "He doesn't usually do that. He always said"—I change my tone to make it sound more like him—"'It doesn't matter what it's in, as long as what's in it is good.'" Smiling, I turn the bottle over in my hand. "He spent weeks with our design team on the bottle shape and the extra materials. It was just after Shelby died." He did a whole lot of things differently after Faye's mother was no longer around.

"Oh, I remember, Ace. You forget I've been here." *I haven't forgotten for even a second.* "I watched Griz turn into mush, falling in love with her." She swallows first before she says, "And I watched how hard it was on him when she was gone."

Hadley's familiar blue eyes dance between mine. The flecks of yellow around each iris are as captivating as her high cheekbones and full lips. Her broad nose and square chin would seem masculine if they'd just been features on their own, but mixed with the rest of her, she's the most beautiful woman I've ever seen.

I clear my throat and twist off the wax that sealed this bottle. "The actual bottle, and not just the bourbon inside it, was what made it one of our most expensive. You already know it's one of our bestsellers." She stocks it at her speakeasy, so she knows, even wholesale, it's a pricey bottle.

She smiles knowingly. "I do. It looks pretty behind the bar too."

So do you.

Around the seal is a small, round ring—it's what kept the round shape of the stamp. Griz complained about it always running and not drying fast enough for the clean shape. It was an unnecessary cost, but Griz was adamant about keeping it. I pop out the deep red wax from inside it and hold up the round metal ring.

"I'll get you something you want, but for now—"

"Ace," she cuts me off, her voice turning quiet as she calls me out. "You realize, this is very romantic of you." She slides it onto her ring finger, and I hide the fact that I like seeing it there.

"It's convenient," I correct, popping the top off the bottle and pouring some into one of the glasses. And while I know it's the wrong thing to say by the way her eyebrows pinch for the briefest moment, it's what will allow all of this to work. Needing a second to focus and remind myself that this is simply a temporary solution, I take a sip.

I make the mistake of watching her as I do. I had planned to tell her that, while this wasn't real, it needs to be presented like it is, but as she stares at her finger and plays with the slightly large metal ring around it, I feel proud to have surprised her with this. A satisfaction that I wasn't expecting.

Clearing my throat, I take another step back, and pour out three fingers into two glasses. I turn and grab a square cube from the freezer for her—since she prefers it that way. "The only way this works is if we have some—" I pause, handing her glass while trying to find the right words as her eyes meet mine. Dammit, this is going to get messy. And I know it. In this moment, I know I'll look back and say that I could have figured something else out, but I want it anyway. The mess. The fallout. The way she's looking at me.

"Rules." She smiles, finishing my sentence.

"Details." I take another step back and lean against the counter adjacent to where she's perched. Pushing my hands into my pockets, I watch as she sets her drink down and leans back, bracing herself with her arms behind her on the counter.

"About how all of this started and we ended up married?" She widens her legs, and I nod, trying my fucking hardest not to look away from her face.

"I expected you to be far more…difficult about this, and you're acting like this is as natural as having a drink."

Putting her glass down next to her, she scoots her hands beneath her thighs. With a thoughtful look, she stares at the floor and says, "You don't want the truth, Ace. So I'll give you some time to work out those details before I change my mind and make this… *difficult* for you."

She has no idea.

She leans forward, plucking another strawberry from the cheese board and popping it in her mouth. Then her eyes lock on mine, and she wiggles her eyebrows. "When's the wedding?"

There's no need to drag this out, so I don't hesitate when I answer, "This week."

"So eager, Daddy," she teases, and like it always does, my breath catches in my throat.

"You can't—That's not something you can just call me. It's gotta stop," I tell her gruffly.

She tilts her head to the side, sizing up the demand. But instead of pushing back or prodding with why that's the case, she says, "Fine." And then she's hopping down from the counter and padding on bare feet out of the kitchen, toward the grand staircase as she asks, "Are we doing a town hall quickie, or are we making a big deal about it?"

"Town hall and a bite to eat?" I follow her up the stairs. "I think most people will be surprised if we don't make a big deal about it, but in an effort to—"

"I'm fine with that," she says before I can even finish, heading toward my room at the end of the hall. "No need to embellish the lie."

I bristle at the idea that this is a lie—it feels more honest than I've been in a long time.

"Where are you going?" I ask.

"Already ball and chaining me?" Turning around, she smirks, but her steps don't slow as she keeps walking backward. "Or is it ball and gagging me? How kinky are you, almost-husband?"

"I can make that my thing if it means making sure I get some quiet when you're here full time."

"I can think of other things worth gagging on," she mumbles, chasing it with a barking laugh.

I open my mouth and not a fucking thing comes out. *I may not survive this.*

"And stop getting your panties all in a bunch," she says with a wave of her hand, turning back and walking through the threshold of the bedroom. "I'm checking out my new room."

This is a detail that there's really no way to work around, especially with Griz living under the same roof. It's a stretch that he's going to believe anything about this situation as it is, but I need him to be satisfied enough to consider the marriage as a mutual agreement and not me exploiting a woman he's considered family for a long time. And while the legal documents will be enough for my other reasons, I want his approval too. Even if he eventually realizes it isn't the real thing.

She drags her hands along the top of the dressers, stepping slowly toward the other side of the room. A part of me likes seeing her in my space. Part of me wants to lean into the lie and believe the illusion of this being real. At the doorway to the en suite bathroom, she turns her head, looking at me over her shoulder, just as I'm glancing down at her muscular legs.

"Goddesses, are you fucking kidding me?" She gasps. "This might just be the sexiest bathroom I've ever seen. I'm never leaving."

Please don't, I pathetically respond in my head.

Her fingers tap along the shiny dark marble. "You cannot possibly have a bathroom like this and expect me to contribute to society." Undoing the top button of her shorts, she keeps her eyes on mine.

I lean against the door frame and sling one hand into my pocket, watching her be very intent with the way she moves her hips left and then right, slowly coaxing the tight jean shorts from her hips and sliding the material down her thighs.

"I'd like to try it out. Test what I'm getting into and see if it…fits." Her eyes drop to my pants as her shorts hit the floor. "Or are we just going to ignore that kiss?"

I try my hardest not to seem fazed by her taunt, even as my attention flicks to the bathing suit bottoms tied at the sides of her hips. I haven't thought through the intricacies of what being physical with her would do now. How even one taste could, and likely would, change the trajectory of all of this. There's too much at stake to fuck around and find out.

"I'm not ignoring it, Hadley. It's just irrelevant now."

Her mouth kicks up in a half smile, but a sarcastic scoff comes out when she says, "Irrelevant? Feels kind of relevant."

"It's impossible to ignore how beautiful you are, but you know that." I watch her swallow, like that information is news to her. "So you can keep peeling clothes off, and I'll appreciate the fuck out of it, but that's all it'll be. A show. Just like what we need to put on in order to make all of this work."

She stops moving her fingers that have been teasing along the hem of her T-shirt. "Is that what you think I'm doing here? Putting on a show?" Smiling, she starts to lift her shirt as she says, "I'm simply not feeling very shy around my soon-to-be husband—"

I leave the room at that, catching only a glimpse of the under curve of her tits. Fuck, just that alone has me wanting to fuck my hand hard and fast.

"I'll be in my office when you're done," I call out, just as I hear the shower turn on. Letting out a ragged exhale, I shuffle down the stairs, but as I'm turning on the landing, Griz is standing there with his arms crossed—and a pissed-off look painted across his face. *Great. A hard-on and a disapproving father figure; it's like I'm a fucking teenager all over again.*

I slow on the last step and smile to myself, looking down first, trying to figure out how to play this. He probably heard just about all of that. I wouldn't be surprised if he was home and just sat quietly listening.

"What the hell are you doing, Atticus?" he asks in a reprimanding tone.

Slightly annoyed at the lack of privacy, I move past him, answering as honestly as I can. "What I have to, Griz."

Chapter 17

Ace

Apparently what I've had to do is wait. Two hours have ticked by, and Hadley still hasn't surfaced from my room. The rumble of thunder shakes the house, just enough that the chandelier in my office sounds like an instrument—something unsettling and out of tune. It's how I've felt since I left her upstairs, thrumming with rootless, unyielding energy.

My phone buzzing on my desk is a welcome distraction.

> **RIGGS:**
> You should come and see the place. Know what you're getting yourself into before you decide to sign on the dotted line.

> **ACE:**
> Does your husband know you're inviting me?

> **RIGGS:**
> Whose idea do you think it was to invite you out? We're coming off our busy season. It's the perfect time to see what a place like this can offer when it's done correctly.

Business comes easily to me. Conducting it and finding where things could flourish and what would inevitably end up costing money. The bourbon industry is consistently growing, orders and fulfillment increasing daily, but the distillery, tours, even the expected turnout for this year's races are far lower than any other year that I can remember. The chaos that Wheeler Finch created with his business didn't just impact a few; it's chipping away at my town, the people, and their businesses. There needs to be something new—tourists need a reason to come other than for the bourbon.

A blur of dark hair catches my attention as it moves past my office door, head down, scribbling in her notebook.

"Hadley!" I shout after her.

She walks backward to the doorway a few seconds later—in my white dress shirt. "Yes, darling?" she singsongs, coming into my space with a pep in her step.

Taking out her phone, she pauses the music that's still spilling down the stairs and through the hall. Shania turned into Florence, which then turned into Britney, and then some girl screaming "please" and "espresso." I actually like the last few. "I needed a little lyrical pick-me-up after today."

If it was anyone else, she'd seem fine and not the least bit jilted by the men trespassing, the hard ride here, the vast change of events that have her in front of me, waiting for rules about our newly decided relationship. But I know her, probably better than Lincoln does; the music helps boost her mood, and the long shower was to relax her tension and calm her thoughts. She had nail polish on when she went into that bathroom, but it's been mostly picked off, except for a little left on her thumbs.

"That's mine," I say, nodding toward her.

She points to herself, and then slowly smiles wide, and I already know she's about to break my first rule before she opens her mouth. "Patience, Daddy."

"Jesus Christ," I mumble quietly to myself. I hate how that word affects me when she says it—like it rolls over my skin and settles at the base of my spine like flint, just waiting for the heat from her to strike.

She kicks up her Kentucky accent and jokingly says, "I don't want you ruining my reputation."

I look down her body—her thick, muscular legs and the rest of her hidden beneath the cotton poplin. "I meant the shirt," I say, trying to appear bored by her. To be clear, I'm never bored with the shit this woman says. But it's like feeding a monster, and sexual innuendos can't be involved in what we're about to discuss. "We need to work out some details. Come in."

She perches herself on the leather club chair in front of the chess set. Pointing to the board, she asks, "Should we play while we chat?"

I prefer to play quietly, but she functions best doing a few things at once. Griz is like that too.

My office is exactly where I function best—a space to work and think, surrounded by some of the things I love the most. Chess. Bourbon. Pictures of my family in black-and-white on the farthest wall. A long bookshelf that holds a fair amount of books I still haven't found the time to read and a few special editions that I've collected over the years of ones that lingered in my mind longer than most.

Staring at the board, she studies the pieces carved from old bourbon barrels. "This is a pretty set," she says, picking up a knight and running her thumb along the natural wood that's been polished and stained. But then she sucks in a quick gasp, jolting as her gaze flicks to the window. "My horses. I completely forgot—"

But I cut off her worry immediately as I shift and fix my pieces inside their squares. "Lady and Fergie are both in the largest stalls. They've been fed, and I guarantee Griz gave them a peppermint or two when he got back home."

She sits back, her eyes watering slightly, legs tucked underneath her. I'm still not sure if she's wearing shorts or even underwear underneath, but I divert my attention to her mouth. Fingers pressed against them, she's trying to decide what to say or what to hold in so those tears don't actually fall. "Thank you," she says softly. It makes me feel like I've done something right, especially knowing that most of this agreement serves me more than it serves her—or at least that's what she needs to believe.

"Your move," I tell her, nodding to the board.

She wipes beneath her eyes and glances at the bar cart in the corner. "I've already been day drinking. Might as well keep going." Her mouth tips up at the corner, that small dimple pinching. "Pour me something?"

She sits up higher as I get up and pour a few fingers in each glass. I pluck them from the cart and find her already looking less frayed. A pawn moves one spot closer to my side of the board as she watches me come back to sit. "Don't you ever just throw on a pair of sweats and relax in your own home? You have the glass of bourbon, a game in front of you, but still all business."

I stop the glass halfway to my mouth. "I am relaxed."

"You're still wearing shoes," she says, like it's an accusation and not an observation. She leans forward, bending at the waist, giving me a ridiculous view down the oversized white shirt. It isn't a secret that Hadley has an incredible body, but I only allow myself specific parts to look at in one sitting. I've already had an eyeful of her thick thighs and toned calves—if I look at more, I'll want more.

"What are you doing?" I ask as she gets frustrated at the distance from the chair to the floor and shifts off, moving to her knees. She loops her fingers in the laces of my shoes, kneeling in front of me, focused on a task I never asked her to complete. When she loosens the ties completely, she pulls off the shoe and tosses it across the room. "If you're going to wear a suit while I'm braless and in pajamas as we negotiate our life together, then I need a little bit of the playing field leveled out."

It isn't fucking leveled by a long shot.

She glances up at me through her long dark lashes, a smirk tugging at her lips when she sees my tightened expression. "Does this turn you on, Ace?" *Yes.* "Me in front of you, on my knees like this?" *Fucking hell.*

My mouth waters, and I run my thumb along my lip, trying to calm my dick down and keep from fucking this up before it even starts. I straighten in my seat as I clear my throat. "Get up. We're going to talk about some rules and limits—"

"Fine," she huffs out, then mumbles something about me not being any fun. "You realize who you've asked to marry, right?"

"I do," I tell her as I move my pawn forward next to hers. A King's Gambit would be her first thought—a risky choice, but it doesn't surprise me. She's always the player to put someone all in after only one round of poker or setback.

But I prefer something slightly less aggressive and more controlled. I take her pawn by advancing my rook. She's going to look at moving more pawns, perhaps even her bishop, but she's a ballsy player—like with everything else. And while I've never played a single game with her, I've watched her wipe the floor with Lincoln plenty of times over the years. She let him win for a stint right after Olivia died—he knew they were pity wins, but she did it anyway.

"Which is why we need to talk about our hard limits." I pause, searching for the right words. She expects me to keep my important pieces guarded, but I move my queen instead toward her pawns and just out of reach. "And expectations."

"I'm listening," she says as she takes one of my pawns.

"It would be believable to tell everyone that we've been quietly carrying on a relationship since Lincoln's wedding. You admitted to always having feelings for me, we slept together, and—"

She barks out a laugh, interrupting. "Sorry, but why is it me who's been pining for you and not you yearning for me?"

I raise an eyebrow as she stares at me, no longer interested in the moves on the chessboard. The funny part is, I'm incredibly good at keeping my feelings and emotions intact and beneath the exterior. *If she only knew how close to the truth she actually is.*

"Are you saying that because it's a more believable story? Or do you think—" she asks softly. "Why would you say that?" Vulnerability is laced in that question, and it makes me pause. I hadn't taken into consideration that there may be truth in it on her end. She's pushed and said plenty, but I haven't ever stopped to think there's more to it than her wanting to challenge me. That kiss aside, I haven't allowed the idea to even be a possibility. I couldn't. And…I still can't.

When she leans against the arm of her chair, my white dress shirt shifts. Her shoulder peeks out along the wide opening where she seems to have forgotten there are buttons.

My eyes follow its movement, and I grip onto my glass so hard I'm surprised it doesn't crack as I swallow down more bourbon. I'm the one who said I'd be honest, and if this is going to work, I owe her *some* truths.

"I won't lie to my brothers," I say, making sure she knows that's a nonnegotiable. "Griz?" I shrug. "I can work around him, but Linc and Grant are a hard line for me. If they ask, I'll tell them the truth of how we came to be married."

"And if they don't?"

"Then they can believe whatever they'd like."

"That *you're* in love with me," she says, pushing the pawn in the exact place I was expecting. I advance my queen, taking her pawn. And she's confused why I'd risk it by the way she studies the board, taking another measured sip of her drink. Her fingers graze along the top of her foot, which she can reach easily by the way her legs are tucked beneath her.

"That we're married regardless of the reasons." I study the board and think about where she'd go next. "And that should be respected."

"I'm assuming I'll be living here?" she asks.

"It makes more sense."

Her lips tilt up just as she takes another sip. "And I'll be sleeping…"

I mirror her movement and take a drink. "You'll be in my room. If Griz wasn't here, it'd be easier to have your own space, but I'd rather avoid the attention it'll draw if you move into the guest suite."

"I don't really cook," she says. "Unless you count my version of girl dinner."

I pause, not really sure what the hell that is. "What's 'girl dinner'?"

She gives me a leveling glare, like somehow I've royally fucked up. So I mentally note that and just tell her. "Besides making breakfast for me and Griz and hosting family dinners on Fridays—although Laney likes to cook for those lately—you've been here long enough to know we have a private chef that does meals for the week. Just leave any special requests."

Even though she nods, I can tell there's more on her mind as she pictures what this is going to look like—us living together. Her bringing up cooking isn't relevant, more like a warm-up. So I keep going with the more important and compromising parts of this arrangement.

"I don't want you to change anything about your business or the things that are important in your life, but you'll need to accompany me to things. You'll need to play the part of a loving and devoted partner."

She smiles, her pointy, red-chipped nail resting on her front teeth as she does it. "Devoted?"

I try to ground myself regarding the next few things I'm about to say. "I don't expect to hear about your life through my brother. He's your best friend, but I'll be your husband for all intents and purposes. There are plenty of things I'm capable of handling, but I can't help or figure it out if I don't know."

Glancing at the chessboard, she visibly swallows.

"And while this might not be a typical marriage, I recognize there are things…" I clear my throat once again. "I don't want to find someone in my home or in my bed."

Her eyes shoot back to mine. "Are you serious?"

I hate knowing how this woman has no qualms about leaning into her sexuality. She doesn't cower behind it or prudishly keep quiet. I respect it, but fuck, do I hate it.

She barks out a laugh when I look at her pointedly. "Are you serious right now? What about you? Does this go both ways?"

"Of course this goes both ways. I won't allow a third party putting this agreement at risk or making either one of us look like we're cheating pieces of shit." I try to read her reaction, but for the first time—maybe ever—I have no idea what's going through her head. "You know how this town talks. The two of us getting married is already going to catch like fire."

"And if I'd rather not follow this particular rule?"

I do my best not to physically respond to her words. Clenching my teeth, I swirl what's left in my glass, giving myself a moment to calm the nerve that remark just hit. "Rules are meant to be followed, Hadley."

She moves another pawn. "I don't think that's how the phrase goes."

I keep my attention on her and not the way my shirt looks better on her than me, or the way she's looking at me right now—as if she wants nothing more than to push every one of my buttons.

Sighing, she rubs at her bottom lip. "You realize you're no fun? You're taking away one of the most fun parts of a marriage, Ace."

"Infidelity isn't a part of marriage, Hadley."

She rolls her eyes and clarifies. "*Sex*. You're taking sex out of the equation with this"—she air quotes—"rule."

"Out of all the things we should be talking about, this shouldn't be your priority."

She raises her eyebrow and smirks. "Is it because you're older? Things aren't as…" she taunts, glancing down at my crotch.

"You're a smart woman. I'm sure you can figure out how to ease your needs," I practically choke out. Like telling this woman to get herself off is as casual as telling her the weather.

"Oh, I'm very well-versed in that department," she mumbles.

Fuck. My dick nudges me at the insinuation.

"How long?" she asks on an exhale. "I'll need reinforcements," she mumbles to herself as she picks up her phone, swiping at the screen. "How long is this marriage and its rules going to last?"

Good fucking question. "It's more than just the bourbon business now. We're talking about your safety, along with a plan that needs…massaging," I say, barely holding back a groan, hoping like hell this all works out.

"Then I have some rules of my own." She sits back in her chair, her fingers gliding along the edge of the leather. "You're not going to treat me like some kind of inconvenience. If you invite me to something, I won't just be an arm piece."

It's amusing for her to think so low of me. That I'd ever consider her as either of those things.

Tipping her chin up, she meets my eyes with her own when she adds, "I'll be your wife, Ace, but don't ask me to turn into something I'm not."

"Like what?" I smile. "Quiet? Reserved? Obedient?"

A laugh erupts out of her. "You know how well that'll end for you, if you ever suggest me to be quiet." She shifts in her chair. "Reserved? Not in my wheelhouse." With a hum, she moves a pawn. "Obedient though?" She bites the inside of her lip, as if she's thinking about a word I so carelessly threw out. "Depends." Her eyes shift to mine, and there's a twinkle there meant to torture me. "Playing with power dynamics has always been intriguing to me. But I wonder…is it 'sir' and 'daddy' that gets you all warm and fuzzy? Or would you prefer a whimpering 'please'?"

She has a way of getting under my skin, and I don't even realize it's happening until it's too late. Answering that question is asking for trouble, and she knows it. So I keep to the point. "You have my respect, Hadley. Always have, but even more so now as my wife. I will not treat you in any way that doesn't show respect. You should know that. And if you didn't"—I clear my throat—"well, now you do." Releasing a breath, I force a smirk to keep my shit together. "What else?"

Fidgeting just a little bit, she's buying time to figure out what else she should demand. "I want a nickname. You always say my name with a little twinge of annoyance—I'm not sure you even realize it. But other people will. So…" She lifts one shoulder like this request is no big deal. "I want a nickname. Something *sweet*."

I watch and wait for what else she'll say, but she lets the statement linger there. She wants me to call her "sugar."

As I study the chessboard, I can't help but crack another smile.

With my silence, she keeps going. "I'm not against something typical like 'babe' or 'sweetheart,' but I feel like you can be more creative than that." She finally looks up at me. "What? Your brothers really stepped up with the nicknames 'Peach' and 'honey.' I'll feel left out." She fiddles with one of the buttons on her shirt when she can't help but mutter, "You seem to react nicely to 'Daddy,' so—"

Jesus, she's trying to kill me. "No. You're not calling me that, Hadley. I've told you this already. It's a hard no."

She blinks at the forcefulness of my words. "Alright. Can I ask why?"

"Your father—" I start to say, taking the opening to shift the conversation. She needs to know my plans, and I'm not going to enter this with her and have it hanging over our heads.

"Ace, are you kidding me? You can't drop a cold bucket of water like that on me. Please do not connect the two. My relationship with that man does *not* have anything to do with that word. Ew!" She cringes. "They're similar words, but they do *not* mean the same thing. I understand limits and can respect—"

"Hadley," I interrupt her rambling, shaking my head. "If you'd let me finish… I went to see your father."

"You what?" She stops the glass decanter from pouring midair, her face turning from curious to angry within two blinks.

"Your father knows more than he should about my business. He threatened to share names of my colleagues. Names he shouldn't know or with whom to share them." I bite down and clench my jaw, trying not to get worked up over this right now. "It puts my friends and their families in danger, and I can't allow that." I pause and take a breath before what I'm about to say. "Unless I convince you to see him and grant him access to the financials tied to Finch & King funds."

She tosses back the entirety of the bourbon she poured. "I have plenty of reasons why I don't want to help that man, never mind see him. Speak with him. And you…" Her anger drifts off just as quickly as she realizes what I'm saying. "He wants access to all of the estate through me, so you're marrying me…to make that impossible?"

I smile and give her a firm nod. "I'm marrying you to gain my share of Foxx Bourbon." Even though it feels like a lie at this point, it makes sense for me to have a selfish part in this. "*And* to make sure you're safe, because despite everything, that matters to me a great deal." I don't miss the way her mouth parts, but no words come out, almost like she's taken aback. "I can't tell you when this will end, because I don't know if your father being sent to prison ends any of this burden thrust upon you. But you're marrying me to help and pay back a debt you think you have, and to make sure your father doesn't have an opportunity to use you again, or anyone else for that matter."

She blinks and stays quiet. Maybe absorbing everything I've just said or planning my demise. Her unpredictability is as enticing as it is terrifying.

"Then what? After you get your portion of the business and after my father…after all of that settles, then what?" she asks, sinking back into the chair. "After all of it, we just stay married? You have to have an exit strategy, Ace."

I grit my jaw. *If it were up to me, there'd be no exit strategy.* The thought of it ending feels wrong, regardless of it being an integral part of an agreement like this. *I'm so fucked.* "I'll let you decide. When it's enough. When you say, then we stop."

She glances at the board, and then back at me. "And you'll be okay with that—allowing me to be in charge of how this ends?"

"Yes," I say, watching her think through her next move. "I would prefer that this marriage look as real as possible. If there are things you need or want, then you need to ask for them. I'm not a mind reader, and I don't want this ending in either of us hating the other."

"I don't think I could ever hate you," she whispers. *And I could never hate her.* "If you meet someone and—"

"I won't," I say, looking her in the eyes, leaning forward, bracing my elbows on my knees and letting the empty glass hang from my fingers. *I won't.* "How and when this ends can be up to you." She doesn't need to know that an end is the furthest thing from my mind right now. Not with the way she's looking at me.

She mirrors my pose—elbows braced on bent knees, looking me in the eye. "While I appreciate the sentiment, I don't want the responsibility. This is a partnership. Plenty of people muck this part up—forget the fact that choosing someone isn't just about the gesture, it's the ride."

"Hadley…"

"I'm not done," she says, glancing at my mouth. "The minute you want to choose something or someone else, you tell me. We've both earned that level of respect."

There won't ever be anyone else for me.

She moves one of her pawns to the right side of the board. A move I knew she'd make. So I take her knight.

"I refuse to be anyone's pawn," she says with a slow smile.

I look at where her eyes just fell and where her rook is set. Wiping my hand across my mouth, I try to erase my impressed amusement. She set a fishhook. In chess, a gambit typically means sacrificing a pawn. But this move sacrifices something higher, a stronger piece to gain the advantage. She isn't only a smart-ass with a dirty mouth. My soon-to-be wife just played me. And with strategy.

She tips her glass all the way back rather dramatically, then gets to her feet and heads for the door. "If you are making plans that involve me, I expect to know about them. I will not be just a player on your board." She lingers in the doorway, my shirt hitting high on her thigh. She looks too good in it. "Careful looking at me like that, I might get the wrong idea…husband."

With a wink, she leaves my office just as she calls out, "Checkmate!"

Chapter 18

Hadley

"You'll marry who I say, Hadley. You think this life you like to benefit from doesn't come with sacrifice?" The words my father tutted not long after my eighteenth birthday replay through my mind. I wasn't surprised that he'd use this as an opportunity to show me off to his friends and see who might step up and make an offer.

I would have much rather been in downtown Fiasco tonight, dancing to bluegrass and country, people-watching, and snacking on Kentucky specialties like Modjeskas and a slice of transparent pie. But instead of Fourth of July fun, I was walking into a stuffy dinner party for my father's associates who either owed a favor or were angling for one. It usually meant being introduced to someone's son or brother. And in Kentucky, bastards had brothers. I was turning twenty-five this year—and even now, by most Southern standards, I was old.

I plucked a glass of champagne from a passing tray and smiled at the few friendly faces I recognized. The newly elected governor *and his brother, a bloodstock agent who had just been folded into the mix, two Russian men who kept to themselves in the far corner of the room, and my father's business partners, the Kings.*

I counted three women—myself included. The other two were slinging trays of hors d'oeuvres. It pissed me off, the lack of women in rooms like this. Fucking boys clubs. Fiasco looked like every other quaint town in southern Kentucky—small and unassuming. But I knew it was filled to its brim with secrets, swimming with liars, and running on agreements. Most of those things usually transpired between people who had similar goals in mind. In this room, it was money and power.

"Heard your girl had a helluva race at the Oaks."

I leaned against the far wall in the oversize room and looked around at the elbow rubbing and bullshit slinging, trying not to laugh.

"You heard right." I smiled. He was a good looking older man. I instantly liked him. "She sure did. My father is still sour that she's not one of his." Some folks here were in the same boat as me, required to make an appearance. Chief Hawkins, like most of the public officials who showed on evenings like this, didn't have much of a choice. It was better not pissing in Wheeler Finch's lemonade by not showing. My father had no problem holding grudges.

"I'm being beckoned," he said as his brother, the new governor, and my father turned toward where we were. He squeezed my elbow. "Let's see how long it takes them to talk about money and bullshit committees." With a wink, he moved away. I shamelessly checked out the way he wore his dress uniform during today's parade, but right now, he was more casual in jeans and his Fiasco FD T-shirt. It made him feel more like a friend than a guest.

"Hadley," my father called out, holding his arm up, as if that was my sign to come and pretend like we were close. With his arm around me, my father showed me off to his other guests.

"My daughter, Hadley. It was her filly that took the Oaks this year—quite an accomplishment." I felt like I was being paraded around, exactly like one of my father's broodmares—to be shown off and used for gain.

James Switcher had a receding hairline and an overinflated ego. And the second my father made introductions, I knew he was angling for a setup.

"Nice belt buckle," I said, trying to get Switcher to stop staring at my tits.

The small group laughed first, and then my father said, "Thought you two might get along—James here was just telling me all about the last rodeo he rode in."

"Been a while now, actually. I did a bit of bull riding when I was younger. Never made it too far, but my brother is a helluva rider and has won a great deal of championships," he said proudly.

"Then why are you wearing it?" I blurted out, with my father's attention flicking around to the dwindling crowd.

Judgment and sarcasm were laced in my tone, so when he stared at me without saying a word, it should have thrown out a warning. It was all I needed to know about him. A man who liked to show off other people's hard work and felt threatened as soon as someone challenged him.

Dinner conversation after that lingered around the latest plans for my father's breeding facility. What started as training and racing had evolved into every facet of horse racing—stallions, mares, fillies, foals, you name it, and my father had a plan on how to capitalize on every step of a horse's life. It wasn't anything new, but for Finch & King, it would make them the kind of powerhouse that made a lot of people a lot of money. It was another hour of smiling and pretending to give a shit before I managed a quiet escape.

I shook out my hands and rolled my neck just as I walked

into the stable. At least it was cooler here. Summers in Fiasco were always unforgiving, but this was one that felt long-winded, like a self-reflective sermon—no one asked for it. I don't remember feeling this hot when I was lounging on the porch with the Foxx boys. Even in the late afternoon heat, they were more comfortable than an evening here. It had always been that way, since the first moment I was in their company. Like I'd belonged there with them.

"Thought you might have run off," a voice said from the side door. I nearly jumped out of my skin. "Your father thought it might be nice for us to get to know one another a little better."

My stomach churned at the idea. The long corridor that led to the horse stalls was a lot of steps away, and he was blocking the closest exit.

He laughed to himself, his tongue pushing along the side of his mouth just before he said, "You're not so good at hiding your feelings." He held his hand up to his face. "You wear them all over."

"Oh, how nice, a man who proclaims to know what a woman is thinking. So predictable," I said with as much sass as I could muster, knowing I was alone with him.

"Made an offer your father seems to like." His eyebrows raised, crinkling his fivehead. He was amusing himself. "What must that be like? Knowing you're no better than any of these horses. Being negotiated and sold off." My stomach clenched as he laughed again. "Maybe we can just play for a little while, test each other out first…"

I couldn't help the laugh that escaped. "You must have missed the part where I'm not interested. So let me spell it out for you and your uneducated ass—"

I didn't know how he moved so quickly. His arm cocked back wide and came down hard. I couldn't brace for it. I hadn't expected it.

My neck snapped to the side so fast that it was going to feel like whiplash later. Later…there needed to be a later. The momentum of the open-hand slap connecting with my left cheek had me hitting the ground. The dirt felt cool along my cheek. I coughed and dusty dirt swirled into my mouth.

"What was it you were saying again, bitch?" he tutted. "Something about my ass, was it?" His overzealous belt buckle was far too close, hovering over me.

Get up, Hadley.

"I didn't want to have to do that," Switcher said with that same muted smile as he wiped his brow and tossed his hat on the workbench just to the left. "I can't go havin' you thinkin' it's okay to speak to me that way, sweetheart. Where I'm from, women know when to shut their mouths."

My eyes instantly watered, and my breath caught in my throat.

The shock of a slap across the face should have left me speechless. It was my mouth that caused this pinprick to get pissed off to begin with. The point of it was to shut me up. Silence and a healthy fear have served me well, apparently, but now what? Violence wasn't a language I knew. I was tough by most standards, but being shoved around and looked at the way he was looking at me wasn't in my typical wheelhouse. I imagined most women felt that way—never ready, until they had to be.

I pushed up on my hands and scurried back up and on my feet in seconds. This wasn't going to be my sad story. Or a preview of my life. I touched my cheek that was now warm, feeling higher near my eyebrow where it throbbed, and I must have hit something sharp because there was blood on my hand when I pulled it away. I blinked back the tears that threatened to escape when I said with a saccharine smile, "Ah yes, where you're from—the land of overcompensating for mediocrity and massive mommy issues, I bet."

He blinked, trying to digest the words.

I took a deep breath before adding, "I should have known better just by looking at you…"

He ran his tongue over his teeth. His tooth was chipped, and where most people had two front teeth, Switcher had one front and center. Maybe someone had broken his jaw and it was never set right. It wasn't noticeable at first, but I was good at pinpointing imperfections. They were what made people memorable. Vulnerable. Human. But the abusive womanizer with a fivehead was not the kind of person I had any interest in remembering.

There were benefits to being best friends with a man—gender roles never registered. I'd barnacled myself to Lincoln Foxx, but the payoff was that he'd done the same. Taking out our frustrations on the world meant riding fast and punching things instead of gossiping and shopping. It was the unspoken agreement Lincoln and I always had—if you needed to cry, do it while punching something. Or swinging an axe. Or slinging rocks at things that would shatter. My best friend was the one thing my father and Switcher never accounted for. He and his brothers and grandfather did something that I hadn't even realized until this moment: turned me more into a Foxx than a Finch.

Shifting my eyes to the left, I remembered how many steps it was from the archway of the farthest horse stall to the double doors that led out to the open fields of paddocks. My car was parked not far from there, and the keys were in the cup holder. Switcher had an easy hundred pounds on me, but the look on the idiot's face gave nothing away, other than the fact that remorse was nowhere in sight. This fueled him. He looked proud of his choices tonight, which meant I would never feel bad about mine.

The clanking of his oversize belt buckle was as loud and motivating as the bugle that started the Kentucky fucking Derby. I couldn't hesitate or second-guess, I could only make it hurt. And then run.

A fire alarm jolts me, and I clasp my chest, sitting up fast. The breeze is pleasant up here in the late spring months, before the humidity settles into the rooftop. I came to my apartment to pack a few things to bring to Ace's. I couldn't keep sleeping in his shirts, and eventually, I'd want the rest of the things that keep me feeling good—makeup, perfume, baseball jerseys, boots, and heels. The sound of pages flapping in the breeze has me glancing at my little black book that must have fallen. It's still open on the page where I had been listing out all the summertime things that made me smile. *Firecracker ice pops, the smell of coconut sunscreen, watching lightning bugs wander in the dark.* I had been replaying the rules in my mind, and the idea of marriage jogged enough of my memories to knock me back to a night I try my hardest to forget.

The door to my roof deck swings open with the breeze. The weather is always ornery in spring, and today the wind moved throughout Fiasco like it has something to say. There isn't much up here yet. The winter igloo that had been here I took down to prep for the lounge chairs, minibar, and plunge pool that I usually set up for summer. I lean along the edge, the chest-height bricks making it so this space isn't dangerous, even if I'm tipsy. Up here, that's been pretty often. The fire station stands across the street and is the gut-check reminder that I need to talk with Hawk. Too much has happened, and he needs a heads-up.

I swallow the dread of having to do it, but I press the bell that connects from here to the fire station. A fun detail that I branded my Pool Boy Bell. It was how Chief Hawkins and I ended up flirting our way into bed together. I press the bell two more times, but it's one of the new recruits that comes out of the station's side door. I call out, "Hey, is Chief there?"

He looks around and then up at me. "Nah, he's out of town with his brother for a family thing. Should be back in a few days. Want me to tell him you're looking for him?"

"All good," I shout back.

Pulling out my phone, I plan to send him a follow-up text from earlier, but Lincoln's name and face pop up on the screen. When I answer, it's like picking up a conversation that was already in progress. I make my way through my apartment and try hoisting as many bags as possible along each shoulder, the crook of each elbow, and the free hand that isn't holding the phone.

"Tell me again why you aren't coming with us tomorrow morning to visit Dottie's siblings?" Lincoln asks. And without letting me get a word in, he says, "Lark and Lily wanted me to remind you that you're the unofficial auntie of the world's sweetest highland cow, and you are, by their laws, obligated to come with us whenever we visit her home turf." Dammit, I don't want to lie here. He's going to find out soon enough anyway.

So as I toss the bags into my trunk, I settle on, "Tell the girls next time."

"I call bullshit," he says in one breath, while in the next, he's negotiating with one of his girls about whose turn it is to choose takeout tonight. "What are you doing right now?" he asks me.

He's going to freak out. "Had to pack a few things." As I sit in the car, I wait for his next question.

"Why? Where are you going?" His eyebrows scrunch, and he stares at me with that look that says, *I better not be the last person to know what you're doing.*

I tip my head back on the headrest and take a deep breath, bracing for what I'm going to say. "Promise me you will not freak out."

"Lily, you chose last time," he shouts into his phone. His face is frozen on screen with one eye closed and a stink face. I can't help but laugh. "I need to talk to Hadley," he tells them.

"Fight it out." Then he's moving through the house, going outside, and closing the door behind him. "Alright. You should not start off a conversation like that, by the way."

"I'm doing something…with Ace," I say, as if it's a confession and not a statement.

I'm met with silence and his face unmoving, only this time, I don't think his screen froze. I've rendered him speechless.

"Are you there?" I ask a beat later.

"I'm listening," he says quickly. "It feels like there's more you're not saying." His hand flaps over his mouth in surprise before he gets even more dramatic. "Wait! Holy shit, Hadley. Did you tell him? *Please* tell me you finally told him how you feel."

I clear my throat and grab a handful of the sour cherry candies that Laney brought during her last visit. Closing my eyes, I spill it. "We're getting married."

He stops whatever he was doing and blinks at me. A moment later, his face bounces on screen as if he's rushing off somewhere. "What do you mean, you're getting married?"

"There aren't too many meanings other than that—"

He holds up his hand, pointing at the screen. "No! You don't get to be sarcastic when you drop a mic like that." Turning back, he flings open the door and shouts, "Faye, I'll be back in a few minutes!" I hear her in the background, and then he's moving like a maniac again, phone all over the place, before I get a view of the ceiling of his Jeep. "Where is he?"

"Right now? My guess is the distillery."

"You're getting married?" He sniffs out a not-so-amused laugh. "Are you pregnant, or is this just a convenient business deal?" Quirking his eyebrow, he looks back down at the screen, still driving. "Wait, why am I not invited?"

"I'm not pregnant," I huff. "I think it's hilariously very eighties of you to think that getting pregnant means I'd get married too."

"Hadley!" he rushes out, groaning as he smacks the wheel.

"And no, fine! It's mostly a business deal." That's the truth. For me, at least, this is convenient and a smart move, but I've been low-key obsessed with Atticus Foxx for longer than I would ever admit. "And we're not making this a real wedding because…because this isn't about love. And I can't…" My eyes water. I want to say, "I can't think of it as real." Or, "I can't be too happy." Or, "I can't pretend it's not exactly what I've always wanted." I hate how pathetic that makes me feel. I can't allow myself to lean into it. If Lincoln or anyone else important were there, I'd start thinking it wasn't laced with so many layers of complication. I'm a smart, strong, and practical woman. The hopeful romantic that lingers below my surface and claws often at my choices for substituting sex for love is unsettled by all of this. It all sounded very logical when I asked the first time. And the second. But right now, I'm wondering if I can keep my feelings for Ace seemingly fake.

"You never answered me. Does he know?" His body sways, and I watch as he parks and gets out of his car. The dark building and the lantern poles are seemingly familiar.

"Where are you right now?" I ask, a bit nervous. Lincoln is nothing if not a protective friend.

"Does. He. Know?" he asks again with gritted teeth.

I can't help but let out a laugh. Lincoln frustrated and slightly angry always makes me laugh a little. The truth is, I never explicitly talked with him about my feelings for Ace, but he pays attention.

"Hadley, I know you. And I trust that you know what you're

doing. But I also know him…" He doesn't say anything else after that. Instead, my best friend in the entire world says exactly what I need him to. "You tell me whatever you want. A party. A minute. I got you, Hads."

"I want this more than anything," I say honestly. "Him. This…" I hunt for the right word. "This arrangement, and I need you to not do whatever it is you're planning to do at the distillery." I know full-well he's going to lace into his brother. "And then you need to be the world's biggest cheerleader. And welcome your newest sister-in-law into the family."

"Already done." He smiles.

As soon as he hangs up, I look at my reflection in my rearview mirror.

"I'm getting married…" I whisper to myself.

I'm in my mid-thirties and drowning in the aftermath of my father's sins. I've earned the laugh lines around my mouth. I look pretty good considering the lack of sleep I've had over the course of the past year, but I stare at myself and feel proud. I've built a successful business, cultivated and nurtured friendships, had vast sexual experiences that have allowed me to discover what I like and what I could salute to and never do again. I'm proud of who I am, and yet, I wonder if, at the end of this, I'll look the same.

Chapter 19

Ace

I'M STILL WAITING FOR REGRET to invade and take over. For at least one, if not both of us. But it hasn't even been a full day since we agreed to a roster of rules for a strategic, on-paper marriage, and I keep thinking about how our chess game felt like foreplay.

I swipe my hand across my mouth and stare at the land deeds and properties that I've just purchased. It'll be worth it in the long run, but I've gone ahead and made sure my lawyer has the papers drawn and ready so that all of mine and Hadley's assets are joint and shared as soon as we sign on the dotted lines.

My phone buzzes next to me, and I glance over, almost expecting it to be him.

THE JEWELER:
I heard an interesting rumor.

> **ACE:**
> I never took you for a gossip.

> **THE JEWELER:**
> It's only gossip if it's about other people. This one was about a fox. Specifically one who's getting married.

> **ACE:**
> I thought Griz was stepping away from things regarding you and our collaborations.

> **THE JEWELER:**
> Gossiped with my dad. Secrets when it comes to women were never their strong suit.

> **THE JEWELER:**
> Need a ring?

Julian is the person I call when Lincoln or Grant aren't an option. There are plenty of uses for a jeweler, but I usually call on him for his *other* talents. Grant or Lincoln believe that Julian and I went to university together, and they've only ever had a couple of random interactions over the years. Before that, his father had worked with Griz on occasion, and we'd been told he was an old boyfriend of our nana's who he enjoyed playing cards with every now and then.

Without warning, Lincoln bursts into my office, looking slightly unhinged. Shaking out his wrists and tilting his neck from right to left, he bounces on the balls of his feet as if he's ready to start a fight.

Ah, fuck. She told him.

"Alright, I'm just going to say this. You probably don't know this, but Hadley's actually really soft in the center, like those fruit snacks we had as kids—gummy and sour as fuck on the outside, but a big, squishy mess on the inside. So I'm going to do my job here and tell you," he says, slowing down and pointing at me. "Don't fuck this up, Ace."

I raise my eyebrows at him, putting my phone down and leaning back in my chair.

"I asked her point-blank if this is what she wants, and without missing a beat, she said, 'More than anything.'"

I stop what I'm doing at those words. An admission that makes my chest feel light.

"You don't do relationships, but you just decided to marry her? Skip the dating part and jump straight into a massive commitment. Explain that to me."

Blinking, I try to keep from laughing. "Should we pour a glass before you keep talking?" I ask, standing up. Walking down the hallway, I head toward the sliding wall that opens to the hidden room at the distillery. If there's anyone lingering around, they don't need to hear any of this. He follows me in as I pluck a bottle of the 1928 Prohibition bourbon from the wall that houses bottles from floor to ceiling. I pour out a heavy three fingers in each glass.

"Sit down," I tell him when he begins pacing.

"I'm good standing."

I stare at him without saying anything for long enough that he takes a seat. And then I tell him exactly what's happened that he's missing. About the men on her property, the meeting with Wheeler, and a few other details that I need him to keep to himself.

"What aren't you telling me?" he asks. It's an out-of-character moment for him. Lincoln rarely asks too many questions.

I hate keeping anything from him, including the role that his wife is playing in all of this, but some of it needs to be quiet until the timing is right. I settle on "There are a lot of moving parts. But I promise you that I won't hurt Hadley."

"Not intentionally," he says, brow furrowed as he looks at me intently. "But this isn't a business deal. Regardless of how you're approaching it." When I open my mouth to speak, he holds up his hand and cuts off my rebuttal. "I will punch you in the dick if she ends up crying over you."

Quirking my eyebrow, I rest my fist under my chin. "You done?"

He nods, slapping his hands on his thighs as he stands. "Done."

I'm going to get punched for the few secrets I still need to keep from him, but it will be worth it, provided everything works out. My phone vibrates in my pocket. I'm instantly distracted when I see it's a call from Del.

"Yeah, Del?" I answer as Lincoln watches.

I hold up my finger to keep my brother from leaving.

"Ace, we couldn't get a confirmation on the men you reported at Finch & King stables, but the plates we pulled from the security footage were registered to a stolen vehicle up in the tristate area," Del says from the other end of the line. "My guess is old associates of Finch, and based on what you said, they don't seem friendly. I'll make sure my guys on the house arrest detail do a sweep between shifts."

It isn't a surprise that Del didn't find much. I appreciated his support, but oftentimes, Fiasco PD got in the way instead of helping.

As soon as I hang up, I throw out a text to someone who will get this done.

> **ACE:**
> I'm going to need you to do a little hunting.

> **THE ARCHITECT:**
> Sounds fun. I'm in.

> **ACE:**
> Two men walked into Finch & King horse stables.

> **THE ARCHITECT:**
> I don't do jokes, so I'm assuming I get to deliver the punchline?

> **ACE:**
> That would be ideal.

I crack my neck. I know she'll find them. She should have been my first call.

"I'll take the fact that you're distracted now as your way of telling me you're done with this conversation," Lincoln says, and I glance up just in time for him to add, "Don't hurt her, big brother," as he's walking out.

That's exactly what I'm trying to keep from happening. This goes beyond some pissed-off trainers and other workers left without jobs and paychecks. There's only one other time in my life when I saw her scared like that, and I'm not going to allow it ever again. Her father is going to pay heavily for putting her in front of his mess.

And it starts by making her my wife.

Chapter 20

Hadley

> *May: Wearing a Saint Laurent tux as the bride. Oh yeah, and marrying Ace Foxx, regardless of whether or not it's "real."*

MaryJune Howser nearly spits out her chamomile tea when Ace steps up to the window at town hall and asks for a marriage license. She snort-laughs, taking in his crisp black suit and the white-collared shirt that's unbuttoned at the top, sans a tie, of course. I roll my eyes at how stupidly attractive he looks.

I've never been one to fidget much when I feel good in what I'm wearing, and today, I feel really fucking sexy. I decided on repurposing the tuxedo I wore for Lincoln's wedding. It was Saint Laurent, and I bought it thinking that I'd only ever wear it once. With my aggressively tall stilettos, it's absolutely the right choice. This is an agreement between friends, for lack of a better explanation, and a marriage of convenience. I wasn't going to wear a pretty white dress. Despite the mixed signals and a life-altering kiss, this is a business deal.

When I woke up this morning, I was alone again in my soon-to-be husband's bed. It's been a couple of days of that, ever since I started spending the night in his room. He falls asleep in his office, and he makes sure he's out of the house bright and early. His distance makes this feel like it should—a business agreement. I'm old enough to know when to read the room. I've been ghosted and simply not picked before—this isn't my first rodeo. It might sting, but it doesn't matter. Today's nuptials aren't leading to a happily ever after.

With a deep breath, I press my palms down on my thighs and drag them down the sides of my pants along the black satin stripe, trying to ease my anxiety.

"I'll just need your license." MaryJune smiles, giving me a once-over, her lips pinching as I hand it over. She lets out a judgmental hum. The town gossips are nothing if not consistent in who they are high and low on. For the greater part of this year, my name has fallen from their lips as if they've always known I was trouble. Just by being a Finch. The funny part is, plenty of them have had some sort of business with my father over the years. They'd been fine with it until they were swindled out of money, needing to hire attorneys to confirm they knew nothing of his illegal ventures. I merely shared a name with him, while they were the ones shaking hands.

Ace is very good at making people feel uncomfortable. It's a Foxx trait to glare long enough and add in enough silence that it makes you question your own morals. MaryJune is currently on the receiving end of it. And it makes me smile so fucking wide. *Bitch*. His hand moves to mine and links our fingers as if we've held hands a million times. It shouldn't be such a big deal, but it's a small comfort that I won't forget—my husband holding my hand publicly on our wedding day. It's a prudish plot twist I never saw coming. I relish watching her eyes glance at our hands. I give her a wicked smile as we leave.

"That's pretty consistent then? The way everyone seems to give you shit for something you had no part in?" he asks as we're pulling up to Church a few minutes later.

"You know people here. They like to make heroes and villains out of the same handful of people. It just depends on what rotation you're on," I say with a brave smile. I try to play off how much it hurts to hear people who have watched me grow up lean into the idea that I'm anything like my father.

I smile as Presh greets us, and I'm a bit surprised that she knew we were coming.

"Presh, thanks for doing this," Ace says to her as if they're friends who go way back.

"Of course," she says with a smile as she comes outside with a small book. Her dark hair is the same shade as mine, and she reminds me of my mother, though I don't think of her often. When a woman decides to leave and never look back, it's easy to let time do its job and help you forget. I wonder if she'd be happy seeing me right now.

"This wasn't planned then?" she asks, curious.

I smile at how extremely accurate that is. "It was unexpected."

She hums, signing the marriage license as a witness and officiant. "I don't know." With a raised eyebrow, she smirks. "Unexpected has its way of being romantic."

I don't correct her, and neither does Ace.

"Come with me. Let's do this over there." She points out at the water, where the river cuts through her property that descends toward the caverns. It's one of the many things I love about this spot; the sound of water is so calming. It reminds me of fishing trips with Griz and the guys. I always feel like one of them when they include me on those trips.

I shed my jacket, feeling that humidity kicking in.

Ace's attention flicks down to my shirt as I walk up along the landing on the river's edge. Swallowing roughly, his eyes trace the edges that are cut right at my sides along my curves, with the way it halters behind my neck and ties low at my back.

"We can keep this simple, if you'd like, unless you have something of your own to say," Presh says as she looks between us.

I smile and nod as Ace does the same.

"Perfect." Presh smiles. "Hadley Finch and Atticus Foxx, two names I'm not all that surprised to hear together. Today is a brief moment in time. The stroke of a pen."

I stand a little taller as I watch the lines along his eyes crinkle just a pinch. His strong jawline tensing then relaxing as his gaze stays connected with mine. My face warms at the way he's looking at me.

"Brief moments, but this one is one that you'll remember."

I think about the small moments that are impossible to forget—the way he gets so flustered with me and can't help but run his palm across his mouth to either keep from smiling or saying something he shouldn't, or the way his eyes always find mine in a room, or the deep sound of a short hum when he kissed me.

It takes me a moment to recognize exactly where we are. I look out across the river at a tree that seems like it should have fallen by now. Its craggy shape and slightly burned branches, and just to the left of it is where I'd parked the night Ace found me. As if Fiasco had somehow planned this moment all along. The same space, only on the opposite side of the river, and years later. A fateful coincidence, the constant in both being him.

Presh wraps her hand around my wrist, pulling my focus back to the man in front of me. The blue-gray eyes, the only color that calmed me on a night that changed everything. The wall of a man who stepped in front of me, worried and angry for me. The only person who has ever fixed my mess and never wanted it to be repaid or even acknowledged.

With a smile, she hums. "*Une preuve d'amour.*" She squeezes my wrist only slightly and continues. "Hadley Jean Finch and Atticus Kelly Foxx, I'm happy to share this day with you. Congratulations." When I look back at her, eyes glassy, she says, "I always like to leave couples on their own to say a few things and enjoy their first kiss as husband and wife privately. Your mom and dad…" She looks at Ace with a reminiscing smile. "They spent so long together that Griz had to request that they get back to their own party."

I can tell he wasn't expecting that. He clears his throat and gives her a brief smile and nod.

After she's made it a few feet away, I say, "I didn't realize she married your parents."

"Neither did I," he says, visibly affected by that detail.

"I thought they were married at the distillery?" I ask, curious now.

He moves his head to the side, looking out toward where I had. "No. It was by the river. My mom would come spend time with Presh when we would go fishing. She said she'd rather be near baked goods than fish guts."

Stepping closer, I loop my arms around him. It takes him a moment, but he hugs me back, holding me against him in silence for a few minutes. His parents have been gone a long time, but everyone in Fiasco knows they were taken far too soon. A car accident that ended up with their vehicle exploding and Ace there to witness it. Plenty of people gossip, but the softness and care most have when it comes to that particular story is always the tone.

"You alright? Having second thoughts?" I say jokingly to lighten the moment. It isn't a normal practice to hug Atticus Foxx, but then neither is marrying him. I suppose it's a day of firsts all around.

"No second thoughts, sugar."

I rear my head back and try not to look ridiculous smiling at him. "Was that…? Did you just call me 'sugar'?"

"It's our wedding day. Seemed like the right time to give you something you wanted," he says, stepping back.

I raise my eyebrows. "Husband, you need to start choosing your words more wisely. There are *a lot* of things that I want."

The sweetness of the way his mouth tilts up just a pinch to the right isn't something I've seen many times in the years I've known Atticus Foxx. He waits for me, and we walk together, back up the path toward reality.

As we approach where Presh is waiting for us, she says, "Hadley, love, I woke up this morning and was eager to make your favorite." And then she winks at Ace. "French cream with brandy-soaked cherries. Have a treat before you both leave?"

"You're my favorite, you know that, right?" I call out to her when she disappears quickly inside, and we take a seat at one of the picnic tables. When I look back, Ace eyes one of them and then plucks it from the box. "I don't think I've ever actually seen you eat a donut," I say as he opens his mouth, ready to take what's gearing to be a big-ass bite.

"It's my wedding day," he says, then resumes his path by destroying the donut in his hands. The easy smile that takes over his face isn't one I've seen often either. Maybe ever, if I really think about it. "Presh has been paying me in donuts and pastries for years."

I take a bite and close my eyes—*damn, that's delicious.* "Why would she pay you? What kinds of things do you do for her that warrants such great currency?" When I glance up at him, I can tell I must've asked the wrong question. I'm met with a suddenly pinched brow as he wipes his mouth and his hands. Standing, he ignores my question, gathers the napkins, and says, "We should get going," then moves toward the house and tosses our garbage. I'm left watching him, wondering what the heck that was all about.

A loud roll of thunder breaks up the quiet conversation that Ace has with Presh, the sky turning grayish purple and angry. Spring storms like to swoop in and remind everyone that we're not as big and powerful as we like to think. The first few droplets force me to abandon what's left of my donut and move quickly toward the car, shouting a thank-you and goodbye to Presh as Ace does the same. Moments later, those few drops turn to a whipping sheet of cold water that douses me instantly.

I yank open the door, and the second I get in his car, Ace is coming in right beside me on the driver's side. Both of us are out of breath from trying to keep from being soaked, but one look down at my saturated tux and a glance at his wet hair, and it's obvious we failed miserably. His hair is darker when it's wet, the silver streaks disappearing as his hand drags through it. He looks like the younger version of himself. The one I crushed on since the moment I saw him—less sure, but still wildly more confident than anyone else I'd ever known. Eyes closing for a moment, he leans against the seat's headrest, his Adam's apple bobbing with a swallow, raindrops trailing down his face. *He's impossible to not want.*

Another crack of thunder sounds in the distance, and his hands grip onto the steering wheel tight as he opens his eyes and lets out a held breath.

Catching myself staring, I clear my throat, and with it, the stupidly dreamy moment I was just having. It also snaps his attention to me, and we both let out a laugh at our currently drenched state just before he starts up the car. Words seem lost on me as I watch him race through town, the reality of what we just did hitting me as hard as the sheets of rain outside the car. *I just married Atticus Foxx.* I bite along my thumbnail, trying to hide my smile. I shouldn't be so impressed with myself. I need a distraction. Leaning forward, I play with the music and settle on something country. "What kind of music do you like?" I ask, realizing I don't know.

He looks at the display at what's playing. "Depends on my mood." I can't keep from looking at his white dress shirt that's practically see-through along his upper arms. He glances at me, similar to the way I imagine I'm looking at him. He reaches to the back seat and passes me a Foxx Bourbon T-shirt.

"And what kind of mood are you in right now?" I wipe the shirt down my arms, unclasping the halter that's buttoned at my neck.

He doesn't answer right away, instead focusing his attention solely on the road ahead. Licking at his lower lip, he shifts his body, gripping the wheel tighter before tapping the gas and kicking up the speed. "Not sure I should answer that right now," he says, swallowing and stealing another glance.

My body heats, even as I shiver. Moving the T-shirt he gave me over my head, I push my arms through, then toss the wet halter onto the dashboard.

He glances at the discarded shirt and clears his throat just as we're pulling into the driveway of his house.

I don't fully comprehend why I do it, but I feel a cavalier urge to say things to this man that I know will rile him up. It's a dangerous addiction. "Why not? Are you in the mood to keep looking, husband?" I angle my body toward him. "Or am I misunderstanding the way you're eye-fucking me?"

Pulling the car toward the front porch and not the garage, he throws it in park. This time when he looks at me, it's like he's working hard to keep his hands on that wheel.

"You don't need to answer me with words." I run my fingers down the front of the damp shirt, between my breasts, and down my stomach. "I'd rather you show me..."

"Hadley—" he bites out, like a warning, and I know I've pushed my limit when he moves for his door handle.

There's a twinge of disappointment that passes through me. So I don't linger; I beat him to it. I shove the door open and rush out of the car.

I hear him shout my name as his car door slams shut. But I keep moving. Running up the porch stairs and through the front door, that's as far as I make it.

His arm wraps around me from behind, his chest pressing against my back, hand splayed open along my waist and holding tightly. My heart races, belly fluttering wildly, as his mouth brushes just below my ear.

"You want me to show you?" he husks. His words spark to life pure excitement and need for him to keep going.

"Yes," I say on a breath just as his arm loosens enough for me to turn to face him.

I don't have time to think or want, only to follow his lead as he pulls me fully into his arms. His hands grip and fist the back of my shirt as his lips find exactly where they belong: playing and prying against mine.

Sighing into the kiss, I wrap my arm around his shoulders, and he lifts me up as his tongue swipes along my lips. He hums like he approves of the way this feels, and it lights me up even more. Working my tongue in a warm and wet caress, he lifts me so that I can wrap my legs around his waist. I writhe against him, releasing a moan, teasing for friction. When his hands grip my ass and squeeze tightly, that move alone makes me want more of whatever he decides to give.

My fingers dive into his hair as he moves us down the foyer, past the stairs, anchoring my back to the wall and then grinding himself into me. And as I feel every goddess-blessed inch of his cock rock into me, another moan crawls up my throat.

If the first time he kissed me tilted my world, then this sets it on fire. I don't know if I've let in any breaths, only that the way his teeth nip at my lips and how his tongue dances with mine turns on every single fucking part of me.

Using the wall as leverage, he moves one hand to my breast and finds my nipple, pinching it first, and then moving his mouth down to it. Over the T-shirt, he teases me with his teeth, pulling another clipped sigh from me, one consumed by desire. He does it again, and then moves back to my lips, nipping my bottom lip first and grinding himself right along my center once again. *Jesus, that feels so fucking good.* A rogue moan escapes his throat, and it's so sexy that I want to drop to my knees this instant just to hear it over and over.

But instead of another moan or growl, it's the sound of car doors slamming, feet running up the porch, and voices of his family getting louder by the second that has us stopping, him retreating and looking at me like he just did something he never should have.

Chapter 21

Ace

A DOUBLE KNOCK, OR RATHER a pounding on the front door, knocks me out of the haze of the perfectly thoughtless moment I just shared with *my wife*. Hadley was just in my arms, and if we hadn't been interrupted, she would have been naked with my cock buried in her cunt in a matter of minutes. I practically groan, having to pull away and put her down. It's too good kissing her; it feels effortless getting lost in her. The way her body molds to my touch, like her skin craves mine. How she submits to me even without realizing it. *Fuck!* I'm making this more complicated every time I indulge.

"Shit." I blow out a breath and let her slide out of my grip. Standing back from her, I don't say anything and move toward my office. I need a minute.

"Oh my gosh, Lincoln has the biggest mouth, doesn't he?" Hadley asks with a clipped laugh, like what we were just doing isn't the bigger issue.

"You already know the answer to that," I say as I run my fingers through my hair.

Her eyes rove down the front of me, mouth tipping up to the side. "We should change. Looks like it's time to play husband and wife."

As she steps closer, I stupidly take another small step back. I know the roles we need to play, but right now, I can't determine what's real and what's not. My head isn't sorted after that kiss, and it needs to be.

A low bark from one of my brothers' dogs snaps us both out of our stare down. The front door swings open, and with it comes the entirety of my family, just as Griz shuffles in from his side of the house. Great, he's already here, probably eavesdropping on all of this. Echoes of congratulations come pouring inside, my nieces practically tackling Hadley as she moves toward them. Julep and Kit jump up with the same level of excitement like they know what the hell's going on.

Hadley has always been more than a part of my family or my brother's best friend. I'd never admit it, but I'm looking forward to seeing her folded completely into our chaos.

"There's no fucking way we weren't showing up to celebrate," Lincoln says, holding up two trays.

"Dad!" Lark shouts at him.

"He paid ahead, Lark," Lily singsongs, likely referring to their lucrative hustle known as the curse purse, where all their adults are obligated to pay up for their swear words. I give them a preemptive hundred-dollar bill each month. I'm not even mad about it; I'm impressed by those two little hustlers.

"You two wanted to go ahead and get married without us and—" he pauses to look at me—"not your finest decision, but I suppose love might make people stupid sometimes." He smirks at Hadley, points his finger at her, and says, "Best friend turned sister is the kind of upgrade I can get onboard with though." Her eyes water as she hugs him. A part of me feels guilty for not having all of them with us. But another part, a more selfish one, likes that I didn't have to share her. That it was just the two of us. When Linc moves toward the kitchen, he shouts, "Peach, did you bring my *Grill Daddy* apron?"

Faye follows him down the hall, rolling her eyes at me, patting my chest as she says, "Congratulations, Ace." She gives me a smile like she knew it was coming. And maybe she read between the lines. My sister-in-law is very good at figuring things out; we're similar in that way—always thinking six steps ahead of the rest. She wraps her arms around Hadley and says something in her ear that makes them both laugh so hard that Hadley snorts.

"This isn't what I would've pictured for your wedding day attire," Laney says, holding up Hadley's arm. "Though I do love the commitment to the Foxx legacy." She smiles as she takes in the damp T-shirt.

"We, uh, got caught up…" Hadley says, glancing at me before she continues, "in the rain. Come help me pick something to change into."

Less than fifteen minutes later, Faye, Hadley, Laney, and my nieces make their way back to the impromptu party.

"What do I tell them?" she whispers, voice panicked. "They want details, and I don't know what's off-limits to share." With a heavy exhale, she rubs along her wrist, looking on at the busy and loud kitchen. "What the hell are we doing? I should've just told them before when I told Linc, but I couldn't get myself to lie. And now everyone's here at the same damn time, and this is way harder than I thought it would be."

Whenever she gets nervous, she rubs along her wrist. I don't like the idea of her being anxious about this, but I don't have an answer. Without thinking, I reach for the same place she's soothing. Her eyes find mine, surprised by my touch. *The hell am I doing?* I shove my hands into my still-damp suit pockets and watch as my youngest niece hangs a sign that says Ace + Hadley. Taking in how easily this just worked and has been accepted, I clear my throat and tell her, "I'm going to go and change."

As I turn away and down the hall, I hear Lincoln call out, "She's finally a Foxx!" He's going to play this up in all the ways that are going to push my limits. I didn't lie to him about any piece of it—I couldn't. If I'm lucky, Griz will call this a win, and then I can focus on building out what I'm intending to. And drown out Wheeler Finch in the process.

Like my thoughts have summoned him, Griz comes up beside me, gripping my shoulder. The strong squeeze is as good as a hug in our family. We aren't ones to carry on with long embraces or unnecessary sharing of feelings, but a long handshake and a shoulder squeeze are the more meaningful equivalents.

"Tell me you've just married that woman because you love her. That you've finally gotten your head out of your ass." We live in the same house; he's watched both Hadley and me dance around each other for years, so I never thought he'd believe that I'd just marry her all of a sudden. But right now, the look on his face isn't one I see often anymore. He looks…happy and content. Only, as the seconds pass without a confirmation from me, his smile falters below that bushy mustache.

He sighs, head shaking while crossing his arms. He moves his hand from my shoulder, and that small shift in body language makes me feel like I've fucked up. "You're somethin' else. The hell are you doing, Ace?"

"I should be asking you the same thing, old man," I say

quietly. He's making a lot of changes lately. Trying to tie things up in a way that's starting to make sense to me.

He steps away, but not before he looks me dead in the eye to say, "Being selfish for once in my goddamn life."

Laney smacks my chest with the back of her hand as I watch him sulk off.

Where the hell did she come from?

"You're a good man, Ace." She smiles at me and tilts her head to my shoulder. Laney fell hard for my brother, and I watched them become each other's most important people. "I know you're going to treat my best girl the only way she deserves. And if you're curious or don't already know," she stands taller and then whispers, "that woman deserves the kind of respect she doesn't expect and the kind of love you're still unsure if you're capable of. Anything less puts you on my shit list."

"Understood, Laney." I smile at my sister-in-law, looking over at my brother, Grant, who hasn't said much other than smiling at what he's overhearing.

She grips onto my arm. "Like a queen, Ace. Treat her like a goddamn queen."

I give her a tight-lipped nod as I watch Hadley smiling, holding champagne flutes while Lincoln double-fists bourbon and prosecco. When her eyes meet mine, I feel it at the base of my spine, in my gut, and in the tingle along my lips.

It should be like any other day with the family—grilling steaks and drinking bourbon, catching up and laughing. It all feels…easy. As the hours go on, I realize it might be the same, but it's also wildly different. It's the first day in a long time when I don't field calls about problems or touch base with the team at the distillery. I'm fully present, taking in each moment, not wanting to miss any of this impromptu wedding reception—my wedding reception. I've witnessed Hadley's reactions thousands of times before today, but never so openly or while not being worried she'll catch me looking. Every time she laughs with her full body, her head tipping back, eyes crinkling, mouth open. When she tells Lark and Lily about her newest combination of Pop Rocks flavors. How she talks comfortably and animatedly with my brothers and their wives, my grandfather too. Or how she glances at me and smiles every so often. I'm not sure if it's because she's feeling that same sense of easiness or if she's embellishing our lie.

There has never been a time in my life when I wanted to settle down with someone and fold them into this life. But then again, the one I just married had been folded into it a long time ago. There's no learning curve or disapproving family members—she fits in here better than I do sometimes. I let myself get lost in how easy it would be to allow it to play out—finish what we started earlier and just...see.

"Why am I just noticing this now?" Grant says with a mischievous grin, looking right at me as we sit around the firepit.

But it's Lincoln who answers. "It's been like that for at least a decade, maybe more. You've just been too into your own bullshit, little brother."

Grant flips him off, looking back at me when he says, "You gave Linc all the reasons why this is happening, but you forgot to mention the part where you're obsessed with her."

I run my hands along the lacquered wood arm of the Adirondack chair. "Obsessed is a little aggressive. I'm merely looking at the woman I just married and thinking..."

Lincoln chimes in, "That you're an idiot."

Grant adds, "That you're not as smart as you thought?"

Lincoln carries on, "That you should quit listing off all the reasons why this isn't real."

I don't finish the thought, because they're both right. For as many times as I've watched her laugh the same way, never, until today, have I thought...*mine*.

"Alright, I brought out the 1923 and a Cowboy," Laney says as she winks at Grant, coming out to the back patio. "Who wants what?"

Hadley spills through the double doors behind her, along with Faye seconds later, holding rocks glasses. Hadley's hair is piled in a messy knot on her head, wearing a simple white tank top cropped just at the waist of her jeans.

Jesus Christ. I grip the arm of the chair, trying to filter my attention elsewhere.

Laney moves toward my brother, pouring out his blend without him needing to answer.

"Here you go, husband." Hadley passes me a glass, then says to Laney, "I'll take the 1923." She pours into the glass I'm holding, watching me as it starts to fill, and smirks when it hits the center of the rock. "Mind sharing, darling?"

Darling? No.

She tips her chin at me and looks at my lap just as she takes a sip. I know what she's asking, and while it's good for show, the last thing I need right now is her ass rubbing on my dick. And in typical Hadley fashion, she doesn't wait for a response. She turns and perches her ass along my left thigh, keeping her eyes locked with mine as she takes another sip. *Here we go.* I move my arm from the chair to around her lower back and rest it along her thigh, letting my fingers grip onto her in a way that seems natural to anyone else looking but for us is entirely new. And fuck, does it feel good to have her close to me. Clearing my throat, I try not to get lost in this.

Laney's been talking about something, while I've been so

focused on my wife taking up real estate on my lap that I haven't been listening. "We have just over twelve-hundred ticket holders, and then down on the main lawn, there will be space for walk-ins. I think the locals are going to love it, but you bet your ass when people catch wind of something exclusive happening here after the race, people will hop in a rideshare from Churchill Downs and wind up drinking bourbon and listening to music at our place."

If we wanted tourists to turn their attention back to Fiasco, we needed to do so when plenty of people were already in Kentucky. The Kentucky Derby was the perfect catalyst, and it's been a massive undertaking, mainly for Laney, who's done the majority of the planning.

"I'll catch the tail end of it, if I'm lucky. I'm hoping Midnight Proof will be packed." She glances back at me, knowing the little detail she shared about the downturn in business she's been experiencing. She plucks the bottle of Cowboy Edition bourbon and adds another splash into the glass that we're apparently sharing now.

Her pocket buzzes, and with both hands full with a bottle and a rocks glass, she gives me a half smile. "Go ahead," she whispers. "Take it out." Her tone is playful as usual, and it's hard not to smile back at it. But when I see the screen, my mood instantly changes.

HAWK:
Thinking about you.

With a slight wince, she puts the phone on the fire pit's edge. I move her off of my lap so that I can stand. But before I move away, I lean into her.

There are eyes on us, so I kiss the top of Hadley's head and mumble into her hair, "Make sure that's over now, sugar." And without looking back—no matter how much I'd like to—I head toward the distillery to clear my head.

I need to focus on what our marriage is going to put into play, so I voice note a series of text messages to my people who need to be aware of what I've just done before the rest of the town, including her father, catches wind of it.

When that happens, we need to be ready.

Chapter 22

Hadley

May: Hearing my husband groan against my lips as he grabbed my ass and rolled his hips into me. Aggressively underrated: A confident man moaning for me.

I STRETCH MY ARMS ABOVE my head, shoving my hands into the headboard and twisting my hips into the dark gray satin sheets of the California king. As I peel a mascara-sewn eye open, I confirm what I'm already fearing might be true: I'm waking up alone. Again.

I feel around the bedside table for my black book, but my fingers hit two pills. As I sit up, I spy two ibuprofen pills, a water, and a clementine next to my black notebook and charging phone. I stare at the bright orange rind and turn over the idea that maybe Griz hasn't been the one leaving these for me all this time. I shake my head and sniff out a laugh, almost not believing that Ace could have done this every time I've stayed at this house.

Gulping down the pills and water, I flip open to the section of my notebook that's marked "May." I didn't like the idea of just unloading bullshit that would fill the pages fast and then be tossed because I wouldn't want to read back the bad stuff. Living the bad stuff once was enough. So I opted for a positivity journal. Throw a metaphorical middle finger up at the bad and find comfort in writing down the good. However small or special it might be. I add "clementines" to the page, and then read back some of the other good things May has brought me over the years:

> *Magnolias blooming along Main. A long ride with one of my girls. Watching the ricker riders run barrels from the rickhouses to the distillery. Winning the Oaks. Derby hats that have ostrich feathers. The fire station opening its garage doors. Firemen sitting in the sun as they wait for their next call.*

Shit. I need to talk with Hawk. I don't want him hearing about me getting married from anyone else. We might not have been officially anything more than casually hooking up, but I'm not stupid. He was looking for more from me. And if Ace's reaction to seeing Hawk's text last night was any indication, he's thinking the same.

I fire off a text as I move into the bathroom, brushing my teeth.

HADLEY:
I'd like to have a chat. Want to meet me for a coffee later?

HAWK:
On duty today. This weekend?

Maybe I should just tell him over text, but the thought leaves me when I step into the kitchen and I'm visually assaulted by Atticus Foxx. He leans against the kitchen counter in mesh shorts and a gray cutoff T-shirt, scrolling through his phone. It's like catching him in goddamn lingerie. Who knew moisture-wicking material in the most basic colors would be such a slutty look? Bravo, universe, you really delivered this morning.

He doesn't even look up when he pushes a box across the marble top. "This package is addressed to you, and it's vibrating."

I'm still not sure how I'm feeling after getting married yesterday. I couldn't tell what was real or simply a performance. I'm disappointed that he didn't search me out for more later on, that he still hasn't come to bed. Maybe we both just got caught up in the lie. I want to stomp my foot and demand a fucking answer. I don't like complicated, so I swallow my pride and play this smart.

I put my black book and phone down, realizing what package this is. Instantly, my mood shifts. "My wedding gift has arrived," I cheerily singsong.

I can see his brow furrow out of my periphery as he stares at the small box. "Who's sending you wedding gifts?" he asks, confused.

When I look at him, I notice his face is red and damp. "Why are you sweating?" I ask, bypassing his question as I snatch a knife from the butcher block.

"Worked out," he mumbles, still focusing on the low intermittent buzzing that's making the box shake slightly. "Who is that from?" he asks again, and then follows it up with, "Is that…?"

"From me, to me," I answer as I flip the top open. "And yes, it's my favorite kind of flower. I forget what color I picked this time." When I pull out the palm-sized vibrator from the little black box, its bright yellow color makes it look like a stemless yellow rose. "The gift that keeps on giving."

He nearly chokes on his electrolytes. A stream of actual liquid spurts from his pretty lips, and I feel mildly triumphant that I've rattled him.

"It's a vibrator," I whisper mockingly. "I know, shocking."

He wipes his mouth with the hem of his shirt, giving me a very nice snapshot of his stomach—lots of lines. Two very prominent ones that protrude inward and disappear into his mesh shorts. *Jesus, he's dangerous, no matter what he's wearing.*

"It's not shocking." He clears his throat. "You just catch me off guard sometimes. When did you order a vibrator to have it shipped here?"

"The night I agreed to a sexless marriage. I was taking pity on myself and decided on a rush shipment."

Swallowing audibly, his eyes linger on my self-given gift, and then he shifts to my shirt. Correction: his shirt. I like stealing his dress shirts. Plus, I was drunk last night and found myself smelling the shirts hanging in his closet. I settled on this one. I even cuffed the sleeves the way he does.

He chugs almost an entire water bottle before he asks, out of breath, "What are you always writing in here?" He's picking up my black notebook before I realize what he's doing.

I snatch it out of his hands. "Off-limits."

"Diary?" he asks, his mouth ticking up at the side. Ace doesn't have dimples like Lincoln, but there's a small divot that presses against his cheek when he's amused.

"Tested sex positions," I say with a sarcastic smile, leaning my forearm on the closed book beneath me. That answer should keep him from ever wanting to finger through it.

He bites down on his molars, those damn tendons popping

in his neck again. *Mm, I just want to lick them.* "I need a shower," he mumbles as he turns away.

"That an invitation?" I call out behind him.

He spins around slowly, his foot propped on the first step upstairs as he stares at me from down the hall. *I love getting under this man's skin.* Part of me wishes I could hear what he's so heavily weighing whether or not to say. But he holds up a finger like he's counting. And without another word or glance, he glides up the stairs.

I flip open my little black book to add another favorite: *navy-blue mesh shorts and a gray cutoff shirt.*

"You're up awfully early today," Griz says from behind me. I didn't hear the side door open, but he strolls through like it's the middle of the day and not the ass crack of dawn.

I clear my throat, trying to quickly come up with a response, but he beats me to it.

"Mind telling me why I didn't know about you seeing my grandson until you both had already signed on the dotted line and promised 'for as long as you both shall live'?" He gives me a pointed look, eyebrow lifted as he circles around the counter.

I squint my eyes, cracking the right one open when I say, "Slipped my mind?"

He lets out a barked laugh. "Is he up yet? I heard him come home late. Must've been quite a few urgent things he had to handle to keep you waitin' on the wedding night." Griz winks at me. At least he's amused by this situation and not lacing into me about what the hell I'm doing.

I shake my head. "He's in the shower." If we're going to lean into this and make the lie believable, I might as well start now. "And I'm more tired than hungry," I lie as I finish peeling my clementine.

"My son used to leave one of those on the boys' nightstands every night. Told me he wanted to make sure they always had something sweet to wake up to." Griz smiles, looking down at the counter, lost in the memory for a moment. Then he taps his knuckles on the surface and says, "Be gentle with him."

He doesn't elaborate any further, only makes his way down the hall and toward the basement stairs, leaving me in the kitchen of a house that's always felt like home, but now suddenly is.

Chapter 23

Ace

"We have a little problem," a voice says quietly over my shoulder.

I turn slightly to see tightly cropped platinum blond hair out of the corner of my eye. With a heavy exhale, I prepare for what inevitable shit comes next.

"There are five names left, and you haven't given me any direction on what you want to see happen. One of those names is coming up on trial, and that's going to make things more difficult if you'd like to see it followed through," she says. I'm instantly uneasy, knowing the conversation I'm going to need to have with Hadley about her father.

I should feel relieved—removing the problems is the only way this ends with my family safe and happy.

"Baldy, the bloodstock agent, left little to no room for error, especially after that outburst here. Julian helped me figure out a better extraction point. No more bodies traveling over the falls. Presh was getting testy about it."

I lean back in my chair as Seraphine joins me at the bar, snagging my bourbon out from in front of me and taking a sip. Peering back to look down the long hallway toward Hadley's office, I'm hoping she continues to take her sweet time talking with Faye. "I know I'm supposed to appreciate this," Seraphine says, holding up the rocks glass. "But I prefer gin."

"Hadley makes a good French 75," I tell her.

She smiles knowingly. "I bet she does." Then she casually adds, "The run-in your wife had at the Finch & King stables you wanted me looking into wasn't pissed-off horse breeders." I wait for her to keep talking. I had a gut feeling this was going to be more complicated than that. Or more dangerous. "Two Russians. Both with last names on your little list." That short list is from a decade ago now and, as it's turning out, not just a list of names from a dinner party.

"Who are they?" I ask.

"Career criminals, nothing original," she says, unimpressed. "Dealers, pushers, traffickers. They're from a small group that split off from the New York Bratva. They were in Nashville but pop into Fiasco whenever Wheeler calls. I've got them on numerous toll cameras back and forth on the interstate dating back at least ten years. I'm surprised the FBI hasn't snatched them up."

"I don't think the FBI has much interest in anyone unless they are high profile when it comes to the Finch & King case," I tell her.

She shifts toward the door, angling herself so she can see more of the room. "You have some high profiles left on your list," she says. "You should also know that one of these guys had been texting your new wife some colorful threats before they showed up at the stables."

Hadley had told me about the text messages, but hearing it

from Seraphine now and knowing who was sending them makes me instantly angry. I was careless to assume the more dangerous partners that Wheeler had wouldn't come looking for payback or handouts with him out of pocket. He left his daughter to fend for herself like she didn't matter, except when he needed her.

"What do they want?"

"Wheeler owed them money—quite a bit, from what I can tell. That, and he likely promised more jobs, but I'm not sure what else. I'll get you answers," Seraphine says with a slow smile that lets me know she has them tied up somewhere, ready to be interrogated. It's laced with a twinge of giddiness that scares most people. And only a select few of us know the real reason why.

Hadley comes walking around the corner just as I'm about to ask another question, her head down, eyes focused on her phone. My new wife isn't going to be happy to see Seraphine again, and I'm not in the right headspace to explain what she's doing here.

"We need to wrap up this discussion," I say, watching Hadley getting closer.

"That's fine. Care to dirty up that suit a little? Julian will be here for cleanup by midnight. Leaves us with a little time for some Q&A."

I don't get my hands dirty often. That's what she and Julian are for, among some other colleagues I've made over the years. But this is personal, and I'm fucking pissed. I give her a curt nod.

"We should look more closely at the last few names on this list. Figure out if they're going to be a problem," she says.

"We can look into them, but I'm not going to make any decisions just yet," I tell her. I'm not going to get rid of people unless they prove me right. I trust people; it's one of the few things I want to keep. Trust isn't something that needs to be earned with me, only taken away.

Seraphine turns on her chair and covertly says, "You might want to tell your bride you're going to be home a bit late then," as she nods toward the bar. "She doesn't look very happy to see me."

When I shift my focus, I'm met with glaring blue eyes. She looks down the front of me as she folds her arms and smacks on a piece of gum. There's not an ounce of amusement on her face as she says, "Already breaking agreements, husband?"

Fuck. I know this doesn't look good, and she's right to think I have something to hide.

"It's not like that, Hadley."

She raises her eyebrows. "Oh yeah?" With her hands on her hips, she sends a sarcasm-laced look of amusement my way. "Mind telling me what it's like then? Because I'm making all sorts of assumptions."

I kick back the rest of what's in the glass. I'm not processing any of this with logic, only emotions. The fact that there were dangerous men trying to intimidate her is enough to set my blood to boiling. Add in that these two tried stealing her horses and have been wrapped up in her father's dealings. I'm not interested in talking about anything right now. "Then you can assume what I'm telling you is the truth," I say, turning on my heel, fully prepared to deal with the fallout of this later.

"And I'm just supposed to believe that?" Her voice raises from behind me.

I don't respond as I move up the stairs and out of Midnight Proof. I hate the insinuation—that she can't trust me. But she's right; there's plenty I'm keeping from her. And the relationship I have with Seraphine is just the tip of it.

My fist hits his cheekbone on the first jab, and he smiles and slurs out, "*Suka.*"

"You like that?" I smile back.

"I think he just called you a bitch," Seraphine says as she sucks on a red lollipop, perched on a metal barrel in the corner.

"I'll take that as a yes then." The cracking sound with my left hook is followed up by a grunt and a stream of blood and spit. A broken nose usually adds enough dramatics to get people talking. "Say it again," I seethe.

His accent is faint, but recognizable, when he says, "He said his daughter wouldn't be a problem."

Two more hooks have my knuckles splitting. I take a step back and try to catch my breath.

Seraphine crosses her arms, as if this was boring her. "Ace, I have other, more *effective* ways to get what you want from him." She glances at an ice pick and mallet that are laid out on the bench beside her. The old tobacco mill along the edge of town is abandoned and condemned, which means there won't be anyone around to witness any of this.

I throw an elbow against his jaw, and his head snaps to the left, where his friend is silent and bleeding out from the slices along his torso, courtesy of my colleague.

"What were you doing at Finch & King Stables? And this time, I'd like something that resembles the truth."

He spits out a jumble of words in Russian, before answering. "We have not been paid what's owed. So we collect. The horses. He said the girl might be worth something—"

I cut him off with another punch, only this time, I don't stop. I know exactly who they're referring to, and I could guess who would give them the green light to take what they wanted if they weren't paid. When I take a deep breath and twist, driving my elbow clean across his face, the eye that had quickly swelled closed busts open, spurting blood along my arm. My knuckles hurt, but I'm long past the point of caring about a little bit of pain. The thought of either of these men coming near my wife is enough to throw my fists without letting up, the only sound bringing me any sense of relief being my fists colliding with his flesh. When I'm satisfied and he's unconscious, I give Seraphine a nod, and she finishes the job. They were never walking out of here, not after knowing what they were capable of and how close they had come to hurting Hadley.

"You never get this angry," Seraphine says as I wipe my hands. "This is about the one you married, isn't it?"

I glance at her, trying to calm my breathing and ease the adrenaline.

"The one who you've mentioned before. Your brother's best friend. The one you look out for."

That makes me pause.

"I know everything, or at least, eventually I do, Ace. C'mon. I think it's sweet. You finally got the girl," she says, softening in a way I don't normally see from her.

"It's not like that." Part of what she's saying is true, but it's not the way she thinks.

"Maybe not, but we both know the only reason I'm here right now is because of her. We'll make sure she doesn't get hurt. Of all the favors, Julian and I both know that this one is the most important."

Thirty minutes later, and I'm pulling up to my house, which is lit up like a fucking Christmas tree. The time on the dashboard on my car reads 2:40 a.m., so there shouldn't be lights on or anyone awake at this hour. I planned on Griz being sequestered in his part of the house, but it was an oversight thinking

Hadley wouldn't be awake with her late nights at Midnight Proof. I've been so wrapped up in the last few hours that I forgot how we'd left things. The low lights on the porch are on as usual, but so are the path lights to the stable, and a warm glow streams out of the ajar double sliding doors.

When I step into the stable, there's music, and Hadley's voice echoes through the stalls. *There she is.* The low chords play as she starts quietly crooning about wise men and fools rushing. The song is poetically appropriate considering we got married this week. I exhale in relief at seeing her, and along with it, the adrenaline from what I just left starts to fall away.

I lean against the archway and watch as she brushes along the full length of her white horse, swaying her hips to the song, zoned out in her own world. It's rare to catch her like this—without putting on a show or a brave face. I like how strong she is, but I respect it even more, knowing that a good chunk of the time, perceived strength is nothing more than stubbornness and bravado. It's something we have in common.

Her tone is wildly off, and she laughs when she fumbles the words. It's part of what everyone in my family finds so charming about Hadley. She's naturally likable and can make everyone around her, including me, smile with her quick wit, raunchy sass, and a lightness that I can never find on my own.

She turns and nearly jumps out of her skin, not expecting to see me—or anyone, for that matter—standing here.

"Holy fucking shit, Ace," she laughs out, her hand splayed on her chest. "Warn a girl when you're creeping up on her."

Tossing the brush into her tack box, she wipes off her hands with the bandana stuffed into the back pocket of her barely there pajama shorts. I'm trying to keep from looking at the very obvious way she isn't wearing a bra with the loose tank she has on.

"Don't give me hungry eyes right now," she says with her eyes squinted and chin raised. "I was waiting up for you... I want answers—" She stops talking as soon as she spots my hands. "You're bleeding."

I look down at my knuckles. They had split and kept bleeding, but some of what's on my forearms isn't mine. I must've missed some of it.

"It's fine." I push off the wall and try to cover the carelessness of split knuckles and blood splatter.

She tips her head to the side and watches me curiously. "I'll play nurse while you answer my questions," she says, her shoulder brushing mine as she walks ahead of me.

Jesus.

Some of her anger from earlier has fallen away, apparently, but I'm not going to keep this from her. Maybe she doesn't need to know everything, but I can tell her this.

As I follow her up to the house, I can't help but crack a smile. And again, all I can think is: *She's here, and she's safe.*

Chapter 24

Hadley

May: Bedazzling horse manes and singing karaoke—Lady and Fergie are the best listeners.

THERE'S ALWAYS MORE TO A story. Anyone who tells you otherwise just isn't privy to the details. I've lived in Fiasco my entire life, and I've always known there's more to Ace. Too bad for him that I'm feeling brave tonight.

Rumors swirl about what the Foxx boys do to people who steal from them. That they like to teach their own lessons and not involve the authorities. To never cross them. But beyond that, Ace has always rubbed elbows with people I've only ever seen once. He takes meetings with governors and senators. He hosts events with sports agents and their clients. Celebrities aren't interesting to him, but he'll always say yes to drinks with anyone in the bourbon business. I've always wondered if Ace ever got his hands dirty. With one look at his knuckles and the blood rubbed across his forearm and splattered on the side of his shirt, I guess I have my answer.

He'd been at Midnight Proof for business tonight. Ace would never just pop by to see me—that wasn't his style—but when I saw him come in and settle at the bar instead of the table on the floor, I thought *maybe* he wanted to see me. Which is why I have on replay the woman with short blond hair and gorgeous bone structure speaking to him. Watching him speak to someone I don't know, and with such familiarity, made me feel like an outsider, jealous, and I hated that. It helped me realize that there's so much I don't know about my brand-new husband.

Yes, I've witnessed plenty over the years, paid attention to small nuances, like his body language and favorite things. But the secretive moments between him and Griz, the minimal details I have regarding women he's seen here and there, and the small whispers around town of a man who people respect, none of those things make me feel any closer to him now.

I splash bourbon into a rocks glass beside him as he runs cold water over his bruised and battered hands. I know what the aftermath of a fight looks like. Lincoln has been in plenty over the years. I'd assumed that he was the muscle, while Ace sat back watching whoever needed a good swat to the face. Apparently I was wrong.

Pulling a hand towel from the rack next to the double-wide shower, I hop onto the bathroom vanity. With my ass perched next to the sink, I drape the towel in my hands and say, "I'm going to need to know who she was."

As he moves closer, I push past the heated feelings I get any time I'm alone with him—swooping stomach and goosebumps along my arms. It's equal parts nerves and anticipation, but I'd like to stay in charge of the conversation. I don't want his stupid blue-gray eyes to distract me.

"When we agreed to this marriage, I told you that I don't like things being kept from me."

His eyes lock with mine. "I remember." With his jaw tensed, he says, "What if the things I've kept from you are to protect you?"

"I call bullshit," I bite back. It sounds like a placating line.

He exhales, and then tilts his head back, staring up at the ceiling for a moment. "It's not bullshit, baby."

Baby? I turn off the water and pull his hands to rest on the towel in my lap. "Don't 'baby' or 'sugar' me. Right now, I'm not your wife, just your friend," I say as I softly pat at the ripped skin. "You think I care if you fucked that woman?" With exasperation, I shake my head. "*Nope.* Don't care. You asked me what I wanted when we started this—I said I wanted honesty. And I want it right. Fucking. Now."

I tamp down the emotion that's threatening to surface. *I will not cry. Hold it together, Hadley.* "Secrets say, 'I don't trust you.' Lies tell me you've got something to hide. And I don't want either of that in this sham of a relationship."

Like he knows I still have more to say, he quietly watches me be gentle with his hands. "I want proof that I can trust you, Ace. I want to know that I can count on you to be the one person who won't hurt me." When I look up at his face, his eyes immediately lock with mine. "So answer the question. Who is she?"

Reaching for the rocks glass, he hands it to me. I take a sip and let the burn of it coat my mouth before sliding down my throat. I didn't drink to ease pain or mask problems, but a well-timed shot of bourbon had its own healing power sometimes.

"There's always a solution to every problem," he says, his tone measured. "You just need to ask the right people to help solve it."

With a pinched brow, I open the ointment and blot some on his wounds.

He keeps his attention on my face when he says, "You've met Julian."

I work through who he's referring to, and the only person I can think of is one I only noticed recently. "Hot, leather cuffs, likes to flirt?" I ask.

He nods. "He's a jeweler. Very talented. He's made some impressive pieces. But that's not how he works with me." Clearing his throat, he adds, "He cleans things up when I require it."

That has my full attention, and I glance up at him to confirm if what I think he's saying is true.

He gives me another nod. "The night that I created a DNA-filled mess in the stables with that asshole, Switcher. Julian is who I called in to clean things up afterward."

My fingers stop moving along the gashes, trying to digest all of that. And the fucked-up part is that I'm more surprised that this is the first time in ten years that he's bringing up what happened that night.

"The blond woman is an architect," he continues. "Seraphine draws up plans for just about every property we've ever built. She's working on rebuilding the new rickhouse now. But she, like Julian, has *other* talents."

The anger and frustration I had about all of this is quickly dissolving into even more questions but of an entirely different tone, like, *Who the hell did I just marry?* I try focusing on what I'm doing while he keeps talking, pulling out a butterfly bandage.

"Seraphine removes problems that no longer fit into an equation. If you're asking if I'm sleeping with her, the answer is no. It's not like that between us, never has been. She has a certain way about her, so I understand why you might have gotten that idea. Like you, she leans into her sexuality. She uses it to her advantage, but she and I are purely business partners."

"Like us?" I ask, vulnerability sneaking into my voice, hoping he doesn't say yes.

"No, Hadley. Not like us," he says quietly, and the words hit me right in the chest in a way I didn't expect. "I'm trusting you here. This is not information that people know. Griz knows; hell, it's part of his legacy. He knew Julian's father, who had done the same. I have no idea when Seraphine showed up, but he introduced me to her as well. But my brothers don't know any of this."

Ace tells his brothers everything. I can't believe that this hasn't been shared with them.

"Seraphine operates on a larger scale, handling things that would be higher profile than Julian or I are equipped to deal with. I've asked her here to remove—"

"Why would they do this for you?" I interject, trying to wrap my head around all of this.

"I help when they need the support. When I step in, it's usually about strategy and connecting people, but I have no issue getting my hands dirty. You already know that though," he says, glancing down at his hand still resting in mine.

I suppose I did. Even outside of his busted hands from tonight. I knew that he hadn't just politely asked Switcher to leave and never come back. I knew he wasn't some gallant knight riding in to do the right thing, just like I knew that whatever it was he had done, it made me feel safe in a way I never had before.

All of it is unbelievable. A part of me wants to swoon over the fact that this man is morally fucking gray. And yet a part of me feels like I'm just making excuses for poor judgment and criminal behavior. I did that with my father for decades. How could I continue to do it now?

He clears his throat, cutting into my thoughts. "It's not right and not my first choice on how to deal with people, but some…" He trails off as he shakes his head. "I would kill Switcher all over again."

I can only stare at him for a moment, staying quiet at that confirmation. It's seven layers of fucked-up, but hearing him say that and how he didn't hesitate to make sure that fucker got what was coming to him…I feel cared for. Taken care of.

Searching my face for some kind of response, he says, "You didn't ask me to do it. Switcher could have gotten up and walked out of there with a bruised face and ego, but there would have always been the chance that he'd try coming near you again." His jaw twitches, head shaking. "No fucking way." He tries to calm his tone, cupping his hand across his mouth, leaning close against the counter where I sit. More quietly, he says, "Switcher put his hands on you, got rough, then ran his mouth. None of that would ever be okay with me."

Nodding, I hop off the vanity. "You're right. I didn't ask you to do that. I didn't ask for any of that from you." It's the second time in my life that a man I thought I knew has been carrying on with things I knew nothing about. But this one's actions only ever show me that I matter to him. That I'm not a commodity or an inconvenience like I am for my father. That means more to me than even I thought it could. "Thank you. It's not enough, but I pushed for answers, and you gave them to me."

Those haunted eyes search mine as he swallows and shifts his weight. Maybe there's more, maybe not, but I want to fall asleep knowing that I'm important to someone. Someone I'm wildly attracted to, despite the fact that he skates along the lines of morally right and just.

"Hadley—" he says, like he doesn't want this conversation to be over.

Ignoring him, I move into the bedroom. "You're going to sleep on your side tonight. Beside me, for once," I say, looking at the massive bed that I've been sleeping in the center of. "Wait, which is your side?" I turn to look at him.

He unbuttons his shirt and moves into his closet as he says, "I don't have a side. I sleep in the middle, like you."

My lips tilt into a slow, knowing smile. "Do you sneak in here and watch me sleep?" I tease, louder for him to hear me. "Very creepy and kinky of you, husband. But that's not going to work if you don't want me cuddling into you. Pick a side, and I promise—" But my words falter when he emerges from the walk-in closet. A very shirtless Daddy Foxx shuffles into the room with loose cotton pants slung low on his hips.

He swipes away on his phone, distracted, and is out the bedroom door without so much as a glance when he says, "There are a few things I need to finish up." There's a coldness to his tone that wasn't there a moment ago. "Goodnight, Hadley."

Relief and disappointment mingle, making my heart heavy as I crawl into his bed and think about the details of what he's shared.

Sleep must've found me quickly, because when I wake up, I've barely moved. The room is still dark, but there's enough light creeping above the horizon that the dim swell of morning bleeds behind the dark velvet drapes hung around the windows.

I turn over and find the space empty, but when I squint my eyes, I notice Ace passed out on the oversize chair just a few feet from the bed. A hardcover book is resting open on his bare chest, his head tilted down and eyes closed.

Ace has always been distractingly handsome, but asleep and vulnerable, he seems lighter, sweeter, younger. Nothing like the man everyone knows. Sexier with a book too. A book about bourbon and grains is the only weight on his chest, while the heaviness of everything he carries is resting. I should close my eyes and go back to sleep, but I don't.

The hardwood floors are cold and the air cool when I shove the covers back. Stepping over to him on quiet feet, I lift the book up and over him slowly to place it on the table next to him. His hand shoots out, grabbing my wrist suddenly. It startles me and pulls a rather pathetic gasping squeak from my throat.

With his intense eyes locked on mind, his voice is low as he speaks. "What are you doing?"

I don't answer. I don't want to shake either of us up more from the haze of sleep than I already have. I twist my wrist in his hand as he loosens his grip, and I hold on to his forearm, pulling him toward me as I move backward to the bed. He follows easily, watching me with long, tired blinks as his knee hits the mattress. I don't have any ulterior motives other than wanting him to find comfort in a space that he's made sure I feel welcomed in.

I crawl across the mattress, moving over to make space for him. He settles toward the center on his stomach, facing me. "Did you mean it?" he asks quietly, just above a whisper.

With his eyes on mine in the dimly lit room, I let the quiet settle around us.

"That you want this," he clarifies.

I nod, watching rare vulnerability last for mere moments around a man who typically never allows it.

My heart beats a little faster as I whisper back without hesitation. "I'm sure."

Taking him in like this, I can't decide if it's the gray or the dark brown hair that I like more. I don't remember when the deep-set "eleven" lines on his brow became a permanent part of his features, or if it's just part of his lifelong seriousness, but right now, he looks content. The only lines that crease his skin are the faint reminder that years have passed since the first time I laid eyes on him.

"Stop looking at me like that," he says with a smirk tilting his lips, his eyes closing. "Dangerous," he whispers as a follow-up. Rolling onto my back, I stare at the ceiling—the wooden beams that look like charred barrels and a vaulted design that seem so far from where we are lying.

"Like what?" I smile, knowing exactly how I was looking at him.

"Like you're mine," he mumbles into his pillow like he's drifting back to sleep.

And all I can think to myself as I lie next to him is: *That's all I've ever been.*

Chapter 25

Ace

Even before I open my eyes, I'm aware of what I've done. I flex my fingers along the satin panties that I instantly know are hers. I'd felt that lace trim and the soft satin sheen with the pads of my fingers plenty of times. The massive difference this time is that it's still on her warm curves. She breathes so calmly that I don't want to jostle and wake her. *Jesus Christ, she's beautiful.*

Moving my free arm above my head slowly, I lift my other hand from her ass as I try to slide myself out from under her. Her body half sprawled over me in the morning isn't the way I had planned to wake up, but I'd be lying if I said it wasn't something I've thought about before. A part of me wants to linger here longer and let this moment play out—the very obvious morning hard-on isn't helping me think straight. As I move quietly from the bed and look at her like this, I can't help but picture a lazy morning with her wrapped around me as I fuck her nice and easy. How we could take our time and learn all the curves and touches that made us both feel good.

The morning light is barely seeping into the openings of the curtains, but one glance at my phone, and I'm already starting my day later than usual. I need to get to the distillery, but before that, I have to make calls and confirm that all loose ends were tied up after last night. My knuckles are bruised, but it's a good kind of pain, the one where you know something came out of it.

I work my way through a solid forty-five-minute leg workout, with some time on the heavy bag before my knuckles split again. Nerves about what's coming and what I still have to address nag at the back of my mind, needing an escape through exertion. While Hadley was content with the answers I gave her about Seraphine and the added information about Julian, I still haven't told her about her father. About the agreements I'd made and what needed to happen.

The kitchen is quiet, neither Griz nor Hadley making noise yet, so I snag a clementine from the fruit drawer and pour an iced coffee to leave on her nightstand. I'd add two pain relievers if she had drunk too much and ended up crashing in the guest suite. It's become a small and secret gesture, one I know she assumes is Griz's handiwork. There's a part of me that likes knowing I can do something to take care of her when she's under my roof.

When I pad back into the room, I notice she's only shifted slightly since I left. I keep my movements quiet as I place the coffee and orange on the side table, then I head into the closet to pick out my clothes before my shower. The space is large enough for both of us to hang our things—I know it was a perk when she realized how much real estate I was giving to her. I smile at the eclectic mix of colors and textures on her side. It's a stark contrast to my very specific hues of black to gray to navy suits and white to black dress shirts. I wear jeans and T-shirts, mesh shorts and sweats, but those things are folded in drawers and tucked away on shelves.

I'm plucking out my suit pants and a white shirt just as I hear the rustling of sheets and her making noises as she stretches. Then a small hum and the mumbling of words, "So tired…need water." I pause my movements when I hear her say, "Ace, you swoony motherfucker." I smile when I realize she's talking to herself. She finally figured out it was me who's been leaving her things by her bedside. "Goddesses," she huffs out. "He looks like that *and* he brings me coffee. Such a lucky bitch." Quiet settles, and just as I choose a set of cuff links I hear a drawer closing and then a whirring vibration. With my body locked in place, in the center of my walk-in closet, I strain to hear what my gut already knows is going on out there.

A small hum from her lips and an audible exhale have my dick instantly responding, almost faster than it registered that she's going to get herself off while I'm standing in the fucking closet.

How the fuck do I handle this?

I place the clothes on top of the center dresser, and then run both hands through my hair, threading my fingers behind the nape of my neck. Shaking my head, I berate myself for not rushing out of here the second I heard what she's doing, just as another small moan comes from less than thirty feet away. *Fuck.*

There's a part of me that wants to watch, to witness how she likes to get herself off, and get a glimpse of how she looks spread out on my bed, making a mess of my sheets. But there would be no coming back from it—the second I step into that room, all bets are off, the floodgates open. It isn't what we'd agreed on.

None of this: kissing her, holding her, wanting her. It feels like a tortured marriage punctuated by my lack of willpower and her insistent habit of settling under every inch of my skin.

The sound of the vibrator jumps higher, and with it, a small wet spot appears right where my dick presses into my navy mesh shorts. I move my hips slightly, and the friction of the material just makes it worse. I want to join her so badly. My body is wrung tight, and my dick is the angriest it's been in a long time. I haven't fucked my hand since she moved in. Hell, now that I think about it, the last time I touched myself was the night of my brother's wedding. I jerked off into a pair of those pretty panties, just like the ones she was wearing now.

"Just like that," she says in a breathy tone, and I damn near lose it. Breathing deeply through my nose, I try to calm my pulse, anchoring my hands along the dresser in the center of the room. My neck is heated, drawing goosebumps along my arms as a tingle makes its way down my back. My dick twitches as I think about the things she could be doing. Does she fuck her fingers as her vibrator sucks and teases her clit the same way my mouth would? Or does her hand rove over her pretty tits and pluck each nipple? My mouth waters, wondering how she'd bow her body if I were sucking on them. *Dammit.* I know if I touch myself and relieve any of this, I'm *not* going to be quiet about it. I'm getting lost in just her sounds and flashing back to the way she so pliably wrapped herself around me when I kissed her. The way her lips taste, the lulling rhythm of her tongue chasing mine, the smell of her skin when I pull her closer and press up against her curves.

The rasp of her breathing kicks up just as a small gasp escapes her. This is wrong on a multitude of levels, but even knowing that isn't going to stop me from listening now. *Not a fucking chance.*

"Please," she begs. I want her to say that to me. Call out my name, whisper "Daddy," and look up at me the same way she did last night. I can feel the telltale build of an orgasm at the base of my spine, and if I can't walk it back by thinking about something else, anything else, I'm going to come in my pants without even stroking myself. She moans, sounding so desperate for relief that I abandon the plan to be distracted and instead think of all the filthy things I could do to her—bite, spank, fuck, lick, all of it on repeat—as if it's a fantasy reel playing in my mind. And when she finally comes with a soft cry, I'm fucked. Biting on my forearm, I fall over the edge. My hips jolt as my dick pulses, and I come so hard that I have to grab my cock and work out the last of it. With my chest heaving, it takes me a few, or maybe many minutes, to gain my bearings.

She laughs from the bed, out of breath, while I stand in cum-soaked shorts and barely an ounce of satisfaction. If anything, I'm more turned on now, my dick still semihard, but if there's ever going to be a moment to turn the tables and push back all of the one-liners and comments she's made to me over the years, it's now. With a steadying breath and a nod that this is a good idea, I walk into the bedroom and clear my throat.

"Finished?" I say, an eyebrow quirked, standing at the foot of the bed. She jolts up with a yelp, leaning back on her elbows, her face flushed and hair wild. Pieces are stuck to her neck as the tank she's wearing clings to her tits.

As we stare at each other, she lets out a nervous laugh, but it's immediately eclipsed by a smirk as her eyes dart to my tented shorts. "I should ask you the same." She tilts her head to the side and asks, "Did you listen to what I was doing, Daddy?"

I swallow and realize that I'm being outmaneuvered. "Fuck," I mutter through gritted teeth.

She sits up higher, the sheet falling lower around her thighs and barely covering her pussy. I didn't think any part of this through. "Did you like what you heard?"

"If I answer that question, sugar…" I shake my head. If I answer, if I don't get my ass out of here, I'll never leave.

A loud knock sounds on the bedroom door. "Atticus, I'm all for morning nookie, but I have business I need to discuss with you that will hopefully change my breakfast status. I can't keep eating at Hooch's. I already had to move a notch on my belt buckle."

I shout back, "Yeah, alright!" Hadley stands up, pussy on full display. Her arm grazes mine as she waltzes right past me and into the bathroom. The knowing and devious smile playing on her lips makes my already spent dick twitch for more.

He knocks loudly again just as I turn to see her sweet curvy ass pass the threshold, and the door closes behind her.

Jesus Christ. I wipe my hand across my mouth and blow out a breath. Tucking my now rock-hard dick up into the waistband of my cum-stained pants, I swing the door open. "You have the worst timing, you know that, right?"

Griz's mustache tics up on the right before he says, "Consider it payback. You know how many times you and your brothers interrupted me from gettin' some?" He glances down at my pants, chuckling. "Happens to the best of us, son."

"Fuck you," I say on a laugh.

"Nah, you have a wife now. Might want to consider doing that with her." He starts down the stairs, calling out over his shoulder. "When you're decent, you can look over the papers for Foxx Bourbon's shares and how I expect my retirement package allocated. Oh, and I'd like an egg-in-a-hole and some of that turkey sausage."

Chapter 26

HADLEY

> *May: Playing a two-finger DJ session with a vibrator assist while my husband unknowingly listens. Derby dress pickup day!*

THE MAGNOLIA TREES LINING MAIN in downtown Fiasco add a softness to the brick buildings and cracked sidewalks. It's the same walk I take after a good night and a great sleep. My townhouse isn't far from here, but I haven't been living in it. Normally I would go for a walk just to have some human interaction. It's the double-sided perk to living on my own. It always feels good to smile at the shop owners on my way to grab breakfast at Hooch's. But my mornings are different now—not perfect, by any means, but I like seeing Griz while I sip on coffee and catch my husband stealing glances at me when he thinks I'm not paying attention.

I smile to myself. *My husband.*

The sign lodged in the front window of Loni's Boutique has me screeching to a stop and catches me off guard. I've been coming to this shop for my Derby Day dresses for my entire life. And when Loni finally took the place over from her mother, she brought in new designer brands. Some more affordable than others, but always trendy enough that Fiasco could be well outfitted when we wanted to be.

"Loni!" I call out when I push open the hefty oak door. "Please tell me that sign isn't serious."

She pops her head from around the corner and gives me a small, reserved smile. "Hadley." Like she's readying herself to tell me what I absolutely don't want to hear, she nods sadly. "I think it's time for me to read the writing on the wall. It's been a rough year. You know that."

I try not to hear the accusations that live underneath those words, things I've been hearing time and time again, like, *"Your father ruined this place"* and *"Fiasco will never be the same."*

I feel it too. Midnight Proof is just barely breaking even. Opening a speakeasy in a bourbon town was smart, I'll toot my own horn for that one, because even in a down economy, the place still managed to usher in drinkers who wanted to either forget the day or celebrate when it was over. It's my fifth year in business but only the first that it's not profitable. Luckily I don't need to consider something as drastic as closing. Not yet, at least.

"I'm not the only one," she says. "The Creamery cut back its hours." She nods toward the front window. "I know Dugan's Hardware is planning to sell. And the girls at Crescent de Lune tell me all the time how they've cut their batches down significantly." That hits me out of nowhere. The bakery is in my building, facing my speakeasy, and the girls haven't said anything to me. "Fiasco's having a rough go of it, and this time, it isn't one I think I can recover from."

I hate hearing it. I feel responsible. There's a part of me that thinks if I had only paid more attention or had done something different, maybe fewer people would have gotten hurt or would be hurting now because of the mess my father created.

I follow her back to the fitting rooms, noticing how much has been removed from the front of the store. More clearance racks than new arrivals.

"My sister is down in Nashville. We've been thinking about doing an online store for a while until we can manage a storefront again. Mom would be sad to see this place close, but I need to live too. Can't keep living for other people."

She wipes the corner of her eye, and then brings me my garment bag. "That's my sad situation." Seeming to shake it off, she gives me a warm smile. "In the meantime, you went ahead and found one of the prettiest dresses I think I've ever seen. Far sexier than the usual Derby wear." She plucks a small box from the top shelf. "But for you, Hadley, it's the perfect choice. The hat too."

I think about what she said, and I can't help it, I want to help.

"Loni, what if there was a way to—" But my words get cut off by the front door shoving open, knocking the bell off the top clear across the room as Hawk barges inside.

"You married him," he says loudly, his chest moving up and down as if he ran here.

Eyes widening, I glance back at Loni. She's holding her phone to her chest, trying to decide if there is going to be a problem here.

I'm not supposed to meet up with him for another hour, but it doesn't matter now. He already knows. "Hawk," I say with a tight-lipped smile. He doesn't really have a right to be so angry. We weren't together, but I understand him being hurt. "I'm so sorry you found out before I could tell you—"

"How long?" he bites back. And without leaving room for a response, he stalks closer. My nerves ratchet as I move a few steps back. His body language is all wrong, and I don't think he wants an answer, not truly. This isn't a version of him I've ever seen.

I glance at Loni again, and then her phone, silently conveying to use it if this gets any louder. Or if he gets any closer. As much as I don't think this man is capable of being violent, I learned my lesson a long time ago not to underestimate someone.

"How long, Hadley?" he presses in a curt tone. With his hands on his hips and adrenaline so clearly pumping through him in the way he was breathing and gritting his teeth, it's the most worked up I've ever seen him.

Vinny from the flower shop next door lingers nearby. I feel a little relieved by the way he's watching and how he's angling his body inside the doorway. He knows something's wrong here.

"I was hoping we could talk over a coffee…" I say softly. "I was planning to meet you after I picked up my—"

"How. *Long*?"

My brow furrows at him cutting me off. But I shake my head and step closer to him. Apparently we're doing this here with a little audience. Fine. "Not long. It wasn't like I was with the both of you. But I handled this really poorly."

I lift my hands, trying to diffuse how intense this is feeling. I owe him an apology for not telling him when things were done and that I was moving on. If the tables were turned, I would be disappointed. Then again, it was only ever meant to be fun. But I'm realizing with certainty that it was more than that for him.

He laughs to himself. Only nothing here is funny. "You use people," he says, shaking his head. "Why am I surprised? You're just like your father in that way."

I flinch back. *Fuck him!* That's probably the meanest thing he could have said.

"That's just plain mean, and you know it," I say more firmly, standing taller. I know I messed up, but I'm not going to cower and listen to him stack me up next to a man who stole, blackmailed, and fucking murdered people. "Like I said, Hawk, I wanted to tell you in person, not over text. I'm sorry you were blindsided by this—"

"You know he's been paying for it? For fucking years," he spits out with a smirk. His tone is laced with such disdain that I almost can't keep up with who he's talking about. *Ace?*

"What the hell! is that supposed to mean?"

Hawk cups his hand across his mouth, holding his next few words. Now I'm curious and eager to hear everything.

"Might be worth taking a walk, Chief," Romey says, walking into the shop with Prue on her side and Marla in hair foils on her heels. The conversation must've easily carried next door to Teasers.

But Hawk keeps his stare on me. I can see him weighing whether or not he should listen and leave or finish what he was about to say.

"Go ahead," I taunt. "What. The. Hell. Does. That. Mean? *Who* has been paying for *what*?"

He shakes his head and turns to leave. Like riling me up and spitting out accusations is enough to make his fragile ego feel better. Over his shoulder, just as he shoves past Vinny, he yells to me, "Ask your husband."

It hits me square in the chest, taking my breath away momentarily. I don't fully understand, only that he knows something about Ace and my father that I don't. It's another thing Ace is keeping from me.

Ask your husband...

I *knew* there was more. Hell, until last night, he's never talked about the fact that Switcher just disappeared. I feel like a fucking idiot. Again. In the dark and stupid. I rub along my wrist, trying to calm myself down, my stomach in knots. *I will not spiral.*

There's a small audience shifting their feet and watching as I try to keep from having a panic attack after being yelled at and embarrassed by a grown-ass man. It's bad enough that people talk about me behind my back, text me threats, condemn me for being my father's daughter, while the rest pity me for being caught in the crosshairs. I don't want any of it. I want answers and to stop being lied to.

Prue and Romey look at each other, and then at Loni. But just before I can rush out of here, it's Marla who cuts the silence when she asks, "Since when do you have a husband?"

Chapter 27

Ace

"Two dead bodies were found, one floating along the output of Fiasco Falls, and the other by the old tobacco farm," the governor says, loud enough that it stops Grant in his tracks as he walks out to the porch. *Fuck*. He passes me a glass and lingers as the governor carries on. I hadn't expected a call from Governor Hawkins so quickly. I'm not sure if it's telling, or if he's trying to sniff out if I can offer him some information. It was presumptuous of him to call me.

"I'm not really sure why this is my problem, Governor. I shared my idea to open up the caverns and hire more folks in parks and rec. If the mayor didn't do the second part, that's a fairly big oversight. Quite frankly, it's a little jarring knowing the intent was to boost tourism, and now there're people getting hurt because there aren't the proper hires or signage about safety. The tobacco farm, well…" I pause. I'm not sure how to spin that one, so I settle on, "That place should have been torn down years ago. Again, this is probably a call for the mayor, not me."

"The FBI brought it to my attention, which means this isn't simply people falling into a river, Foxx." I'm waiting for him to share the details that I already know. "I have media calling me, asking for a statement." I know who those bodies are, but does he? He would have been in their company at least once. Maybe more. But his tone feels more like he's asking if I have an ear to the ground about it. He doesn't need to know it's far more than that.

"Governor, I agree this isn't the kind of attention Fiasco wants by any means, but again, I'm not sure what you're looking for from me."

"They're unidentified bodies. The FBI wouldn't share. Even if I asked, they look at me cross-eyed for the limited funding I had from Wheeler fucking Finch more than a decade ago. I'm asking you if this is something that I should be concerned about happening again."

I stay silent. Maybe the governor isn't as embroiled any longer. Maybe the disaster that has become of Finch & King shook him the same way it has everyone else. "I think bad things have a way of surfacing eventually. Whoever those bodies are tied to, I'm sure that'll surface too. But if you're asking me any more than that, I can't help you."

He swears under his breath and says, "Appreciate that, Ace. Speak soon." Then the line goes dead.

I clear my throat and glance up at my brother, who's now sitting casually on his porch, listening in. He invited me over for a late dinner. Laney and Hadley are working tonight, so it was a good excuse to spend time with him.

Grant folds his arms over his chest and just stares back at

me. "Is this something that falls into those gray areas we don't talk about?" he asks as we move inside, both taking a seat in his living room.

I rub along the back of my neck. "This is me trying to figure out if my trust has been misplaced." Leaning back, I glance at the time. "I promise I'll tell you everything when I'm able."

He nods once. That's enough for him. And hell, I respect him for giving me the space to not have to explain more when I'm not ready yet.

"I can tell you that Del is at his wit's end with the FBI field office trying to interject. They're scrambling, trying to tie the bodies to Wheeler. But that asshole has an ankle bracelet and hasn't left his home in months. I swear to god, most of the bad shit that lingers here has to do with him though."

There's truth in that, just not in the way he's assuming.

"I still don't understand how he's on house arrest and not at the Montgomery Jail"

I always enjoy listening to Grant get fired up about things. It beats the shell of a man he was before Laney.

"Expensive lawyers and likely favors that will never be repaid, or ones that were owed," I say in response.

I don't need to bitch about the loopholes Wheeler scurried through to remain in Fiasco. It isn't a question of if he had anything to do with the threats that Hadley's received. I now know that he sent people after his own daughter considering he wasn't getting what he wanted. I'm still working through how I can make that hurt in a way he never sees coming.

"Brought something for you to try," I tell him, pulling out a bottle from my private reserve. I wanted to share it with him and Lincoln—hear what they have to say about it. Enjoy it together instead of trying to make it about the bourbon business. I'm ready for them to see that I'm still good at this—making and recognizing great bourbon. I want them to see that I'm more than just the suit and numbers.

He takes a small sip, allowing the alcohol to burn his palate so that on the next sip, he'll taste the hidden notes. I can tell he likes it by his body language. His shoulders settle and the side of his mouth tips up when he pulls back the glass. That, and the instant change in conversation when he says, "You have a wife." Smiling now, he shakes his head.

I exhale, thinking about her. "I do."

"And it's Hadley."

I smile to myself before I confirm it. "It is."

He flashes a smile and then combs his fingers through his mustache.

"You look like Griz with that thing." I point to my upper lip, mimicking where it has grown in thicker.

"Laney likes it," he says with a shrug, his smile turning into a smirk. "She's the boss. I'll do pretty much anything that makes her smile and eager to get naked. This, for some reason, accomplishes both."

I take another look at my phone to check the time. It's late, and regardless of her job, there have been too many threats lately to ignore the fact that Hadley left my messages unread.

ACE:
> Are you staying at the Midnight Proof apartment tonight?

She hasn't done that yet. She always comes home, but it's a possibility.

> **ACE:**
> It's late and the bar should have closed well over an hour ago.

When I look back up at him, he's watching me. He's been doing it for years—assessing my social cues and making sure I'm okay. He's the only one who asks every now and then if I'm alright. I don't need it, but I appreciate it anyway. "You've been taking care of all of us since we were kids, Ace. It's 'bout time you got your happy."

I send her another text as I smile at my brother and say, "What makes you think I haven't been happy?"

> **ACE:**
> I'm coming down there if you don't answer me.

Grant lets out a clipped laugh. "You're more of an asshole than I am most of the time; happy is not the adjective I'd ever assign to your natural state."

> **SUGAR:**
> Don't.

She never uses one-word answers. And my gut is telling me that something feels off.

When I look up, my brother's examining the color of his glass of bourbon. "This is good. Is it single barrel?"

I nod.

He hums, and then takes another sip. "How long?"

It's been a long time since I shared a bourbon I made. "About six years on that one."

"It's different. Not sure what that after-bite might be…"

"I smoked out the barrel. I let it rest and charred it again before I added the white dog. Wanted to see if it'd hold the added smoked flavor." I take another sip, recognizing the notes he was appreciating. "I was right. It did," I say proudly.

With his eyebrows kicked up to his hairline, he says, "You tried something new then?"

I did. "Griz has a way of getting under my skin. He's been telling me to take more risks for years. He just thought I wasn't listening."

"Well…" He polishes off what's in his glass. "You got married, and now you're finding ways to bend the rules of bourbon. I'd say he did more than just get under your skin."

Julep gets up from the floor and sits with her tail wagging by the door a minute before it swings wide open.

Grant smiles as Laney waltzes inside. "Julep, my best girl in the world!" she laughs out, then notices me. "Hey, Ace, what are you doing here? You're lucky I didn't strip as I entered—Grant's been rocking that mustache lately." Raising her hand next to her mouth, she whisper-shouts, "I'm feral for it."

"Honey," Grant says, his voice low.

"Yeah, cowboy?"

He crooks his finger at her.

I try to hide my smile. "Alright." Knowing it's time for me to go, I glance at my brother. "Grant, dinner was good. Appreciate the company, as always." I nod to him. "Let's keep that blend between us for now."

Laney plucks the freshly poured bourbon from Grant's hands. "This smells delish."

I look toward the front windows, waiting to see headlights, or at least the roar of a very loud engine. "I didn't hear the Mustang come flying down the road. Is she still working?"

"Your wife?" she hums, giving me a knowing look. "It was quiet tonight. A lot of locals, not too many faces I didn't recognize." She glances at the bourbon she just drank, and then brings her attention back to me. "I like this. And she was still there when I left—" Laney leans against the top of the couch, looking like she wants to say more. I've known her for long enough now to know that Laney rarely holds back.

I glance at Grant, and then back at her. "What am I missing? What *aren't* you telling me?"

"Gossip. A few people were talking about a little confrontation at Loni's today with the fire chief. He got loud about her being married all of a sudden. Then there were lots of questions about you and her from the town busybodies. When I came in, she was…upset."

That's all it takes for me to slide my shoes back on and head for the door. "Is she alright?"

"You know Hadley," she says thoughtfully. "She'll tell you she's good even when she isn't."

That isn't good enough for me. And hearing it out loud doesn't sit right. How many times have I listened to her tell Lincoln or Griz she's "good"? Especially after this past year. I'm realizing quickly how I could have missed the shit she's been dealing with—she doesn't want people worrying about her.

"You have the keys?" I ask.

"To Midnight Proof, yeah, but if she wanted—"

"With respect," I say, looking at Grant, "Laney, give me the fucking keys." Julep lifts her head up and barks at me, as if she knows I just cursed at her favorite person.

Laney smirks and digs into her back pocket. I catch them as she chucks them my way. "Thanks," I call out. I'm out the door and in my car seconds later. She shouldn't have dealt with any of that on her own. I gun it through town and make it to the main drag of Fiasco a handful of minutes later, running through the roster of things that asshole could have said to her. She's a grown woman and can handle herself, but fucking hell, I didn't like the idea that I'm hearing about this from someone other than her. And hours later.

"Ladies," I say as I walk past the sisters starting their early morning prep at Crescent de Lune.

"Hey, Ace," they both reply with a smile as I rush down the back stairs and toward the double doors of the speakeasy.

The music's blasting loud enough that she doesn't hear me unlock the doors and disarm the alarm. Anything this loud makes me uneasy, but for Hadley, she gets lost in it. Her codes are too easy to guess—she likes to tell people her favorite things, like numbers and dates, far too frequently. I always listen.

When I walk through the long black velvet curtains, she's perched on the bar, shoes off and legs folded, a Boston jersey draped on the bar next to her, leaving her in a simple white tank. She's concentrating on writing in that black notebook. I don't know why I'm so interested in what she scribbles in there. It's been the same one for as long as I can remember, and I don't understand how she hasn't run out of space.

She's different when she's distracted—still beautiful, but it's something softer and more vulnerable when she isn't spitting out sarcasm and insults at me. Her hair is gathered to one side, still messy and wild. She drains what's left in her glass, and then pours out another shot of the most expensive bottle of bourbon on her menu. I should know, it's mine.

"Why are you still here?" I ask, loud enough that she'll hear me over Britney fucking Spears. "You closed two hours ago."

Her head whips up, eyes meeting mine. She's pissed off and ready to lace into someone. I've seen that look only a few times over the years—Hadley isn't very good at hiding her emotions. And she typically carries a lighter mood. Right now, whatever looms over this room feels heavy. Angry. It's a stark contrast to the exchange we had this morning as she sauntered past me with her bare ass and pussy out for show.

Lowering the volume on her phone, she hops off the bar. "I'm not interested in talking to you. Get out."

Alright, I did something to piss her off.

She plucks the shot off the bar, and noticing I'm making no moves to leave, she asks, "How did you get in here?"

I walk farther into the speakeasy. "Your alarm code is predictably 6969."

With her head cocked to the side, she gives me a dead stare as she tips back a Glencairn filled halfway.

"You're drinking a six-hundred-dollar bottle of bourbon like a Jell-O shot."

It's dim in here, but with the glow of the chandeliers splashing across the room, it's bright enough to see the soul-cutting glare she's giving me for that comment.

She walks around to the front of the dark oak bar and grabs the bottle next to her. Tipping it, she holds it high for a long pour, and with precision, fills the glass to its brim while her eyes stay pinned to mine. "I'll drink my bourbon however the fuck I want, Daddy."

"Don't" is the only word I get out before she's tossing the full shot of bourbon at me.

Every drop in that glass splashes up my chest and across my face.

Turning her back to me, she slams the glass upside down on the bar top, then stalks off down the hall to her office.

I pluck open the top three buttons on my shirt as the bourbon drips down my chest, but before I can even untuck it to reach the bottom buttons, she's hustling back to me.

"You've been working with my father." And without pausing to let me answer, she grits her teeth. "How long?"

Well, shit. This isn't how I wanted to tell her.

"What have you been paying for, Ace?" She lifts her chin, finger pointed my way, chest heaving as she waits for my response. "Hawk said something, and it just didn't—" Releasing a frustrated breath, she shakes her head. "Tell me you're not in business with my father."

I take my time to finish unbuttoning my shirt. When I finally do, I unclasp the cuff links and pocket them. Taking off my dress shirt, I wipe what's left of the bourbon from my chin. "What is it you think I've been paying for, Hadley?" I ask as I gather the hem of my undershirt and pull it over my head.

She swallows, looking down at my chest, more distracted. I know this warrants a conversation, but I need her to calm down if she's going to understand all the moving parts. "You think taking your clothes off is going to chill me out here? Not happening, Foxx."

"Liar," I breathe out, taunting her. Hadley pissed off is a fucked-up drug that feeds me. I look down the length of her body, appreciating each curve in a way that I rarely ever do. Allowing my eyes to linger in all the places I want to touch and suck. Eyes narrowed, she plucks the bottle off the bar and pours out another shot, kicking it back with her eyes still on mine. It's fucking sexy.

"I've spent my entire life being dealt half-truths and bullshit answers to appease me." When she looks down, I feel her dejection competing with her anger. "I'm done with that now."

My stomach bottoms out. The last thing I ever wanted was for her to think I'm anything like her father. "I made a promise to him," I tell her, taking a step closer.

She blinks back tears just as confusion settles in the way she's looking at me.

"And in return, he agreed to keep men like Switcher away from you. No more pushing for some bullshit marriage to some asshole you didn't want." I sniff out a laugh, realizing that's exactly where she ended up anyway, only the asshole now is me.

She stands taller, pushing back her shoulders and watching me closely as she asks, "What was the promise?"

"Your father capitalized on my weakness, and he had stipulations." I clear my throat. "After I killed Switcher, I confronted your father. I walked right into his house, pissed off and without thinking." I shake my head, still angry at myself all these years later for being outmaneuvered by him. "I wasn't going to watch shit like that happen again, Hadley. You being traded or auctioned for the best offer, like you were some kind of property of his." Rubbing along the back of my neck, I take a deep breath before telling her the rest. "But he had leverage that I didn't see coming. Switcher didn't matter. He got what he wanted—an upper hand on the Foxx brand, through me. I gave him a percentage of earnings. I became the private investor for the Finch & King breeding facility. And…" I pause as I look at her. "I paid out monthly the remainder of your trust."

Her eyes widen. She stares at me as if she's waiting for more, but I know it's just because she wasn't expecting any of this.

"Nobody knows. Not even Griz. I covered any trails that

connected the Foxx brand to Wheeler. I promised to stay away from what I wanted if he left your relationship status alone—no more pieces of shit being paraded around as marriage material to you."

She closes her eyes for a moment, and when she opens them, a single tear falls down her cheek. Swiping it away, she tries to put on a brave face, still looking angry, but possibly even more emotional. "If you keep something like that from me ever again, I swear to every goddess from Aretha to Zendaya that I will make your life feel like the tenth ring of Hell," she says firmly, hardening herself.

It's the one thing that equal parts pissed me off and served as the thing I crave. She walks up to the things that would scare the hell out of most, and then flips them off with a charming smile. She's the kind of woman most men don't even try to approach or handle—to them, she's too much. Too confident, too smart, too attractive for those who would never come close to measuring up. It makes her that much more dangerous because she has no idea. When enough people who are supposed to be important to you tell you and show you that you're not, you start believing it. She has no idea how much power she wields. And she needs to know how important she is to me.

"There's one thing I still don't understand…" She trails off, pouring out another shot.

I eye what she's doing this time, not trusting that her bratty side won't toss another right at me.

"You said you promised to stay away from what you wanted…" Tilting her head, her eyes collide with mine again as she asks, "What was it you wanted—"

"Want," I cut into her question, anticipation thrumming

through my veins at what this admission is going to mean. "Ask me what I want."

Her lip quirks slightly, that small dimple puckering, like she knows what I'm going to say. It's written all over my face right now and along the lines of everything I've done. "What do you wa—"

"*You*. I want you."

She closes her eyes for a moment, absorbing my confession and allowing it to settle into the space left between us. Quietly, she says, almost to herself, "All these years…" With a huffed breath, she shakes her head. "I thought this was one-sided." When she focuses back on me, she looks angry all over again, maybe even more so. "You pushed." She steps closer, and my heart pounds more powerfully. "And kept pushing me away. I thought I was crazy, that I was seeing things I only wanted to see when you looked at me."

"It's not that simple," I say, but before I can elaborate any more, she lets out a sarcastic laugh.

"Oh, it's pretty fucking simple, Daddy."

Every hair on my body raises, any atom that contributed to my arousal practically vibrating to take what I want.

"You want me the way that I want you. The way I've *always* wanted you," she says, taking one last step closer. Confirmation of how she feels for me is like a match dropped to gasoline.

"Hadley—" I warn, but it's too late as the single barrel, small batch bourbon splashes across my face.

She's going to pay for that. I close my eyes, breathe in and out slowly, trying to remain calm. When I blink my eyes open, I watch as she tries her hardest to bite back a laugh.

"Are you done?" I ask, licking my bottom lip. The bourbon's still wet and lingering.

Her lips slowly tip into a smile as her blue eyes stay locked on mine, challenging me. As always. "Not even close," she says with all the attitude she's got.

"Good," I growl. And I tell her exactly what she's going to do. "Now clean it up."

We've barely explored each other, but every inch of my skin is buzzing. It's like a switch has been flipped, and now we get to play.

She doesn't hesitate or ask what I mean; she merely closes the small gap that's left between us, puts her hands on my hips, and lowers her body until she's looking up at me, eye level to my very turned-on and hard dick. She sticks out her tongue and licks a path from the waist of my pants up my abdomen, swiping through the center of my chest and straight to my neck. As if it's the best blend of bourbon she's ever tried, she hums deeply, then licks up my neck again, not ready to be finished. My body is so heated that I nearly pant at the way she's taking my direction like the *good fucking girl* I know she can be.

A groan escapes my lips as she draws a line across my throat and up to my chin, ending the slow, wet path just below the curve of my lip.

She exhales and breathily asks, "How's that?" It's a question eager for praise. Her pretty blue eyes are wide and curious for more of whatever that just was, like she isn't used to a dominant partner.

"You can do better."

She looks down the front of me and moves her slick lips across my neck and along my pulse, her tongue caressing the same path on the way back.

She pulls her lips away, just enough to whisper, "Yes, Daddy."

I asked her not to call me that, but now I crave hearing it. Something about the way she practically moans those two words has every muscle in my body pulling taut. My fingers flex. My mouth waters. My cock is so hard that its slit fucking weeps with an eagerness to fill her.

As her tongue teases my lips, it unravels the very last thread of my control. I wrap one hand around the back of her neck and the other around her waist, pulling her against me as my mouth collides with hers. Her legs wrap and lock around my waist without effort as her fingers delve into my hair. The small sounds that she makes are like fuel for me. I hold her so tightly, trying to erase every inch between our bodies as our lips press and play, tongues dancing together to savor the guttural need to consume the other. Anything less wouldn't be enough. When her teeth nip my lips, wanting more, I happily oblige.

I move us back toward the bar until her ass is perched on the edge, her legs staying wrapped around me as we take our time to really feel the other. The collision and heat burn lower and slower as I work my mouth along hers. "Feels so good, kissing you," I say between breaths.

She hums against me, her lips tilting into a smile. I can't help but run one hand along her side, palming the curve of her tit, my thumb rubbing her hard nipple. She lets out a soft gasp at the touch, and I pull back to take her in. Even fully clothed, it turns her on. Watching my hand move over her in ways I've only ever fantasized about is dizzying. I've never wanted anything as much as I want her.

Pulling me closer, she licks at my lips. "It'll feel even better fucking me."

"I know it will, sugar. But not before I taste what I've been craving." I lift her higher to sit on the bar, and she lets out a laugh, leaning back on her hands, with her arms braced behind her. I tuck my fingers into her waistband and roll the painted-on black pants down her legs and tug them clean off. When I see exactly what's waiting for me, I barely hold back a groan as I toss them aside. "Where're your panties, Hadley?"

She smiles at me, biting the puffy bottom lip I just finished sucking on. "Why do you care? You would have just taken them off anyway."

I reach forward, and with my thumb, I swipe up and down, parting the lips of her pussy, spreading her wetness from cunt to clit.

Her mouth parts as her neck tilts back and she audibly exhales, "Oh fuck, Ace—"

"I care because I need to know if my wife's pretty pussy is all wrapped up in white lace or black spandex," I say, moving my thumb slowly to tease her. "I think a husband should know how many layers stand between him and his wife." Circling around her clit, I slide my thumb between the lips of her slick pussy. "Just like I need to know that the next time you're serving a drink in this spot, you'll think about what I'm doing right now. I bet you'll soak whatever you're wearing. And then come home to show me."

Grabbing the bottle of bourbon off the bar, I stick it in my mouth, tucking the pourer between my teeth to pull it off. I take a step back and sit on the bar chair behind me, a front row to my wife's spread legs. With my thumb coated in her arousal, I circle it around the rim of the bottle.

"Show me the rest of you," I demand as I take a pull from the bottle. A bottle that retails for more than it should simply based on the fact that it took its time. Aged in a barrel for nearly a decade, a proof that heightened, working over the sugars from the wood when it swelled in the warm summers. But now, mingling with the taste of her, it has me savoring it in a way I never have before. I groan and unbuckle my belt as I watch her tease the tank top up her waist.

"Stop," I demand. The bottom of the white ribbed cotton stops, still covering her pebbled nipples but revealing the swelled skin of her tits below. *Fuck, why is that so hot?*

She stops moving, her arms dropping back to the bar top just as she raises her legs, bending her knees and spreading herself wider. Her pussy glistens for me.

"Is it your turn?" she teases.

I take another pull from the bottle and raise my hips, pushing my pants just past my ass and reaching into my black boxer briefs to pull out my already leaking dick. Swiping at the slit, I spread my arousal around the head and then grip myself tight.

"That all for me?" she asks as she bites on her thumb. Fuck, she's even better than I imagined. Submissive and playful, sexy and mouthwatering.

"You know it is," I growl as I slowly rock my wrist up and down.

She tries holding back a smile, like there would be any other answer. "Can I?" Her eyes meet mine as if she's nervous. As if I would deny her anything.

I do exactly as she requires—give her the direction she's craving. A moment not to think or calculate, not to worry about the hand she's been dealt, how she'll play it, or doubt the outcome. "I want you to come all over it. Can you do that for me?"

Sighing, she tips her head back. "Fuck, I knew this would be good."

And that makes me smile, knowing that she's thought about us like this too.

Without wasting any more time, she lifts herself off the bar and plucks the rest of her shirt up and over her chest. Full tits and soft, peaked nipples are needy for my mouth. I lick my lips, the taste of her and bourbon still lingering.

When she reaches me, her thumb brushes the head of my cock before moving that thumb across her tongue. Then she holds out her hand for the bottle I'm still holding. When I pass it to her, she tips it back for a sip and bends to put it on the floor before she moves to my lap, straddling her knees on either side of my thighs. "I've always used condoms," she breathes out as her pussy hovers over me.

"Same," I tell her, holding my breath and waiting for her lead on what she wants. I'll take her however—condom or not. She lowers just enough so I can drag the head of my cock up and down, combining her wetness with mine. "I want to feel you, bare, but only—"

She interrupts me with a kiss. And with a devious smile, she says, "I have an IUD. And I've had far too many fantasies about how you're going to fill me."

"Fuck," I exhale harshly, gripping onto her hips as she rubs the head of my cock along her clit. Her hips angle just right so that I'm lined up where she wants me. She exhales as her cunt takes the first part of me, and I hold on to her tighter at the warmth of her perfect fucking pussy.

"I get it now," she says quietly as she slowly stretches for more of me. "The confidence and I-don't-give-a-fuck attitude…" She slides down farther, halfway to where I want her to be. "Your cock is so fucking good," she says, determined, with one hand on my chest and the other on my shoulder for leverage. A breathy whimper escapes her lips.

"You can take it," I tell her, and her eyes flick to mine, a smirk across her lips.

"Oh, I know, I'm an overachiever," she says as she rotates her hips, opening herself up so it feels good. I lick my thumb and find her clit to ease her pussy into relaxing. Her mouth opens and her head tilts back, her fingers digging into my shoulders. "Daddy, you're going to make me come, and I'm not even all the way—"

Her words cut out to a guttural groan as I thrust my hips up and fuck into her tight, wet pussy. That fucking nickname makes me feral for this woman, and I'm not the least bit mad about it. I moan into her, my teeth grazing the skin just above her tits. She feels so fucking good. As her arms move around my neck, all I can think is, *How are we only just doing this now?*

"Ace," she exhales. "I just need—"

I lean down enough to suck one of her nipples into my mouth. Her fingers thread into my hair as I drag my teeth and suck on her, enjoying the sweetness of her skin and the way she hums with appreciation.

Her eager pussy clenches around me with every swipe of my tongue and pull of my lips.

I roll my hips the slightest bit to see if she's ready for more, and I'm instantly greeted with a long, low moan and a gushing wetness as she shudders against me. "Fuck, did you just do what you were told? Did you just come for me?"

She bites her lip and rolls her hips, her body still pulsing. "Tell me what to do, Ace." Tilting her ass back, she jerks her pussy forward. *Perfection*. "And I'll do it."

I wrap my hand around her throat to guide her to me, and she smiles just before her lips meet mine. "I thought that was obvious by now," she whispers against my mouth.

Our tongues collide and move in time at the same pace that her hips roll and grind. She leans into me, pulling me deeper, both of us moaning out at the angle. My dick stretches her, and I can't help but pull back to see it.

"Look at how pretty you are on me."

She moans out softly in response as she follows my gaze.

"That's it." I swipe my thumb over her clit, needing another taste. "Make a mess all over me, sugar." Her pace is slow but intentional. A fill and retreat as her pussy grips me so *fucking* well that it has me on the edge. My vision starts to blur. A dark haze seeps into my veins and finds purchase down to every square inch of me. This is the kind of orgasm that's chased and hunted.

Hers crests and her greedy cunt works me over until she's coming again. As soon as she cries out, I'm letting go. Every muscle in me tenses, from my neck to my thighs, as I suck in air and moan against her neck. I chase every last beat of an orgasm that I know will leave me wrecked and eager for more.

Her body trembles beneath my hands as I hold her.

Chest heaving, I feel as my cock pulses, still hard inside her. *Fuck.* I move my hands up to her face and neck, pulling myself away from her slicked skin. "Look at me," I say, out of breath.

When her heavy lids open, she leans forward, kissing me again, her tongue gliding along my lips like she's hungry for this to keep going. Snaking my hand between us, I groan as I feel my cum leak out of her. I pet her clit like it should be rewarded for giving its owner the pleasure she deserves.

She hums sweetly, and leaning into my right ear, she whispers, "Please tell me that wasn't just a one-time thing."

It's a fake marriage. A convenient agreement. A contract with a smart strategy. At least it was. Now I want to be a husband to my wife in every way that matters. Being attracted to her was never the issue. And I can control my wants, stifle physical desires, but this is more than giving in or being taken. It's not about getting lost or falling. It's a shift. The players are still the same, but now, the game has changed.

I lick the side of her neck, and then kiss below her ear, telling her what she wants to hear. "That wasn't a one-time thing, sugar."

She sits back to look at me as my fingers trail up her skin and delve back down between us again. With a smile, her blue eyes sparkle, cheeks flushed pink. "Prove it."

Chapter 28

Hadley

May: The smell of oak, oranges, and orgasms

The real perk to this marriage, outside of breakfast made daily and copious orgasms, is waking up next to Atticus Foxx. *Why does he smell so good?* Maybe I never truly appreciated the weight of a man's body, or perhaps it's the faint smell of him and me lingering in his hair—sex and oak. Damn, I wouldn't mind bottling it up and saving it for later.

He twitches, and then his tensed muscles relax as he hums against my neck. "Are you sniffing me?"

"Pinch me," I say, smiling.

As he lifts his head to look at me, his hair a tousled mess, scruff longer, and eyes puffy with sleep, it's stupidly sexy to see this man disheveled and barely awake. His cock's hard, pressed against my calf with the way he's sprawled over me. Leaning down, he drags his teeth along my bare shoulder, and then moves his arm down, pinching my outer thigh.

"Just needed to make sure this wasn't a lingering fantasy from a really great self-induced orgasm."

"Have I been a part of many of those?" he asks, resting on an elbow. Those gray-blue eyes become more aware of my naked body as he licks his lips and draws the pad of his thumb under the curve of my breast. Back and forth, and ever so lightly.

"More than I should ever admit."

At that, his lips tip up. "Good," he says before he leans down and licks across my breast. His teeth drag along my warm skin just before he draws my nipple farther into his mouth. I'm painfully aware of how wet and needy nipple play makes me as his tongue plays with me. Or maybe it's any kind of play when the other player is Atticus Foxx.

I suck in a breath as his thumb brushes up along the lips of my pussy, up and down. He adds the slightest pressure, just enough to slip between the lips, reaching my clit and then moving lower. *Up and down.*

With his eyes locked on mine, I let out an exhale. My body feels relaxed and ready for whatever he desires. "It's almost unfair how sexy you are when you're looking at me like this," I mumble lazily. He doesn't say anything in response, just hums and keeps the same lulling pace as his thumb glides effortlessly up and down. I'm almost certain it's the single most erotic moment of my life.

The thickness of his cock rubs up against my outer thigh as he shifts his body, moving higher beside me. Draping my leg over his hip, he opens a path to exactly where I need him. And holy shit, do I need him again.

"How many times?" I ask just as he slides into me, both of us moaning as he stretches me.

He drags his cock back out slowly, just to its tip, as he asks, "How many times what?" Lifting my leg higher, from his hip to his waist, he angles himself deeper.

"How many times did you picture this when you were touching yourself?" I ask as I tip my chin up and absorb how fucking good he feels. The way he fucks isn't passive or aggressive, it's confident and curious. He fucks me deep and holds himself there, moving his hand from roaming along my body up to my chin so my eyes meet his.

"I've come to the sound of your laugh, picturing your lips on mine, your hands wrapped around my dick, my cock fucking your throat. I've fucked my hand just by your smell…"

My eyebrows raise. "Holy hot," I rush out. A smile lingers on my lips when I praise him this time. "Dirty fucking Daddy."

Kissing my shoulder, he pulls out of me, moving his body from beside me to hover above me. "Say it," he says as he drags the tip of his wet dick through my pussy.

I hum as I spread my legs wider. "Please, Daddy." Without pause, he easily glides his slicked cock into me with one slow thrust.

The change in angle and the pressure of his weight on me has him hitting the right spot so fully that I get lost in it. With his mouth running along my neck, arms holding tight, he fucks me with intention.

I exhale a breathy plea. "Please."

"Not yet," he answers. His voice is strained as he shifts his weight to his knees, gaining more leverage as his hips grind into mine. Holding me tightly, he moves me exactly where he wants, and I push my fingers into the short hair at the nape of his neck. His forehead rests against mine, breath labored when he says,

"I'm going to fill this pretty little pussy and you're going to moan my name when I do. Got that, sugar?"

"Yes," I gasp as he fucks me harder. My body feels weightless. Tingled sensations heat my skin, and I can barely hold off what I know will be an orgasm that's going to wreck me. His body jerks, and he fucks his hips forward twice more before he moans a loud and deep groan. The change in rhythm pushes me to the brink, and I moan the simplest answer to what he's asked. "Yes, Daddy."

My orgasm barrels through my body, and I suck in a breath, barely registering the way my thighs shake and the sounds I make. It's not until we're both breathless, slightly delirious, and momentarily speechless that I realize there's no coming back from this.

And I can't stop smiling about it.

May:... orgasms that end with heavy breathing and permanent smiles until sleep takes over. Nipple play, being called "sugar," and screaming out "Daddy" while the world's sexiest man moans against my ear. Perfection.

I scribble small stars around the words I just wrote. It's a page I know I'll come back to repeatedly throughout my life. It's the laziest day I've ever had with another person. Getting lost in the low music that's playing on the record player I brought from my apartment, Ace roams his fingers along my thigh as he checks emails on his phone. If anyone were watching this right now, it would look very coupley and domestic—so out of character for who we are separately, and yet, it feels like the most natural thing being together like this.

It's new for me. Eagerly getting up and moving on with my day is typically how sex ends. If I have an orgasm, it's good, and if I don't, then I'll plot how to get a few minutes in with my vibrator before I have to move on with the day. Even before Hawk, it was like that. A couple of sexy encounters, but fleeting.

"You're thinking very loudly," he says without even looking up from scrolling.

"That," I say, looking at the messy bed across the room, "and this"—I watch his fingers skate slowly along the crease behind my knee—"seems to be breaking, or at least bending, the rules we outlined for this marriage."

But instead of entering my anxious thoughts, he asks, "What happened yesterday?" Taking a sip of his coffee, he nods his chin for me to feed him a bite of the croissant. The easiness of this moment feels too good not to enjoy.

"Hmm, well…" I give him a bite and then take one myself. "Holy hell, this is delicious. And should I be concerned about your memory? I'd like to think what we did was kind of memorable—"

He pinches my side, and I can't help the laughter that bubbles past my lips. "I might be older than you, sugar, but you're the one who's been moaning my name. I didn't forget a single thing about it. And quit calling me old; I'm in my forties—you'll be here soon enough."

"It's too early to make such mean jokes, Atticus." I smile.

He doesn't hesitate to move closer to me, nudging himself between my legs. Curling a piece of hair behind my ear, he looks more serious when he says, "At Loni's yesterday. What happened?"

Ah, yes. "Hawk happened. He found out we got married, threw a bit of a nutty inside Loni's, and it attracted an audience."

I tilt my head to the side, thinking through that piece more. "Actually, it was Vinny, Prue, Romey, and Marla who stepped in and told him to cool off. Then it was a series of questions that I'm not even sure I answered. You know how they all get—"

"Was it over?" he asks as his hands move along the sides of my thighs, almost soothingly. "With Hawk. When you kissed me—asked me to marry you—was it over?"

"Our situation was never more than casual. It was over as of Lincoln and Faye's wedding. I let that linger on for longer than it should have. But I was the asshole. I used him for sex. I just thought he knew that. I thought that was what he'd been doing too."

"Do you think that's what we're doing now?" He clears his throat and leans back to look at me. "Using each other?"

I wrap my legs around the back of him to get him to stop moving away. "I think it's how this started. Using each other to get what we needed. Maybe that's how everything starts—people looking for something and trying to get it from another."

His phone starts vibrating on the counter. When I glance at the time, it's well past a typical morning for him.

Looking at his texts, he says, "Laney is cursing me out about a shipment, and Griz is whining about not having breakfast this morning."

He doesn't see it, not like I do, but he takes care of everyone in some way or another. And he's been doing it for so long that I don't even know if he realizes it.

"You have everyone fooled, you know. You're not all that intimidating; you just care a whole helluva lot."

"Is that what you think?" he asks as he pushes my hair behind my shoulders, dragging his lips along my jaw. "Don't start thinking I'm a good guy here, Hadley. You'll be disappointed."

Doubtful. I've been near plenty of bad people throughout my life. I know the difference.

He frames his hands around my face as he says, "I want you in my bed tonight, wife."

Smiling, and way too giddy, I lean in to kiss his disturbingly perfect lips. "People just do what you want, don't they?"

The scruff along his chin and cheeks is thicker this morning, and all I can think about is how much I like the scrape of it against my skin. He hums as he leans into my neck, dragging his teeth while peppering kisses. "I think you already know the answer to that."

Chapter 29

Hadley

May: Charcuterie, a dirty martini, and a side of Griz

"Alright, Griz," I singsong as I pad down the stairs. Griz has an entire space down in the basement of the house. It's a wine cellar that weaves into a finished theater room, and then off of that is Griz's. The walls are lined with shelves of books and that messy clutter that feels more warm and cozy than hoarding and chaotic. When he said he didn't want to go to the Oaks race this year, I was a little surprised. Every year since I can remember, Griswald Foxx would attend. He'd don a hat that reminded me of *Newsies* and wore his nicest pair of Wranglers and boots.

I stop short when I hear two voices. Before I turn the corner, the smell of cloves wafts from his office. He isn't much of a smoker; sometimes, he'll puff on a cigar for a special occasion, but even then, it's rare.

"I've tied up as many loose ends as I can," Griz says to

someone. "It needs to be enough. I'm not getting any younger. And I'd like to finish out this life my own way."

I swallow down the emotion that statement pulls from me. I haven't thought much about Griz not being around. His age isn't lost on me, but he's healthy, and if you asked anyone, they'd confirm he looks more like he's pushing sixty and not eighty.

A woman's voice says quietly, "You know the deal with how this works, Griz. You can't just pack up and go there."

I'm clearly not supposed to be listening to this, so I move back upstairs quietly and take a look at the car that's parked out front. An old truck, not one I recognize. I sit in the kitchen and wait for her to leave, neither of them seeing me sitting and sipping on a drink as she makes her way out the front door. Griz isn't expecting me to be at the house right now. Ace is at the distillery, working through all of the last-minute Ditch the Derby prep with Laney and Lincoln. Everyone else is heading to Louisville for the day or taking it easy before the entirety of the Foxx properties is inundated with bourbon lovers and tourists.

My phone vibrates along the counter. It feels like my stomach knots every time I hear it telling me there's a text.

> **UNKNOWN:**
> You realize that by ignoring this, it's not going away?

> **UNKNOWN:**
> Do not push me. You may be fucking my brother, but do not fuck with me when it comes to paying for what's been promised.

> **HADLEY:**
> Governor?

That asshole. I smirk, knowing he has no plans to answer my question. I'm not shaken knowing who this particular threat came from. I'm starting to replace anxious thoughts with anger every time another unknown text comes through.

"Are you going somewhere?" I ask as soon as Griz walks back inside. His head swings up fast, not expecting me to be sitting at the long counter, casually enjoying my sparkling water. He changes course and pads into the kitchen, sitting down next to me. The size of this house makes it feel inviting, but it also gives a sense of privacy. I imagine that's one of the perks that's kept Griz and Ace living together all this time.

"How much did you overhear?" he asks, swiping a piece of cheese from the cutting board.

"I'm not sure," I say honestly. "I know better than to listen in on conversations. Eavesdropping never did me any good." Popping a grape in my mouth, I take a minute to decide if I want to know the answer to the question I'm about to ask.

"Go ahead, ask whatever it is you're going to ask, Hadley Jean," he says, and then swipes a slice of apple.

I inhale deeply, my heart beating a little faster as I ask, "Are you dying?"

He barks out a laugh, followed by, "What? No, I'm not dying. At least not as far as I'm aware. Hell, don't jinx me like that. You hit my age, and even thinking it might be bad luck."

I can't help but get teary-eyed as I laugh with him. "Between taking your official retirement from bourbon—"

He cuts me off. "I ain't never retiring from bourbon, Hadley Jean. I'm pretty sure that's what's keeping me alive at this point."

"You know what I mean. Handing over the company." I glare at him and add, "With stipulations. And now, hearing that you're tying up loose ends…"

"You said you didn't eavesdrop," he tuts with a quirked eyebrow.

I pinch two of my fingers together, leaving the tiniest gap. "A smidge."

Plucking two pieces of cheese, he pops them in his mouth. "Is this girl dinner that I'm eating right now?"

I smile at him, nodding. "My version of it, yes."

He hums. "You realize it's charcuterie, right?"

"Yes, but I have French fries in the air fryer and need to whip up a martini. Then it's perfect. Want to join me?"

He nods, giving me a look like it was silly to even ask, and then rests his elbows on the counter. "I would rather not tell you all the details. I had that meeting purposely so nobody, especially my grandson, would ask too many questions."

"Griz, if you tell me we were just here eating a delicious girl dinner together tonight, then that's our story. A perk of officially being your granddaughter-in-law," I whisper.

His eyes look glassy, but in typical Griz fashion, he makes the emotion disappear with a simple tilt of his mustache. "I like the sound of that—not just the innuendo of keeping this between us either. I mean the part about you being something I've felt in my heart for a long-ass time now."

My chest warms, the backs of my eyes burning. "Don't get sappy on me. I need to get my bearings for what will hopefully be a rowdy and packed house at the bar tonight."

He nods, and just like that, switches the mood. "Alright, you need to tell me what we'll need for these martinis."

"You're going to have vodka?" I laugh out as I pull out the blue cheese from the refrigerator.

"I'd prefer gin, but I'll have whatever you want to serve up." He gets up from the counter, on a mission. "And in case I forget to tell you, having you in this house and married to Atticus feels like it was always meant to be."

A part of me agrees. The part that's fantasized about more than just being with Ace Foxx. The part that wanted to be a part of this family in any way I could. I swallow down the nerves of knowing that this all began as an agreement. A convenient, contractual marriage, and now, after all that's happened, I don't know how the hell I'm going to ever want to leave it.

Thousands of people come to Kentucky early in the week leading into the Derby. Bourbon tours are nonstop, day and night, and guests who want to experience the sexiness of a hidden speakeasy know to look for Midnight Proof. There isn't a sign out in front of Crescent de Lune; instead, it's a series of clocks stuck on 12:00 that serve as breadcrumbs toward the staircase that lead to the double doors of my establishment. It feels secretive and seductive for out-of-towners. Part of the fun is hiding and finding—almost as much as building out cocktail menus curated specifically to the season. Or in this case, the occasion.

"A mint julep," a woman's low voice says as I make my way down the length of the bar. I'm one of those people who thinks someone looks familiar. I know a face if I've seen it—there's no need to play coy about it either.

I didn't need to study her to know that I've seen her before. "That's rather predictable—would you like me to make my version of one? It's not on the menu."

I hadn't seen her face, only her profile before. I expected her to be pretty, but she's striking—high cheekbones on par with Geena Davis, full lips with no bow in sight. I wanted to absorb just a fraction of her confidence. "If you'd like." She nods.

"We haven't met," I say as I flip a chilled shaker. "Officially, at least."

She rests her elbow on the bar, her long white nails matching her platinum hair. "I know who you are," she says with a slow, menacing smile. "For quite some time now, in fact."

I pluck three brown sugar cubes, along with a stalk of mint and a small scoop of crushed ice. Slightly more aggressive than usual, I jam and twist the steel muddler into it. "Mind elaborating on that?"

"I've known Ace for a long time." She tilts her head to the side, pausing for a moment as her eyes rake over me. "And I know how important you are to him. I take it he's told you about me?" She sits back in her chair, just as the music for Faye's burlesque performance ramps up. "The Jeweler? Maybe more?"

I nod as I swipe a lime wedge along the side of a short rocks glass, and then dip the edge into mint-infused sugar. Pulling the bottle of Foxx 100 Proof, I eyeball two and a half ounces, give it a shake until the shaker frosts on the outside, and double strain it over one large ice cube with a lime frozen at the center.

"Good," she says, as she slides a hundred-dollar bill across the bar. "Welcome to our fucked-up little family, Hadley Foxx. My number is in your phone."

My phone buzzes in my pocket, but I ignore it and turn back to give her change, but she's gone. With my brow pinched, I peer over the crowd and along the main room for her, but it's like she was never here. The only thing that remains is an untouched mint julep and text on my phone that reads: *If you ever need a favor, let me know.*

Somehow, her name is already in my phone, along with her phone number and email. I won't overthink how it got there, but it seems like I passed some kind of approval having met her and knowing who she is to Ace.

I take inventory of the faces that pack the house tonight. Some I recognize, but there are more I don't. Oversize hats and fasteners are still on most who had been in Louisville earlier in the day, on their second wind of drinks and fun by now. I smile at my busy servers and keep an eye on the overserved that Brady consistently keeps turning away at the door.

I'm eager to duck out and see how Ditch the Derby is going. Laney sent out pics of her and Lincoln clinking glasses and another handful of images that showed off a crowded distillery that bled into the hill along the main building. They had set up a main stage for bands to play throughout the day and a row of food trucks to keep everyone happy. They managed to do what they had set out to do—offer something different for a day that thrives on tradition. I'm proud knowing how much hard work it took to put on an event like that.

As I glance at the clock, and it's only just after 9:30 p.m., I decide that a perk of being the boss is leaving when I want to. "Faye, are you going to the distillery?"

She smiles and leans against the bar. "Lincoln said the girls were fading fast, so he took them home. I'm going to see my crew after my last set." She glances around the room. "You should go. Your crew can handle it."

The truth is, I want to see Ace. It's always been that way. While Lincoln was the reason I found my way to the main house or the distillery most of the time, Ace was my quiet reward. But now, it's wildly different. Of course I want to see Lincoln and support Laney, but I'm going for him. To see my husband, show off a little, stir up some gossip, and know that when he kisses me hello, he won't hold back. Not anymore.

Chapter 30

Ace

THERE ARE PEOPLE FROM ALL over peppered around the distillery throughout the day. The tastings started early, but when the Kentucky Derby kicked off, it was broadcast over the massive screens on either side of the stage that's currently playing some decent bluegrass. It was over quickly, but the Derby is always about the show of it—the races and the experience. Fiasco has had enough of racing this year, so when Laney suggested Ditch the Derby, it felt like the perfect way to cater to locals and still celebrate an event that ushers in massive amounts of bourbon drinkers.

Grant and Lincoln join me on the balcony just off the upper floor offices. With them is James Dugan Sr. in his hardware store polo, and Del, who quietly surveys the crowd in his typical cop-like fashion. My brothers welcomed the plans for investing in Dugan's Hardware. It wasn't even a question for them—trying to find ways for us to invest in our town. They're good men.

Plus, the three of us have been absorbing the fundamentals that Griz always spouted, like, *"You'll find success more palatable when you watch others find it."* And the one that seemed to hit hardest lately, *"Take care of where you're from and it'll take care of you."* Today is a great day to bring our partners up here to show our appreciation. Their last name might be different, but they're a part of the Foxx family.

"Helluva view from up here, Ace," James says.

I nod, taking it all in. It's been a while since the distillery's been this crowded and the warmth of pride laces its way through me as I admire all of the hard work it took in getting this event moving. Winter is never as busy as the summer, but it hasn't been this full of life since our 100-year celebration. And that was just after Laney had moved here, after the rickhouse had burned down, and along with it, some of our oldest bourbon. I look toward the main road, hoping to hear the roar of that damn Mustang coming up the drag. I was hoping Hadley could duck out early and enjoy some of this.

"I didn't think you were going to opt to rebuild it," Grant says, looking at the newly constructed rickhouse frame. It's just past the distillery, in between the path to the stables. I haven't told him yet that it's not going to be a rickhouse—I have ideas and, hopefully, with a little bit of research and time, those ideas will turn into plans. They just aren't ready to share yet. I need to pitch an idea to my wife first, and then take it from there. I cover my mouth, trying to hide the smile those words cause—*my wife*.

I can still taste her on my lips. Hell, every time I think about her sweet, sugary smell, I get hard and want to say fuck it all. I knew the moment I woke up with her beneath me that I'd want all of it all over again—and on repeat. The sounds she makes. The way she does exactly as I request. How she doesn't hold back. How it feels to lie with her and just be exactly who we are—no masks or lies. It's a quiet proof that I'm never going to let her go. If she allows it, this will be it for us.

I clear my throat and tell him, "I have a few ideas of how we can use that space. Maybe something a little different instead of just barrels and bourbon." It's one of the reasons I'm heading to Colorado. I want some time with Hadley, to work out what we're doing and to share with her what I've been thinking through for the past year. That new, empty building we were looking at, I'd be lying if I said I hadn't thought of her when I first had the plans drawn up.

"Heard some big name in Thoroughbreds, a bloodstock agent over in Lexington, was found face down at Fiasco Falls. It's all the guys down at the station were talking about yesterday," Jimmy Dugan says to his dad as they make their way through the first pour of their tasting flight. I try not to be obvious in listening, but I know exactly who they're talking about.

"The bald guy from Midnight Proof? The one who got tossed out after getting in Hadley's face the other night?"

Del glances at me, looking to see if he should be playing interference. But instead of giving him anything, I add to the conversation. "The guy was a real hothead. I remember him from auctions over the years—fought like hell with plenty of people." I look at Lincoln and ask, "He was at the Blackstone auction last year, if I'm not mistaken?"

My brother remembers that night pretty damn well. It was the first time he realized his now wife was more than just a burlesque dancer. A private investigator who worked closely with Fiasco PD and the FBI field office. Every single person I recognized at that auction had a tie to Wheeler Finch in some way or another.

I can feel Del watching me. He knows I had something to do with this, but I'm not about to show my cards.

The roar of her Mustang nearly drowns out the new country blasting out over the speakers from the main stage. As Hadley tears up the long driveway and into the lot, rocks spit out and dirt flies. Fucking hell, she barely slows below 20 mph as she reaches the guys at valet.

Lincoln is smiling at me when I look up from my hyper-focus on her arrival. "No offhanded comment about 'Lucifer arriving' or asking, 'Who summoned her'?" He's still looking at my profile as I watch her get out of her car, like he's working through what might have changed in the past week between my last conversation with him about our relationship and today. With a curse, he hits me in the back. "Well, holy shit. You're sleeping with her."

I give him a sideways glance, and then focus back on her. Those gorgeously toned legs are all I see before I'm turning toward the double doors and heading back inside to make my way down through the distillery to meet her. I hustle past a handful of people who want me to stop and chat, but I'm having a hard time hiding how happy I am to get to my wife.

"Atticus Foxx," someone calls out in the crowd, but I wave and keep walking. When I make it to the front lawn and through a small crowd of sloppy drunks and the country band that just finished up their set, I finally spot her again. The dress she's wearing isn't something that would be considered attire for the Kentucky Derby. And while there are plenty of dress codes depending on where you're watching the event, this one in particular wouldn't fit anywhere. The short black dress looks like it's made of the same leather as the black cowgirl boots that hit just below her knee. Her hair falls down her back in smooth waves, and a gathering of feathers with black netting is fastened off-center. I bite back a smile—damn, she's beautiful. When she finally sees me, her pouty, glossy lips tip into a smile that hits me right in the chest.

"You're here," I say as I stride closer and erase the distance.

With a coy smile, she shrugs her shoulder. "I own the place, so I snuck out early. Figured I should be here to support my husband." She glances to her right, where a few sets of eyes are paying attention to us. The rumors have already thoroughly circulated and marinated about our marriage. People are looking for more than confirmation. They want to see for themselves if it's true—a Foxx and a Finch happily in love.

"We've been showing off for long enough. Think it's time to stop pretending?" she asks, leaning back to look up into my eyes. Then, without missing a beat, I lift her against me, bringing her lips to mine. With a moan, her fingers glide from my cheek and into my hair, holding me close while holding nothing back as we kiss like we've got something to prove.

I hum against her lips and kiss her again before I tell her, "You look incredible."

"Somebody call up the western winds! I need to cool off after witnessing that!" Romey says to her sister—and just about everyone else standing around willing to listen.

We pull back just enough to let her feet find the ground, but she catches my lips once more and kisses me again. I smile against her mouth when we hear, "Why are there not more of you Foxx boys?" Romey huffs. "Prue, we need something stronger. Hadley, send me the website with all those vibrating flowers, please. Might need a bouquet after spendin' time 'round the two of you." With a laugh, they move inside to the tasting bar.

Hadley laughs heartily and salutes them. "You bet, Romey."

"You're still giving people vibrating presents?" I ask her, already knowing the answer.

"It's the gift that keeps gifting," she says, raking her eyes down the front of me. "Maybe I should buy one just for you, husband."

I hold up two fingers. Her brow furrows again, like it did when I ticked off the first time I'd almost reached my limit with her bratty mouth. But I don't explain what I'm counting; instead, I wrap my arm around her and lean in close enough so my lips skate over her bare shoulder.

"Say that again, sugar."

I tilt back to look at her questioning blue eyes, but before I can ask her to call me her husband again, I see someone stalking toward us out of the corner of my eye.

Lincoln must've seen him coming, because he's already standing next to us at the same time I slide my arm from around Hadley. Lacing my fingers with hers, I pull her closer to my side.

Chief Hawkins looks at her, and then at our laced hands, jaw clenching. "Your party is blocking all the way down the main road, Foxx. Not to mention, there are capacity limits inside that tasting room that I'm sure are well over." His eyes lock back onto Hadley, trailing down her body and lingering where they shouldn't be, and I feel her tense.

Lincoln tries to cut through the thick awkwardness as he holds out his hand and says, "Thanks for the heads-up, Chief—"

"Get your eyes off my fucking wife," I grit out.

He tuts, and I know just by the way he so casually crosses his arms that what he's going to say next is going to end with a hook to his face.

"Hawk, don't," Del says, coming up to try to defuse the situation that has the potential to escalate quickly.

But he ignores him. Apparently, a public confrontation is on his bingo card tonight. *Fucking sloppy.* "I've had more than just my eyes on your wife. Isn't that right, Hadley?" Hawk says with a shit-eating grin.

"Ace..." Lincoln says quietly, trying to keep me from losing my shit. Hadley squeezes my hand, which is all she needs to do for me to keep myself in check. But I can still run my mouth.

Something hasn't sat right with me for a while. After seeing a list of names from a night about ten years ago, there's one person who didn't seem to add up. The exception is that he's the governor's brother, but there's more to it. I feel it in my gut, and I'm about to call it out. "Remind me again how you got your job, Hawk? Always made me wonder whose elbows you were rubbing or dick you were sucking."

He raises his chin and takes a step closer. *Ballsy.* "You're one to talk, Ace." And then he sniffs out a laugh. "Or do I have it wrong? Maybe she was sleeping with me because she wasn't getting what she needed from you." Again, he looks at Hadley, and my chest nearly rumbles. "Are you that hard up for a man to take care of you? Daddy couldn't anymore, so you ran to the next closest thing?"

This motherfucker. It's enough to make me snap. Grant comes up to my left just as he says it, flanking me. Both of my brothers are starting to box me out, even though public violence is never the way I handle assholes like this. But everyone's dismissing the biggest wild card here. The subject of the discussion.

It happens too quickly for anyone to stop her, including me. Hadley steps in front of Hawk and slaps him clean across the face with the hand that was just holding mine. Quietly, maybe just for him, but the small group gathered around us hears her say, "Let me make this clear for you." With his hand pressed against his face, it leaves her an opening to cock her leg back and give him a knee right to the dick. When he groans in pain, I have to hold back a chuckle. "Every time I came, it was because I was thinking about that man behind me right there. The one who, I promise you, is not going to forget this."

Goddamn, I'm in love with this woman.

Hawk's hands are braced on his knees, gritting something out as Del tries grabbing his arm to help him. The music still echoing around the commotion we caused drowns out any of their muttered conversation. But from body language alone, it's clear Hawk's ego got checked.

Faye steps closer, bending down and lifting a phone from the grass. "Here, Chief, you dropped this," she says, handing him his cell phone and smirking at me. He swipes it out of her hand without so much as a thank-you, then stalks off with some of the guys from his department witnessing all of it. Instead of caring about the crowd that's gathered or the repercussions of kicking a public official in the dick, Hadley turns on her boot heel and rushes back to me. I don't hesitate to lift her and follow the same momentum, meeting her lips with a kiss that very well has no business being on display. My tongue crashes with hers, and her arms wrap around my shoulders, fingers diving into the hair that meets the nape of my neck. When she pulls back, her lips hovering against mine, she says, "I need you to get us out of here right now, husband."

I smile. "Who knew my wife would be so eager for me?"

She lets out a laugh. "Literally everyone."

Chapter 31

Ace

The shift of the clutch is addictive in her car. "I get it now," I say as I downshift to make the turn into the driveway. Throwing the clutch and shifting up so I can push it, and then cut the corner and floor it, I glance at her in the passenger seat to see she's smiling. She's looking at me like she either wants to murder me or devour me. "I like your car."

"I'd like to do very naughty and delicious things to you right now," she says, rubbing her thighs together. "Who knew that Atticus Foxx could drive a car like this?"

Putting the car in park, I point at her. "Stay," I tell her and throw the driver's door open. Walking around the front, I open her door and take her hand to help her out.

"This entire vibe—I'm going to burn the world, drive like the devil, open my door—is really working for me."

I kiss her forehead, lacing my fingers with hers. "Kicking your ex in the dick for being a mouthy asshole is working for me too."

"We're not going to the house?" she asks as I veer her toward the stables. There's something she needs to see, and as much as I want to show her exactly how turned on that little show and what she spouted off to fucking Chief Hawkins just made me, I promised her over a game of chess that I'd be honest with her.

"I want to show you something first," I say as we make our way through the stable doors and to the back, past the horse stalls. Her two horses, Lady and Fergie, have been calling this place their home since she moved in, but upstairs isn't a spot I ever let anyone see. There are plenty of hidden places inside the main house, at the distillery, and inside the main offices, but this spot is just for me. Griz knows it exists, but nobody else.

"How did I not realize there was an entire space up here?" she muses as we make it to the top of the spiral staircase. It's tucked behind the last stall and looks more like it leads to a utility space. I've always liked the idea of things hidden in plain sight; it makes for the best reveals and reactions, much like the way her breath catches as I open the door. It probably says a lot about my feelings for her too—*hidden in plain sight*.

Up here has the same footprint as the stables below—more long than wide. The sprawling counter along the length of the space operates like a workbench, with its dark oak top. Its drawers are made of the staves of oak barrels before they were fired and bent into shape. The tools and hung notes look more like Lincoln's work benches inside the distillery. But she knows what all of this is right away.

"You've been making bourbon up here?"

I shake my head and move toward the limited barrels stacked along the opposite wall. "Something just for me. It's nothing like Grant did with his Cowboy Edition or what Linc does every day, but I was so caught up in the business of Foxx

Bourbon that I started forgetting why I loved it. The core of what we did. So I messed around, got lost in discovering what I loved about it all over again. This"—I tap along the side of one of the barrels—"is mine, just for me."

It isn't as nice of a space as the secret room upstairs at the distillery or meticulously decorated like the main house, but it has things spread throughout that are reminiscent of a younger version of me. There's nobody to impress up here, no expectations, just the things that I like the most. The sound system is connected to an amplifier and a nice-looking record player. My mom had a huge record collection that collected nothing more than dust for a lot of years when cassettes and CDs took over. It was a jackpot find when we dug through forgotten storage.

There are sketches that my father created when he was younger, framed and hung—some of them better than others. And there are a lot of pictures—moments that seemed insignificant at the time. Nothing like birthdays or holidays, just the random summer afternoon or breakfast for dinner. A collection of moments that don't need to be measured, but simply looked at and remembered every so often.

I nod toward the end of the room—the oversize couch perched under the large round window. In the summer, it's hot as hell up here, but this time of year, especially at night, it's exactly the kind of spot that pairs well with a glass of bourbon and a refreshing Kentucky breeze. On the draft table, there are maps of Fiasco layered on top of one another.

"You do know they have computers where you can access all of this now?" she asks as she runs her fingers along the papers.

"I'm aware, but some things need to be laid out like this." I point to the map I have spread out on the floor. It's a massive bird's-eye view of Fiasco. "That's a view of every business that's currently in the process of taking out loans from the bank that they can't afford or ones that are tapping into their owner's savings just to keep the doors open and electric on." There are more than a half dozen prominent businesses highlighted and another five coming really close.

I watch her eyes scanning the properties of her favorite places, sadness filling them as she lingers on Crescent de Lune, then Hooch's, and Loni's, even the hardware store and flower shop. She cares more about the community than she does her own business, even when she's struggling too.

"Some have been hit harder than others. Marla inherited the building from her father. And she's never relied on tourism to keep her doors open. But the hardware store needs an investor, and you've seen the signs for lighter hours at the flower shop, and then Loni's closing." All of them had nothing to do with Wheeler's bullshit, but they're suffering just as bad, if not worse, than some of the horse businesses that were directly impacted. "Your father made a mess and had no idea the impact it would have."

She closes her eyes and exhales, like she's absorbing the burden, and that wasn't my intention. I want to show her how we can help make it right. "Hadley, look at me."

As her eyes open and lock on mine, they shine like she's holding on for dear life to not start crying. "Why do you have all of this?"

I rub at the back of my neck and take a leap at pitching this to her. "I have it because I'm not going to sit back and do nothing about it. I could easily invest, bail them out of the debt they're in, but it's a Band-Aid. It'll keep happening unless we can boost tourism and get it back to what it was before."

Her attention goes back to the paperwork, and she takes in

the architectural plans, blueprints, and 3D renderings. When she realizes what I'm saying, what she's looking at, she turns to look at me over her shoulder and smiles. "You're giving people another reason to come here."

I clear my throat. "I'm going to try."

"What else aren't you telling me, darling husband?"

There's plenty. But the most important thing to discuss is what would affect her the most. "You've been given the keys to your father's entire estate while he's under house arrest, and providing he's incarcerated. I know the ballpark numbers of what that looks like."

She nods, letting me finish my point.

"I want you to use all of it. Pay debts to the people who did nothing wrong, and the rest, invest it where it could count."

She rests her thumbnail between her teeth, working over what I just proposed. At the end of the day, I may have access to what's hers, but it isn't my decision. I simply want her to take the lead and stop allowing her father to have any type of power over her. "And then what happens?" she asks.

I'm not going to sugarcoat it. Maybe initially that was the plan, but she needs to understand the moving parts and the main player. "Your father will inevitably find out there's nothing left. Likely from his attorney. Then they would need to choose either to abandon him or work pro bono. And if we're lucky, then he ends up exactly where he belongs. And the mess he made might not be fixed, but it'll be funded. And that's a start."

She nods, biting her lip, knowing all too well how risky this will be. As she's about to say something, she does a double take at the far side of the room. Squinting and head tilted, she sets the blueprints down and heads right in that direction. It doesn't hit me what she's looking at until it's too late.

One of the drawers along the top was left open and the papers that were covering it must have shifted when I opened the big window. She holds up a pair of dark-pink satin-and-lace panties, and below it, the unmistakable black envelope with cursive white handwriting. I swear I stop breathing.

"Hadley," I say, coming up behind her.

"How do you have these?" she asks, turning around to look at me. I can tell that she hasn't worked out why or how just yet. "I send them to a person in Colorado who pays me exactly one thousand dollars per pair. Every month. For the past—"

"Five years," I answer, swallowing past the lump in my throat. "Give or take."

Her eyes nearly bug out of her head. "You? This was you?" she says, flustered.

There aren't too many times in my life where I've been at a loss for words, but right now is one of them. And it seems the same can be said for her as she stares at me, and then the panties, and then me again. I never considered this ever happening—her finding out and realizing the level of crazy this turned into.

I pluck the pair out of her hands and walk back toward the other side of the room. The muscles along my forearms twitch as I grip the satin. It's a habit to feel the material, smell what she left behind on them, imagine exactly how she looks wearing them.

"That makes no sense. How do you even know about—"

With nerves thrumming through my body, I lift the pair up to my nose, and she watches, curiously and quietly. Keeping my eyes connected with hers, I inhale.

Her lips part, and she takes a step closer to me—still far enough away that I can't tell if I'm turning her on or scaring the shit out of her.

"How?" She shakes her head. "Better yet, *why* do you have these?"

The simple answer is one I'm not sure she's assuming. I lower my voice when I say, "You were talking to Lincoln about needing to make money. The fact that it didn't dawn on you to just get a job I thought was a bit hilarious. I thought that was where you were going with it, that you were going to ask him to work at the distillery, but instead, you went on and on about selling your panties on a website." I laugh to myself, even though she might not find it all that amusing.

She clears her throat and lifts her chin. "It was easy money. And I needed to be able to pay for things like food and my own bills. I had just used everything I had to my name to—"

"Buy that building and start renovating for Midnight Proof, I know."

Eyes on mine, she takes another step closer. "You were paying attention."

I chuckle at the ridiculousness of that statement.

She points at me. "Don't do that. Don't laugh or have a conversation about this with yourself. I've just found my panties in your drawer. I should be the one with the attitude."

"I was always paying attention," I admit. Undoing the top button of my shirt, I then unbutton the right cuff and fold it back, once, twice, three times. I do the same to my left, moving the panties to my other hand. Releasing a breath, I sit down on the leather couch, legs spread wide, and take a long look up her body, savoring every second that she'll allow for me to look at her this way. If I'm going to tell my wife I've been obsessed with her for far too long, then I'm going to do it while I'm comfortable and staring at what I've wanted for longer than what would be considered acceptable.

Without a word, she watches me do all of this while taking small steps closer, allowing me to be in control. But she's the one holding all the cards.

"Stop there," I demand.

Her steps falter and she does exactly as I ask, almost begrudgingly, by the way she sends me a glare. Her hip cocks out, chin raises, and shoulders straighten like she's squaring off for a fight. But that's the last thing I want from her right now.

"Tell me why," she orders, just as she moves the left strap of her dress over her shoulder and down her arm, exposing the top of her gorgeous tit and its pretty, puffy nipple.

A trickle of relief seeps in at her developing reaction. I lick my lower lip, my mouth flooding with the need to wrap around it and suck on it until she's moaning. *Jesus*. Shifting in my seat, I watch her take another step closer.

"At first, I was curious. I wanted to see what you listed. What they looked like. I wondered if they were panties you had already owned, or if you had worn them before."

Pausing her steps, she pulls down the thin leather strap of her dress and exposes her other side. Fuck, her body is always something worth looking at, but like this? Knowing that it's mine as she fucking offers it to me, knowing exactly what her skin tastes like and how she likes to have her nipples tugged and played with…it spurs on an entirely new level of attraction. My dick strains behind my boxer briefs and pants, a wet spot already formed just from the sight of her.

I can't help but bite back the smile that this is causing. Stripping for me as I'm under her interrogation. "Are you pissed?"

Lips pursed, she makes me wait a moment. "I haven't decided yet." Moving the dress lower down her waist, she lets it gather at her hips. "Keep talking, Daddy," she says in a raspy voice, as if adding her nickname for me wouldn't set me off all on its own.

I undo another button along the center of my dress shirt and keep going. "So I created an account, a fake email, and offered more money than what you were asking." As I unbuckle my belt, she takes another step closer, her chest bare and still wearing those fucking boots that make her toned legs even sexier. I stare at where her dress still covers her body, and just like the story I'm going to keep telling her, I need more.

Like she can hear my desires, she shimmies slowly from side to side, working the tight leather dress over her hips and ass until it moves to her thighs, and then her knees, and then finally dropping to the floor.

"You're not wearing panties."

"Somebody has been buying them all," she sasses, resting her hands on her hips, naked and in boots with enough attitude that my dick twitches.

I rub my thumb across my bottom lip as I take in every inch of her skin. "The first pair were black lace. A small scrap of material that shouldn't have done anything to me, but they smelled so fucking good, Hadley. I couldn't decide if I should be disgusted with myself for holding them to my face when I was jacking off or pleased that I had a way to—" I cut my words short, swallowing roughly.

She moves closer so that she's right in front of me, less than an arm's length away. "A way to what?"

"To have you. It was the only way that I could have a piece of you without hurting you, without breaking rules and promises."

"And how do you want me?" she asks teasingly, those blue eyes sparkling as they stare down at me.

As I take one more lingering perusal of her body, I don't hesitate to say, "Better question is, how will you have me?"

Her lips curl into a sultry smile. "I'll always prefer you on your knees for me, but there's something that I'm feeling hungry for right now," she says as she lowers to her knees. Looking up at me, she smooths her hands up my thighs and toward my waist, finding the button on my pants. She flicks it open, and I lift my ass up so she can pull them down. My cock springs free, hard and ready, practically pointing at what it wants.

Lust flaring in her eyes, she wets her bottom lip with the tip of her tongue as she looks at my cock.

"Get your fingers nice and wet, sugar. I want a taste first."

She releases an exhale that could be mistaken as a breathy moan and moves her hand to do exactly as I requested. Now with her pretty eyes searing into mine.

"The idea of you sharing your panties with anyone other than me was never going to work, so every month, I'd wait. Pay what I promised. I'd fuck the fabric, feeling like I was claiming what I wanted. Imagining the way you'd feel wrapped around me. How wet your pussy would get if I told you all of the ways I craved you. And then I'd burn them as soon as the next pair arrived."

She holds up two fingers. The length of them shines with her arousal.

I open my mouth, and she climbs onto my lap, swiping around my lips first and then between them. The taste of her melts onto my tongue, and I can't help the moan it draws from my throat.

She smiles that sexy, confident smile of hers and whispers, "You're obsessed with me."

"Isn't that obvious by now?"

Moving her body closer, she presses her tits against my chest and grinds her pussy over my cock. Before our lips even meet, she's licking into my mouth. Her hunger for me amplifies every sensation buzzing beneath my skin. She reaches between us, and we both watch as she rubs the head of my cock along her clit and cunt.

"No more teasing. Let me see you take me like a good fucking wife," I rasp out, watching as her pussy lips part and slide up and down my cock.

A moan catches in her throat. "You're much larger than what I'm used to, Daddy," she says as she works herself over me. "I need the tease."

I wrap my arm around her and flip us so she's lying flat. "Then let me make things a little wetter so I can slide into your pretty little pussy."

"Oh my god," she groans, writhing against me. "Say that again." Biting her lip, she looks down at me as I push her knees wider.

"Pretty." I spit where I'm about to eat. "Little." I rub my thumb along the hood of her clit, and then work two fingers into her. "Pussy."

She moans, long and loud, head tilted down to watch everything I'm doing.

I twist my wrist and curl my fingers deep inside, finding the spot that I know is going to flood me if I can work her just right. Moving my fingers faster, I add more pressure and lean in to use my tongue against her clit, humming at her taste.

It doesn't take long for her legs to tense. So I lift my mouth, and instead of easing up, I add more pressure, working her harder, knowing she's going to fucking come. "That's my girl. Come for Daddy."

That's all it takes.

Hadley exhales harshly, her body tremoring, neck arching back, and like a wound-up fuck toy, she cries out as she douses me. Coming so hard that her pussy squirts and makes a fucking mess of us. I couldn't care less. Smirking, I kneel up and tap the head of my cock along her clit, knowing she's extra sensitive. She lets out the cutest whimper.

"You okay, sugar?"

Opening her eyes in a daze, she drags her fingers along her mouth. "I'm more than okay. I want to do that again."

"Mind if I fuck you first?" I say, still petting her swollen pussy with the head of my dick.

"Still not sure how this fits, but yeah, let me see you slide inside, Daddy."

Fuck. I nudge myself into her cunt and watch on eagerly as she stretches for me. Slow and soaking wet, her pussy accepts every fucking inch without pause. My eyes flick to hers, making sure she's alright. "Good?"

She smiles, nodding eagerly. "Exquisite."

I move over her and settle close to her chest, kissing her lips and letting my tongue dance with hers briefly. I lose all sense of where my mouth goes from there as I roll my hips into her deeply. Pulling back, I graze my teethe along her chin, and she moans as I thrust a little deeper. It's exactly what I need to let go and take her how I need to. There's been too much time spent wanting this, and adrenaline still courses through me from earlier. Her legs wrap around me as I pull her higher onto the couch so she's propped up for me to gain better leverage to fuck her hard and punishingly, only to do it all over again.

Dragging my hands up her center, I swipe at the sweat that drips between her tits. "Do you have any idea how fucking sexy you are?" I breathe out.

"Show me," she says, her hands gripping onto my shoulders. "Fill me up."

My hips move at the same pace, only deeper, bottoming out and hitting her where I can feel her orgasm building. Every muscle in her legs holds tight until they're shaking, her breath hitching as she starts to whisper, "Oh god. Oh god. Tell me I can. Oh god, please, please, please."

Jesus Christ, she was waiting for me to tell her to come. My good fucking wife doesn't even need the direction. She asks for what I crave without even realizing it. I roll into her with three more powerful thrusts that have her whimpering and tell her, "Come for me, Hadley."

And she does. Her pussy grips me just as she screams. It's enough to make my vision blur, and the pressure that had been building finally releases as I come inside her, filling her with every pulse and thrust. I can barely catch my breath as my orgasm works its way through me, her fingers somewhere in the background, gliding along my skin as I rest my forehead against her chest. Opening my eyes, I rub the cum that's started to leak out between us around us both.

"You're so fucking filthy, Foxx," she says through a hazy giggle.

I smile at her and swipe it up her stomach and around her nipples. "Now you are too."

When I start to pull my hand back, she grabs my wrist and guides the cum-soaked fingers to her lips and sucks. As she drags them out, I'm speechless. "Tastes like sugar, Daddy."

I nearly come again just at her words and the sight of this perfect fucking woman.

When I finally let my cum drip out of her, I shift us both, draping her body on top of mine. The fucked-up part of me wants to hold her here and allow us both to linger in the mess we've made.

I trail my fingers up and down the center of her back, along the curve of her spine and down to her beautifully curved ass. "Will you go somewhere with me?"

She hums, and then props herself up on her elbows on top of my chest. That's when I notice her boots are still on. "If it's a place to go and have a lot of sex, then that's a rhetorical question." Studying my face, she draws her fingers around my jaw and up toward my hairline. It feels so good; I can't help but shut my eyes and enjoy every second of it.

"I have some friends that I want you to meet."

"Ace, are you already trying to introduce a swing couple? I mean, I'm not against it, but it feels kind of fast—"

I pinch her side and laugh with her. "I don't share, sugar. Sounds hot in theory, but I can barely handle the idea of you fucking around with other people before me."

"Ace, I'm a thirty-five-year-old woman who's always leaned into her sexuality. Be thrilled that I've figured out the things I like. And the fact that I've just realized there hasn't been a single person I've ever had before you who's satisfied me as completely."

Warmth blankets me at the admission and how I feel exactly the same. How it feels to have her this way—the ease of it, the way I'm not sure I'll ever get enough of her. The way she's looking at me.

"What I was saying is that I have friends in Colorado who I'd like to go see. They've turned their small town into a tourist hot spot, even beyond the mountain sports attractions. I'd like to show it to you. See if you think it might be something we can do here."

"We?" she asks while grabbing the packet of Pop Rocks

from the side table. I can't help but smile that she didn't ask where they came from, just saw them there and dove in. She shakes out some onto her tongue. The sound and smell of cherry is too good not to sample.

I run my thumb along the center of her neck. "Yes. You and me." Moving my fingers around the nape of her neck, I bring her lips to mine. The way this woman kisses me feels like I never understood the power of lips and tongues. I feel it everywhere when she slows it down and the popping rocks tingle. The taste of too-sweet cherry mingling with the taste of us is too good.

She smiles against my lips and pulls back to sprinkle more in her mouth. "When do we leave?"

"Maybe in a week or so. But right now, I think I need to taste you again." I slap her ass and grab it tight.

A laugh bursts from her as I move her body up until she's where I want her. She moves up, her knees on either side of my head, and I run my hands along her thighs, encouraging her to sink down farther.

"My Pop Rocks weren't cutting it?" she teases. "Wait, where did these come from—Oh god," she exhales as I tilt my head up and swipe my tongue along her slit.

"I like how you taste better. Now stop hovering. I need you on my mouth. Make it hard for me to breathe, sugar, and ride my fucking tongue."

Chapter 32

Hadley

June: An iced coffee waiting for me just the way I like it (except I think he swapped out cream and honey for his protein shake... It's not terrible.)

An All-Star jersey signed by the greatest pitcher of all-time, Gray Turner.

My car has been cleaned spotless—I've discounted the idea of it being sprites who have a hankering for muscle cars and decide it must be the husband.

I ROLL MY HIPS AGAINST his plush lips and relish the way he holds my thighs so I can grind myself at just the right angle. It's the perfect amount of pressure and so fucking freeing to practically smother a man as he eats you out. Tipping my head back, I hold on to my breasts, pinching both nipples as I get lost in the rhythm of chasing my orgasm.

He growls just as I'm about to come again, running his teeth along my clit as I jerk against his mouth, moaning my release until I'm out of breath and still wanting more. "I could do that every fucking morning and never tire of it."

My lips tilt up, cracking a dazed smile. "You making threats down there?"

He hums first, and then pauses a moment to say, "Promises."

It's one of the many things about Atticus Foxx that makes him so successful. He does what he promises. My days look different from his most of the time. My nights end late, anywhere between two and three in the morning. And he's always waiting for me. It doesn't matter what time his first meetings are happening or if he has to host a breakfast with vendors; every night, no matter what time I walk in that door, he's waiting.

Often, he's in his office, sipping on something and in some roundabout way has a snack prepared for before I go to bed. A nonchalant bowl of carbonara or casual grilled chicken pita.

"What do you mean, you didn't eat dinner?" he asked when I shoveled a handful of grapes into my mouth from the refrigerator at 2:45 a.m. before he lifted me up on the counter.

My eyebrows rose at his bossy tone. "Well, it was busy. I was down a server, and typical nights like this mean a bag of Dot's Pretzels and an apple for balance."

He was not a fan, and that was when the heated dinners started. A plate of something delicious would be hot and ready next to him when I came home.

We have a chess game in progress that's been ongoing for days by now. I know I'm going to end up winning, but I've entertained a move per night before he either licks my pussy while sprawled on his desk or finger fucks me as I brush my teeth. He's ravenous for me, and I never in my life, even with a decently confident self-esteem, have felt more sexy or beautiful.

"Hadley, do you think Duchess Fergie might like silver or pink?" Lily calls out.

I stuff my pen into my journal and slip on my boots. I didn't realize what time it was. Time seems to move quickly when the days are filled with more than just me to look after. While Ace is a very capable man, I also take Griz into account. Spending time with both of them whenever I can.

Faye and Lark come up behind Lily, holding two buckets and a Caboodle. After watching the horses in the winner's circle displayed on the big screen from the Kentucky Derby, Lincoln's girls decided that my horses needed to feel pretty too. I agreed.

"Alright, this is nontoxic, biodegradable, cosmetic-grade, silver-and-pink glitter all-natural oil for what I'm betting will be the prettiest fucking horses in all of Kentucky," Faye says as we move into the stables.

"Faye!" Lily and Lark call out with knowing grins.

"Yeah, I know." She exhales. "Curse purse. I already paid ahead, knowing I was coming to see your Auntie Hadley." The girls are eleven and thirteen now, and while their curse purse started when they were much younger, I'm betting that if they could swing it, the little swindlers will have the curse purse in effect until they start having to contribute.

The blaring music of Stevie Nicks pulls right up to the stables and flicks all of our attention to the double sliding doors.

Julep comes barking inside, practically announcing her favorite person's arrival. And the music doesn't turn off; instead, it gets louder, and with it comes Laney yelling the words at the top of her lungs—ones that all of us know pretty damn well. We croon in unison about midnight skies and white-winged doves.

I smile and shout to Lark and Lily, "How do you two know these words?"

They shout back, "It's Stevie and Miley!" As if that's a completely reasonable answer. It is, but I don't know if I've ever been prouder.

It's a core memory moment for me, one I never thought I'd be lucky enough to have in my life—badass women who match my energy and make me feel all levels of warmth and love.

Laney laughs as she lowers the volume and says, "Do you know how excited I am for a girls' day?"

I bark out a laugh. "Clearly."

"I brought the important things—Red Vines, chocolate-covered gummy bears, and sour straws for my favorite preteens." She winks at Lark and Lily. "Girls, help me put all of this out and pour some lemonade before we dive into brushing out the horses."

Laney hands me a Red Vine, but I shake my head, pulling out a clementine from my back pocket. I meant to eat it before heading outside this morning. "How's married life?" Laney asks as we watch Lark and Lily brush Fergie's mane.

I don't even try to bite back the smile. "Better than I expected."

Faye hits my arm with the back of her hand. "You're happy."

It isn't a question. It's an observation.

"I'm enjoying all aspects of it." I glance at them both. "Especially his filthy, delicious mouth and the way he touches me." I swallow as I think about what he really does to me. "He makes me feel safe, cared for, and..." I sigh. "I just sighed, didn't I?"

"Yep, and I love it," Laney says, picking up the tack box to go help the girls.

"You did," Faye says over a mouthful of gummy bears. "But I fucking love it too. Welcome to the wonderful world of being obsessed with your husband. It's highly underrated."

I smile and pop another piece of clementine in my mouth and think, *Been here for a while now.*

Over the course of the morning, we manage to bling out both Fergie and Lady with silver sparkle hooves after a full grooming—from wash to brush.

Faye gives me a smile. "What did you think about the new set from last night?"

My phone buzzing pulls my attention to a local Kentucky number this time.

> **UNKNOWN:**
> You have no idea what you're doing... funds have been promised to me and already allocated. I expect the deposit that has been promised.

> **UNKNOWN:**
> Do you really think ignoring this is going to make me go away?

It's the kind of distraction that would usually make me feel anxious, but today, I'm not going to play the victim. I block the number, delete the messages, and focus back on my stunning friend.

"I love all of your choices when it comes to music and costumes, so until the day you're telling me you don't want to do burlesque anymore, I'll always be on board with your sets."

She nods. "I've been having so much fun with the new singer and band too. It's a great addition, Hadley."

She glances at her phone, and instead of keeping the conversation on burlesque, she peeks at where Laney is with the girls, making sure they're out of earshot, and says, "I wasn't sure if I should mention this, but there's been some discourse at the station between my FBI contacts and local PD in regard to your father."

"Anything I should be concerned about?" I ask, suddenly uneasy once again.

This is one of the few crossed lines we have to deal with every now and then. Faye and her sister are who helped bring all of what Finch & King had been doing to light. Their mother had worked for my father as a horse trainer. I never once had a negative thought about Faye or her sister, Maggie. Only that I wish they had shown up sooner and found a way to get my father locked up before he had hurt so many people.

"Not right now, but the guys at the station are pissed off about his house arrest deal. FBI went hard and heavy, and then the district attorney eased up by not making him sweat it out in central lockup while he awaited trial."

"I don't disagree with them," I say to her. But then noticing she looks a bit nervous too, I ask, "You doing okay?"

She lets out a clipped laugh. "Am I okay? I want to make sure you are." With a leveling, tight-lipped smile, she says, "If everyone does their job like they're supposed to, he'll get exactly what he deserves. And then I think the both of us will be just fine."

Reaching out, she squeezes my hand. I give her a squeeze back and a genuine smile. I'm planning to do what I can now to help make things right and use whatever power I have to fix some of the wrongs my father and his business partners caused. And serve a little punishment of my own in the process. It won't undo any of the loss or hurt, but it will put pieces of our town back together again. Starting with getting business owners out of the red and spending as much of the Finch & King money as I possibly can to help them do it.

"That will be a complete closing of the account, Miss Finch. Are you sure that—"

I cut him off and make it very clear that I don't want to be asked if I know what I'm doing. "Rethink asking that question, sir. If I were my husband, I bet you would never consider such a condescending curiosity."

This afternoon, I walked into the bank with Ace, invited the realtor who handles all of the commercial real estate in Fiasco, and felt confident with a solid plan that should feed a long-term strategy. And it started with cleaning my father out and doing it with fucking flare.

He swallows down whatever uneasiness he may have had, face turning red as he nods.

"Gentlemen, I'm currently the executor of my father's entire estate, which means you're going to do as I wish. Roy?" I smile and turn to my left to carry on. "Roy is my attorney and is present to be sure that I don't have any problems. On top of this, I'd like what's left in my trust fund to be rolled into a high-yield savings account. I have a plan for it, but we can discuss that at another time."

Kentucky isn't full of prudish misogynists, but they do still exist. They're peppered in throughout just about any state where the main sources of income lean more masculine. Here, there's still a boys-club mentality in most arenas. Specifically the arena where Wheeler Finch has a lot of money tied up, and I'm planning to reallocate all of it.

It takes just over two hours to wipe the accounts clean. My father no longer has the means to hurt anyone else. And he's going to be in for a very rude awakening that there's no longer collateral considering that's how he had kept his attorneys.

When everything is transferred to Ace's and my newly formed joint account, I turn to the real estate broker and tell him, "I would like to purchase all the commercial real estate on Main. I don't care who from; make the offer worth their while, and I'll pay cash. You know I'm good for it." I wink. "If the bank has any liens or outstanding loans for those properties, I'd like to take care of those as well. Oh, and when that's set, I would like to sell them to the following people for one dollar."

I slide a sheet listing out all the business owners on Main. Ace covers his mouth, trying not to laugh at the way the group around the table nearly chokes on their own saliva.

"Roy, please make sure that all of these business owners receive their offers within the next two weeks…"

Their wide-eyed and slack-jawed expressions are priceless. And I'm ready to tackle the pushback on my demands.

"I'll be outside when you're ready," Ace says, kissing my forehead as he stands and excuses himself. I could have done this on my own, but I wanted him here. He made me feel like this is as much his burden as mine, and I feel stronger having him at my side.

Just over an hour later, we pull up to the house, and I haven't stopped smiling. We stopped for a celebratory donut and chatted with Presh. Her raspberry-filled beignets melted in my mouth as Ace asked her if she had seen his grandfather again recently.

"Heard Griz came for a visit a little while ago."

She eyed him warily and shook her head before she said, "He knew it was strawberry season and that I'd have some chocolate-covered ones."

"Is that all?" he asked her. "No other side business exchange?"

It felt like a strange question to ask. The only other business she ran besides her incredible baked goods were fake IDs. And I'm not sure why Griz would ever need one of those.

"These won't be as good tomorrow, but for breakfast," I say, kissing the tips of my gathered fingers, "waaaaaay better than your overnight oats."

He smiles, throwing the car in park. "You're welcome to make breakfast, sugar."

I shake my head. "Nope, that was a very specific item in our agreement. And I love everything else you make, but that was a tad too healthy for me the other day. Griz knows where it's at with his breakfast orders."

Reaching his hand out for mine, he pulls me closer as I add, "You handle the cooking. And cleaning. It's yours and Griz's place, after all."

He stops us from moving any farther along the side path of the house. "Would you want a place that's yours? Or ours?"

My heart stutters. Hearing him say the word "ours" with such vulnerability makes me warm and cozy. It feels really good to make up a part of a whole. "I like it here," I say, looking at the modern farmhouse. "This house has felt like home to me for so long. I think I need to add a little more of me to it, but I wouldn't want somewhere new."

He clears his throat. "Living with my grandfather wasn't something I planned, but it just worked out that way. You know that he and I butt heads, but I like having him around. He was the only one who made me feel like I wasn't going to drown from trying to be everything for my brothers when my parents passed." Tipping his head to the side, he gets lost in the memories for a moment. "And then it just became convenient. It's big enough here that if we didn't want to see the other person, we wouldn't have to."

"Let's put it this way. Griz is my family now in the most official way that I'm going to get. And let's not pretend we're living in close quarters. There are, what?" I smile, thinking about how many nights I stayed here and I wasn't sure if either of them noticed. "Three bathrooms on our side of the house alone? It's not like we're sharing much space.

"Why are we going this way?" I ask as we skirt around the side of the house and down a little farther until we come parallel to where the newly constructed rickhouse is being built. It goes right over the space that burned down with their oldest barrels inside. It was a helluva mess. It went up in flames a couple of years ago; we were lucky it didn't spread, but Griz was smart. They had built the places that barrels of bourbon would age with enough distance between them for that exact reason.

"Do you know what barrels will end up in there yet?" I ask him, eyeing the new wood and frame.

"Yes. None," he says so matter-of-factly that I look up at him, thinking I heard him wrong.

"None?" I chuckle. "Are you about to make a joke about it being none-ya business?"

He lets out a sniffed laugh. "No. But I'm thinking about doing something else there. I'm not entirely sure what yet, but

I'm hoping to pull some inspiration. And it's very much your business."

I brush off how much I love that he said that and instead ask, "Inspiration from where?"

His arms wrap around my waist. "The friends I mentioned in Colorado. They've invited me to see some of what's new out there."

I smile at the idea of these friends of Ace's that exist in the world. He's charming and a businessman, but seeing him as a friend isn't something I've witnessed outside of his brothers.

The light from the day is long gone. And back here, there isn't much light pollution, not facing in this direction. The only glow comes from the summer string lights hung around the entertaining space behind the house. I lift his hand to my mouth and kiss his knuckles. There are plenty of sexy things that I'm fully capable of doing, but for some reason, that simple gesture makes him growl softly while his other hand grips my hip. He kisses my eyebrow, right over the scar I had gotten a long time ago. On a night when he made me feel as safe as he is right now.

"Make whatever arrangements you need for the bar. We're leaving tomorrow."

I must be punch-drunk because I let a laugh bubble out of me. "Tomorrow? How do you expect me to pull that off?"

He props his crooked finger under my chin to lift my attention to his handsome face as he says, "I just watched you dismantle an entire business in a matter of a couple of hours. You're a badass, wife. That's how."

His words linger, seasoning and simmering under my skin. He challenges me. Impressing him is a nice payoff, but more than anything, making a person who truly cares for you proud is my biggest motivator. He's always my biggest motivator. Less than an hour later, I have a full schedule for the bar and staff to step up and have a busy weekend. And I'm more than ready for the same.

Chapter 33

Ace

Griz crosses his arms, cutting me off, "What is it you think you know about Hawkins?"

I move around him as I say, "Been curious for a while. But didn't know anything until he confirmed it for me at Ditch the Derby."

Griz asks, "Confirmed what?"

"He's more than just pissed off, Griz. He made some kind of agreement with Wheeler, and I'm not about to trust a single thing he does next." I glance at the mint-green box on the counter. "Is that box of donuts fresh?"

"I went to see Presh," he says, clearing his throat and swiping his thumb along the edge of his mustache. It's a nervous habit of his and makes me pause. "Hadley loves those donuts. It was a nice morning for a drive. Just finished tuning up the golf cart."

It's a long ride all the way to the edge of town, even with his cart souped up.

"What're we tasting here?" he asks as he sidles up to the counter. He watches as I pull out an unmarked bottle of bourbon. I want him to know that I'm not angry with him. I want him to see that everything he's said to me I take and figure out a way to make it happen.

A loud thud at the bottom of the stairs has both of us whipping our heads around to find the source.

"Just my suitcase," Hadley singsongs. "All good."

My phone buzzes in my pocket.

> **THE JEWELER:**
> A little something is waiting for you at your desk.

> **ACE:**
> What we discussed?

> **THE JEWELER:**
> I took some liberties, but you'll be pleased.

"This trip an unofficial honeymoon?" Griz asks. Looking at the color of the bourbon and examining it in the light, he continues without me answering. "That mean you finally told'er how you really feel then?"

I haven't. I show her, but I haven't said those words to her yet. Lust is easier. We have that in spades. A part of me feels selfish to say something so permanent to her, like that I love her. "How do you think I really feel about her?" I ask, curious to know what he's seeing from the outside looking in.

He laughs. "Atticus, that woman has had you by the balls

since she came back from college. I honestly wasn't sure if you'd ever get out of your own way."

When he takes a taste, his eyebrows raise. "Nice notes. Simple. There's a smoky aftertaste that feels different."

I've never felt more pleased with myself at hearing both of those things from him. "You mind telling me exactly what it is you're planning, old man?"

Without skipping a beat, he says, "No clue what you're talking about." He shifts for another sip, and then, before I can say anything else, he lets out an audible exhale. "You've done everything I've ever asked of you. Even when it turned you into someone else, crossing lines and bending rules in the name of what was right for our brand and our family. Even now…" He tilts his head to the Glencairn glass. "You did something different, found something and someone to care about more than just this business."

The confession isn't something I expected. I'm not too proud to realize I still need his approval, regardless of how old I am. He raised me, and there's nothing that feels better than making someone else proud of you. I forgot what that felt like.

"There are things I need to do now. And I need you to let me do them," he says, knocking the reality back into the moment. I've known he's been making arrangements, but I'm not ready to let him do it the way he believes he needs to.

I fire off a text to be sure there isn't something worth knowing.

ACE:
Anything interesting on our friend's phone?

> **FAYE:**
> Incoming text from the chief to his brother just now.

> **FAYE:**
> We do not have the luxury of ignoring him. You need to come with me.

I could make some assumptions, but it's a waste. By the time I'm back, most of my concerns will be resolved.

> **ACE:**
> Let me know if there's anything more while we're away.

"Alright," Hadley says, coming back and leaning against the archway of the kitchen. "Griz, don't eat all of the cheese I have in that fridge. Your body will *not* like you."

He gives my shoulder a squeeze, and I nod. I have plans of my own that will end up fixing some problems and get him what he wants. He gives me one more glance before he turns to look at Hadley. And like the conversation didn't happen, his mustache twerks up as he says, "I think you should rename it to 'Griz dinner.' It has a nice little ring to it, don't you think?"

While they carry on, I decide it's time for me to call in a favor I've been keeping in my pocket for a while now.

> **ACE:**
> Things will be clear by July 5th. Make your way back to Fiasco with her then.

"This might be the most beautiful view I've ever seen," Hadley says, awed, as she stands out on the balcony of our suite. A four-hour private flight and a gondola ride to our resort has both of us more eager than tired to enjoy some time away from things in Fiasco.

"I've always thought so," I tell her, smiling at the way she takes it all in. Her hair is up in a messy bun on top of her head, and she's wearing a New Zealand rugby club sweatshirt, black leggings, and black shiny stilettos. She's fucking cute, sexy as hell, and the best view I've seen in a long time.

There's a term in chess called a zugzwang. It's what Wheeler Finch had done to his daughter. She was put at a disadvantage because she was forced to make moves she wouldn't have made otherwise. The only problem is, he never factored in the idea that it would backfire if the board had suddenly fallen and then restarted. That's what my wife did with his entire fortune. From real estate to tied investments, she took all of it and started a new game. Only this time, she knows she's in it. And if there's one thing about Hadley Foxx, she's fucking phenomenal at strategy and wearing a proverbial crown. Smart and thoughtful decisions have now been put into play that will impact our town in ways they don't even realize yet. It's the least selfish thing I've ever witnessed, *and fuck*, do I love her even more for it.

When she realizes what I've said, she turns to look at me with a broad smile. "Took you long enough to say something, Daddy."

I move fast, wrapping my arm around her waist before she can pull away. "What did I tell you about throwing around that nickname?" I smile into her as I drag my lips along the side of her neck and breathe her in.

"Maybe you should remind me. The air is really thin up here." With a hum, her hands run up my neck and her fingers push into my hair. It's the simplest thing, but being touched by her feels so damn good.

A buzzer rings out, signaling someone is at the door, and it has her slipping out of my arms and moving toward it. When the door swings open, it's a familiar face. A friend I never expected to have, but a friend nonetheless.

"Holy shit, Atticus Foxx is in Strutt's Peak. I can't fucking believe it."

I cross my arms as Law Riggs leans against the doorway and smiles wide. His easygoing demeanor is contagious, and I find myself mirroring it. "Then come to find out you're bringing your wife?" He holds out his hand for her and says, "And she's even prettier than you are, Foxx." Even though I know he's happily married, and the fact that I probably speak more often to his wife than him, I still find myself not liking his hands anywhere near her as he pulls her into a hug.

They both stop abruptly and turn to look at me.

Hadley's eyebrows pinch as she says, "Did you just growl?"

I don't say anything; instead, I lean against the wall and try to dial back whatever the fuck that was. I also observe two people who I'm just realizing are guaranteed to cause trouble together.

"Holy shit, you did." Hadley looks at Law with lifted eyebrows. "Quick, hug me again, let's see how mad we can make him."

Law barks out a laugh. "I think I love you."

"Hadley Foxx. It's a pleasure to meet you, but I am very taken." She turns and smiles at me, and then says, "I really love how Hadley Foxx sounds."

I try not to react to how much hearing it hits me square in the chest.

"Law Riggs, and the pleasure is mine. And my wife does the whole brooding thing too. They're a good time together. I think you and I will balance it all out very nicely." He claps his hands in front of him with a shit-eating grin. "Now, how about I show you around this place. Then we can talk about our newest addition." He looks over at me, and then back at Hadley. "I think it's the motivation for coming here."

I met some of the Riggs family on my last trip out here, but this time, it's less about being schmoozed for selling them some great bourbon and more about seeing firsthand some of the big tourist boosters they've created in the past few years. The Riggs family, much like mine, wants to see their small town thrive.

We head on out and get a complete tour of the small mountain town, with Law's wife, Contessa, joining us. I've only ever been once when we were first negotiating a specialty bourbon for Law's exclusive events and VIP adventures, but I didn't take the time to see the parallels of this place and Fiasco. The landscape is entirely different, but there's originality to what they offer. For them, it's mountain sports, and for us, it's the mix of horses and bourbon. Riggs Outdoor is busy, the offices bustling with people working on ad campaigns and social media shoots. There's an expansive indoor rock climbing facility that hosts Olympic climbers as trainers and a sports rehab center that works with the U.S. Olympic Ski & Snowboard team.

"We've tripled the amount of people we can host and accommodate during our busy seasons, and then doubled it during the summer months as well. The mountains absolutely draw the most attention, but it's the exclusive excursions and adult-only adventures where we've seen the most growth."

Law's almost too excited when he says, "My sister-in-law runs a tattoo shop if you were feeling like something to mark the occasion. And I know that, Ace, you enjoy rock climbing. You should consider an adventure outside since it's the perfect season for it."

"Atticus Foxx, how have you kept this place a secret?" Hadley asks with a smile.

Tessa cuts in and says, "Ace tells me you own a speakeasy?"

"Midnight Proof," she answers with a nod. "Doors have been open just over five years now. It delivers on that sexy, sultry 1920s Gatsby glamour. I have a phenomenal cocktail menu, and I brought in a resident burlesque dancer who performs with a talented jazz trio." Her smile shows her pride. "It's a labor of love, and I'm lucky for its success."

"It's not luck," I say as I look at my wife. "You work hard, know what people want, and deliver. You're a helluva businesswoman."

Tessa looks at me with a knowing smirk. "Marriage looks good on you. I wasn't sure I'd live to see the day."

"That's part of the motivation behind our trip," I tell her, taking a sip of my bourbon blend. I forgot how good this one came out. It was a small batch—four barrels only. "Enjoy some time away from our businesses and maybe research a little of the magic you've packed into this place. See what might translate to our corner of the world."

The truth is, I didn't tell Hadley exactly what places we would visit while we're out here. The progress and investments the Riggs family had made to see their town flourish are impressive.

"Tomorrow night, if you're up for something a little taboo…" Law says, and then pauses, glancing at his wife. They have a private exchange of some kind, and then he continues. "There's a place here that I can imagine your wife might find… inspiring."

It's what I was hoping they'd suggest. A place that aligns exceptionally well with a bourbon brand, a speakeasy owner, and adults looking to play on a getaway.

Hadley's blue eyes bounce around the table before landing on me with interest. I try my best to hide my smile, but end up moving my hand across my mouth and jaw.

"Oh Foxx, you didn't tell her what she was getting into, did you?" Tessa asks. She leans closer to my wife and speaks quietly to her. The moment I see Hadley's smile crack, then eyes widen, I know I made the right decision in making it a bit of a surprise.

She fist pumps. In the middle of a restaurant, thrusts her closed fist into the air, and says, "I'm sorry, but if I had told myself that I would be sitting in this exact scenario, like, a year ago, I would have laughed so hard that I would have peed a little." She points at me, giddy as can be. "I love you."

But she realizes what she says a fraction of a second too late. Her mouth snaps shut, and she only blinks, knowing she can't backtrack. Not in this company.

So I lean into it. It feels too good to hear it. My brave fucking girl. I let those few words, whether she meant them or not, linger for just a few more seconds. Moving my hand under the table, I slide it onto her thigh and squeeze. "I know, sugar. Me too."

I watch her throat bob as she swallows, eyes locked on mine as Tessa continues to chat with her and Law with me. We both said something that was never meant to be said when you're in a supposed fake marriage.

"I have a few masks you might like to choose from for

tomorrow evening. Since it's an anonymous club, all faces must be covered in some way," Tessa says, pulling my focus back to the plans forming in front of me. She glances at Law. "It's how we met though. Women were the only ones wearing masks at that particular establishment. It was ladies' choice, so the men had to be brave enough not to wear a mask if they wanted to participate. For men at our place, it's optional." Bringing her attention to Hadley, she says, "I know Law wanted to try to convince your husband to make another small batch of his specialty bourbon for us, so how about you come with me and tell me all about your speakeasy. I want to hear more about this burlesque dancer."

Hadley nods, already grabbing her purse. "Well, she's incredible and my sister-in-law, if you can believe it."

"Oh, I can. I have a small handful of those myself," she says as they get up from the table. When Tessa moves to leave without saying a proper goodbye to her husband, Law calls out, "Bunny, do not leave this room without kissing me."

Hadley smiles at me as she watches Tessa roll her eyes and walk over to her husband begrudgingly. I crook my finger twice, telling *my* wife to come to me. And she doesn't hesitate, looping her arms around my neck and sitting sideways on my lap as she says, "I have a feeling we're about to have way more fun this weekend than I expected."

I think she's fucking right.

Chapter 34

Hadley

June: Following the white rabbit

Anything worth talking about and remembering is always heavily impacted by the way it's presented. It's why Midnight Proof is half as successful as it is. The experience is just as impressive as the lighting and mood of the curated style. It's exactly how I feel riding the elevator to the highest level of our hotel. I would've never known it's here, and I think that's the point. While places in Strutt's Peak are named after the mountains and lean into the vibe of mountain sports, this place is hidden in plain sight. It can only be accessed by key cards that were delivered to our room, and I learned that the vetting process to even be allowed entry is quite extensive.

The doors to the elevator open, and along each side of the hallway are full-length windows looking out onto what appears simply as a darkened sky lit up with stars and the outline of peaks shadowed in the foreground. At the end of the hallway, there's a single door. There's no name or words, simply a gold statue of a rabbit head wearing a monocle. It opens with the swipe of a card, and a greeter stands behind the door.

"Miss, how may I help you this evening?" a beautiful woman asks.

I clear my throat and smile. "I'm here to follow the white rabbit."

When I chose a black lace mask from Tessa's rather eclectic selection, she informed me that I needed to respond to that question correctly; otherwise, I'd be escorted to a bar on the other side of the hotel. She said, *"It keeps curious patrons from gaining access who haven't been properly selected to join."*

I did a little bit of shopping for tonight too. Law's sister owns a gorgeous boutique of casual wear and lingerie. There were a few cocktail dresses, and one in particular that caught my eye. It matched the mask perfectly. I was in the mood for bold. The black lace dress is long-sleeved, cut to a midi-length, hitting right at the calf, and hugs every part of me. Since it's lace, there's a matching black balconette bra I paired with cheeky panties covering barely anything. It's exactly what I would imagine wearing to a sex-positive club like this one.

When the next door opens, the low lighting feels moody and glows just bright enough around the bar that stands in the center of the vast room. It isn't crowded, but there are plenty of people peppered throughout. Men in formalwear and women in complementing attire are more and less covered than I am. Too-large chandeliers hang low for ambiance, the light reflecting off the walls lined with a dark design that looks tactile. I want to touch it. A low beat of drums and an accompanying bass feels familiar—similar to Midnight Proof. This one thumps through the floor as a swoony higher trumpet or sax hums along the edges of the space. I can't tell if it's live music or a DJ, but I can feel the low notes do the work and set the tone of the night ahead.

Tessa has explained they'd kept with the "women's choice" concept that had been a part of the London sex club she and Law had visited. Women's choice simply meant women are allowed to approach men, but not the other way around. Other rules applied as well. Mask colors depicted interests. And if anyone had a hard limit or didn't want to play, then they simply kept to the center room and could watch.

My skin is already flushed, the heat creeping into my cheeks. I'm eager to watch what's happening around me and to find my husband. It's the kind of place that makes you feel like you're being admired. And maybe it's just confidence in knowing who and what's waiting for me, but I'm feeding on it.

I smile at a cocktail waitress who stops in front of me, a sheer black mask covering only her eyes, with bold, red painted lips. "French 75 for the beautiful woman in black lace."

I have to tamp down the sheer anticipation of knowing exactly who ordered this for me and that he's in this room right now. As I take a sip, the botanical taste of gin mixed with the sour splash of lemon eases down my throat. I practically hum at how well it's made.

"You're the most delicious thing I've ever seen, sugar." Ace's voice vibrates along my neck before he presses his lips against my skin. I knew he'd find me.

My mouth waters, thinking about his words and how often he's tasted me. When I turn to look at him, he's not wearing a mask, the cocky bastard. In a tux that isn't too different from the suits he usually dons, he's exchanged the usual white-collared shirt for black. And of course, no tie. It's buttoned up just to the point where his chest hair is covered. I'm almost lightheaded at how intensely sexy this man is—broad and so much bigger than me, borderline arrogant, combined with well-manicured facial scruff that leaves the best kind of burns, and his salty dark hair…he's my fantasy. No, better—he's my fucking husband, and damn, do I want him.

"I could say the same thing about you," I say, leaning into him as his hand grips around my hip and squeezes like he needs to hold on tight. "Tell me we get to play here tonight."

"We get to play here tonight," he says quietly, his words like a caress. "Tell me what you'd like to do." For as much as I melt for his dominance, I can't help but feel devotion at the way he defers to my wants.

As I focus on the details of the people around us—their closeness, the motion of their bodies—I swallow roughly. "Have you ever played in front of an audience before?"

"I have," he admits. And the smile on his face is all that I need to know whether or not he liked it. "And I'd love nothing more than to allow strangers to watch me fuck you in all of your tight, wet places." He pulls me closer into him as his other hand moves around me and down along my ass. His fingers dance along the lace of my dress, tracing the line where my panties end and my pebbled skin begins. "That what you want? For me to show everyone how much you're mine?"

My mouth parts, and an escaping breath follows, my core aching already. "Yes," I exhale.

"Yes, what?" he says as his mouth drags across the sensitive skin on my neck.

I know exactly what he wants to hear, even without looking at the smirk I can feel playing on his lips. "Yes, Daddy."

"I'm going to ask for a room with a view." His hand circles

my waist tighter, and he growls as he peppers another series of slow kisses along the same path. "I'd like some of my bourbon to splash across your tits and drip into your pussy when I'm fucking you." That visual has me suppressing a moan as his nose runs up and down the path he just kissed. "Now be a good little wife and go get our bourbon."

This fucker. "Good little wife?" I can't help the way those words make me tense up and smile at the same time. He knew it would rile me up, too, simply by the smile he's trying his hardest to keep from cracking. The low laugh that vibrates against my skin drenches my panties instantly. Hell, it's the first time I realize I can be a feminist and still melt over dirty talk when it comes from Ace Foxx.

"Just go do it." He pinches the curve of my ass. "We both know you're the one who can boss me around every fucking way you want."

With my French 75 forgotten, I smile at the bartender. "I'd like that bottle of bourbon," I say, pointing to the Foxx Reserve on the top shelf.

"The entire bottle?" he asks.

When I nod, he doesn't balk at the request, simply plucks the bottle and asks, "How many glasses would you like, miss?"

"Two would be nice," I answer.

The woman to my right at the bar asks, "Do you think men like that are as good as the fantasy?"

I glance at the man she's referring to. And of course, it's my husband. "I do."

She hums to herself first, and then says, "He's got that daddy vibe, doesn't he, with that silver raked through his hair? And the dark suit."

I can feel her looking at me as I watch him and wonder how a place like this would do in our small town. A place where a woman can feel completely safe and able to act on her wildest fantasies. Whether it's just for one night or a succession of visits. I know why he wanted me to see this place. It isn't just for the playing and payoff. He wanted to see if this is something that I thought could work—maybe in tandem with Midnight Proof, or maybe just on its own as something new.

The chatty woman runs a finger along the edge of her glass, sizing up a man who's legally and unequivocally mine.

He's watching me now that he's finished speaking with one of the staff, and I hold up the bottle of his bourbon. His stoic gaze has hints of a smile, as if he knows exactly what's happening over here.

"Oh, I think Daddy likes you," she says with a hint of humor.

Biting my lip, I pluck the two glasses off the bar. "Oh, Daddy more than likes me." I raise an eyebrow as I lean in to tell her, "That's my husband."

I miss the look on her face because my eyes are locked on his. I know he was watching this entire exchange.

"Are you behaving?" he asks as I reach him.

"Never," I say on a laugh, taking a sip of bourbon directly from the bottle.

Reaching up, his hand cups my face as he whispers against my lips, "Such a brat."

I smile and wiggle my eyebrows. "Want to punish me?"

I nearly combust on the spot at the way his eyes flare. As butterflies flap wildly in my stomach, he lifts my arm above my head and gives me a spin. "I want to show you what happens when you trust me." Pressing a kiss to my wrist, he growls, "And, fuck yes, I want to punish you."

It feels like walking into box seats of an intimate theater. Our host ushers us to a grouping of plush leather chairs sectioned off only by waist-height partitions. The open-air space is the voyeur's lounge, with the focal point on the space slightly below. There's a satin bed and velvet chair in the center, and a wall lined with toys that range from crops and floggers to dildos and nipple clamps and everything in between. It's not nerves ticking my pulse higher; it's the sheer anticipation of watching something taboo—and doing it with a man who turns me on in the simplest of ways.

"A reminder," the host says. "This is not a performance. There will be no need for clapping, cheering, or other auditory remarks from the audience. You're welcome to enjoy it in any and every way you would like. Please feel free to press that button there." He nods to the small, framed button on the wall not too different from the one on the roof deck of my townhouse. "I've been informed that you are both VIPs, so whatever you need, at any time, please do not hesitate to ask." His attention shifts to me. "And if at any time, miss, you are uncomfortable, or would simply like something from the house, please press that button as well." He looks to Ace. "You may ask your female guest for something you would like, but this is a reminder that regardless of how you arrived, this is a ladies' choice venue. What she prefers is respect. Always."

My husband simply nods at the host in confirmation, and then he leaves, the door snicking shut behind him. It's the one thing I never questioned with Ace. He isn't the kind of man to take what isn't offered. And while I love that this particular establishment caters to the way things should always be, when it comes to him, I've only ever felt safe.

As soon as we sit, his arm drapes over my crossed legs, his

hand feeling the lace of my dress that goes past my thighs and halfway down to my calves.

The woman who steps into the space ahead draws my attention; it's the same woman I spoke with at the bar. That same confidence she had out there is in overdrive in here as she shrugs off her wrap dress, walks around the room, and sizes up her partner as if she's deciding if he's worthy.

Ace leans closer as he asks, "Are you ready for this?"

My mouth tips up into a coy smile. "I'm not sure watching people toy with each other will ever be as good as watching you slide your cock into me."

He barely lets me finish the thought before he's kissing me momentarily breathless. Shifting back, his lips still hover over mine as he says, "Right answer. Maybe you're a good girl, after all, *wife*."

I laugh at that. "Of all the things I am, dear husband, a good girl is not, and never will be, one of them." I tip my head to the side. "But that's exactly what drives you wild, isn't it?"

His hand squeezes my thigh. The eagerness I feel whenever he touches me sparks along every inch of my body, well aware of where we are and that we're not alone. Maybe that makes it even more heady.

"And you like it when I say things that make your tighties tent," I tease.

I smile and gaze into his pretty eyes, intense as they look back at me. His plush mouth and the way he smells like the oak barrels at home and the clementines on my nightstand have me dizzy for this man.

He exhales a low hum. "Then what kind of praise would you prefer?" he asks while working his hand slowly down my leg. He gathers the lace of my dress as he moves from my calf up to my knee and settles on my thigh again.

I glance around and make out the shapes of other people, but it's too dim with the way the lights are strategically placed to see much more. The space is intimate, and if I had to guess, no more than twenty people are spaced throughout. Cocktail servers are taking drink and prop orders before things begin. My body nearly shivers with excitement at not knowing who or what we'll witness, but I'm turned on simply by the vibes and the man molded against my side.

"I'll settle for adjectives that better describe me—exceptional, exquisite. And then you can always throw in, queen, wife, sugar, or simply…" I pause and articulate the last with a bratty smile. "*Mine.*" I've thought about all the things he's ever said around me, and *those* are instant panty-dampers.

I sink into the side of his body as his fingers move lightly over my shoulder, aimlessly. Turning my head, I watch him pour and sip his bourbon. When he glances at me, his lips tilt up. "How are you feeling?"

"Warm and a little needy," I say honestly. A part of me swoons at him even asking.

The huskiness in his voice sends a delicious shiver through me as he whispers in my ear, "Still trust me then?" He pushes my hair away from my neck so that he can drag his lips across the edge of my shoulder.

I release a breathy exhale at the slow and deliberate pace of his movements. "Yes," I whisper with a smile.

His fingers glide across the edges of my dress, along my collarbone, and down the slope of my breast. When I part my lips, he's quick to remind me to be nice and quiet. Dragging my dress up over my hips, he fists the lace so it pulls taut against my skin. "This looks beautiful on you."

"It will be more beautiful off of me." He's too much fun to

push. I bite my lower lip. "I know you have a thing for panties. These are rather pretty, don't you think?"

His thumb grazes my lips before his hand cuffs around the column of my throat. "Such a smart mouth," he teases as he tilts me where he wants me, but instead of kissing me, he bites at my lower lip first, and then runs his tongue along it, making me whimper.

Ace hums against my skin, his lips ghosting just below my ear. "You will not come until I let you."

My head whips toward him, thighs clenching. "Sounds like a bad idea."

His eyebrow quirks. And he lets out a muffled growl. "Then it sounds like you'll be self-servicing tonight."

I smirk, narrowing my eyes, thinking that he can't be serious. But his glare and lack of humor are an easy tell. He's serious. I let out a frustrated groan and sit up a little taller, peering back at him when I say, "I'm very good at self-servicing, if you remember."

His sexy mouth doesn't say anything else. He just gives a simple nod, knowing that I've heard his demand. But he's still waiting. "Say it," he whispers.

I squeeze my crossed legs as his fingers skate along my outer thigh.

"Tonight. You are not coming unless I permit you," he says, voice like gravel. "Now say, 'Yes, Daddy,' and watch."

I'm dead and on my way to heaven. I'm wet past the point of my panties. And I'm not sure I want to simply watch any longer.

"Yes, Daddy," I say, just as his fingers push lightly against my knee, encouraging my legs to uncross.

"Knees wide, sugar." He shifts his body beside me, wrapping his arm along the back of the oversize chair, and focusing on the scene unfolding in front of us. "And eyes on her."

The woman from the bar is lying out on a plush, round platform, her sheer lingerie set framing her lush figure. The dynamic between her and her partner feels like it's changed. She's no longer in charge while the man standing across from her takes his time choosing tools and toys from an expansive display. "Has anyone ever used those types of things on you before?" Ace asks.

I shake my head, keeping my focus on the long bar with leather cuffs on either end. And then the riding crop wrapped around the man's wrist. I'm chastising myself for never having thought of having a spare one for pleasure in addition to the ones in the stables. I glance along the tabletop with various straps, plugs, and gags. I know the mechanics of most of it—romance novels and falling down a rabbit hole of curiosity in a post-*Fifty Shades* era will do that to a woman. But witnessing them in use, or being on the receiving end, has yet to be on my experience card. "Do you find her attractive?" I ask him.

"She's very beautiful," he says, and then takes a drink of his bourbon. When he places it back on the side table, he leans into me, and with his lips dancing along my ear, says, "But she's far too obedient for my liking, and like every other woman, her curves aren't the ones I want in my hands. She doesn't rub her wrist when she's nervous. Her hair isn't wild. She doesn't have a freckle on her left cheek, just beside her nose that I love to look at. And her lips don't tilt up along the right side when I talk."

My heart beats faster as I turn my head to him. "That was very detailed of you."

But instead of answering me, he wraps his arms further around me, just as he kisses my forehead. Then he's lifting and shifting me effortlessly into his lap as if I'm not a solidly built woman. There's something wildly sexy about being manhandled with the right man. I'm not tiny. My legs are long and muscular, and I have a softer center and round hips. Thick and fit. I learned a long time ago to love all the parts that make me whole, but I also take notice of that reality. And Ace lifts, shifts, and holds me without much effort.

With one arm still around my waist, he encourages me to relax, pressing my back to his front. It feels so good to be handled like this—carefully and dominating. My body warms as I sink into him. I'm rewarded with his hard cock pressing into my lower back. His hands fist the lace of my dress, exposing my panties, and cool air brushes against my pussy as I watch. "Be nice and quiet for me," he says quietly.

The items the man in front of us has chosen seem tame enough, but perhaps it's the determined way he's chosen them. Thoughtfully, but confidently. He bears that same dominant energy that practically billows off my husband. My mouth waters as he pushes one hand into the woman's long, dark hair and the other down the column of her neck.

Ace's hand snakes up between my breasts and to my neck, mimicking the same movement. His thumb rubs gently along my racing pulse, his lips beside my ear. "When are you going to realize that there could be thousands of beautiful women presented to me just like that…" He widens his legs, which in return, widens mine. His fingers skate along the edges of the panties that still cover me, with a slow glide back and forth over the gusset. "My attention has always been and always will be…" He trails off as his fingers dip beneath the fabric to find the lips of my pussy. A low growl escapes him as his fingers slip along my arousal. "On. You." He punctuates his point with a pinch on my clit.

My lips part as I gasp.

"Remember my rule, sugar."

You will not come until I let you. I groan at the reminder.

"Take these off," he says, pulling at the fabric of my panties. I lift just enough to loop my fingers into the material and do as he says. When I settle back where I was, so garishly displayed on top of him, he grabs my panties from my hand. "You're right, these are pretty, but your bare pussy dripping on my pants is so much better." One hand goes right back to wrapping around my throat, my body pressed into his as his fingers play with me exactly like I would be doing myself. "Eyes on her," he demands.

Her fingers trail between beautiful breasts that spill from her balconette bra, circling around a nipple that peeks through the red sheer material. Her mask is still in place, that deep red matching her full lips that part as she teases us—an exhibitionist at her finest, confident and ready to entertain. I admire her flair.

A gasp echoes from across the room, catching my attention. I forgot that we weren't the only observers.

"You're so wet for her," he hums against me. I hold on to his forearm, keeping the pressure of his hand against my throat. The way it feels to be touched this way, it's like ownership, and goddesses, does this man own me right now.

I move my head to the right so he can hear me when I say, "Not for her."

He must like that, because his fingers move to the hood of my clit and slap her twice before curving down and shifting into me. The change in pressure is so unexpected that I can't help but moan.

"This all for me then?" His lips drag along my jawline. "Show me. Squeeze my fingers nice and tight with your eager little cunt."

"Goddesses," I whisper. I do just as he demands, contracting and gripping, trying my fucking hardest not to squirm as he fingers me with a slow *come hither* motion, grazing parts of me that have my body heated and tensing.

"Watch what he's doing," Ace says against my ear.

I open my eyes and watch as the man lifts the spreader bar, forcing the woman's legs high and wide just as his mouth drags from her asshole up. He spits on her pussy, and then pushes the flap of his pants down just enough to take out his dick and slap it against what he just made wet. At the same time, Ace's fingers retreat, and he taps at the hood of my clit again. It stings as he does it twice more, and it's taking sheer force of will to keep an orgasm at the edges of my body.

"You're doing so well for me, wife. Are you ready to come yet?"

I swallow. As much as I want to, the torture and edging of this is too good to be done with just yet. "No," I breathe out. "Are you?"

He huffs a laugh as he shifts his legs wider. Two fingers fuck into me, but this time, his thumb presses onto my clit. The angle and the pressure are downright criminal. "More like ready to fuck you."

I let out a small whine. *I'm feral for this man.* "Tell me how," I basically beg. I watch the woman in red writhe in front of me with legs high and wide. The man sinks into her and stays there. One fast thrust, and he's to the hilt. She wants more, her thighs shaking at the stretch of him, and I feel it too as Ace tilts his hand, his fingers filling me wider and never stopping their delicious teasing.

"I think I'd like to see your mouth filled. Ease my cock into your throat," he whispers along my skin as his fingers against my neck ease their pressure. "Would you like that, swallowing me down? Taking everything I spill?" He lets out a small, humming laugh as another whine escapes me. "I think you would."

His fingers disappear, then slap my pussy again—one, two, three times. I moan and try to keep from giving in to the tingling sensation that's started to build behind my knees and up my back. "Please," I quietly beg once again. I have no shame about being so needy. Or for publicly bearing part of my body, or for garishly panting as I watch, feel, and want.

"No," he says as his hand from my throat moves down the length of me. His legs move even wider, opening me farther and rubbing his hard dick between us. One hand plays with my clit, while the other rubs along the edges of my pussy lips, not giving me what I want. "Now press the button."

The screaming moan from the woman in red steals my attention. She comes so hard that her whole body shakes, but the dominant man doesn't wait for her to finish. Instead, he uses the spreader bar, turning it over, and with it, her body follows. With her legs still spread, he pulls her to the edge of the surface, and then sinks into her again. He fucks her at a punishing pace as he holds her arms behind her. It's filthy and aggressive, but not nearly as enticing as the man holding me by my fucking pussy.

"Press the button, Hadley," he growls. I look to my left and see the framed Press for Service button and do what I'm told. I slap at it twice just as Ace sits up, taking me with him. Sitting higher and out of sorts, I blink slowly, pussy tingling, with my dress hiked to my waist. He takes his glass of bourbon and presses it to my mouth. With my eyes locked on his, I take a sip. Moments later, the host comes to us, and Ace loops his arm across my lap as I still sit perched against his straining dick. Without breaking eye contact with me, he says, "I want everybody out."

My lips tilt up at the request. And not only that, but at the dominant tone in his voice. Of course Atticus Foxx would be so bold as to demand the show stop and the place be vacated.

"Sir?" the host asks, not expecting it.

But it's me who breaks eye contact when I look at the host and say, "You heard him. Everybody out."

The host opens his mouth, but instead of saying anything in response, he simply nods and exits the way he came.

Ace smirks at me like he's proud. Fuck, do I like making this man proud of me. *Kink unlocked.* I sit on his lap sideways, eyes back on his, when he says, "I want a taste."

It's not rocket science to know exactly what he means, so I widen my legs, swipe two fingers along my soaked center, and then swipe them along his lips. As I pull back, he grabs my wrist, holding my hand in place to suck off the arousal he just played from me.

Around us, the room is uneasy with people moving. The couple in front of us both moan one more time before silence settles. Ace grabs the bottle of bourbon by its neck and takes a sip. Once he swallows, he says, "On your knees, now. Let me see exactly how brilliant that mouth is when it's choking on me."

I let out the tiniest sound, like I can't help myself with a request like that. When have I ever been so eager to suck a man off? Arrogance billows off of him as he watches me unbuckle his belt and unzip his pants.

"I do think *you* look so much better on your knees, Daddy," I say in a sassy tone.

He takes another pull from the bottle of bourbon, his gaze never leaving me as I take out his cock.

"Is that so?" he asks just as I grip and lick from balls to tip. "Eyes up here when you're tasting me, sugar," he says as I rock my wrist along the length of him. "I think you need your mouth nice and full to keep from making those bratty little comebacks."

It's exactly what I want—to submit to him, but not without a little verbal foreplay first. The sound he makes as I run my tongue along his length has me clenching my thighs as my knees dig into the floor. I do it again before I answer his request and take his beautifully fat cock all the way past my tongue and down my throat. It's not my first rodeo, so I breathe through my nose and swallow. Then I do it again, with a moan this time.

"Fuck," he breathes out.

A groan escapes him as I do it yet again, dragging my hands up his thighs, even though I want nothing more than to touch myself. I know if I do, I'll come. This room, what we've briefly watched, his words and direction have left me edged and ready.

His fingers glide along my jaw and dive into my hair as he rises to stand. "Open your mouth."

With his cock still between my lips, I open as best as I can.

He leans over, pulling my hair to tip my head back, and then holds his bottle of bourbon above his cock and my mouth. "No more talking back to me, sugar. You're going to swallow everything I give you now. Don't let it spill. I want all of it down that pretty throat of yours."

As the first splash of bourbon hits his hard cock, and then drips down toward the tip and spills into my mouth, I work my throat to swallow both his cock and his bourbon at the same time. It's messy and warm, the taste of his arousal as it leaks from him and the heat of the bourbon.

"So fucking hot," he grits out, and then tilts his head back and releases the sexiest moaning sound. I swallow again and wait for more of whatever he wants to give to me.

Making my husband moan and feel good is powerful. I

may be on my knees and submitting to him, but I have never felt more in control. I dig my fingers into his thighs, trying to keep measured sanity as my core clenches around nothing. But as I ease up and drag my tongue along his length, whatever calm Ace had settled into breaks away. Suddenly he puts the bottle down, and then guides me up from the floor, pulling me with him as he sits back and captures my lips in a messy, urgent kiss.

I straddle his lap eagerly, kneeling above his cock as it points up at my pussy. He licks the pad of his thumb, then rubs it over my clit. I let out a gasp at the pressure, so sensitive and ready for him. With a smirk, he drapes his arms along the side and back of the plush couch, and says, "Let me see you ride your husband."

Within the next second, I sink down onto him, his cock filling me so fucking well that I cry out. The stretch is as punishing as it is pleasurable. Rolling my hips, I hold him deep, my body pulsing around him. I keep the same rhythm with only one plan in mind: making him come. And to do it soon, because I'm going to unravel.

"That's it," he groans, tilting his head back. "Just like that."

His hand moves between my breasts, pulling the material down so that the lace swipes across my nipples. It feels like sensory overload. I'm breathing heavily, practically panting. "Look at me," I hear him say as he palms my breasts, leaving a path of kisses all over as he leans forward. I roll my hips again, grinding down, and this time, his cock hits a spot that has my walls crumbling. I'm lost in how fucking good we feel together.

"Look," he pants, just as on the edge. "Look at me, Hadley."

When I open my eyes, I lock onto his as he pulls my body forward. His hips roll with mine, and the change in pressure has me begging. "Please," I rush out as his upward thrusts become unrelenting. "I can't…"

Holding my body to his, he kisses me, his tongue swooping into my mouth as I whimper. When he pulls his lips back, he grits his teeth and says, "I'm going to come. Are you ready?"

I can't find words, only nodding.

"Good," he says with a strained voice. "Now let me hear you scream for me."

Pulling me down on his lap, he somehow anchors his cock deeper, and as I roll my hips, he moans, "Come."

It doesn't take anything more than that. My body is overcome with a rushed wave of energy, causing my limbs to convulse as my hands grip onto him for purchase. A darkness that danced along my vision rears forward before stars take its place, and the only sounds are my throaty groan of relief and the moaning of a well-fucked man.

With my body draped on him, his cock still inside me as we come down from our high, he mumbles a word that feels even more true now than it ever has before. "Mine."

I smile, eyes closed as I kiss his neck and agree. "Mine."

Chapter 35

Ace

I FEEL AROUND IN MY suitcase for what Julian left for me. It's a small black velvet drawstring pouch that holds a ring that I never expected to have made, never mind give.

Morning light filters in through the sheer linen curtains. The cool breeze of a Colorado morning forced Hadley to burrow into the bed deeper as soon as I snuck out of it. I could barely make out her shape beneath the plush covers. It's a lump and wild brunette curls that drape over the pillows.

Once I find what I'm looking for, I bring the tray of coffees and croissants from the bakery in the hotel lobby toward the bed.

"Please tell me you have breakfast and that I'm not just dreaming about coffee right now," she says in a raspy morning voice. When she surfaces, her face is flushed and sleepy. Wisps of hair block her eyes, and even like this, under the covers first thing in the morning, I feel so many things for her. Lust, attraction, love, want, and the need to be whatever she needs.

It feels like the right time. On a day when she can be carefree, away from our life at home—between running a business and dealing with the chaos we started, now is more than the right time to ask for the right reasons.

"We're not at my place, so I couldn't find a clementine, but I have iced coffee—splash of cream and a squeeze of honey. And some water." I glance at her sitting up, looking like a perfectly worked-over woman. *My woman.* "Why are you looking at me like that?"

She smiles wider and singsongs, "You are so obsessed with me."

I lean over the bed to get closer to her lips and say softly, "You're catching on." When I steal a quick kiss, she smiles.

She rips off a piece of croissant and shoves it in her mouth with a hum. "Breakfast in bed delivery from my sexy-ass husband? Best. Honeymoon. Ever."

I pull off my Foxx Bourbon T-shirt and toe off my shoes to join her, opening my mouth for her to give me a bite of the flakey croissant. She's right; it's the kind of morning that gets stored away and taken out when life feels complicated again. Sitting here with her, watching crumbs from her breakfast stick to her lips and the way she closes her eyes when she sips her coffee, is the kind of easy I never realized I could have. I feel around in my pocket, knowing without a doubt that there isn't a more perfect time for this.

As I lean back against the headboard, giving her a place to rest up against, she traces the cursive lines along my torso and whispers, "The Bourbon Boys." She offers me another bite, and then, with a mouthful, asks, "It seems like something I should already know the answer to, but did you always want to make bourbon?"

"I thought I had a choice." I smile to myself. "So I thought

I would want to choose something that wasn't what everyone in my family said I was supposed to do."

"But you seem to love it. You've always seemed like you love what you do here."

I nod, agreeing with her. "It became my choice. Bourbon, and proof that if I made enough things right, I might find the kind of life my parents had. Full, hard, happy, and brimming with so much love that everyone who knew them felt it."

I run my fingers along the top of her knee, back and forth, as if touching her in some way is necessary. An eagerness thrums through me as I reach into my pocket with my other hand.

"Did you never settle down with someone because—" she starts to ask, but I cut her off.

"Because anybody else wasn't you." I hold up a ring pinched between two fingers. It's something she would wear—gold and lined with diamonds. Nothing too over-the-top, but something that's comfortable, beautiful, and just for her. Julian outdid himself with this design. It's entirely original. "We did this all wrong, sugar."

Gasping, she moves her hand over her eyes like she's too overwhelmed to even look. She pulls in a breath first and blows it out slowly, moving her hands away from blue, tear-filled eyes. "I don't know why I'm so overwhelmed; we're already married," she says with a watery laugh.

"That was for show. This one's for us," I tell her as I take her hand, sliding the ring above the one that already occupies it.

"Ace…" she breathes out, and I swipe away the tear tracking down her cheek. "This is beautiful."

It feels pretty spectacular to take this woman's breath away and make her speechless as she stares at the ring. But I need to tell her how much I *want* this life with her. "I've been trying to catch my breath since the moment you walked into my life. And I know that I've done this all wrong, but I want to make it right." I steady my voice when I say, "I'm in love with you, Hadley Foxx. We may have already gotten married, but I want to be your husband in every fucking way if you'll have me. And I don't want this feeling to ever go away, so I'm asking you to stay married to me. Throw out the rules we've barely followed and just keep choosing each other. Let me love you, sugar, like I should have from the start."

She barely lets me finish as her hands find my face and pull me into a kiss. "Yes. It's always been a yes from me," she mumbles across my lips. Wrapping her arms around my neck, she practically tackles me back onto the bed. "I thought the first ring was romantic, but asking me to stay with you…" A soft smile brightens her face as her fingers graze along my hairline. "You would've had to find a way to get rid of me because I was never going anywhere. Even when I was pissed off at you, I was already stupidly in love with you."

I can't help the smile that pulls out of me, knowing that she's been feeling the same way I have. She looks at the ring on her finger, above the metal band from the bottle of bourbon. "I think I'll wear both. One for loving you and pretending I didn't, and the other for being able to say it whenever I want now."

I push her hair back behind her shoulders and look up at my beautiful wife. It's a view I don't think I'll ever forget—her smiling at her ring as she lies on top of me and the word "love" being thrown around like it's the easiest thing in the world to say to someone. To her, it is.

She glances at me and cracks another smile. "What are you thinking about?"

"You."

A few pieces of her hair fall from the knot on the top of her head as she looks at me curiously. "Why are you smiling at me?"

"A lot of reasons," I say, drawing my fingers along her bare shoulder. "You don't have any idea how brilliant you are. Sexy, yeah, absolutely, but…" I tuck a piece of her flyaway hair behind her ear and tell her the simplest truth. "I'm in awe of you. Always have been." I smile at the way she's looking at me, like this isn't obvious to her. "You drained your father's money and bought up most of Fiasco's commercial real estate. And you did it to help people." I shake my head. "Not out of greed or to take something for yourself." Leaning in, I kiss her pretty lips. "I love touching you, tasting you," I breathe out. "But I also love the way this thinks," I say, dragging my fingers along the side of her forehead. "And the things you say." I swipe my thumb along her lips.

She closes her eyes, smiling. Jokingly, she says, "I'm awesome. We've already established this. Plus, I didn't need any of that money or real estate—that's what I have you for." Wiggling her eyebrows, she bops her finger on my nose. *Such a brat.*

I pinch her nipple, making her screech a laugh. "Kidding. I'm kidding," she says, out of breath. "That's what I have Midnight Proof for—"

"And Foxx Bourbon," I say, cutting her off. "And whatever else we build out from there."

"Baby, Foxx Bourbon is yours and your brothers'."

That hits me right in the chest. I close my eyes for a second and hum, "I like that one," I tell her.

She furrows her brow, trying to work out what I'm talking about.

"'Baby' is good when we're like this," I say, and then drag her closer to my lips again as her body wraps fully around mine. My cock rubs up against her barely there satin shorts. "But when I'm hard or you're wet, I want you to be a brat and call me 'Daddy.'"

Her cheeks flush pink immediately, and then she bites that pretty bottom lip.

"Say it," I demand as I drag my nose along the column of her neck.

"Yes, Daddy," she breathes out.

"And your last name is Foxx, which means Foxx Bourbon is just as much yours as it is mine." I wrap my hand around her neck just as she settles her pussy right on my dick. She grinds herself over me as I tug her bottom lip with my teeth. "Tell me okay, so I can flip you over and fuck you again."

A breathy chuckle escapes her as her eyes blink slowly. "How are you ready to go again?"

"I have more than a decade's worth of sexual frustration to work out on this pretty pussy." I move my other hand below the covers to her already slicked clit. Petting it with my thumb lightly, I'm hoping to hear her beg me for more.

Her head tilts back as she lets out an audible exhale. "You've had sex in the last decade."

I sit up with her on my lap as she tries to grind her pussy into whatever I'll give her. Dragging my teeth along her pebbled skin, I suck one of her nipples so hard that she cries out. When I pull back, I lick and soothe the divots I just made. "Yes, but I've been fantasizing about having it with you for just about that long."

"You're..." She trails off as I slide two fingers inside her. "Oh god—"

I flip us over and tease my cock along her slit. "I could see why you'd call me that, but you can do better."

She squeezes her eyes shut and barks out a laugh.

Sliding into her all the way, I make her whimper and writhe. The sounds of her pleasure fuel me. As much fun as it is to deny her, I get off on hearing her come loudly against me. I pull myself back, inching out of her slowly. Tapping the head of my cock along her clit, I say softly, "Tell me what I want to hear, sugar."

I glance at the gold band that's proudly displayed on her hand. With her breath labored, she smiles up at me and says, "Fuck me like you mean it, husband."

I barely let her finish the words as I thrust into her hard and deep, both of us moaning together. And I do exactly as my wife demands.

Chapter 36

Hadley

June: I went to a sex club.

That's it.

Full stop.

I went to a sex club!

A FANTASY IS A DANGEROUS thing. It's meant to live inside your mind as a way to play out exactly as you want. Sometimes I'd fantasize about mundane things, like racing my horse or my car so fast that the only thing I could feel was the wind in my hair and the adrenaline pumping through my veins. There wouldn't be the worry of a bend in the road or an end to a path, just a wide-open space to feel alive. And then other times, like right now, I'd fantasize about something as simple as a stroll. Holding hands with *my husband*. And I'm so blissed out and happy that my face hurts from smiling.

"You alright?" he asks, nudging my hip as we walk.

I exaggeratedly sigh. "More than alright. I'm happily married. The guy is intense and sexy. My body is still recovering from"—I point up and down the front of him—"all of him."

He barks out a laugh and pulls my held hand to his lips.

"Plus, he makes me feel—" I stop short when I catch the steampunk-style sign in the window with bold letters and the perfect idea of what I want to do. *Hideaway Ink*.

Turning to face him, I give him a mischievous smile, barely containing my excitement. "I think I need a tattoo."

He kisses my forehead and says, "Then let's get you a tattoo."

Easygoing, do-whatever-I-want Ace is not who I expected, but I'm more than happy to accept this version of him in the daylight.

The bell on the door is a riff of "Go Your Own Way," and instantly, I think of Laney; she would love this place. The shop is clean and pretty, a bohemian vibe of bright colors mixed with masculine and dark lines. A gorgeous tattooed woman with an easy smile and flawless makeup turns on her rolling stool when we walk in. She pauses the tattoo she's doing on an oversized man in biker leathers and says, "Hello, gorgeous," and then does a double take at my husband. Plopping the tattoo gun down, she stands, taking off her gloves as she walks over. "My sister-in-law mentioned you two might come on through." She doesn't stop until I'm wrapped in a hug. "I'm Giselle, but please call me G. Welcome to Hideaway Ink."

"G, how are you?" Ace asks.

She gives him an air-kiss on his cheek and says, "Fucking magical. But apparently"—she smiles, eyeing me—"you're better! You went ahead and fell in love with one of the hottest women I've ever seen."

I turn to Ace, smirking. "I love her."

"I feel like the two of you in the same space is messing with the balance of the universe," Ace says warily.

She slaps his chest with the back of her hand. "You know I don't do walk-ins, but your name precedes you. Let me finish up my current client, and pick what you'd like. I'll be with you in a bit." She winks at me and leans into Ace, whispering loud enough for me to hear, "Haven't seen you here in a long time, but marriage looks good on you, big guy. You look happy."

He doesn't even hesitate when he looks at me and says, "I am."

We both study the wall of the mini-tattoo options. "These are all really cute, but I'm leaning toward maybe the logo for Midnight Proof or something having to do with being a Foxx now." I tap my finger on my lips. "Or maybe a bourbon barrel? What do you think?" I say, turning to him.

He looks at a small and simple series of fruit, and then stops at a line drawing of a bird. "Can I make a suggestion?"

Too much laughing and less than thirty minutes later, I stare at the elegant cursive ink drawn along the inside of my wrist. It was his idea, and then he decided he needed to get one too. The words are a reminder of our vows—*Une preuve d'amour*. Proof of love.

"I'm telling you, Hadley, if you want to fuck around with a French 75, then try it with cognac instead of gin. It'll make all of your lips pucker. I promise," G suggests as she wipes away the excess ink on Ace's skin.

Strutt's Peak, Colorado, is in many ways the complete opposite of Fiasco, Kentucky. I look out the front of the shop and take in all its details. Picturesque mountains and a brisk chill that rolls off the snowcaps in the distance. When we walked here, it wasn't the kind of temps we have in early summer back home, but in other ways, it feels so much like our small town. The quintessential town center with shops intended for tourists woven in with familiar hangouts for locals. There's something special about small towns.

"No way," I say under my breath when I peer out toward the town green. "Please tell me they're setting up a movie night."

Giselle smiles as she looks out the front windows, and then focuses her attention back on Ace's tattoo. "From the first week of June until the end of the summer, Riggs Outdoor hosts a movie night on our green every week. You're here in time for the start of the season," she says.

"Any idea what they're playing?"

"It's always something from the eighties or nineties. Last week it was *Field of Dreams*—tonight it's another cult classic named *Romancing the Stone*," she says, wrapping Ace's tattoo, and then tossing her gloves in the trash. "Alright, I think this is incredibly romantic. I can't wait to tell my husband." She smiles. "And Hadley, I might take you up on a visit. Midnight Proof sounds right up my alley."

Not even an hour later, and after a little more window shopping, I'm watching from one of the open benches along the sides of the town green as Ace carries back a tray of tacos in one hand and two horchatas in the other. The smile on his face as he looks around the now crowded space is one of contentment. I've been slowly falling for Ace for most of my adult life. I've fantasized about the man, obsessed over the bourbon boy, challenged the arrogant businessman, only to find myself exactly where I always wanted to be: deeply in love with my husband.

It feels like a moment to remember, so I slide my phone out of my bag and take two pictures: one of him staring out at the movie that just started and another of him smiling at me when he looks back and realizes what I'm doing. I can't help but smile back and all I can do is think, *That man is mine.*

And because I'm curious, I stupidly swipe off Do Not Disturb for the first time during this trip. My phone buzzes wildly just as I'm about to set it back down. I just want to be sure things at Midnight Proof are running smoothly. Laney and Faye took the lead and said if there were any problems, they'd handle it. And that must be the case because there aren't any messages from either of them. Instead, there are twelve voicemails, all from different phone numbers. A few text messages from Lincoln. And there's a flagged email, which means it's from my father's attorney.

Miss Finch,

As you know, we have represented your father with the understanding that payment for services would come from the Finch & King estate once the trial had been completed. At the time of his arrest, the estate had been valued at more than $200 million. However, I have been informed that payment via the estate is no longer viable. We regret to inform you that we will be stepping aside as his legal representation. He will be offered a state-mandated, court-appointed attorney in time for his trial that is now set for later this month. We will no longer handle any legal matters or negotiations on his behalf as of today.

"What is it?" Ace asks, noticing the change in my demeanor as I sit taller, reading through it again.

"Looks like my father will find out soon that he's been royally fucked over." I swallow down the nerves of what all of this means. It's what I wanted; the money that had been so carelessly left in my control is now invested in Fiasco business owners. I should be feeling ready and relieved that the choices I've made are finally making an impact, but instead, an uneasy feeling shifts over me.

When I hold the phone up to listen to the first voicemail, my stomach turns when I hear my father, and my eyes shoot to Ace's. My father's tone is laced with anger as he spouts his version of venom: promised threats. "Do not think your actions here will go unanswered, pumpkin. You want to hit me where it hurts? Your new husband making you feel like you have a stronger backbone than you really do, is my guess." He tuts. "Be prepared to feel what it's like to cross me. If I've taught you anything, you should remember that betrayal deserves punishment."

I toss my phone next to me, hating that his words make my eyes water. Scratching along my wrist, I try to pull myself together and think about my journal of good things: *June is iced coffees waiting for me, a new Boston jersey…and now I can add tattoos and a real proposal.*

"He's backed into a corner," Ace interrupts, framing his hands along my face and trying to pull my attention back to the present. "You're safe. Do you hear me, Hadley? He's not going to hurt you."

I want to be strong and pretend like my father's promise doesn't shake me. I want to lean on my husband and know that he won't let anything bad happen. I'm exactly where I should be and can't let anything ruin it. I want to stand tall and calm, knowing that money went to fix the things that he helped break. But I also know my father better than most. And his threats are never veiled. He meant what he said: He's going to try to find a way to hurt me.

I want all of this good to linger, to keep breathing easy and settle into being this strong and capable woman Ace so adamantly believes I am, but in my gut, I know if there's a way, my father will ruin it. He'll tear it down, find my weaknesses, just to get what he wants. And what he wants now is more than just money or freedom. It's to hurt me.

"Look at me, Hadley," Ace says, his tone soft as he rubs into my shoulders to soothe me. "Breathe for me, sugar. You are okay," he says slowly. My chest heaves as I start to slow my breathing, matching his measured breaths. I hadn't even realized I was gasping for air. "I will not let anything happen to you. Do you hear me?"

It takes a moment to really hear what he's saying. I nod, listening to the steadiness of his voice. Tears that were brimming finally fall as I say, "I'm happy, actually. Stupidly happy."

"Yeah, you are," he says quietly, the right side of his lip tipping up into an easy smile. "That's it, just breathe." He blows out a breath in time with mine. "That won't be how things end, you hear me?"

"He ruins things. That's who he is, Ace."

"Maybe so. But this is our life, yours and mine. Not his. Not anymore," he says as he wipes away the tears from my cheeks, pressing a kiss to my forehead. And the only thing I can think as he breathes with me, calming this tailspin, is, *Goddesses, I hope he's right.*

Chapter 37

HADLEY

July: Being cliché as fuck and getting matching tattoos with my husband. I love it so much.

When it comes to the Fourth of July in Fiasco, the Independence Day festivities are more than just barbecues and sparklers. We have vendors out the ass, from kettle corn and yards of slushies to the best burgoo and fried just about everything. It's always an illustration of my small town at its best. The weekend hosts the largest craft fair in the county, while the evenings mean good music, warm beer, great bourbon, and lots of dancing. This year will be the first time that I can dance with the one person I've always wanted. Even if it's still begrudgingly.

"Leave your brother alone and come dance with me," I shouted after him.

He stopped in his tracks and turned slowly like I had no business telling him what to do. And for the record, I didn't. But that never stopped me from trying. "Don't look at me like a dance is the craziest thing in the world, Atticus Foxx." *I smiled, just to taunt him.*

But his blue eyes pinned me in place and practically made me whimper when they drifted down the front of my top and kept roaming down past my short skirt and cowgirl boots.

"Why don't you go find someone you can boss around? There are plenty drooling over you tonight," *he said, crossing his arms over his chest, squaring off like he was readying for a fight.*

"So you are paying attention." *I stepped closer. I watched as his nostrils flared and he bit down on those back molars. The tendons in his neck flexed as I said,* "You think just because I ask you to dance with me, that gives you the right to talk to me like I'm not worth your time?" *I looked down at his body—Wranglers and a Foxx Bourbon T-shirt that showed off exactly where he spent his extra time. He glided his thumb along his bottom lip, his bicep straining against the sleeves. The crack of a firework caught us both off guard, and he flinched.*

I didn't think, I just reacted, digging into the small front pocket of my skirt where I stashed some Pop Rocks. I'd seen him flinch at loud noises before and watched him trying to find a quiet space when things got too loud plenty of times. He never watched fireworks with us and was usually long gone before they ever even started. His hand shot up, stopping me from moving any farther.

"It's just a little bit of sugar. It's a nice distraction when I get anxious," *I told him, just as Laney and Grant came hustling back from wherever they snuck off.*

"No," *he gritted out.*

I stared at him, silently swearing at him for being an asshole when I was trying to help. So I did exactly what I always had when Ace was involved—I put up my defenses and mouthed off.

A loud whistle has me whipping toward the commotion happening at every angle. Food vendors, families setting up to watch the upcoming events, and the last of the horses being loaded into their respective trailers post-parade. There are rails all along the center of the town green for barrel rolling contests. Grant Foxx is a powerhouse, and if you add his cooperage team, then they're unbeatable. A couple of other distilleries from Louisville come down and a few from out along the craft bourbon trail join in too.

Faye, along with Lark and Lily, wave like loons from across the street when they spot me. Each of them holds kettle corn bags. Lily has an arm stacked with flower crowns that she's selling for ten dollars, as written on the front and back of her white shirt. Lark holds a giant stuffed Highland cow that looks a lot like her real cow, Dottie, while Faye has a neon plastic yard cup filled with a frozen pink drink.

"I'm going to need some of all of what you guys have." I laugh as they get closer.

"Hadley, please tell me you were able to talk him out of it," Faye says as she looks out across the field.

I furrow my brow and follow her line of sight. Sure enough, Linc is stretching his arms out, wearing a *Foxx Bourbon Crew* T-shirt. Grant's calling a huddle next to him, and with his arms crossed, looking less than thrilled just off to the right, is my husband. "I had zero knowledge of any of this," I tell her, unable to hold back the chuckle at the look on her face.

"I think Lady Brittany Christina Pink is the prettiest one in the entire parade. Don't you think so, Faye?" Lily asks.

Faye passes me the yard glass of frosé. "Lily, I think Lady is the prettiest horse I've ever seen. I mean, with the exception of Dutchess Fergie, there isn't a single horse in the entire county with sparkling hooves and bright pink horseshoes." Faye leans into me, adding, "The paint is awesome, but I didn't realize you were getting them fitted with colored horseshoes too. I kind of love them."

"I have great taste, but you already know that." I give her a wink. "It trickles down to my horses."

"And your nieces," Lark says over a mouthful of kettle corn. She decided to borrow one of my baseball All-Star jerseys, and I'll be honest, she's a whole vibe now. Cute jean cutoffs, the jersey, high-top Converse, and a bright orangey-pink gloss that I know Lincoln wasn't thrilled about.

"Obviously," I say, giving her a high five that morphs into a pinky promise. It's become our version of a handshake, and truthfully, I'll take however much attention and goofy moments as she wants, because I know soon they'll be fleeting.

Lily starts shouting, "Go, Dad!"

And like the nerd he is, Lincoln flexes like a WWE wrestler and tries knocking chests with Grant, who shoves him off.

Laney comes up from behind us, whistling loudly and yelling, "LET'S GO, FOXX BOURBON!" She's smiling wide, her red hair piled high. "I know I'm biased, but what the hell are Ace and Linc doing out there? They're going to slow Grant and his guys down."

"They're all showing off," Romey says, laughing next to us. But it's her sister, Prue, who tells her to pipe down. "Let's just enjoy the small blessings today. Like the way those boys look like they might've sized down in those shirts and are about to burst out of 'em."

On the other side of Romey, Marla sips on a glass of iced tea and says, "Ah, Fiasco." She smacks her lips. "Old-fashioneds and old biddies objectifying men."

"Oh, fuck off, Marla," Romey says, shoving a candy in her mouth.

I snort a laugh. "Romey, you had better pass me one of those Modjeskas," I tell her, just as Del steps to the center of the green, and over the loudspeaker, he announces the start of the bourbon barrel relay.

"LADIES AND GENTLEMEN, IT'S A RACE AGAINST THE CLOCK TO SEE WHICH DISTILLERY CAN HANDLE THEIR BARRELS BEST…"

I glance toward the edge of the green, taking in the massive turnout of people, and my eye catches on someone leaning against my car. It's not uncommon for people to pay attention to a deep-purple muscle car—she's beautiful. But the dark hair and pressed uniform leaning against her makes me do a double take. It isn't like the fire chief is hard to pick out in a crowd on a day like today. Hell, the fire department and police department marched down Main, tossing candy and collecting donations. But him lingering there seems strange, especially after our last interaction. I don't want to witness another fight, or start one for that matter, but that fucker said some shitty things to me. He isn't allowed to lean on my car.

Marla nudges my arm, interrupting my internal back-and-forth about what would happen if I marched over there and demanded he move. She gives me a tight-lipped smile before she says, "You look happy, kid." It's a rather nice thing to hear from her. She's always been rough around the edges, but she looks out for people in her own way. "You always put on a brave face. I know those; I did those most of my life too." She glances out to the announcer's podium, where Del's standing. "But when you find a good one, the kind of partner that shakes up everything you ever thought you knew about yourself and allows you to be exactly who you are, you learn that being brave and being happy don't need to look the same."

The horn sounds off, and the girls around me start yelling and hollering for Lincoln to hustle and for Grant to pick up the pace. Ace hauls his sweet ass down the rail tracks faster than both of them, steering the barrels exactly where they're meant to be placed and positioned with the bung side up. And in less than three minutes, the entire cooperage crew from Foxx Bourbon are chanting, hooting, and cheering. Ace breaks from the crowd, and with an easy smile, starts walking right for me.

I can't help but peacock a little as I watch Romey and Prue nudge each other as they witness how he's looking at his wife.

Shaking his head, he laughs out, "Please tell me you saw that."

"Oh, I saw it. Are you trying to impress your girl?" I say, smiling up at him.

Just as he wraps his sweaty arms around me and mumbles the word "always" into my neck, I glance back at my car. Hawk is gone.

"Look at him up there," Lincoln says as he sips on his beer. The evening crowd is picking up as the kids have all filtered home with their parents. Lincoln has his girls doing sleepovers with friends so he and Faye could enjoy the night.

"Griz looks like a natural on that stage," Faye says as we all look on and watch Griz pull a solo on his accordion.

I point at her. "Do *not* tell him that. You know how long it took for me to convince him that he wouldn't want to perform at Midnight Proof because the crowd barely notices the jazz trio?"

Laney chuckles. "Oh, I remember. He moped around for a solid week and threatened to take away your book club privileges if you didn't reconsider."

"How was he when we were away?" Ace asks Grant at his side, low enough to not make it a group conversation.

"Same. Still more quiet than usual. You think something is off?"

Ace rubs along his lip when he says, "Nah, probably just missed me." But I know that tell. He's worried about something or knows something that he isn't ready to share with everyone. Swiping on his phone, he types something out before he pockets it. I don't love secrets being kept from me, but whatever's going on with him and Griz isn't my place to know until one of them shares it.

When the song changes over from Bob Dylan to Dolly Parton, the crowd cheers wildly. Griz stands, taking off the accordion and lifting his hat to the crowd. We drown everyone else out with the whistling and clapping. Ace raises his arms, cupping his hands around his mouth to cheer out for the patriarch of our family.

I catch a glimpse of the inside of his forearm and smile proudly. From his wrist to his elbow, the same cursive words that run along my wrist are written even larger on him. It's the only tattoo that's visible for the world to see. I swoon a little at the matching words we both wear proudly.

Griz makes his way over to more claps and whistles. "Y'all are the best cheering section," he says, snagging Lincoln's beer from his hand. Then he promptly makes a face. "I hate this stuff. I'm going to go find Hal's moonshine."

"You want to head home soon?" Ace asks him.

He turns from where he was just walking. "I'm sure you'll be fine without me. You take the horse back, and I'll drive Hadley's car."

"You treat her with the kind of respect she deserves, Griz. No moonshine please," I call out, narrowing my eyes playfully.

He rests his hand on his chest. "Hadley Jean, I would never…" He winks. "The fried dough soaks it all up; they cancel each other out."

"Griz…" Grant groans after him.

He waves his hand over his head like he's exasperated. "Fine, y'all are no fun." But he gives us one more smile. "But I love ya."

The short ride on the keyboard tees up a twangy version of "Little Lies."

"Oh c'mon, cowboy. It's a Fleetwood cover," Laney says, locking her arms around Grant's neck. She stares up at him, and they have their own wordless exchange.

"Alright, honey, one dance." He loops his fingers with hers, pulling her onto the dance floor.

"Let's go, Foxx." Faye claps after she sucks down the rest of her peach daiquiri yard. "Time to show me those sweet dance moves." Linc rushes toward her, mumbling something in her ear and shuffling her forward, but then halfway to the dance floor, he shouts back to us, "You two coming?"

I glance at my husband, and he's smiling and running his fingers around his almost empty glass.

With a sassy smile, I turn to Linc. "We'll snag the next song. Your brother looks like he's really feeling his forties right now." I tilt my head at my husband. "Aren't you, Daddy?"

He wipes his hand over his smirk, muttering, "Jesus Christ." With a huffed laugh, he says, "Sugar, you like to make fun of how old I am, but I can run circles around most of those guys—my brothers included. And while I might be a little thicker than I used to be, you know I can lift and move what counts."

I scream out a laugh when he bends quickly and scoops me

up in his hold. With one arm cradled under my knees and the other around my lower back, it feels exactly like the way someone would carry a new bride over a threshold. But instead of moving inside, he keeps moving toward the center of the dance floor. There's something to be said for not giving a shit about what people around you think and doing something or having a moment with a person despite how uncomfortable it might make others. I've always felt that way, but Ace? He likes quiet. To observe. To steer clear of the center of attention. But with me in his arms, at the center of a dance floor, surrounded by most of our small town, the smile on his face and the way he's looking like he wants to kiss me might mean I've assumed all wrong.

Round globe lights strung up around the dance floor let off a boozy glow. The slow bass and a drumbeat make way to an unhurried version of "Fools Rush In," and I can't help the smile it pulls from me. "Did you know that when I told Lincoln we were getting married, he asked if I was pregnant?"

His arms wrap around my waist and pull me closer as the dance floor gets more crowded. Smiling at me, he says, "That so?"

I nod, taking in his somewhat serious expression.

"That something you think you want?"

I move my fingers into the hair at the nape of his neck, and his eyes blink slowly at the feeling. I love how much he loves being touched.

"I like the idea of having a family, but that doesn't need to include babies. I don't think I ever allowed myself to want things like kids." I swallow whatever little bit of fear I have in saying it, because I wonder if he feels that way too. "Why? You offering?" I ask lightly.

Ace cuffs a piece of hair behind my ear. "You should know by now that I'll give you whatever you want, Hadley." With that, he holds me closer, like he can't imagine letting go. "I think hearing you tell me you love me was one of the best moments of my life."

I glance up at the sky, trying my hardest not to gush about this not-so-casual conversation on a dance floor. "So it was 'I love you' and not, 'Fuck me harder' or 'Yes, Daddy'?"

He leans into me, and just below my ear, says, "Those are a close second and third." Peering back, he smiles. "I never could understand what it felt like to build a family of my own—my brothers and Griz will always be that, but you and me..." He kisses my forehead. "Having you is more than I ever expected. So truthfully, sugar, I'll take on whatever makes you happy. You want more horses, babies, two more speakeasies? It's fucking yours."

But before I can say anything else, Linc interrupts, leaning into our space. "I'm just going to say it..."

Faye sways with him, trying to pull him back. "Foxx, you're cutting into their dance."

He kisses her on the lips. "Love you the most, Peach. But"—he points to Ace, moving his finger up and down—"you two look"—he makes an *O* with his pointer finger and thumb—"really fucking good together."

Faye just rolls her eyes at him and smiles at me.

Linc holds out his fist, and I bump it, followed by the wrist flick, elbow tap, and jazz fingers to round out a handshake that we made too many years ago. I smile when he says, "Couldn't be happier for you, Hads." Then he glances up at his brother. "You too, asshole."

Ace just grunts at him, but I know he likes hearing it.

I look around the crowd and see Marla swaying with Del, while Romey and Prue twirl each other with cocktails in hand.

And a bit farther out, I see Griz with his arms crossed, talking to Hawk. I squint through the crowd of swaying bodies to gauge their body language. Griz isn't much for confrontation, but as he walks off with the fire chief, I glance at Faye and notice her watching too.

Something doesn't feel right.

Chapter 38

Ace

"Can we get out of here?" I ask, moving my hands lower, down her back. As much as it's been a great day, I want to go home and get my wife naked before the fireworks start sounding off.

She leans in and lightly kisses my lips. "What's in it for me?"

"Sugar, if you need me to remind you exactly what being this close to you does to me, then I'll happily bend you over the closest table and show you."

Her eyes widen as she nods excitedly. "You feel like putting on a show this time?"

That sounds like far too much fun, and my thoughts move back to Strutt's Peak and the scene we very much enjoyed watching. I hum against her and say, "You're going to be the death of me." Grabbing her hands, I lead us away from the dance floor. "But I'd happily show off all the ways I can think of rewarding my bratty wife." I slow so I can say to her quietly, "I think I'd like to tease people and give them a glimpse of what they'll never get to have."

A few folks wave as we head away from the dance floor. There are plenty of eyes witnessing the oldest Foxx brother openly adoring his unexpected wife. It feels good to do. I look down at the way she's shuffling her feet and the fact that we're moving at a snail's pace. "Need me to carry you?" I ask as we hit the edge of the grass.

I smile as she slips off her boots, and then holds them in one hand.

"Yes, please," she says. Between walking the green and making the rounds, hunting through all of the crafts tents, and just dancing now, I'm betting she's reached her limits.

I raise her hand to my lips, kissing along her knuckles, and then turn her wrist over to kiss along the healing tattoo. I love that these words are here—something for everyone to see, but it's just for me and her. "Alright, let's go," I say, bending forward, nudging my shoulder into her waist, and then hoisting her up and over my shoulder.

She yelps before cackling a laugh, and then gives in to it. "How about a game of strip chess? We haven't done that one yet," she suggests.

I give a tight-lipped smile to the older couple that passes us and clearly overheard her suggestion. Grabbing a handful of her ass in these cute jean shorts, I say, "Strip chess sounds like you hustling me. You should just ask me to take all my clothes off for you, because we both know how that game will go."

"Okay, take all your clothes off for me then," she says through a giggle.

Chuckling, I glance at the horse trailer at the end of the road. Her horse needs to get out and stretch. She's been in there for long enough. "One second," I say, moving us toward her Mustang instead. "Leave your keys in your car for Griz to take. I'm guessing he won't be too far behind us."

The road is lined with parked cars. And it's mostly quiet, except for a couple making out in the back of a truck, and the muffled sound of a transistor radio playing some bluegrass from the ice cream truck at the far end of the block. But almost everyone is down by the stage and dance floor, getting rowdy over the cover band that I can hear is just starting a new set.

I walk around the exterior of her car. It's loud as hell and an eyesore, but she loves it. And it drives like the devil. Placing her down on the trunk, I kiss her smiling, waiting lips. I can get lost while kissing this woman. It's exactly how I like—lips pressing, tongues wet and warm, lulling the other into a promise of edging foreplay and blackout orgasms.

She hums against my lips, and *fuck*, do I want her right this second. I wrap my arms around her and slide her closer, letting her feel the way she's already made me hard.

But the sound of her horse kicking the side of the trailer has us both stopping. She's probably more than ready to be out of there. "She sounds ticked off."

"I think she's ready to go home." She runs her fingers along the back of my neck. I kiss her again, and she hums, "Me too."

"Keys," I mumble against her lips.

She smiles and drags her tongue along my bottom lip, laughing at my frustrated exhale. Patience when it comes to her has never been my strong suit.

I squeeze my hands around her waist. "Hadley, give me the fucking keys, or else I really will fuck you right here."

"And that's a bad idea, why?" she asks coyly.

I consider it for a moment. The street is quiet, but the thought ends abruptly when she says, "Oh shit." And with an exaggerated exhale, she adds, "They're in my bag, which is still at the high top table, down by the dance floor. This is what you do to my brain!"

I know that feeling all too well. I rest my forehead on hers for a moment. "Alright, let's go," I say, scooping my arm under her to trek back down to where we just were.

But she taps my chest. "I'm fine right here. I'll hang with Lady. You'll be faster not having to carry me down and back anyway."

I hesitate for a second. I'm not too keen on leaving her by herself up here. After the bullshit message from her father, I've been more watchful. I haven't left her side for more than a few hours at a time since we've been back. My schedule is flexible at the distillery, and on her nights at Midnight Proof, I've met someone there for a drink or two, and then stayed until closing to give her a ride home. It's overprotective, but after witnessing her having a panic attack, I knew she'd reached her limits. When her father is finally out of the picture for good, I'll be able to breathe easier. Until then, it's like torture leaving her in a vulnerable spot like this.

"Go." She smiles. "I'm fine."

I exhale the breath I'd been holding. "Okay, give me a minute. Don't go anywhere." With another kiss to her lips, I turn toward the town green and the music. I hate that, in the back of my mind, all I can think about is something going wrong. I never believed in the fucking rumored curse about falling for a Foxx, but now there's a small part of me that fears it. It's the distant kind of fear, but it's still nagging.

"That's a nice view!" Hadley shouts. "Hate seeing you go, Foxx. But goddesses, do I looooovvvvve watching you leave."

"*Jesus Christ*," I say to myself with a smile I can't tame. I rub my palm over my mouth, and I can't seem to wipe the smile off as I hustle faster.

From here, Fiasco looks like it should—thriving with people

celebrating, and with that lick of nostalgia that the nighttime summer humidity always ushers in. I glance around, looking for where Griz might have wandered off to, but I can't spot him. I look on as Grant moves his foot in time with the harmonica cupped in his hands. And I could watch Lincoln swing Faye around the dance floor and Laney cheer my baby brother on from the side of the stage forever. I'm still grinning without even realizing it.

When I turn back to where I left Hadley, her attention is on her phone. And just then, my phone vibrates in my pocket. I'm expecting it to be her sending me something dirty, but instead, it's Jimmy. *Shit.*

JIMMY DUGAN:
Heads up regarding the visitors' log from today.

That came in over an hour ago now.

ACE:
Who?

But he doesn't respond right away, so I shove the phone in my pocket and quickly grab Hadley's bag from the high top. I hustle back toward the road, not seeing Hadley sitting there any longer. That has my nerves kicking in.

"Hadley!" I call out slowly. I'm not seeing her.

A loud, bursting noise rings out, like a tire being blown, followed by an earthshaking boom that has me moving before I even register what it is. I don't think or look, I just start hauling ass back to her. "Hadley!" I yell, frantically looking down the street toward the horse trailer, and then back toward the car. I'm not moving fast enough. I shouldn't have left her side. *Fuck!* The corner block erupts in another explosion where I had just been, and my stomach sinks to my feet.

"Hadley," I exhale, just as car alarms sound off, and the pressure from the blast hits me as if I've been shoved hard and quick. The wind is knocked from my chest as I try to stand up. Blinking away the haze, the only thing I see is her 1969 purple Mustang engulfed in flames. *No, no, no. This isn't fucking happening.*

As soon as I find my footing, I pump my arms, running as fast as my feet will go. But it's not fast enough. "HADLEY!" I scream at the top of my lungs, my whole body shaking. *Please don't do this.* No matter how much I tried to forget the details, the sound of a car exploding was the same. Destruction and chaos. And the common denominator was always losing someone. I can't lose her.

The only thing I can see from here are flames inside the car and all along the top and trunk, right where I left her. "HADLEY!" I scream again, my voice catching from the force, but the angry fire and creaking of metal are my only answer. An uncontrolled blaze envelops the hood as black smoke rises and the blurred heat roars. I don't see her. She was *right there*.

Another small burst ruptures inside the car, and the glass from the back windshield blows out, forcing me to turn to avoid shards of glass flying. Ducking lower, I fumble in my pocket for my phone and the only thing I see is Jimmy's message returned.

JIMMY DUGAN:
The governor and Chief Hawkins.

My phone buzzes again.

> **JIMMY DUGAN:**
> He's gone. Took my gun. Knocked me out. Just called it in.

From behind me, I hear someone say, "This isn't a part of our deal."

But before the words and who they belong to register, a blunt object hits the back of my head, knocking me forward. And then again. My knees collide with the concrete. Shooting pain erupts up my legs, and then along the side of my face.

"I don't have a choice," a deep voice says as I try to stand. But another blow to the back of my head keeps me down this time.

Chapter 39

Hadley

"Lady Brittany Christina Pink, I know it's been a long day for you. Daddy just went to go get the keys," I say as I walk up to the open side of the trailer. She huffs out and kicks the side of the trailer again, like she's agitated. It's out of character for her; she doesn't usually mind her trailer. I peek in and see her white mane, tall stature, ears flicking toward my voice. "You're my very best girl, but don't tell Fergie I said that," I say, and then click my tongue.

But then a whirring sound startles me. I take a step back from the trailer, and the sound of the truck trying to start without the engine turning over happens again. I didn't see or hear Ace come back this way yet.

"You technically do not own this horse, pumpkin," a voice says as the driver's side door creaks open. I know that low, slow Kentucky drawl better than anyone, and it makes my hackles rise, forcing me to immediately raise my defenses. *He shouldn't be here.*

My father slams the door shut and stalks closer to me. I feel around in my pocket for my phone, but my hands are shaking as I try to press the side buttons and swipe blindly for the emergency alert. He looks thinner, his hair slightly longer than how he kept it all my life, and it's the least polished I've ever seen him.

"As promised, pumpkin, I'm going to take what's mine," he says, holding up a gun and pointing it at me.

My body tenses at the threat, nerves making me shiver as I stagger back.

"Wasn't referrin' to you. You proved you're fuckin' worthless to me. Thought I'd help myself to this Thoroughbred, but the truck doesn't seem to be cooperating. So I'll settle for what you took from me."

Tears start falling, and my throat feels like it's closing. There isn't an ounce of love left in my bones for him.

I hear Ace call out my name over the pounding in my ears, but I can't see him on this side of the trailer.

"Don't do that." My father tsks. Waving his gun in my face, he says, "Perhaps he just needs a little bit of motivation."

I try to think of what I could possibly say that'll shake him. "Leave him out of this—" But my plea gets cut off when a loud boom sounds out from behind us, followed by a massive wave of heat. My body flies forward, hands hitting the pavement first, then my chest, just barely stopping my face from colliding with the gravel. Before I can put together what's happening, I hear, "HADLEY!" That's Ace again. And that scream is one of distress.

A response to my husband dies in my throat as I'm shoved back down, and this time, my face hits so hard that it slaps against the surface, and with it comes a biting burn that has me cursing.

With his foot pressed into my back, my father grits out, "You stay right there."

"HADLEY!" Ace shouts from what sounds closer, but not close enough to see me.

Glass bursts and shards rain down on the pavement, a handful reaching where I'm flat out and face down.

"The truck won't start," my father says. "I'm leaving the horse. Come get me." He pauses, then adds, "You're done when I say. We have a new deal now."

I move my head to the side to look at him. He seems in control and calculating despite the chaos around us. With a phone in his hand, he continues in a biting tone. "Get him in your truck and get here. *Now*, or I promise, I *will* kill your brother."

With my thoughts racing, I try to make out what he's saying or who he's even talking to.

I steady my voice the best I can. "FBI and Fiasco PD are probably already looking—"

His foot and full weight push into me as he leans in, making it difficult to breathe, and seethes, "Fiasco PD and Fire have their hands full. Nobody's looking for me, Hadley. Now do what you're told for once in your pathetic life and be quiet."

His words make my eyes water as anger rages within me. I'm shaking from getting slammed against the ground and literally stepped on. Swallowing my panic, I focus only on the anger. *I will not let him do this.*

The brakes of a truck squeal to a stop next to us, and a false sense of relief hits me as I glance up enough to see a red stripe along the side of the cab. The big, bold letters that read, Fiasco Fire Rescue, and below that, Fire Chief.

"Hawk?" my voice rasps, barely audible for anyone to hear it.

"Quiet," my father reprimands, shoving me back down just before he rushes for Hawk's truck.

From the back of the parked truck, my father yanks out a zip-tied and muzzled Governor Hawkins from the back seat. *What the hell?* He presses a gun into the governor's back, moving him into the cab of Hawk's truck. I look around desperately, but there's not a single person around paying attention with the chaos of the explosion behind us. The governor tries resisting, but my father knocks him on the back of the head with the butt of the gun, his body going limp as my father's getting him into the back seat.

"Hawk!" I call out this time, but instead of rushing to help, he simply looks at me, eyebrows pinched, and then floors it, just as the sound of more glass blows out behind me.

Jolting, I cover my head with my hands, staying against the ground until I only hear people yelling from a distance. Panting, I shift my entire body, turning over and pushing myself to sit up. I blink slowly as I get my bearings, staring down at my hands. Small cuts are bleeding over embedded pieces of gravel.

When I look up, that's when I see the fire, and there are people calling out my name. My world stops for a fraction of a moment as I struggle to pull a full breath in—*Ace*. I don't hear him shouting for me anymore.

"Ace," I try to yell, but it comes out pathetically quiet. My legs tremble as I push myself up to stand. There's blood on my knees, and the air licks like an angry wind at the side of my face. "ACE!" I bellow out, dread filling my veins at what could have happened to him.

I turn toward the chaos and see my Mustang—or what used to be my Mustang—engulfed in flames. *My father blew up my fucking car?!* My head spins with rage and unease as I watch people running around and shouting for their loved ones while smoke billows upward in a black cloud around us.

"Ace!" I yell out again, a sob catching in my throat as I walk closer to the back of the trailer. Lady kicks at the sides, whinnying. She's as spooked as I am.

"HADLEY!" is shouted again from the direction of the town green, catching my attention.

As I turn and lean against the trailer, Grant rushes toward me, Linc and Faye not far behind him. The looks on their faces have more tears trailing down my face.

"Hadley? Hadley!" Grant calls out. "Hadley, fucking hell," he says as he reaches me and moves quickly to help me, looking at the gash along my face.

"Hadley, fuck!" Linc's beside me seconds later, pushing his brother aside and pulling me into his chest. "Oh, thank fuck." He holds me close, and it's enough to have another sob tearing from my chest. Faye stands next to us with Grant, both of them looking around, trying to make sense of what just went down.

Fire engine horns blast loudly as they come barreling down the road, with a series of police cruisers following close behind.

"Holy shit, you scared the life right out of me," Lincoln breathes out, turning my hands over to examine my bloody palms.

"Where's Ace?" I ask shakily, tears blurring my vision. "I heard him call my name, but then—"

"He's alright," Grant cuts off my worry. I exhale heavily, my shoulders slumping with relief.

Lincoln removes his glasses and wipes his forehead. "I really didn't want to have to tell him you were inside that car when he came to. Hawk was helping him over to his truck to wait for a paramedic. Said he must've gotten knocked out, but you weren't with him."

"How the hell did your car blow up?" Faye asks, brow pinched as she looks over at the flames.

And then I register what Lincoln just said, and my stomach drops to my feet. Relief morphs into bone-deep terror. "What do you mean Ace was with Hawk?"

Grant and Linc glance over to where they'd left their brother.

"Hawk wasn't helping Ace," I say in a rush as I look down the blocked-off street and can't see anything other than red-and-blue flashing lights and panicked faces. None of them belong to my husband. "He...He took him," I tell them, making sense of it. "The governor was tied up and..." Spotting my phone, I step over to the sidewalk on wobbly legs.

"Hads?" Linc says as I'm calling Ace. Only it goes right to voicemail, and I just about lose it. "What are you talking about? Who took Ace?" He glances at Grant, who's watching me now with concern.

"My father was right here. Tried taking my horse, but the fucking truck wouldn't start. Then my car exploded," I say with my arms moving wildly, stuttering over my words. "He had the governor, and a gun, and then he got into Hawk's truck."

"Your father?" Lincoln spits out.

"Fuck!" Faye barks out, just as she takes out her cell phone.

Grant is studying me, and then looks out over his shoulder. "Let me find Griz. Something isn't—" He cuts himself off, looking like he just worked something out as he rushes off.

My head pounds as painfully as my heart, the only certainty bringing me any clarity being the fact that I don't trust a single thing when it comes to my father. He's desperate, pissed off, and he wants what he's "owed." I'm betting he took Ace to get the payout he needed to disappear. I don't know what the hell Hawk has to do with any of this, but he's involved somehow, and I'm not just going to sit here and hope the monster gets caught. I've already waited and paid for it. I refuse to do it again. I'm done being quiet.

I call Ace's number again, but it rings straight through to voicemail. My face squints as I try to tamp down the anxiety attack wrapping around me. I catch a glimpse of my wrist, reading our tattoo again. If someone had taken me, Ace wouldn't let panic consume him; he'd think like them. *Where would my father go?*

"He needed chaos to cover his tracks and give him a jump on getting out of here," Faye says, and I think through what that would mean next. "They've stopped right along the town line before the interstate." She swipes away on her phone, eyes locked on the screen.

Lincoln's attention whips to his wife. "You've got to be kidding me."

She kisses the air. "Love you, Foxx, but I'll fill you in later." She raises her phone to her ear. While she waits for whomever she's calling to answer, she says, "Your father could easily get a money transfer with a mobile phone and pin number access from Ace, or any of the Foxx family, for that matter."

I watch as Faye relays what she knows. She's a private investigator, but she also helps Fiasco PD from time to time. I want to trust that Ace will be okay, that there are enough people moving to make sure, but I can't just sit here.

I try thinking six steps ahead. If my father was going to make a run for it, he'd need a new passport and ID. And there's one person who lives right along the river at the edge of the town line, where he could get that fast and without much notice. The realization lights a fire within me. I know where they're going. Now I need help to get there.

Taking a breath, I swipe at the newest contact added to my phone.

Without so much as a hello, she says, "What do you need, Hadley?"

"Are you still in Fiasco?"

"I am," she says in a curt tone. "What happened?"

"I think my father—"

"Text me where," she cuts me off. And then the line goes dead.

Immediately, Linc's asking, "Who was that, Hads?"

I ignore his question and text the location of where I'm hoping Ace is. Lady kicks the side of that trailer again, snorting her frustration like she knows the mess we're in. Flexing my hands, the gravel still embedded deep in my palms, I shake them out as I look toward the chaotic mess of the street. The road is blocked off, police cruisers at one end and the fire trucks at the other, with more and more people crowding around. I don't see Griz anywhere and Grant is lost in the sea of bodies, still calling out for whomever they came with.

No, I can't just sit around here and wait.

"Linc, you need to find Del, and tell him he needs to get to Presh's place." Spinning around, I flip the pin and open the latch to the trailer. "My father's making desperate moves."

Lincoln's face squints as I ease Lady back and out of the trailer. "Wait, what? What the fuck is happening? I don't—"

I'm shaking my head as I turn to face him. "Lincoln! I don't know. I told you, Hawk and my dad took Ace. And right now, I can't freak out, I just need to go."

"You're not going anywhere," he shouts, loud enough that it has Faye turning back from her phone call. When she widens her eyes at him, he huffs out. "Unbelievable. Both of you. Sit down and let me get a paramedic. You're fucking bleeding," he snaps back at me.

"LINCOLN!" Swallowing, and more even toned, I say, "I need a minute."

He searches for what I'm asking of him. A simple few words that we agreed on a long time ago. A request, or rather a demand, for support. No questions asked—it's a way of telling the other that we need time and space. And maybe an alibi. He told me once that *"It's what best friends do."* And now, I need to collect on it.

As I ease my Thoroughbred out, Lady Brittany Christina Pink's ears shift toward me when I click my tongue. She leans her head down and huffs like she's equal parts relieved to see me and annoyed I took so long to get her out of here. "You might have saved my life having a temper tantrum in there, you know that?" I pet along her neck. "That's my girl," I coo.

"Hadley, there's no reins or saddle," Lincoln says, rubbing his temple, eyes wild. He's about to combust. "You're not riding her—"

"Lincoln Foxx," I argue back. "I'm not wasting any more time. I need to get to my husband, and this is the fastest way I know how. Now give me a fucking boost! I said I needed a minute."

Glancing back at Faye, he's hoping for backup, but she hangs up the phone and calls out, "Don't think, Hadley. Just move!" Linc nods immediately, his face shifting to me with a soft smile. Moving next to me, he squats down and links his fingers together so I can use them as leverage to get onto my horse's back. Dammit, this is going to hurt. My body is sore from getting knocked down, and now I need to ride bareback to the town line. "Linc, remember what I said. Find Del and get the police to meet me at Church."

"Fucking hell," he breathes out as I turn Lady in the direction we need to go. "I'm right behind you!" Lincoln yells, and then he's pressing a quick kiss to Faye's head before turning and running to where Grant was headed.

Gripping onto Lady's mane, I wrap her hair around my wrists, squeeze my thighs, and lean forward. "Let's go, girl!"

For so long, I've fought with the idea that I could be anything like my father, that I've seen enough and absorbed enough of the ruthlessness and narcissistic behavior, so I know how to turn it away. That I can recognize those things and close the door on them before they ever have a chance to hurt me. Some people are meant to cause hurt. They have no way of turning it off because it's who they are. And then there are others who would burn the world down to keep that kind of harm from ever touching the ones they love. That's the difference between a Finch and a Foxx.

With the wind whipping my hair, I squeeze my thighs tighter and turn into the last bend in the road. I ride her ruthlessly through the dim evening and hope like hell I'm going to the right place. That what I know about my father might help me this time around.

The sign for The Holey Donut isn't lit as I approach, but the lights in the house bleed enough onto the patio so I can see it's empty.

Any noise coming from the property is washed out by the rushing river, making it difficult to know which way to go. I swallow down the nerves that are making my hands and arms shake as my eyes frantically flick around the trees and open space, the change in terrain leading to the river. Squinting when I see some movement and the outline of bodies kneeling with their hands behind their backs, my breath catches, and my heart nearly stops.

"Ace," I breathe out, just as fireworks go off in the distance.

Chapter 40

ACE

ALL I HEAR IS MY heart beating too fast and blood rushing in my ears, the dizzy vertigo making it feel like I'm on a Tilt-A-Whirl. My head's heavy, and I try to pry my eyes open, but more than anything, I want to sleep. I'm coming in and out of consciousness as my body slides down and knocks into metal. Then the sound of muffled voices, a truck engine, and someone saying to "wake the fuck up" has me groaning. Until I hit the ground with a dense thud, grass pressed along the side of my face, and a musty, earthy smell permeates my nose. *I'm near the river.*

With my arms bound together, my ankles too, I flip to my other side, trying to gauge where I might be. It's dark, and I can barely see more than the dim glow of the house up ahead, but I know this spot. I married my wife out on the landing not more than a hundred feet from here. *My wife.*

"Hadley!" I yell without thinking. I pull and yank at what's restricting my hands, every nerve ending in my body vibrating to get to her.

"She's not here," a man's voice says from a few feet away. I know that voice—*Hawk*.

I swallow down every ounce of fear that the worst thing could have happened to the only woman I've ever loved.

"Fuck you," I seethe. I wish I had ripped out his fucking voice box when I had the chance. I knock my shoulder against the ground with a huff, realizing from the pinch of the restraints that they're zip ties. If I twist them just right and pull with enough force, I could snap them.

As I turn my body again, I freeze, seeing the governor at gunpoint, duct tape around his mouth, handcuffed, with blood all along his left side. But it's the gravelly groan and my name being mumbled by a voice I've heard my entire life that quiets my thoughts. Griz sits propped up against the side of Presh's house. Face pinched tight with pain, his hands behind him, zip-tied like mine, if I had to guess.

"Griz!" I shout, then try to take in the entirety of the situation. My mind is running like a ticker tape on what the hell is happening. What I missed.

"Still here," he groans again. "Pretty sure my shoulder is out of sorts because of these fucks, but I'm here." He makes a pained sound as he tries to adjust himself. "Ah shit."

"Quiet down," Hawk says from just a few feet away, holding his hand against the governor's side. He looks like he's been shot or stabbed.

Griz yells, "The hell are you doing, Chief? This ain't you. Tossing an old man in the back of your truck, and then helping that asshole over there."

"I hope you're planning to kill me," I say with an even tone to Hawk. "Because there is no way this night ends with you still breathing." When he finally glances up at me, I grit out, "Where's Hadley?"

A fist slams into me in the next second, my mouth flooding with warm copper, and knocking me more awake. It must be the *asshole* Griz was referring to. I spit into the dirt, smiling as I turn to find Wheeler fucking Finch five feet in front of me. "I don't think the fire chief plans on killing anyone tonight, but I'm more than happy to take your request. After you transfer the funds that you and my fucking daughter stole from me."

I let out a sarcastic laugh. "I didn't do a damn thing. My wife went ahead and paid out for all the damages *you've* caused. She was really generous about it too," I sneer as he disregards me and moves toward Hawk and the governor.

Whatever had the Hawkins brothers walking into Wheeler's estate earlier today turned sideways for them. The governor is bound and bleeding out while Hawk does what Wheeler demands.

Presh's place is the last stop before the highway out of here—and she has a side hustle that would deliver what Wheeler needs. A new ID and passport if he's really looking to flee. That, and now I know he wants money. Which is why Griz and I are here. The dark plays in my favor, the same way as the noise from the whistle and flare of fireworks starting to go off from miles away downtown. If I can rile Hawk up enough and get closer without them noticing, maybe he'll realize that between the two of us, we can overpower Wheeler.

"Was it the fire chief position?" I taunt him. "They handed over a position like that, one you barely earned, and now you owe them." An annoyed huff passes my lips. "Some brother you've got. He might have gotten you a job, but did you know he was angling for Hadley?"

"Fuck you, Foxx," Hawk bites out. And I keep going.

"No thanks, heard you weren't all that great at it."

That gets no reaction as Hawk runs his hands through his hair and paces back and forth while Wheeler lists off whatever the hell he needs him to do. Hawk is a piece of shit, but he's only helping because of his brother—that much is clear. There's no other reason for the governor to be here, injured, unless it's motivation to keep Hawk in line.

Wheeler casually holds a standard-issue Glock, the one he probably lifted off of Jimmy. If Wheeler was going to get the drop on anyone, it would be that kid.

With them distracted, I lift onto the tops of my hands, trying to shift them from low behind me to under me. I need leverage and tension or, at the very least, some fucking miracle so that I can maneuver myself free.

"You're pissed she chose me? That it, Hawk?" I call out, sitting taller as Hawk finally glances my way again. "You hear me, Hawkins? She told me how often she had to fake it with you. Must really hurt that small dick pride you're barely holding on to, knowing that you couldn't keep her."

He stops walking mid-step and points at me with a snarl. "Shut the fuck up."

Smirking, Wheeler turns to me. "You know, Atticus, she was never *yours* to keep. You did the one thing I asked you not to do." He takes Hawk's phone, then strides to stand before me. "Now, you can pay me what you took, or I'll linger in town a bit longer after I've killed you and fucking Griz."

As I release a growl, chest tight from his threat, Wheeler tilts his head. Looking down, his gaze flicks to Griz before returning to me, holding the phone in front of my face. "You will authorize a transfer of that money to my offshore account. Otherwise

I'll happily kill each person in your fucking family until one of you is smart enough to do it."

Before I can even grit out a response, Griz yells, "You can eat crow and choke on it, Wheeler. He's not giving you jackshi—"

The loud bang of gunfire cuts off his words, followed by a wailing shout from him.

"Griz!" Shuffling in a panic, I try to get up, seeing enough to know he was just shot in the leg. "Griz—*Fuck*." I turn back to Wheeler. "Don't."

"There was approximately two hundred million in assets," Wheeler says, completely unaffected. "You're a smart man, Atticus. I know you can easily make an offshore transfer with a simple call to your bank."

Griz bellows, "Fuck you, Wheeler!"

"Quiet." I raise my voice while keeping my eyes locked on Wheeler's.

My grandfather keeps going though. "Don't you fucking give him a goddamn dime, Atticus, or so help me—"

"Shut up, Griz!" I watch as he tilts his head back, eyes squeezed shut as he deals with the pain of being shot. If we're lucky, the bullet went right through.

Wheeler turns on his boot heel and taps the barrel of his gun into Hawk's chest, who's now standing right behind him. "You're already in over your head, Chief. You plan on coming out of this with yours and your brother's lives still intact, then you're going to need to get rid of them once I have what I need."

This time, I flinch at the sound of another firework sounding off. It lights the sky just enough for me to look farther out into the space that was just blanketed with darkness. I do a double take. Then another one shoots high, and as soon as it claps and explodes, scattering like white rain in the sky, I see her.

Hadley. My fucking wife, racing like the wind on the back of her white horse like a goddamn knight. Thank fuck, she's alive. With her head down along the side of Lady's neck, and not slowing, she's headed in a direct path, right for us.

Just as both Hawk and Wheeler hear the hooves of her horse, turning toward her, a series of things happen in succession. She's the perfect diversion. Hawk hauls himself and his brother away enough so that Wheeler is shoved and almost trampled by her horse. She doesn't slow until she starts to turn. The horse is barely coming down from a trot before she launches herself off its back and is running straight to me.

"Ace," Seraphine calls out. "Down!"

Seconds later, the whirring sound of two bullets coming from a silencer hit Wheeler. One in the hand, forcing away his weapon, and the other blowing out his knee, taking him down. He screams as he hits the ground. Presh comes from the corner of the house, moving straight for Griz, whose eyes are still thankfully open, chest still rising and falling steadily.

"Ace!" Hadley calls out, arms pumping fast with her eyes locked on mine.

"I'm here, baby," I say as adrenaline courses through my veins, mixing with relief that she's okay. I rock myself forward once more with enough force and leverage to finally snap these zip ties.

As soon as Hadley reaches me, she sits right on my lap. Our arms wrap around each other just before our lips collide in a kiss fueled by the fear we've just experienced. A short cry bursts from her lips as she pulls back to catch her breath, my forehead resting against hers when she frames my face in her hands.

"I thought you were—" The words cut off as my voice cracks, and she kisses me again.

"Nope." She shakes her head. "You're not getting out of this marriage that easily," she says through a watery laugh. As she peppers kisses along my jaw, my chest burns with the emotions crashing into me.

The moment I saw her car explode, I stopped breathing. My life has been intertwined with hers for so long, before she kissed me or looked at me the way she is right now. I don't believe in anything resembling religion, but there's something that's woven itself around me and this woman in a way that's bigger than both of us. Coincidence and misfortune, sure. But reverence and appreciation for getting to love her is something I feel deep in the marrow of my bones.

"I kind of like the idea of you tied up. Should have left those ties on." She makes me chuckle, even with tears streaking down her beautiful face. "Maybe later, yeah?" Kissing me once more, she shifts off of my lap just as Seraphine approaches.

"Let's get you on your feet, Foxx," Seraphine says as she flips open her pocket knife. With a quick swipe, she cuts the ties at my feet and helps me stand, my wife getting up with me. "Nothing like the women riding in to save your ass, huh?"

But just as I let out a laugh, Hadley gasps as Wheeler yanks her arm and pulls her against him. With her back to his front, his arm is looped around her neck; his hand is nearly blown off, so he holds her tightly in a headlock by the crook of his elbow. She cries out as he digs his gun into her side with his other hand.

I step forward without thinking, my gaze on Hadley's terrified expression, but Seraphine blocks me with her arm, holding me back. The action nearly has me feral, until she steps in front of me slightly, and I see the gun tucked into the waistband of her pants. She knows I'll have a better chance of grabbing it without being seen than she will.

"You really"—he breathes hard, spit drooling from his mouth as he limps, trying to pull her farther from me—"made a mess of this, pumpkin."

Hadley's eyes water as she tries to gain her footing from being pulled back, her bare feet slipping, unable to gain any traction. Digging her fingers into his arm, she tries to hit the mangled flesh. "I'm not your pumpkin."

Wheeler tuts like her words mean nothing to him.

I've never wanted to kill him more than I do at this moment. I'm seconds away from tearing that arm right off his body. "Take your hands off my wife."

"Not yet," Seraphine grits out quietly.

"My name is Mrs. Hadley Foxx," my wife seethes in a strained voice and through a clenched jaw, just as Hawk comes to his full height behind Wheeler. It has my nerves ratcheting even higher, until I see the look of disdain on his face, aimed right at the same man I'm staring at.

The cocked gun Wheeler holds digs into Hadley's ribs and his mangled hand turns up, his arm tightening around her neck even more, which has her eyes widening and body straining. Even if Hawk makes a move to protect her from Wheeler, there's no guarantee his gun won't go off.

"Hadley, look at me!" I shout to her.

"Shut up, Foxx," Wheeler hisses, along with other scathing words, but instead of letting them sink in, I lock eyes with her and shuffle for one important thing that she'll understand.

"Where you think all men should be," I say, pushing past the roughness in my throat so she can hear me clearly. Her eyes dart around my face, more tears streaking her flushed cheeks. "Where. You. Prefer. Me."

And like the good fucking girl she is, her eyes widen as it

registers what I'm asking her to do. She deadweights her body and drops to her knees. Hawk moves fast from behind them, taking the opening and shoving Wheeler just enough that it knocks him off-balance. I tug the gun from Seraphine's back, and in one fluid motion, flip the safety, raise, aim, and fire off one clean shot.

The sound of sirens is faint in the distance just as another firework pops off above. The glow of red and white bleeds from the sky and lights up the mess around us—Wheeler slumped over on the ground, eyes open with a bullet hole in the center of his forehead.

Hadley's in my arms again in the next breath as I lift her to her feet, her chest heaving from crying. "You're okay, I've got you. I've got you," I tell her softly, holding on and kissing the side of her head.

Pulling back, my hands frame her face now covered in tears and dirt.

Her face squints as she kisses me. "Tell me this is over now," she says with a labored breath.

"It's over. You're safe," I say, taking a few deep breaths to get her to calm down. There isn't a single ounce of regret for killing that bastard.

She lets out a choppy exhale from pursed lips, head jerking in a shaky nod as she repeats, "It's over."

I run my fingers through Hadley's hair and hold her tightly, pressing my lips to her forehead. "We're okay. I've got you." I keep repeating it to soothe her, and maybe myself as well.

Like I need to confirm it one last time, I look over and see there's no movement from her father. It should've happened sooner, but at least now he's gone. Hawk hovers over his brother, who doesn't seem to be moving either. Seraphine collects the gun that Wheeler had and holds it to her side.

"Don't think about going anywhere," she says, pointing at Hawk. He doesn't seem ready to up and run. If anything, he looks numb.

Hadley's attention flicks around, following where Seraphine just was, before her head turns to look behind me. My chest aches as it registers where she's looking. Her body tenses, eyes widening, just before she's sprinting from my arms and in the direction of…

"Griz!"

Chapter 41

Ace

"You're thinking awful hard over there," Hadley says as the triage nurse cleans and bandages the road burn that's scraped up her torso. She said she hit the concrete hard when her car exploded. If I believed in it, I would think it was divine intervention and coincidence mingling like old friends trying to keep one of the best people on this planet alive and okay. Whatever it was, I'll never stop feeling grateful.

Sitting on the gurney across from me, she stares at the ceiling, and I give her some quiet moments to process what we've just survived. Her chin wobbles, trying to hold in what she can. I can tell she doesn't want to shed any tears for a man who had hurt her in so many inconceivable ways. And that pain is only amplified by the fact that she watched her father do monstrous things tonight, threaten her life, and then be shot dead.

"I'd like to hold you." I look down at the stitches being sewn into my wrist. "As soon as this is done…"

She nods and wipes away the tears, batting them away like she's mad they're even falling. "I'm not crying over him dying. It's for everything we've just survived." She pinches the bridge of her nose, eyes closing as she speaks softly. "Wheeler and I had the same taste for spicy foods. We're both left-handed and thought horses should have ridiculous names." A breath whooshes from her mouth as she shakes her head, working through it. "But that's it. That's where our similarities ended. The things that made me feel close to him when I was younger didn't outweigh all the lies. He showed me how much he *didn't* love me for much longer than showing me he did. I don't want to be sad about him being gone now."

"You mourn however you need to, but don't for one second feel bad about it. You can be sad and angry or forget about him tomorrow. Doesn't matter to me. That's for you to handle and for me to make sure you're okay. I'm here when you need me. And I'm not going anywhere." Inhaling deeply, I try to ease the tension in my body. I'm still wound so fucking tight from everything that's happened. "I didn't expect all this…"

She tilts her head to the side, listening as her eyes search mine.

"This wasn't how this was supposed to go down. In the end, Wheeler still ended up dead, and I should be content, but I almost lost—" I close my eyes, trying to wipe away the thought. I can't even think about the reality of losing her; it makes me sick to my stomach. "Your father and Hawk…" Meeting her gaze again, I shake my head. "I had a gut feeling that something wasn't right, but I didn't—"

"Save the day?" she finishes for me and stands to move closer. With her bottom lip pouting, she settles into my lap, ignoring the nurse still suturing my wrist. "Sometimes it's the unexpected hero. And baby, I saved the fucking day on a white horse and all," she says with a beaming smile. "Well, me and Seraphine."

"You called her?" I ask, a bit surprised.

Her arms slide around my neck. "She decided to try one of my cocktails, have a chat, and leave me her number in case I ever needed it."

I huff out a laugh. "'Course she did."

She leans in to kiss me, and it feels so good to have her in my arms and safe.

Smiling against her lips, I say, "You saved my ass, and I'll be honest, I feel like you've been saving me without trying for a long time."

"Just following your lead, baby," she responds. "Saving each other kind of feels like our thing."

Fiasco General isn't all that large, but between an explosion during the Fourth of July festivities and the showdown that took place along the riverside at The Holey Donut, the entire place is buzzing. We both didn't want to leave until we knew what was happening with Griz. It had been six hours since he arrived by ambulance and was wheeled into the ICU. Soon after we were cleared from the ER, I passed out in a chair in the waiting room with a sleeping Hadley in my arms.

Buzz buzz buzz.

My phone buzzing incessantly wakes me from the most uncomfortable sleep of my life. With a stiff neck, I swipe on my phone to find a wall of texts from my brothers.

LINCOLN:

Going to need an update about what's going on, Ace.

GRANT:

I'm on my way down to the hospital now. Laney is going to head over to your house, Linc.

LINCOLN:

Sounds good. Faye had to tap in and help Del with something. Any word on Griz?

ACE:

Nothing yet.

LINCOLN:

Alright I'll be down there soon. How's Hadley?

"Tell him I'm good but could use a little best friend time," she says, reading over my shoulder.

I pocket my phone after firing off one last text and hold her hand as we make our way toward the nurses' station. "I'd like to see Griswald Foxx," I say as the nurse types away on her computer.

She gives me a tight-lipped smile. "Sure thing, I'll be right back."

Never underestimate the power of a well-placed pawn, Griz said once when I was young. It seemed like there were millions of ways to play the game, but the smartest moves happened when you were thinking at an average of six steps ahead. He's always been the best at that part—seeing what might happen and a dozen different alternatives. He'd never do anything that would sacrifice his queen. On the board and in life.

Hadley tilts her neck as we wait, working out the kinks from being knocked around last night and sleeping in waiting room chairs. "Can I ask you something?"

I kiss her fingers that are clasped with mine. "Anything."

"Before we got separated, you wanted to talk to me. Was it about finding a way to"—she clears her throat, lowering her voice—"make sure my father was out of the picture for good?"

Just then, the nurse returns to the station desk with Del on her heels. I know exactly what's transpiring behind the double doors. It has my chest tightening all over again. "Del." I nod, holding my hand out to shake his.

Hadley tenses up, brow furrowing. "Del, is everything okay?"

He glances at me, and then tilts his head to follow him back. "I swear, you and your brothers are really going to force me to retire. C'mon, Faye's already here. She said you two were out cold in those chairs when she arrived."

I clasp his shoulder. "You're a good man, Del. Thank you."

As we reach a room at the end of the hall, I lean closer to Hadley to answer her question. "Making sure your father was out of the picture was to protect you…and to help him." I nod at Griz as we walk into his hospital room.

I cross my arms over my chest as Hadley rushes to his side.

"Griz," she says on a clipped cry, wrapping her arms around his neck. "You scared the shit out of me."

I can tell by his widened eyes and the quick glance at Del

that he wasn't expecting to see us. He was planning to use this unfortunate situation to his advantage if he could. It would make a planned exit a little easier on him.

He's bandaged up, arm in a sling, but he's dressed, no oxygen or wires anywhere. He looks fine, minus the bandage and splint covering up the stitches from a bullet hole in his knee.

"A bit surprised to see us?" I ask him, and then mumble, "Pain in my ass, Griz. If you'd just waited or talked to me." I glance at Del. "Is she here yet?"

He shakes his head, then checks his phone.

Griz tilts his head at me, probably assuming I'm referring to Agent Bea Harper, a U.S. Marshall, who's shown up countless times at our front door for some reason or another. The last time led to Laney finding a life here after she was deposited on our doorstep. I know Bea's found her way back to Fiasco a couple of times since, but I was still looking to cash in a favor the U.S. Marshall owed me. I'm done losing people.

I smile at Del. "Del, mind taking a walk for me?" I ask, just as Grant comes in.

"What's going on?" he asks, looking around the small hospital room.

Faye nods, knowing what I need to share. A plan that she's been helping to make happen, long before my focus had shifted to marrying and keeping Hadley safe.

Del gives me a pointed look as he laughs to himself. "You know, some might get the impression that I take orders from you, Ace." He glances at Hadley and then again at Faye, who's sitting with her arms crossed. "I don't, for the record," Del says as he clasps my shoulder. "I'll keep an eye out."

We all watch the detective exit, silence taking over the room before Griz speaks. "Atticus—"

"There were nine," I cut him off as I take a seat. "It was a nightmare trying to figure out who was an actual threat and who just needed to be paid back what Wheeler had taken from them. But in total, we figured out nine, including Wheeler, who would rather see the dead stay buried."

Griz locks eyes with me, but I keep talking because he needs to hear all of this. "Two were already dead—the King brothers." I shift my attention to Faye, who has a past with the King brothers, then look to Hadley when I continue. "A list of men from a Fourth of July dinner party about a decade ago helped narrow down the rest. A coming together of Wheeler's closest business dealings that were guaranteed to go south eventually." It was a lucky assumption to keep that list of people after all this time. "Two criminals who defected from the Russian Bratva, a bloodstock agent, Governor Hawkins and his brother, the fire chief, and a cattle rancher who liked wearing rodeo buckles that weren't his.

"And then Wheeler, of course. He was the largest threat if he still remained alive." I keep my eyes on my wife's. "Then you started getting threats." Shaking my head, I huff out a laugh. "You refused to say anything and made all of them sweat."

Griz wraps his good arm around her and squeezes, mumbling, "Brave and thickheaded. That's our girl."

"Those threats changed my motivation," I confess to them, as if it isn't obvious. "The only two I hadn't considered a threat were the fire chief and the governor. They weren't supposed to be part of the plan. Until the governor decided he should still expect the financial backing that Wheeler had promised." I shake my head. "Asshole," I say under my breath. Swallowing roughly, I lean back, head pressing against the wall. "But that was irrelevant because the plan had always been to remove

Wheeler. If he went to prison and was still alive, then there wouldn't be a way to guarantee her safety," I say, lifting my chin to Griz. "Or Hadley's."

Hadley grits her teeth, eyes closing as she whispers, "The damage my father caused…I'm so sorry…"

"Knock it off, Hadley Jean," Griz says. "You're done apologizing for anything your father did. None of that was ever on you."

Griz's brow furrows, trying to work it out. "I understand that. I understand what it means and the lengths a man will go to keep the woman he loves safe."

"I know you do. Been doing that for a while now, haven't you?"

Grant shifts his attention to me, putting his coffee down and leaning forward. And Faye leans against the wall, arms crossed with a knowing smirk on her face.

"You've been making plans to join her, haven't you?" I ask Griz, eyebrows lifting.

"What the fuck?" Grant interrupts. "Who's he talking about, Griz?"

But I keep going. "You needed to tighten things up here as best as you could first." I watch my grandfather try to keep a brave face.

Hadley looks at me, and then at Griz, trying to read between the lines of what isn't being plainly said.

Griz crosses his arms and shakes his head with a huff. "Dammit, Atticus."

"Such a romantic, Griz," Faye adds.

"I found an old postcard in the mess that you like to call your office downstairs. It was from a town in Montana that when I asked Julian if he could look into it, he said didn't exist, but he found it anyway."

Griz smirks beneath his mustache, almost like he was proud of me, albeit pissed off at me for finding it.

"The town wasn't on any map," I say, glancing down at my phone buzzing in my hand. "Then a little over a year ago, when Faye went missing for a couple of weeks with her sister Maggie, who never came back, I knew my hunch wasn't wrong. Those girls were given a chance to see their mother. Shelby Calloway was in hiding because of Wheeler. She trained for Finch & King for too long not to know what they'd been doing, and that put a target on her back. You ensured her safety and haven't forgotten about her for one day since."

"He hasn't. But I'm betting neither did she," Faye adds.

Grant stares at both of us, and then shakes his head with a disbelieving laugh. "What the hell? The both of you."

I drag my fingers through my hair. "I've been trying to make it right, tying up loose ends. As soon as you started making arrangements about work, I knew you were planning on leaving. And that fucking marriage stipulation only sealed the deal at confirming my suspicions." My phone buzzes again, twice more in succession. "That meant that anything or anyone who might make it unsafe so that Shelby could come back here, and so that you would stay, needed to be handled."

Hadley gets up from next to Griz and rushes to me. She ignores the rest of the room and wraps one arm around my neck as my arms circle her waist. Brushing her hand along my brow and down my jaw, she says, "I love you."

I look down at her sweet smile and blink back the tears that have been brimming in my eyes.

"I'm right here." She lifts onto her toes to give me a soft kiss, and I lean down to rest my forehead on hers. When I take a breath and focus back on my grandfather, my phone buzzes again.

> **HARPER:**
> Just pulling in. You had better be right about this. If it's not safe here, we're going to have a bigger problem on our hands.

> **HARPER:**
> I hope you know what you're doing.

> **HARPER:**
> Ah fuck, what the hell is Del doing here?

"I'm not ready to see you go anywhere, old man. You and I butt heads, but I need you around here to piss me off as often as possible."

Hadley covers her mouth, a small gasp escaping just as the side door opens. The timing of it couldn't have been any more perfect. A wafted breeze of clove cigarettes enters the room first, followed by a weathered and annoyed U.S. Marshall. And behind her stands a teary-eyed, and very much alive, Shelby Calloway.

"Oh hell." His face squints up, standing as fast as a man with a bullet hole in his leg can. He rights his emotions quickly when he asks, "What are you doing here?" Without waiting for an answer, he wraps an arm around her as she moves with him back to sit. She releases a cry filled with longing, burying her face in his neck.

Hadley squeezes her arm around me as she loops her other around Faye's shoulder while we watch two people find their way back to one another. I let out a breath, knowing that it was all worth it for this moment, right here.

Shelby rests her forehead against Griz's, and I can hear her tell him, "Every day." Her lips press softly to his. "I think of you and my girls every single day."

Griz swallows audibly, holding her tighter, and I can tell there's not much he can say at the moment, his eyes closed as he whispers something to her that makes her choke out another sob. When she looks up and sees her daughter, she rushes toward her. Griz watches on as she and Faye hold one another. Loud words of "missed you" and "so happy you're here" are peppered between cries. I know regardless of how we got to this moment, it was all worth it.

Hadley glides her hands around me once more and searches my face, tears falling from her eyes as they meet mine. "You're a good man, Atticus Foxx." She leans in closer, kissing my lips first, then my cheek as she says, "So much better than the fantasy." We both smile as she whispers, "I love you, baby."

Hearing those words, feeling them from her, hadn't been in my plans for a long time, but not a single part of me is anything but thankful for it. I brush away the wetness on her cheeks and rest my forehead against hers, letting those words seep into me. Wrapping my arms around her, I hold on to her tightly, burying my face in her neck as I mumble out what all of this unknowingly proved.

"I love you, too."

Chapter 42

Hadley

September: Teaching Lily and Lark how to beat their dad in chess.

Frozen grapes dipped in Pop Rocks…genius!

"It's a downgrade when it comes to square footage, but it's yours for whenever you might need it," I say, walking through the foyer and into the main living space of my townhouse. I still have furniture here and paintings on the walls, but I've slowly been folding my things into our house.

"*That black cat clock yours?*" *Ace asked as he flipped a pancake.*

"*So fun, right? The eyes tick back and forth, and the tail vibrates on the hour,*" *I said with a smile as I added the protein shake into my coffee.*

With his lips tilted to the right, he huffed a small laugh. Then he took a sip of his coffee from a hot pink mug with bright orange letters that read, "Slut for Smut." "Could have done without the dick-shaped appetizer plates, but the rest of it feels like you." His eyes flicked up to mine. *"Feels more like a home now with you and your things in it."* Popping a strawberry in his mouth, he smiled, and I nearly slapped myself just to make sure this was, in fact, real life.

I squeeze Ace's hand as I walk through my old galley kitchen. I wasn't sure what to do with my townhouse at first, but keeping it means I can rent it out or, in this case, allow family to use it. "The walk to Hooch's is about ten minutes from here, but with your golf cart, I bet you could make it in three," I say to Griz with a wink. "And everything on Main is footsteps away. If you want, I can have the girls at Crescent de Lune keep a standing morning croissant order. Just say the word, and they'll drop it off. It's a nice little perk."

"Might be nice to have some space of our own while the farmhouse is built," Shelby says to Griz as she looks out the floor-to-ceiling windows in the living room.

Griz gives me the biggest Cheshire cat smile. And I can't help but mirror it and follow it up with a fist bump. I know exactly why he's considering moving into this space. I assumed he'd want some privacy to enjoy this fresh start with Shelby, but the urgency came when Ace decided to check on him early this morning. My husband got a full frontal view of his grandfather as Shelby rode his face.

Ace rushed into our bedroom and shut the door behind him. Leaning against the door, eyes wide, he said, "Just saw Griz's dick waving in the wind and far too much of Shelby." He rubbed his eyes, looking like he didn't know whether to be appalled or proud.

I think this townhouse might be a good way to ease the adjustment of all these changes around here. First me, then

Shelby. The eldest Foxx boys were going through some growing pains, and a little space wouldn't hurt.

"Since my grandson is being so prudish about how I like to fit in a morning ride, it looks like you've got yourself some new tenants, Hadley Jean."

Ace wipes his hand over his mouth and grumbles out, "Jesus Christ."

"It's a big adjustment from where I was, but I like the change," Shelby says as she sits on Griz's lap. She combs her fingers through his gray hair. "But I'm ready for all of this with you. I spent too long thinking about what-ifs and now I'd love to lean into the why-nots."

"Me too, sweetheart," he says, tipping his head back to look at her.

"Want to go for a little walk while they look around a bit?" Ace tilts his head toward the door. When he holds out his hand, I weave my fingers through his. We ride the elevator down to the main floor and walk along the sidewalk up the north side of Main.

I glance at the fire station. Hawk was removed as fire chief after he was charged with a short list of things after the Fourth of July. He'll likely do community service and help his brother wade through the fallout. I doubt the governor will continue for another term when this one runs out. And though he came out looking like an innocent kidnapped bystander, Faye had gathered plenty of text exchanges between him and my father, not to mention the colorful texts he had sent me. All of it would tank his campaign in a minute.

"You doing okay?" I ask Ace as he quietly observes the bustling downtown. Fiasco is setting up for the Fall Festival that's gearing up now that September's finally starting to feel a little less like summer. There are at least a handful of weeks left of warm days, but everyone's eager to start their apple ciders and pumpkin spices. The Downtown Business Association is readying for a film festival to come through as well. They aren't instant fixes, but the progress on tourism is moving in the right direction.

"I've lived with Griz almost my entire life." He swallows and glances at me. "As much as I don't want another viewing like this morning, I'm going to miss having him so close."

I squeeze his hand and rest my head on his shoulder. Catching another glimpse of how this man is so caring and soft for the people he loves makes me appreciate the many sides to Ace even more.

I smile when I look out and see the new sign for Loni's Boutique lit up. The soft-pink neon and the pink-and-white awnings are only the first of many upgrades she's made to the store.

"I don't know how it happened, but I have a feelin' you had something to do with it," Loni said when I saw that her Closing sign had been removed. *"My sister is coming up from Nashville, and the online shop opens in the fall."*

Two whistles sound from across the street. Romey and Prue sit outside in front of Teasers, likely gossiping about something going on around here. "You two are still hot as hell," Romey calls out with a wave.

"Just appreciatin' the view," Prue echoes. "OH! Hadley, are you coming to book club this week?"

"You know it, Prue!" I shout back.

"Good." She looks at her sister, and then asks us, "Any chance we can host it at that new place you two are keeping under wraps over there?"

We both know the locals are going batshit over rumors of a

private, adults-only club being built. And while most of Fiasco loves tradition, the conservatives are just as nosy as the rest of them.

Ace and I glance at each other, smirking, before we both say in unison, "What place?"

"Jimmy, the rules are simple." I exhale to gather some patience, trying not to get frustrated with having to repeat this again. "This isn't a resume builder. If you're taking this job, then you're going to make it yours. But under no circumstances do you talk about what you see when you're here."

With eyes wide and excited nodding, he says, "I'm not going to let you down here, Hadley. The police force just wasn't for me. I've jumped around a bit, but I think if you can trust me with this, I'll be exactly the kind of manager you need for this place."

I can't help but smile. Jimmy Dugan lasted only a few more weeks with the Fiasco Police Department after getting knocked unconscious and relieved of his weapon. My father could have killed him. I'm still not sure if Jimmy was truly knocked unconscious or just passed out from the chaos, but he'd helped Ace, and my husband trusted him.

"We open next weekend. Our VIP list has been vetted, and there's no such thing as walk-ins. We'll figure that piece out as we move along. I'm trusting you with what could very well be one of the most taboo things to ever happen in Fiasco. Are you sure you're up for it?"

Before Jimmy can answer, my husband comes down the dark staircase in his signature suit pants and white dress shirt.

Damn, it's hard not to smile at the way this man looks at me. He carries a long white box in one hand with a devilish smile painted on his full, handsome lips. "He's up for it," he interjects. "Right, Jimmy?"

Jimmy stands taller and nods once more. "Yes, sir. You both can count on me."

Ace nods, and then wraps his arms around me. "Hey, sugar."

I melt against him. "Hi, baby."

"Jimmy?" Ace says, his attention still fully on me. "You can go now."

"Oh, yup. Sure thing." He looks around him and feels in his pockets for his keys as he turns toward the stairs. "Have a great night."

I watch as he jogs up the steps, and I wait to hear the door slide shut behind him. "You think he'll actually keep this position?" I ask. Ace leans into my neck and kisses along my throat.

"He'll handle it. The man is coming up on twenty-four. This just might be the best job he'll ever have. And there's a little bit of fear in knowing I don't like to be disappointed."

I hum against his lips and kiss him. When I lean back, I look at the white box he dropped on the bar. "Did you bring me a present?"

He pushes it toward me with a smirk as he shifts around to the back of the long black bar in the center of the room.

The Foxx Den is an adults-only club. A place to experience and explore fantasies and desires. It's not the kind of place Laney's writing press releases about, but rather finding VIP guests who show interest by word of mouth. Law and Tessa Riggs have shared it with some of their clientele, and we're ready to open this coming weekend. It's not a place for Fiasco townies, though there are benefits to locals. It lives under the umbrella of a Foxx-branded business, but it adds to the allure of Fiasco, boosting tourism.

Between here and Midnight Proof, my evenings are full. The architectural design that Seraphine planned with me is exquisite. If Midnight Proof is a Gatsby-style speakeasy, then The Foxx Den is its bohemian sidekick. The place is bathed in deep golds and blues with rich textures like satins and velvets, and with lighting that ranges from moody to eclectic. It's as welcoming as it is arousing. It's unusual, pushes boundaries, and is a gamble, but that seems to be our specialty.

When I open the white box, I cover my mouth and bark a laugh. "These are very *beautiful* flowers, Ace." I glance up at him as he sips on the bourbon neat he just poured. The tip of his lips lets me know he's more than pleased with himself. Inside the box are a half dozen flower vibrators and, from what I can count, three different-sized dildos arranged in a way that they truly look like the best kind of floral arrangement anyone has ever given. At its center is a riding crop. Not just any riding crop or one that I would use for a long ride on anything other than my husband's mouth or cock.

I hold up the long leather piece. One end has folded soft black leather, and the other, closer to the handle, a plume of black ostrich feathers. A rush of shivers rolls through my body, thinking about how we watched something just like this used at the club in Strutt's Peak.

"You've been working so hard." Looking up and around at the space, he adds, "The place looks incredible. I'm impressed—as usual—but I'm proud of you," he breathes out, and the softness of his smile melts me from the inside out. "So…I think my wife deserves an evening filled with rewards."

Taking his glass of bourbon from his hand, I sip once, then

twice, with my eyes locked on his. "An entire evening, huh?" I glance at the box of goodies he just gave me.

He watches me with the dangerously arrogant disposition he always seems to have. With a deep, low hum, he circles from behind the bar, standing in front of me—his tall and broad frame so close makes my pulse tick higher as a flutter settles between my legs. Pushing my hair behind my shoulder, he leans down to place a kiss along my neck. "You'll take everything I plan on giving you tonight," he says, lifting my chin to look up at him. "Do you understand?"

I shift my body closer. *Oh, I understand.*

I exhale the words I know he's waiting for. "Yes, sir."

Hooking his finger with mine, he scoops up the floral toy arrangement, tucking it under his arm and guiding us down the corridor, out of the lobby, and toward the room that we've deemed our observation space. A space purely designed for exhibitionism and voyeuristic fun. Sprouting off from here are more private areas, all specifically curated for different tastes. Each spot can transform into any variety of fantasies the guests choose—as simple as sex with a stranger to other kinks that range from bondage to primal play and every unique and exploratory experience in between. It's all been quite educational, and I love to learn. Tonight, however, we have the entirety of The Foxx Den to ourselves. And my husband seems to be in a *giving* mood.

Ace shrugs off his jacket and drapes it meticulously over the turquoise velvet chaise longue. The chandelier lighting bounces warm tones and shadows along every surface as he cues up a playlist on his phone that's perfect for the evening ahead. A low bass echoes through the speakers built into the ceiling and walls.

He circles behind the chair and taps its back before he starts unbuttoning the cuffs of his shirt. I do as he requests and watch with rapt attention as he rolls his sleeves up, showing off his slutty forearms. I can't help smiling at how stupidly sexy he looks. Leaning forward, I tease out my tongue and he swipes his thumb along the path I just licked. "This feels rather sweet," I whisper.

He smirks before he takes a small step back, and then holds up three fingers.

"Don't threaten me with three fingers, baby. You know you're at least as thick as that."

But instead of cracking a smile or mumbling out a curse like he usually does when I say shit like that to him, he inhales slowly, and on the exhale, the dominant man that lingers around his edges is in front of me now. Strong and demanding. Patient and measured. Singularly focused. "I've been pretty lenient with how often your bratty mouth goes unpunished, sugar. I've kept a tally. Every time you've said something that warranted more than a good, hard fuck, I've kept count." He cracks his neck to the side. "I think it's time for me to indulge and deliver a little discipline."

I'm dead. I'm already wet and needy from the anticipation of this, but that confession just soaked my pathetic excuse for panties. My nipples are hard, and I'm craving his mouth, his fingers, his cock to fill me in every filthy way he wants.

He stands in front of me, wiping his thumb along his lower lip. "Tell me what I want to hear." Unbuckling his belt slowly, he pulls the dark brown leather through each loop.

I nibble at my bottom lip. "Yes, Daddy."

When his eyes shift to mine, he gives me a nod in approval.

His hands frame my face, thumbs caressing along my jaw and drifting over my lips.

From behind me, he lifts my skirt and asks, "Spanks or bites, sugar?"

I swallow the laugh that tries to bubble out of me.

"Either one works for me. I'm marking up this perfect ass tonight before I clean up how much you've already dripped for me."

Fuck it, I'm so turned on that he could throw down a list of all the BDSM options and I'd take whatever he's willing to give me. "Bites."

He doesn't move, and then I remember what he would be waiting for.

"Bites please, sir."

This part of who he is—leading, playing a role, and leaning into it with such confidence, holy goddesses does it make me want to play with him right back. I can see the hard, thick outline of what this is already doing for him, and my stomach swoops, knowing that he's pleased.

His hand moves gently up the center of my back, easing my body down. "Face down, ass up, wife."

I almost squeal and clap my hands at his direction. Facing him, I kneel, draping my body forward. My chest reaches the soft surface, and I tip my hips back, making it so that my ass is nice and high, just as he likes.

He pushes my dress up and over my ass and then tucks his finger along the string of my thong. Pulling it taut, he rolls his fist around it so that the lace material rubs tightly against my clit. That move alone has me audibly exhaling.

"Yes, please," I mumble into the velvet chair.

As he settles behind me, his lips skate along my ass cheek. It's so soft that when he swipes his tongue and then bites at the skin, I let out a tiny yelp and laugh. He does it again, and I know he's holding back. Maybe I like a little bit of masochism, after all.

"You can do better than that," I taunt.

And I know he wasn't expecting it, because I can hear a small laugh huff out of him.

His wrist twists again, pulling the lace tighter along my pussy as his hand moves in between my legs to rub along the material covering my clit. "What did I say about that bratty mouth?" He grips my skin, twisting the material until it rips.

"Oh god," I rush out. It steals my breath when he follows it up with a graze of his teeth, and this time, opens wider, biting down. *Fuck.* He runs his tongue along the indented marks that his bite left behind, and for reasons that I'll never understand, I'm panting and needy.

He leans from behind me, over my body, and says quietly, "Tell me what I want to hear."

"More, Daddy," I beg. I don't think twice about what he wants from me.

Moving back, he kisses my shoulder tenderly. I can hear him reach for the box of goodies he brought me, and I peer over my shoulder just as he finds my favorite little vibrating rose. He turns it on the slowest mode and drags it to the front of me, nestling it right on top of my clit. It offers the perfect suction that I know will set me off almost immediately. With the toy firmly placed, he drags his thumb from his other hand up and down my slick slit, never pushing inside, simply teasing and making me wetter with every pass. He hums in approval as I moan and hold my breath just as my orgasm hits, tingles running down my spine and settling deep in my core. My skin heats as I gasp for another breath. On my exhale, he flips me over and then nestles his shoulders between my legs, shoving them as wide as they'll go. With his eyes locked on mine, he licks up my cum, making me whimper.

I blink slowly, still aroused and half-dazed as he says, "Another one, sugar."

Before I can register what he's demanding, he focuses on my

pussy, kisses my thigh, and then slowly fucks two fingers into me. My clit is so sensitive that I can feel the pressure of his entry there too. "Yes," I draw out, ending with a moaning plea of his name.

He curls the tips of his fingers, searching for my G-spot and finding it within a few seconds, like some sort of sexual GPS that's been integrated into his digits. His other hand trails to my lower abdomen, increasing the pressure. I lose track of anything other than the build of another orgasm as his fingers quicken their pace, as if he's chasing and coaxing an orgasm that I know is going to tear through me.

"That's it, soak my hand, sugar."

My eyes are watering, breaths stuttering, legs trembling, and he doesn't slow. If anything, the motion of those two fingers increases until the muscles in my stomach tighten, and suddenly I scream out as Ace removes his fingers and with them a flowing release that feels like a fucking awakening. My body shudders, and I try catching my breath, but Ace's palm rubs wildly, drawing it further out of me.

I open my mouth, but the only thing that comes out is a quiet laugh. "You just made me squirt," I say, trying to sit up, never not in awe of what he's capable of doing with my body. But he doesn't let up. Instead of letting that be his trophy, he wants more. My limbs feel weak, spent like putty, but he's doing just as he promised—whatever he wants. His mouth covers my clit, sucking it into his mouth, and my hands grip onto his shoulders like a lifeline.

"Please," I pant. "I can't... I need..."

He tips his head up from between my legs, and with my arousal glistening from his lips, he says, "You can tell me what you need, but we both know you're not in charge right now." Reaching for something, he shifts slightly, and seconds later, his lips are softly kissing my clit. He peppers more kisses along my pussy lips and softly draws along the edges with his tongue. It's soothing and slow, and my eyes drift closed momentarily until one fast, stinging slap hits my pussy. And then another. On the third, when my eyes fly open, I realize he's using the riding crop. But it's the fourth time that the worn leather meets my sensitive skin that has one more deliciously earthshattering orgasm erupting from me, and with it, a throaty moan that I barely recognize as mine as stars fill my vision.

"Look at you dripping for me." Kissing the inside of my thigh, he runs his fingers up and down the other, easing my body down and adding the perfect version of praise. "That's it. My beautiful fucking girl."

I should be depleted, but I'm riding whatever kind of high this is as I smile and drag my fingers through his hair. "I thought you said all night, husband…"

He wraps his arms around my waist and lifts me into his arms, shifting us to the other side of the room and depositing me right onto the edge of the bed that's nestled against the wall.

Moving away, he grabs his bottle of bourbon. "We're nowhere near being done. And you fucking know it."

I grow more and more giddy as he twists the top and rocks off the stopper to this particular bottle.

"Open," he demands. The dominance laced in his voice has my body buzzing all over again.

I open my mouth. And because I'm an overachiever when it comes to what this man desires, I stick out my tongue and spread my knees.

He practically growls in response. "That's my girl."

I hum and let a smile break at hearing him call me his girl. Every time, it's the same feeling—special, safe, loved, worshipped. I never understood what it meant for a man to worship my body until I experienced the way my husband touches me, kisses me, teases me, tastes me.

"I want to see you tease my cock with the taste of bourbon on your tongue."

My mouth waters. Whatever that says about me, I couldn't give a shit.

"Play with that pretty pussy for me," he demands.

His tongue reaches the rim first just as he flashes a smirk with his eyes locked with mine. He takes a pull, and I watch as he works it down his throat, Adam's apple bobbing, lips and chin wet.

"Would you like some?" he offers.

I nod slowly.

He glances down at his pants. "Take it out."

It feels freeing, allowing him to take the lead. In every other part of my life, that's not the case. I run a demanding business. And with that, lead and take on every challenge that comes, all on my own and with feigned confidence in making it seem like I know what the hell I'm doing. I'm a strong feminist. There isn't a single person who would consider me a pushover, but in this moment, submitting to what he wants and doing as he asks, it's a heady combination of letting go and still being in power.

I practically pant as I flip open the button and lower the zipper of his pants, then pull the waist of his boxer briefs out over his thick, fat cock.

As my fingers graze his skin, he hisses.

I swipe my thumb along its head and gather his arousal before leaning in for a taste as my hand moves down to my pussy.

He lets out an approving hum, low and sexy. He likes that.

I glide my fingers teasingly along my slit as I wait for what he wants me to do next.

"Look at how wet you are, sugar. So needy for me," he croons. "Go ahead, tease your pretty little lips, just like that, nice and slow."

I smile up at him as he holds the bottle of bourbon above me, and then slowly tips it. Honey-colored bourbon pours out, and the sting of it splashes onto my tongue and across my lips.

"Let it dribble down your chin and lean forward." As I let it drip onto his cock, I smile, wanting more.

He holds himself at the base and then taps the head along my bourbon-soaked tongue. Letting it rest there, hard and ready, he tilts the bottle above. And more of the bourbon pours. Another splash of warmth colliding with my tongue and along his waiting, eager dick. *Jesus, this is filthy.* And it takes every effort not to smile at knowing how this must look.

"Swallow for me, sugar," he growls.

Humming as my lips close around him, my eyes lock with his as I swallow him down. Taking him deep and then opening slightly so I can drag my tongue along the underside of his cock.

"Making such a mess for me," he grits out. He tips his hips back, teasing himself, pulling out of my mouth to the tip, and then slowly moving himself back in until he hits the back of my throat.

The sounds of wet skin and small moans escape me as I play with my pussy. I'm so needy for more that I ease two fingers in and out of me just to hold myself over for the stretch of him.

He looks down at what I'm doing and then focuses back on my mouth. "Fuck," he rushes out. I try to take more of him in, but instead, he pulls away. His knees hit the floor, and then he's throwing my legs wide with both hands as his mouth hovers just above where I'm still playing. "Feels too fucking good. My turn," he says on an exhale, just as he flattens his tongue and runs it from my cunt to my clit with a savored moan.

Resting back on my elbows, I watch as he does it again, moaning as I writhe against his face. And then my attention shifts to the mirrors around the space. Watching him on his knees feasting on me and moaning for it is one thing, but to see it mirrored back, and to watch myself in the reflection, is intoxicating. Even more than the bourbon he poured out. He takes his time, fucking me with his tongue and then running his knuckles along my pussy lips. My breath hitches at the roughness of his skin and the change in motion.

"More," I plead as my chest rises and falls more quickly now.

But he ignores me and focuses only on what's in front of him. He edges me with the slow movements of his tongue, knowing exactly how to play with my clit as if they're better acquainted now than I am. He draws out every movement, slow and steady, bringing me exactly where he wants me. My thighs tingle, body tensing tightly, and I fight to keep my eyes on him when my orgasm shifts to the surface. With rapt attention, he slides a third finger into my cunt and draws pleasure out in a way that I will never quite understand. His lips and tongue settle on my clit, and with precise pressure and intention, he doesn't ease up until I'm coming so hard that my body bows off the bed with a feral scream.

When he sits back on his heels, I practically beg for him again. I lean up to see what he's doing, and he takes the bottle and runs the rim of it up my thigh and toward my pussy. The cool bottle grazes each of my pussy lips as he makes sure to coat it with exactly what he wants.

"Two of my favorite things," he hums with focused attention. "This is exactly how I want to drink this from now on. The taste of you on the rim as I sip whatever blend I'm in the mood for."

"Holy shit," I mumble with a disbelieving smile. This man is something else.

He pulls the bottle back, takes a lick of the rim, and then tips it into his mouth. I know exactly what he's planning the second I see him move closer. My lips part as Ace wraps his hand around the back of my neck and spits his whiskey laced with my arousal into my mouth. I swallow, letting just a little dribble down my chin, just like he's asked for before.

"Fuck, I love you," he groans, just as the lip of the bottle moves to my clit. He rubs the smooth glass in circles. I'm so sensitive and aware of every sensation that it only takes seconds to be on the edge of another release.

I cry out so loud that it echoes out in the room, the orgasm shoving me forward, forcing pebbles along my arms. Every inch of me is slick with sweat and completely unraveled. Every thought focused solely on my body and how he's not finished.

I can feel him smile against my leg, already thinking about the next punishingly sufficient orgasm he's going to pull from me as he settles his hips between my legs, his stiff cock at my entrance.

I smile, dazed, as I ask, "What are you smiling at, baby?"

He lowers himself over me, kisses my neck, and slides his cock in slowly before he says two words that I'll never get tired of hearing: "My wife."

Chapter 43

Ace

A few months later...

"Five blends," I say with my fingers steepled in front of my mouth.

Laney laughs out, "You're serious?"

My wife smiles as she looks at Lincoln, who's biting on the tip of his pen, waiting for me to keep talking. We've worked together for long enough that he was eager for the other shoe to drop. There was always more with me. However, new blends are something I typically shoot down without pause.

Hadley's pretty blue eyes shift to me, knowing what else I plan to tell them. They're going to flip their shit.

"Hadley, if you bounce your legs any faster in that chair, you're going to take off in flight."

Giggling with mischief, she leans her elbows on the table. "Then stop stalling and get to the good part." She waves her hand to urge me to keep talking. "And aside from moral support, I was hoping to fit in a quickie before I need to open."

Lincoln barks out a laugh and holds up a fist for her to bump.

And I give my wife a look that just reads, *You're in so much trouble later.*

As she bites at her lower lip, I focus back on the entire purpose of this meeting—to get them on board with this. I ran the concepts by Griz this morning during breakfast, and I don't think I've ever seen the man so damn happy.

"Proud of you, Ace," he said. "For a lot of things, but you listen. That's not something I take for granted." It came with a shoulder squeeze and a smile from Shelby, who had witnessed it even though she was pretending she was listening to Hadley carry on about the horse sanctuary they'd been talking about building out.

"We'll have five specialty blends, providing you both like them and they're differentiated enough. And they'll be distributed and exclusive only to five selected resorts worldwide. Plus—"

Lincoln cuts in with, "There's a plus?" He turns to look at Grant, head rearing back. "Are you hearing this?"

Grant glances at Lincoln, and then focuses back on me. "I'm right here, Linc. Yeah, I'm listening to this."

"You're both so damn ornery sometimes it's almost funny," Hadley says.

Lincoln rolls his eyes at her, but he's still smiling.

"The Den will have one as well, a specialty bourbon that my wife has so kindly poured a sample of for everyone."

With that, she passes the tray down the long table in the conference room. We could have had this chat after dinner tonight, but Faye and Shelby always looked bored out of their minds when we started talking about business, and Griz was doing his best to try to steer himself away from the everyday decision-making.

The glasses are held up to the light—a darker amber than normal, thanks to the double barrel and its storage. "It's finished in its own smaller barrel, meaning it never leaves oak until it hits your glass. It's sweeter." I glance at Lincoln, since he'll understand the numbers. "It'll be the highest corn percentage we've used, clocking in at 73 %, with 19 % rye and 8 % barley."

"And what are we calling it?" Laney asks as she sips, humming her enjoyment at the taste.

I glance at my wife, and I'll be honest, the level of excitement she has right now I can't possibly take from her. Giving her a wink, I nod for her to go ahead.

"It's the Sugared Daddy blend," she bursts out.

Grant glances at me with a shake of his head as Laney giggles beside him. "You're serious?"

I shrug my shoulders, wiping my hand over my mouth to keep from smiling as excitedly as Hadley. *Jesus, I love this woman.*

But she cuts in even before I can start explaining. It's her logic, anyway. "Grant, this is an exclusive blend being served only at two locations in the world—Midnight Proof and The Den."

"One," I correct with a quirked eyebrow. "I said yes to that name because it will only be served at one location. Our adult, invite-only club, the Den. The number of people who will ever taste that blend will be so small that the name barely matters."

Hadley gives me a sarcastic glare and rolls her eyes. "Fine. The Den." She covers the side of her mouth and whispers to Laney and Linc, "And Midnight Proof."

"I like it," Lincoln says, with Grant nodding as well. "It's good bourbon, with some bigger adjustments to the mash, but you're keeping all the rules intact. It's smart."

"Alright, my job here is done. I need to get moving," Hadley says, getting up from her chair. "I love you all—you, especially." She points at Laney, giving her a big hug, and then slides her ass on the table next to Lincoln. "You, almost the most." She holds out her fist to him, and they do their ridiculous combination of a secret handshake.

"Are you coming to Lark's game tomorrow?" Lincoln asks.

"Obviously," she says. "I told her I'd bring the speaker. I think they could really use some walk-out music when they're going up to bat. Lily has been working on the playlists."

Then she stops next to me. "Husband." Leaning down, she wraps her hand around my throat, much like I enjoy doing to her, and kisses me as if we're the only two in the room, taking what she wants. Honestly, I couldn't give a shit. If the other people in here weren't my family, I'd throw her down on this table and have my way with her. When she pulls back, her lips flushed and wet, I'm ready to tell everyone to get the fuck out.

"See you in a little while?" she whispers.

I smile up at her. "Yeah, see you in a little while, sugar."

"Whew!" Shaking her head dramatically like she's hot and bothered by our kiss, she wiggles her arms as her dark hair waves behind her. Swaying her ass away, she shoves through the glass doors, starting off down the hall, shouting from just outside, "Missin' you already, baby!"

"You two were giving Faye and me shit about overdone displays of affection, but you both are out of control. You realize that?" Lincoln says with a smirk as he stands.

I can't help but cover my mouth and try my best to hide my laugh.

But it's my baby brother who surprises me when he says, "Nah. Keep it up, Ace. We like to see it."

Laney clasps her hand with his as they move toward the door. "You might not remember this, but it was the first time I'd ever met Hadley. I'm sure people had been seeing it for a while, but the minute you saw her getting out of her car, you smiled, just a pinch. Your whole body language changed. I've been hoping it would happen for the two of you ever since." She smiles at me and says, "I'm so glad it did."

The bottle top makes a popping sound, and I whip my head around to find her pouring a finger into each glass.

"Ace, you're the one who told me great bottles were meant to drink, not sit." She passes me a glass, clinks hers with mine, and sips. "We're doing something incredible, and that deserves a minute and a few fingers of bourbon."

She smiles as I take a sip of the only bottle left from my father's last reserve. The entirety of his barrels had been lost in a fire. They weren't anything special, just a higher proof single barrel. It's the last of him that I have, and I've been afraid to let it go.

"Whoa." She coughs, covering her mouth. "That hugged all the way down. Please tell me it was either expensive or nostalgic." With watery eyes, she rubs at the center of her chest, right where you feel that Kentucky burn.

"One hundred and forty proof, give or take at this point," I say, resigning to having a sip. It's been poured, and I don't need to get worked up about what's already done. "Cheapest bottle we used to sell. But there aren't any more in circulation. It was the last batch of my father's specialty reserve."

She blinks and stays still for a moment, maybe not realizing *exactly* the level of "special" this bottle really carries. But she's right—bottles were made to be enjoyed, not just stored. She has a way of reminding me that life is meant to be enjoyed too, savored and shared. She glances down at the table and then slides her small black notebook across the desk. "Go ahead. You shared with me, so I'd like to share something special with you."

"You don't have to—"

But she cuts me off with a smirk and a raised eyebrow. "I'm very aware of that. But I want to. It's all good things."

I glide my thumb along the worn leather. I've wondered for a long time what she puts in here, and now she's offering it to me like it's the last secret to be out in the open. When I flip the pages, she's written in small letters a variety of details about my brothers and Griz, observations about the horses she's ridden, as well as her own, descriptions of the weather or delicious foods or random things that make her happy. Then there are pages solely about me and how I make her feel, something that has my chest warming. One that stands out is filled with words swirling around my name at the center—*asshole, kind, strong, wickedly smart, stupidly sexy,* and so many more, she had to squeeze her writing onto the page. There are some months that she simplifies into short sentences, and other spots that hold lists of things that I know are her favorites—Luxardo cherries, horses with glitter hooves, song lyrics that I know she's used as advice for Lark and Lily, words of affirmation, and a whole page dedicated purely to insults, including—*swashbuckling cunt bag, twatwaffle, asshat, titty-tally-whacker,* and *dick-cicle.* My smile widens at that, and I realize I've been smiling more with every new section, getting this special glimpse inside her mind.

As I flip through more of the book, there are descriptions of mash bills and whiskeys, and the process of bourbon as a whole, as if she took notes when Lincoln explained it to her.

I glance up at her, surprised to find it.

She's watching me and how I'm taking it all in. Without looking up, I say, "On your left, top drawer." There are lists of what looks like every barrel we've ever made. It's more proof that she's always belonged here—and she made sure of it.

This is her, an entire collection on Hadley Jean Foxx scribbled on pages.

Out of my periphery, I can see her move to the right first, then the left. She drags the drawer open, but she stays quiet. When I look up, she's flipping through a stuffed drawer of just about every flavor of Pop Rocks. "These all for me?"

I move closer and pluck a pack out and tear it open. "Someone told me once that these sweet things make you feel less anxious. Figured it couldn't hurt to stock up." I pour some into my mouth and they instantly start crackling some gross blue-raspberry flavor. She opens her mouth, and I tip some in as she giggles. Pulling her against me, I push the hair from her shoulders, tossing the packet aside and framing her face with my hands. I rub my thumb along her bottom lip as the sound of crackling rocks rings out and makes me smile. "I don't have a book. But I promise to make enough memories—good ones—that'll help you fill even more pages."

She smiles, kissing the pad of my thumb.

"*Une preuve d'amour*," I say, and she hums sweetly in my hold.

Her eyes glisten with emotion, relishing the words Presh said to us on our wedding day. The same ones marked along our skin. They were our truth long before we ever said the words or recited the vows. She is that for me and maybe always has been *proof of love*.

Epilogue

Griz

I never pictured the end of my life. There was never a moment that I didn't spend enjoying the present. I had no interest in thinking about when it might end, only that I hoped it was a long and healthy one. I liked seeing the forest for the trees and all that nonsense, but I always knew that life needed to be lived. There's a difference between settling and being settled. Pockets of feeling like things were locked in place and how they should be, while others felt like cruelty was a path we, as Foxxes, were forced to follow. And then there were moments over the past decade when I would be reading a book in my book club or simply having a spiked coffee on the front porch and it felt like something wasn't right.

I smile at my beautiful wife. Now it feels right. I should've married Shelby long before today, but life had other plans for us. That woman went through hell and back again—saying goodbye to both of her daughters at various points, leaving the only place she ever considered home just to be safe from men who had no business breathin'.

"Griz," she calls out, arms wrapping around Lily and Lark. Her cropped silver hair is beautiful and just as bright as her smile. "Get your ass over here for a picture."

My mustache kicks up, and I can't help but bark out a laugh. If I died tomorrow, I'd die happy. Fulfilled and whole. Sidling up next to my girl, I smile.

"That smile looks awfully handsome on you," she says with a wide, toothy grin.

"Looking at my favorite things," I say, peppering three kisses along her forehead and then across her lips when she tilts her head back. "Love you, darlin'."

She turns around in my arms to look out at the people most important in this world. Her youngest, Maggie, is the only one missing. The Calloway women are, if nothing else, magnets for trouble. But I have my ways of making sure we see her every now and again.

"Love you too," she says on a wistful exhale. "We're so lucky, aren't we?"

We watch as the dogs sit proudly next to my great-granddaughters, waiting for treats for being so well behaved. One of Faye's hands gives them pets while her other rubs along Laney's swollen belly, both of them releasing tear-filled laughs when she feels a kick. It's a beautiful snapshot of how the Foxx name is growing. "Luck feels too easy," I hum. "We can do hard things, us Foxxes. I'd say we worked hard for every moment of it. Never been more proud."

Raising and protecting my family is the most important thing—it always has been. I take a deep breath and let the chill from the autumn afternoon linger inside my lungs for a few seconds longer. There are plenty of memories locked up at the distillery, even dozens more throughout the rickhouses and stables, within the houses I've lived in, and even my souped-up golf cart. But this right here, along the water that's laced with limestone, are the memories I hope I never struggle to remember.

"You taking stock of your crew, old man?" Lincoln says, gripping my shoulder.

"It's a good-looking bunch, I'll tell you that." I try to bite back the emotion.

"A birthday and a wedding. The man turns eighty and gets married," Grant jokes as he steps closer. "Honestly, I'm not surprised, Griz. You've been either falling, talking, or pushing for love our entire lives."

"Where the hell did Hadley and Ace wander off to?" Lincoln asks, looking behind us.

I laugh out, "Careful, don't look too hard. You might not want to see them once you find them."

"Nah, they just went for a ride," Lincoln says as they ride up on their horses. Hadley's dress is on backward, and Ace is wearing a helluva grin.

"They went for a ride alright," I say through a chuckle.

Ace and Hadley make their way to where we're standing, leaning against an old oak tree beside a river we've fished in a hundred times before.

"How are we feeling, Griz?" Ace asks as he comes up next to me, his hand laced with Hadley's. I smile and feel such pride when I see it. It only felt right that she ended up with one of my boys.

"Like a lucky son of a bitch. Just look at this—all of it. Could use a swig of bourbon right about now…"

Hadley cuts in, "Oh! I can do that." She pulls a flask out

from the strap she had belted around her thigh, laughing when she sees my quirked eyebrow. "What? It's a wedding, which means there should always be a flask filled with Foxx bourbon, ready to either celebrate or forget."

"What are we toasting to?" I ask, holding it up as I look at my grandkids' smiling faces. They'll always be the best part of my life.

Lincoln squeezes my shoulder once more, then Ace moves in on the other side. Grant comes around and clasps Hadley's as she holds on to Ace. A shoulder squeeze in the Foxx family is stronger than any hugs or *I love you*s.

I kick back a swig, letting that warm bourbon flavor fill my mouth and coat my throat. I barely feel the burn of it anymore, but my taste buds know a strong one.

It's the one thing nobody ever expected in a small town like ours. We have gossip and curses, lore and loss, but mostly, we have love for each other. The book club ladies are vipers when it comes to rumors. There are plenty of gripes about new businesses and noisy tourists. Marla will never serve out-of-towners anything more than water. Bourbon is as much a vice as it is a medicine. We aren't upstanding or perfect, but it doesn't matter. Fiasco means a woman can feel safe again after a husband raised a hand, cared for when a father chose greed over his daughter, loved when three boys lost their parents. Maybe it was a curse or just a bored asshole spreading bullshit, but the kicker is that it was never dangerous to fall for a Foxx. It's simply proof that, regardless of any secret or lie that might have been tied to a woman, when a Foxx falls, they do it as bold and strong as our bourbon.

THE END

Extended Epilogue

Ace

"He's got it," I say to Lincoln with my attention focused on the unsure seventeen-year-old behind the counter. I know the kid is low-key freaking out since his last shift ended in two customer complaints and Marla having to use the fire extinguisher, but I know he wants this. When he turned sixteen, I told him that if he wanted to drive, he needed to earn the gas money. Hadley rolled her eyes when I said it, and I know she tucks twenties into the visor of the 1971 Mustang she gifted him, but she agreed that outside of school, he needed to stay busy and out of trouble. It was the one thing that he and I seemed to have in common, trouble always found its way into our path.

"Shepard Foxx," Marla glares, shaking her head.

I feel fucking proud when I hear his full name. It took us a long time to get to this point, for him to officially be a part of our family. Shep showed up in Fiasco at fourteen, trying to break into the distillery looking for a place to sleep. There were plenty of reasons for him to run from the life he'd been given, but the second that child and family services got involved, something didn't feel right. If Griz hadn't been around, my brothers and I would have been in the same position. He was built like me, had glasses like Lincoln, and a chip on his shoulder like Grant. I knew in my gut that life was going to be different all over again. He had barely said two words for the first six months he was with us.

"I swear to all things holy in this town, if you spill one more cup of coffee, I will not allow you a single slice of buttermilk pie for an entire year," Marla promises without so much as looking his way. Instead, she glances at me, winks, and bites back a smile.

When his eyes meet mine again I give him the slightest nod hoping that it'll convey all the things I'll tell him later like— *you've got this* and *I'm fucking proud of you*.

"You know Del said it wasn't him that started that fight," Grant says quietly, crossing his arms and leaning back in his chair to my right.

"Oh, I know," I say, rubbing my bottom lip with my thumb. I knew exactly who was starting shit with my kid, just like I was more than happy to hear that it was Shep who ended it.

The front bell rattles against the door, but before it finishes, high-pitched giggles take over along with an echo of chattering teenage girls. My niece, Lily, leading the horde. The group makes their way to the counter and starts quietly chatting as Lily says, "Hey Shep, can we get four dirty Dr. Peppers and fries to go?"

He smiles at my niece, pulling the pen from behind his ear and jotting down the order. I can't hear what he says to her, only that he stops mid-sentence and looks up as my oldest niece, Lark, wanders in moments later. She barely spares a glance as she looks toward the back where we're sitting. "Dad, I can actually feel myself slowly losing brain cells every moment that

I spend having to entertain Lily's idiotic friends." She glances at Grant and then at me. With a genuine smile, she says, "Hey, Uncle Ace."

"Hey, kiddo," I say, giving her waiting fist a bump. When I glance back at the counter, I notice exactly the kind of look Shep is trying to play off when he's watching Lark. It's the same damn one I had every time I looked at Hadley throughout the years. I smile to myself, knowing the level of shit a look like that could stir.

"Uncle Grant, can you come back to the animal shelter this week?" Lark asks. "We've just received two dogs, both just under a year old, that I think would be ideal for training, but could use your thoughts."

Grant rattles off some questions to her that I stop listening to as my phone vibrates on the table.

> **SUGAR**
> How's he doing?

> **ACE**
> He's fine. Stop hovering.

> **SUGAR**
> That's it? Just fine? And you're the one who's there!

> **ACE**
> He's looking at Lark right now in a way that I think might turn into a fucking problem, but he hasn't burned the place down or pissed anyone off yet tonight.

SUGAR
Great. And I noticed that too. Don't tell Linc, just let it play out. Crushes come and go.

ACE
Says the woman who had one helluva crush.

SUGAR
Oh, Daddy...I don't know if you're remembering it accurately. Maybe that old age is finally catching up to you.

ACE
That's three, sugar.

SUGAR
Exactly. Now get your sexy ass home and punish me. I'll be in the stables.

I rub my hand along the back of my neck and bite back the smile my wife so easily gets out of me.

"Alright, I'm going home," I say to my brother. I squeeze Grant's shoulder. "There's a barrel request in from the Tennessee distillery if you're up for it. Julian asked if we'd make an exception."

He nods. "Just let me know how many and I'll get my guys working on it."

Lincoln points at me. "Faye and I have Foxx Den rotation this weekend."

"Talk to Hadley, not me. You know that's her universe," I say back as I grip his shoulder and move towards the door.

"Still waiting on the invitation," Romey from three tables over says as I walk past.

"You know the rules, ladies," I say with a charming smile at both Romey and Prue as they slice into their waffles and throw out a handful of colorful words. I'm less than a few feet from my car when I hear "Ace!" in a familiar deep voice.

I turn to see Shep jogging after me with a takeout bag in his hand. "She told me this morning Marla's savory waffles were proof that goddesses existed." He lets out a clipped laugh, "I figured she was telling me to bring one home for her."

"Good man," I say taking the bag from him. "You up for some fishing tomorrow morning?" I ask giving him a tight-lipped smile. "I hid her hat, don't worry," I say giving his shoulder a squeeze.

He laughs out. "Wouldn't miss it."

"Shep," I call out. "You good?"

He gives me a tight-lipped nod, "Getting there."

It was an honest answer. It was the one thing I asked of him—honesty, no matter what. And when it came time, if he asked me for answers to things, I would do the same. The rest we'd figure out. It wasn't something I ever thought I wanted, to be a father, but Griz said something to me once about Hadley that I could never shake. And for some reason I kept thinking about it the first time I met Shep. *Family isn't complicated. It's choosing to show up for people. That's it. That's the secret. Show the fuck up.*

Hadley

"He keeps calling Grant 'cowboy,'" Laney says laughing. "Grant can't decide if he loves it or hates it." She sips on her coffee as we both watch Sam chase after the dogs. "His four-year-old son says it like his dad is the coolest guy in the world and I say it when I want to go for a ride."

I snort out a laugh. My brother-in-law in all of his grumpy glory has a soft spot for only three things in his life: Laney, Julep, and his son, Sam. "I have a feeling you're going to need a new nickname," I say tipping my head back and letting the morning sun warm my face.

"Alright," Faye shouts as she shuts her car door behind her. With a pair of oversized sunnies and her blonde hair wildly piled in a top knot, I know she must have had a later night than even I did. "I'm here. What are we gossiping about?"

I hold out an iced coffee with a double shot of espresso for her.

She takes a sip and with a satisfied breath says, "Delish." Popping a strawberry from the lavish tray of breakfast treats Laney put out, she says, "Do not ask me about the night I had after my set at Midnight Proof." She raises her glasses and looks at the spread. "Laney, I want to eat every last thing on this platter. What is that, bacon-wrapped dates?"

"With feta, honey, and pistachios," Laney answers.

"I brought the iced coffee," I smile.

Faye plops onto the porch swing, "I brought myself." A bark rings out from the yard, followed by another. "And Kit."

Weekend brunch or even just coffees on rotating porches are something we've made it a point to show for. That's what it's about right? Showing up. And these moments when it's just the three of us, I feel like it's a way to recharge. Sometimes it's gossip and feeding into the stereotype that we've become: small town women with quieter lives and salacious rumors to help circulate.

"Oh!" I say slapping my knee, "The sexy couple from Oregon came back to The Foxx Den this week."

Laney's eyes bulge out. "What is it about those two?! I mean, I'm a very happily married woman, but holy smokeshow."

Over a mouthful of croissant Faye says, "It's the mystery. I mean, they could be boring nine-to-fivers or serial killers. It's the mystery that makes them hot."

"Or it's their banging bodies," I clap back.

"That too," Faye adds.

I watch as Laney glances at Faye before she says, "How's Shep doing lately?"

I smile thinking about a kid that I never planned on. "Started therapy, which I think will help him more than anything, but he's got a short fuse and I can't get too mad at him for standing up for himself…or other people."

The part that everyone wants to talk about is the one where my adopted kid has a rough past and a bad temper, but what most don't know is that he's so much like Ace and his brothers, protecting what he cares about and standing up for what he believes is the right thing. If anyone understands blood relatives that'll fuck you up, it's me. But that's a story for another time. Right now, I want to enjoy my coffee and then walk back to my house for a Saturday morning fuck.

"What I really want to talk about is the music festival you're booking up for the Fall. I need to know exactly who is in that line-up," I say to Laney.

She smiles wide, "It's going to be at least a two-day festival…"

Just over two hours later and enough carbs and caffeine to call it a good morning, I stop and lean against the stable doors. The sounds of Jimi Hendrix riffing on the guitar echoing loudly throughout the space is the soundtrack of this morning's eye-candy. I watch aptly as my husband hoses off his horse with his Foxx Bourbon T-shirt tucked into the back pocket of his wranglers and bare-chested body on display for my personal viewing pleasure.

I tuck two fingers into my mouth and blow out a loud whistle. Both the horse and Ace swing their heads in my direction. He smiles wide, dropping the hose and walking right up to me without a second thought. It's been years together now and this man looks at me like he wants to devour me if I'm up for it. Spoiler: I'm usually up for it.

Without a word, he wraps an arm around my waist, buries his face into my neck, and mumbles, "Morning, sugar."

I smile and breathe him in. This never gets old. The way he stops and shows me that he's happy to see me. Life isn't always easy moments, but being together, in this way, is the payout. "Morning, baby."

"He's fine, before you ask," he says, lifting me up so my feet dangle just above the concrete floor. "There were no burned hands, small breakout fires, or impromptu fighting words at eight-thirty this morning."

I let out a relieved breath. We were late to the parenting train, but I don't think it was supposed to work out any other way. Shep was ours after the first night he stayed here. There was a story behind a kid who would run as far away from the home he'd known as possible. But I felt a connection that couldn't be explained. It was like finding like. Or just a way of history repeating itself—finding solace and safety with a Foxx. While

I love Lark and Lily and Sam as if they are my own, this is different. Being Shep's mom is the one thing I never saw coming, but feels as right as when I fell in love with Ace. We're a family.

He tips his head toward the bench to our right. "He sent me home with Marla's waffle special for you."

"Damn, I love that kid," I say as I loosen my arms from around his neck. I look behind me in the direction Ace starts walking. "Where we going?" I ask playfully, even though I know exactly where he's heading. "I thought we were going to go for a ride."

"Oh you're going for a ride alright," he says dragging his teeth along my shoulder. "And I'm going to do exactly as you've asked, sugar." He hoists me up so I can wrap my legs around his waist. "Careful, I don't want you throwing out your back."

He leans up and swipes his tongue along my lower lip. "You're going to pay for that comment. We have about an hour now until he's home from his shift."

"Should we put your mouth to work then, Daddy?" I ask with a teasing innocence to my voice.

But it's the growl in his throat that turns me instantly into a malleable piece of princess putty in his arms. "Abso-fucking-lutely, sugar," he says as he kicks the door open at the top of the winding stairs. A laughing yelp escapes my throat as he props me up on his work bench. He kicks over a low-sitting, rolling stool that's the perfect height for what he's planning. "I hope you wearing the satin red ones I picked out for you," he says as he tucks his fingers into the waist of my shorts. This man with his fetish for pretty panties likes to pick out a pair for me to wear each day. He left these on top of my dresser, like most days. On the rare occasion I'm pissed off at him, I'll pick out something else and wear it. Oh the little things that can piss this man off. I smile the second he sees a flash of satin red. His eyes lift to mine and I know he's going to use every last second he's got before our kid gets home from his job. I lick along my bottom lip as he drags his finger tips along the sides of my thighs. When he drags them to the sides of each knee he smiles and says, "Now open nice and wide for me, Sugar." His fingers guide my knees open, making space for him. He grips beneath my thighs and slides me closer to the edge when he says, "I'm feeling a little extra hungry right now. Be nice and loud for me."

My chin tilts up just as his tongue finds what it wants. It's the only time, when we're like this together, that he knows I'll do exactly as he says.

Can't get enough of Victoria Wilder? Keep reading for an exclusive sneak peek at her brand new book *Rumors & Whiskey*—available April 2026!

Prologue

It's been one-hundred and twenty-two days since I've heard the sound of my own voice.

"Isn't he clever, Professor?"

I don't answer. Ignore the question. Stifle the fear that unwantedly rises up into the back of my throat, threatening to come out in the form of a plea or scream. Quiet is smart. If I'm anything anymore, it's smart.

"Am I misreading things?"

"Professor?" he chews. He clicks his tongue as his mouth tips up in his version of a smile—a perverse smirk laced with false emotions. "Isn't our new friend the most clever one yet? Aside from you of course."

I don't blink, I maintain a stoic gaze and motionless posture. Feigning disinterest in the disruption will keep him focused on me. I'm not brave or heroic, but I can at the very least make him enjoy it less. The way he entered just now, though, is anything but usual—out of breath and seemingly disheveled. As much as I try to keep my expression impenetrable, he knows that despite my best efforts, I've noticed the large body he's dragged inside, in plain sight and not stowed into his black leather rolling bag.

My mother would be fucking appalled knowing I'm choosing to be silent. But she'll never know. I blink back the blurred tears that unexpectedly swell in my eyes. It happens every time

I think about her. I block out images of Stevie and Jo. If I allow myself to remember the last time we laughed until we cried or yelled until we laughed, I will die. If I soften, even a little, he will know.

He's not looking for me to answer. He slowly sharpens his filleting knife along the roughed leather hung between the shelf and metal table. The room that has been my home, is so small, that despite being in its furthest corner, I can see flecks of dust kick up around him from the spotlight-like desk lamp as he drags the smooth edges back and forth. My chest tightens with every scrape and scratch. It sounds like an old park seesaw—creepy or comforting depending on the memory surrounding it. Much like here.

"Professor," he tuts like I was being an unreasonable or just plain silly. He smiles, his crooked front tooth escaping just enough to show how pleased he is with my predictability. That tooth is one of many imperfections that would otherwise seem mundane on someone's face. A man I would have never looked at twice. Ordinary on the outside in every way. But inside, he is the kind of monster I never prepared to encounter. *"You are my most prized possession—so smart and beautiful. What makes you think I would ever let you go?"* I realized rather quickly that it was what he wanted—to play and taunt as if I were his special brand of entertainment. I never liked entertaining people, that was my sisters' and mother's arena. My highs came from learning and teaching. Researching, testing, and waiting. I took comfort in being the one that people underestimated but who always outperformed.

I swallow the tangy-false sweetness of my spit. It's a reminder that my last sip of water was nearly two and a half days ago. It's been just under three days since I've eaten the food he laces with a form of barbiturate. Lethargic movements in exchange for not dying of hunger. I miss the way it feels to have my belly full and pants tight. *Stop it, Wyn.* I grind my molars, snapping away my nostalgic feelings.

It took seven days into my captivity to realize he liked screaming and begging. His pants bulged when I pleaded for him to let me go. He smiled, petting me like I was his fucking pet. I screamed so hard and so loud it burst a blood vessel in my eye and made my throat burn for nearly a week. That was the last time. Above everything, I'm smart. Smart enough to recognize that my pain was fuel and a turn-on for him.

A shiver rolls up my back and through my body, anchoring my anger. It's the only emotion I allow myself to focus on. Tempers are the unmistakable signature of being a Crowne. The monster was right, I am smart and a realist. I know I'm going to die in here, but I'm not going to make it easy. Or rewarding. When he kills me, I will not give him what he wants.

So, I bit the inside of my cheek as he cut along my skin—in an effort to disperse the pain. I clenched my fists and breathed only through my nose. Screaming and pleading was encouragement. He craved it, so I denied him of it. I thought about the things I could control once I realized I'd lost any sense of what that used to be for me. Being quiet and obedient is my method of maintaining control now. He doesn't restrain me anymore, maybe he knows I've accepted my fate.

Control in chemistry is about creating a baseline for the variable being tested. I am the control now, not the variable. Moments like this, where something ugly and evil is a glance away, I think about my favorite ways to apply what I'd learned. The processes that led me to my academic career. I think about whiskey. The taste of it, yes, but also the process of making it—*the head, the heart, and the tail.* Three components that came off the still, but only one of them worth keeping. *I want to be the part worth keeping.*

"You've wandered into something, friend, that I don't think you quite comprehend," he says to the still breathing body. "But you will." The pitch in his voice is elevated, like he's readying to show off. I hate knowing that this is where I'm going to die and that his voice is the last one that I'll hear.

My eye catches on the blood draining from a discarded limb in the far corner. As usual, nausea rolls through my sweat-slicked body. I never met its owner. Not officially at least. She looked a lot like me. Similar build, the same color hair, cropped short like mine had been when he first took me. I hated that haircut the moment I watched the stylist start drying it.

I cycle through the things that comfort me. The smell of burning oak. The first taste of whiskey when it's ready. The way charcoal smooths out its bite and how barrels can change the chemistry completely, helping it become something new, something better. I mix up the order sometimes, but I think through each process and dissect what could be done to bend "the rules." As soon as my mind drifts to who taught me, I redirect. I can't allow that—it'll have me unraveling. Instead, I shift course. Frozen honeydew melon balls in pink lemonade make me think of summer. Summer rolls into the picking of a banjo. It's a Pavlovian thought that tricks my mouth, making me salivate picturing smoked meats and tangy barbeque. I stifle my instant curiosity of what season it might be right now.

I clear my mind again as he parades a new person into the snug space. It's the second person he's brought here—wherever "here" might be. The first, I thought was only here to scare me. To show me what he planned to do to me next, but it was like he wanted to impress me. I recognized the act of it—the posturing and flaunting. My experience was only with intellectual sophomores with overzealous five year plans in my chemistry lab, or a cocky graduate student who cared more about hearing himself speak than the response he garnered. Someone finding my opinion of them important always felt strange. But this was entirely different—watching the inner workings of a monster unfold and trying to remain unaffected. Other people's opinions of me had always mattered—maybe too much. It's the only part of him that I can relate to—caring how someone else sees your accomplishments or lack thereof. My indifference now, however, is a performance that I'm banking my life on. He won't see approval from me, or disgust. The moment he sees it, he will have won. I won't give him that satisfaction over me. *Ever.*

Regardless of how many ways he enjoys toying with me—the way he cut parts of me and then sometimes ate them, I never got sick over it. I play over and over in my head the one thing my mother always said to me when life got sticky: *"You're a Crowne, Wyn. Start acting like it."*

A sliver of light catches my attention as it bleeds in beneath the pull down metal door. That's new. A foot above it, the lever that locks the door is perpendicular to the floor. It's not locked.

He made a mistake.

His shoes make a scuffing noise—the only warning to look away from his error as he turns toward me. I shift my focus to straight ahead at the same crack along the dark gray cinderblock eye level from where I sit and to the right of the metal door. I can see the pleased-with-himself smile he has plastered on his long thin face as he opens the small rectangular case from his bag. I keep my tongue resting at the roof of my mouth and take measured breaths in and out of my nose. I ignore how he grows more and more amused rubbing his hand along the bulge in his pants just as he turns towards his newest "guest" with a scalpel. "There's something so pretty about decolletage, don't you think, professor?"

I don't answer. I don't look. The last "guest" he brought in here, he had slowly sliced the skin that rested along her collarbone. He said, *"It's just like peeling an apple, professor."* When I didn't answer and tried to keep my eyes from watering, he asked, *"Did none of your students ever bring you an apple?"* As if that was why I had been struggling to keep tears from falling and not the meticulous violence playing out in front of me.

He tsks—like I'd given him a response. "I hadn't planned for it, but when the world decides to deliver," he pauses. "You take."

A grunting sound echoes—deeper in cadence than what I've become accustomed to hearing. It instantly registers that his newest guest is *not* another women.

I glance just as he says, "I have always admired men who grew too quickly. That's all that makes up an Adam's apple—rushing to grow bigger than the body is ready. But it is lovely when it protrudes like this." He smiles at me, knowing that he's got my attention.

I messed up, because I catch him smiling.

I shift forward and look to the sliver of light again. I messed up…but so did he.

The latch isn't pulled closed. The door is not locked. He isn't this careless. His guest hadn't been planned. It was reactionary.

Within the same handful of seconds of realizing this, a loud thump echoes off the wall and the crunch of bone rings out as two bodies hit the floor. The monster and his newest, quite large and very much still alive, guest. Grunts and yells have me breaking awake. My hands shake as I glance at the sliver of light again and then back to the chaos on both men wrestling for purchase on the floor. But it's the gruff voice that cuts through the chaos that knocks the smarts back into me. "Go!" he yells as he pins the monster. I stand, my legs barely holding me upright. Another grunt and the sound of flesh being punctured. I shuffle forward, bend and grip the latch. I pull the door up and bright white light blinds me. I squeeze my eyes just as the deep voice bellows out, "Go! Wyn. Runnnnn!"

Chapter 1

Wyn

Technically, I'm not dead. But it fucking feels like I'm on it's doorstep when my heart stops for what feels like a power ballad after being startled awake by a rapid succession of closed-fist knocks. I suck in a breath, sitting up. My left arm is asleep from the awkward angle it had been draped on the toilet paper holder. My cheek is sore, nearly numb from the cold marble sink it had been resting on.

"Are you alright in there?" a woman's voice calls out followed by another hurried knock on the other side of the door. I stand too quickly shifting in front of the mirror rendering me light-headed as the haziness blacks out the edges of my vision. I squeeze my eyes closed and take in a slow breath. When I exhale, I lean against the sink, elbows locked straight as I stare at my reflection in the mirror.

"Fucking brilliant," I whisper sarcastically, confirming that I look as great as I feel at the moment. Smudged mascara, nothing left of my long-wearing lip stain except a line edging my lips that somehow makes me look more pale than I should for early August, and a nice little same-day hangover headache lingering just behind my right eye-socket. I turn my head and spot a crease along my left cheek. I rub my fingers along the indentation, trying to erase the evidence of my mid-party power nap.

"All good," I sing-song like it's totally normal for a woman in her mid-thirties to get tipsy and then power nap it off in the bathroom. "I'll be right out."

What time is it? I turn over my phone over to check—*fuck me.* I blink hard and focus on the blurry glow of 1:26 a.m.. Below it, a wall of texts in response to my rescue request I sent out nearly two hours earlier.

I turn the faucet on long enough to mimic hand washing, dip my wrists under the cool water and then press my palms against my cheeks. My face is flush and the lingering buzz will give me just enough courage to pretend like this didn't happen.

I glance at my phone, below my request from before I passed out, and scroll through the texts I missed from my sisters.

WYN:
I need a ride.

STEVIE:
I got pulled into covering at the bar tonight.

STEVIE:
Jo, will you go pick her up?

JO:
I am literally next to you watching you text this and there's a crowd stacked 4 rows deep of drunks and

> cranky bikers. Neither of us are going anywhere anytime soon.

STEVIE:
> Text mom.

JO:
> Again, do you need your eyes checked? She's on the shot swing.

I wasn't going to text my mother anyway. The last thing she said to me was that *"I'm boringly predictable."* I told her she was a narcissist to which she replied, *"At least I'm not boring."* I swallow the guilt of hating her again.

STEVIE:
> Sorry Wynnie. Go a little wild, call a ride share.

JO:
> Come to the bar before you go home.

JO:
> A bachelor party just walked in and Stevie has that ready-to-stir-some-shit look in her eye.

I sniff out a laugh. I missed them more than…I look up trying to coax the tears back from falling. I should go to the bar. I didn't like leaving after an argument—life was too short, despite wanting to flip Lu Crowne off regularly. I thought I would never see any of them again, never mind hear them laugh or listen as they continue to make the most ridiculous life choices. And then by some karma-level turn of events, life threw me a curve. Again.

A shiver runs across my skin and settles low. Goosebumps track up my arms, but it's not from nerves or panic. It's the kind that have my cheeks warming and thinking about a different place. An entirely different life. About *him*.

I swipe to the ride share app and find that there isn't a car available for at least 35 minutes. *Superior timing, Wyn.*

"Wyn," a woman's voice calls out from the other side of the door. Tonight's host, my boss and head of the university's chemistry department, knocks again just as I swing open the door. "Are you alright?"

Giving her a smile, I say, "Your wife's spritzers were too good." Smiling and playing off the fact that I just took a two-hour nap in her half bath, I add, "I'm so sorry if I wandered for too long."

She flaps her hand at me like that was a wild thing to say, and then loops her arm with mine, "Not at all. I thought you had left and I missed you."

I didn't think I would return to work. At least not right away. But small counties have an impeccable way of rolling out townie news like thunder from a summer storm. Quiet at first, and then fast, furious, and without invitation. Before I could consider the audacity of declining, I had my position at the University back—tenure isn't taken lightly in academia. So when the department head and tonight's host said, *Wyn we're going to throw a little welcome back party in your honor*, I was appreciative. Now, I can't get out of here fast enough.

I side-eye three of my colleagues playing an intense game

of Catan in the dining room as I extricate myself from any further niceties and drivel about the research I'm supposed to be returning to in the coming weeks.

The moment I step outside, it's like an open-handed slap of skin-slicking humidity. My shirt sticks to my lower back, as if sweat was readying itself to flee from my pores the moment I remembered it was August. I hated it and missed it all at once. I tilt my chin up and close my eyes hoping for a wave of relaxation to wash over me. I should have opted for a maxi dress instead of the typical work attire I'd always worn. I'm not sure what it was about chiffon and tweed that said well-respected chemistry professor, but it worked. I slid into the clothes and persona as if I had never left—like memorable armor, or a mask. Right now, though, I wanted breathable cotton, the less the better.

I work my fingers through the first two buttons of my vest before I hear a deep voice cut in from my right. "Thought you left, Dr. Crowne."

I practically choke, shuffling to my left. "Holy fucking shit," I rush out. My mouth tilts up into a smile as soon as I realize I'm okay and who it is. "Reed," I breathe. "I didn't see you there."

"And I didn't know you had such a colorful vocabulary, Wyn," he says in an amused tone. He glances at the sharp weapon gripped in my hand. Catching me off-guard wasn't safe for anyone.

I glance down at it. A matte black metal cat head with finger-sized eyeholes where my middle and ring finger fit snugly and razor-sharp pointed ears that protrude perfectly to puncture skin with the right amount of force.

I shift my weapon into my back pocket as he passes me my phone that I had fumbled to the ground.

The ride share app displays the abysmal arrival time just as it buzzes and then powers down, turning black and then flashing the dead battery logo. "You've got to be kidding—"

"Come on, I'll give you a ride." He says in that warm country drawl of his, nodding towards the black Porsche Cayenne.

From afar, Dr. Reed Andrews looks like an upgraded version of the man I once knew. Instead of golf polos and baggy cargo pants, now he wears a crisp white oxford button down and well-fitted suit pants. His sandy blonde hair is short and nearly buzzed at the sides, tousled waves are impeccably placed along the top, and his smile is kind above a cleanly shaved jawline.

"That's yours?" I ask, smirking at the car he's moving towards. I always looked at those cars and thought: *Someone's trying a little too hard.*

He smirks and says, "Jealous?"

My brows pinch and I laugh out, "It screams finance-bro or at the very least, 'I won my fantasy football league three years in a row.'"

"Two years," he smiles, knocking on the roof of it. "Want to drive?"

"It's fine," I say, waving off his offer. I wasn't sure how I'd feel seeing him again. Everyone I knew had moved on with their lives.

Four pairs of eyes study me trying their damndest to politely ignore the fact that they had been to a memorial service for me nearly three years ago. And despite being back, I can't help but feel like a fraud. I had my job back—it's a luxury, truthfully, but my desire to dive back into work, the passion I had for it, hasn't followed me home.

"A published article from that long go should not still impact grant distribution…"

I maintain a tight-lipped smile, trying to ignore the audacity of that remark, along with how bored I am. Did I use to enjoy this?

I spent years working, studying, to practically erase any signs of my origins. It's what I had always wanted—difference and distance. But now, it feels more like a punishment than an achievement.

I clear my throat again and call out to him. "I'm living in Rumor now, closer to where my family lives, it's a bit out of your—"

He closes his mouth and smiles slightly. "Wyn, I don't mind," he says, leaning on his open door. "I've got nowhere else to be at this hour. I'm a bit of a night owl anyway these days." He looks at his phone and taps away at the screen.

I need to get out of this heat and my head already hurts from the lack of something greasy. I'll have to let at least one of my sisters know that I got home safely. And maybe Lu is still wrapping up at the bar—she owed me an apology.

I nod making my way down the front stairs and think about how this is the second time tonight he's managed to rescue me.

"Isn't that clever, professor?" my colleague asks.

The smile I've been faking falters. My fingers tingle and a cold chill runs up my spine and down my arms.

Don't pass out.

"Prof-professor?" Another voice says in a stutter and nausea takes shape.

"Dr. Crowne?" my colleague in the center prods. "Are you alright?"

I shift my weight to shove the panic down. My chest burns from holding my breath and the lack of oxygen is making me dizzy.

Breathe. In and out. Say something.

They glance at each other as if I should have something prolific to say in response. It's been more than three years and all it takes is a combination of two words to trigger me. I am stronger than this. The lead scientist of the chemical engineering department adds,

"*The grants you've secured are really quite—*"

"Remarkable," *a deep and familiar voice cuts in.*

I instantly exhale the breath I'd started holding again and smile at him. A friend, and for a brief moment, a something more. Reed flexes his superpower—making everyone feel at ease.

"*She's been back what?*" *he says tilting his head rhetorically asking.* "*Six months? And she's been able to secure funding for the next year.*" *He gives me a wink and a smile.* "*Brava, Dr. Crowne,*" *he says with a teasing smirk.* Flirt. *He was one of the only teaching assistants, better known as TAs, who didn't flounder in his first graduate year. Instead, he could command a packed lecture hall with grad students who were his own age. Just another reason why I wasn't surprised to find that he had been hired as full-time faculty while I'd been gone.*

"Put in the address," he says as I click my seatbelt.

When he glances at the screen he asks, "The Whispering Fool?"

"I need to check in on my mom about something before heading home," I say, watching the campus lights off to the left, once envious of the luxury of being this close to campus. But now I see the appeal of space between work and home life. Maybe I just like the idea of having more of a life outside of work.

I look over at Reed as he focuses on the road. I knew Reed had spent some time with my grandmother after I disappeared. "Birdie said you came around quite a bit after I left." He glances at me and I feel the need to add, "Thank you for that."

He simply nods, nothing more. Maybe an old friend wouldn't be the worst thing to have right now. We had been that to each other some time ago. Reed always had the easygoing, All-American vibe. An athletic, rule-follower was my type. *Your tastes have changed, I think to myself.* I lean my arm against the door, propping my chin on my fist as I look out into the dark as he flips through news talk radio on satellite. All I know is that Reed was the opposite of the type of men I grew up around—rough around the edges, bleeding masculinity as thick as their facial hair, it was a rotating door of plaid or leather. MC's and blue collar boys. It was never steady or sweet. My mother preferred loud—in every way. And I didn't want anything that resembled that.

I try swallowing, my throat feeling suddenly dry, and my face flush as I play with the worn, brown leather cuff on my wrist. A shiver runs along my skin as I recall the scratch of a beard along my neck. Clearing my throat I focus on where I am, and the person I am now.

"Are you still packing lecture halls?" I ask him teasingly.

He smiles, looking ahead. "The novelty of being a young teaching assistant isn't in my favor anymore," he says.

"Wait, stop, that's Stevie's," I say as he scrolls past my sister's widely listened to podcast—The Distilled Truth. I smile to myself, loving hearing her do this and how it was the only touchpoint I had to this place once. I'd been listening to my sister's podcast for longer than she knew.

"Do you plan to use a TA for the Fall semester?" I ask. It was a poor choice of words, considering he had been mine.

If he took it the wrong way, he plays it off quickly with an answer. "My last assistant decided to leave mid-semester, so one from the shared pool will have to do for the Fall," he says.

The drive here hugs the river after a few exits on the highway, and just as the view of it starts to get lost behind trees, the 'Welcome to Rumor' sign flies past. Rumor is only a twenty-minute ride away—a small town that lives up to its name. It's where I grew up, where my family lives, and where I wanted to return to. I spent so much of my life wanting to feel close to my family, but needing distance. Growing up a Crowne was not for the weak or sensitive. My family's business thrived, while our reputations had been dragged through too much mess to ever really come out seeming clean.

I click the button to roll the window down and immediately catch the warm breeze and savory smells of earth and herbs that linger in the air here.

Dry dirt kicks high under crunching gravel, likely dusting his shiny black sports car a matte brown tint as we pull into the oversized parking lot. The neon sign is dark, but still big enough to see. The Whispering Fool is the kind of bar that that encapsulates all the things I don't want for my life—a beacon where most of the nasty rumors about the Crowne women began.. And every woman from my grandmother to my youngest sister fueled those rumors in varying degrees of bold displays of careless and crass behavior. A bar that's as much of a show as the life I'm trying to fit back into again.

Reading Group Guide

1. The Foxx family dinners (and arguments) are always memorable. If you could sit at their table for one night, who would you want next to you—and why?
2. If *Bourbon & Proof* were turned into a film or series, what songs would make the perfect soundtrack for Hadley and Ace's relationship?
3. The book grapples with justice—both through the law and through personal accountability. Do you think justice is truly served by the end? Why or why not?
4. Hadley and Ace's relationship continues to evolve under pressure. How does Wilder portray love not as an escape from pain but a vehicle for healing? Were there moments when you doubted their bond would endure?
5. "Proof" has many meanings—alcohol strength, evidence, and personal conviction. How do different characters seek to prove themselves, and to whom?
6. Several long-held secrets come to light. Which revelation surprised you most, and how did it reshape your understanding of earlier books?
7. Wilder introduces a new layer of generational trauma and resilience. How do characters like Ace reconcile the need to honor family while forging a new path?

8. Throughout the series, bourbon has been both symbol and craft. In *Bourbon & Proof*, how does the process of distillation parallel the characters' search for clarity and truth?
9. How does Kentucky itself evolve across the series? In this novel, does the setting feel more like home, battleground, or mirror?
10. How does Wilder explore spiritual or philosophical ideas of fate in this novel? Do you feel the story leans more toward destiny or choice?
11. Small-town dynamics continue to influence every decision. How do loyalty, gossip, and forgiveness shape the Foxx family's public and private lives?
12. Wilder's women are flawed but formidable. How do female friendships or alliances in *Bourbon & Proof* evolve compared to previous books? Which woman commands the most agency here?
13. Despite the tension, Wilder weaves in humor, warmth, and tenderness. Which lighter moments stood out or provided balance amid the heavier themes?
14. Does the ending feel like true closure, or does it suggest new beginnings? Which threads do you think Wilder intentionally left open?
15. If the trilogy could end on a single toast—words that capture what the Foxx family has endured and become—what would it be?

Acknowledgments

I knew the minute I was ready to type THE END on the first book in this series that it was something special. And there are a lot of incredible people I need to thank for working with me and supporting me throughout the last year of releasing these books.

To my editor, Mackenzie, damn, these Bourbon Boys turned into one hell of an adventure. I am so grateful for your time and creative brainpower. For seeing the big picture and the tiniest of details. And even more so for the time, attention, and care you took when working with me. Thank you for talking me through all the lows and helping to find ways to make some of my crazy ideas work and flow. I am so ready for what's coming next.

To my incredible team member, Amy. The title of PA doesn't even begin to show off the things that you've helped me do in order to bring this series to life. Thank you for all of your time, from brainstorming to beta reading, organizing my business, proofreading, and everything in between. I am so lucky to have you in my corner and on this wild ride with me. Cheers to so much more!

My beta readers are a team of total badasses who each helped to make this story even better. From the broad strokes to the small bits, I am so grateful for your time and attention. Kate, your voice notes and big picture thoughts; Kelsey, your eye for the suspense hooks; Jill (Foxx), for your keen eye for detail and wildly hilarious blips about spice that let me know I'm doing something right; Sierra, your eye for hooks and the heart; Nicole, for reminding me I'm supposed to be writing in present tense (and for the hawk-eye level of detail); and Laura, for seeing the details that matter and for your endless hype.

To Loni, the Whiskey Ginger, I will consider this the most important choice I made in this series: finding a creative partner that not just delivered, but inspired. I will forever be grateful for your friendship, talent, and the wildly incredible way that you brought these characters to life through your art. Thank you for taking the chance.

To Lauren (Lemmy) at Luna Literary, thank you for all of your support. The creative pieces you've made for this series are simply stunning. Thanks to you and your crew at Luna in helping to bring *Bourbon & Proof* to new readers.

A massive thank you to Colby who guides my TikTok adventure (and fixes it when I mess up the algorithm).

To Julia Connors, Ashley James, and Jenn McMahon: Thank you ladies for being such an incredible support crew and cheer squad. Good kinks!

Blair, I have to say it. With a hand enthusiastically raised, "We stole a car!" Thank you for the brainstorms laced with snorting laughs and exaggerated hand gestures. Here's to what's coming next. Thank you for white-knuckling this ride with me!

To my brother-in-law, Ryan, for talking with me about a bourbon podcast which ended up sparking the idea for this entire series.

To a few fabulous women who lent their expertise and insight. To Shelby, for your knowledge and willingness to talk to me about Kentucky and the Kentucky Derby. To Leticia, for your keen eye and excitement in reading this series—thank you so much.

To my ARC Team, you are incredible! Thank you for reading and taking the time to hype this story. Thank you for ignoring the warning to NEVER fall for a Foxx, and instead, being the good girls that you are and intentionally falling HARD for Grant, Lincoln, Ace, AND Griz. I am very lucky to have readers, never mind the kind that want to read what I write early and then hype the hell out of it. Ladies, thank you.

To my mom, I know you will devour this book in one sitting. It makes me insanely happy to be in your reading rotation. I love you. And thank you to my dad who will only crack this book for the dedication and acknowledgments (keep it that way, Charlie). Thank you both for being my biggest fans and the kind of cheerleaders every kid, no matter how old they are, deserves.

To Mr. Wilder, thank you for the big and the little things. You are the best thing.

About the Author

Forever a hopeful romantic, author Victoria Wilder writes contemporary romance with deliciously witty and wild characters. Her stories merge small-town with romantic suspense that feature swoon-worthy men and fierce women who aren't afraid to ask for what they want.

She's an East Coast girl living in southern Connecticut with her husband, two kids, and Yorkie, Linus. She's always chasing the next season and believes in romanticizing whatever you can along the way. You'll always find her either reading, writing, or ready to dish about movies and books.

instagram.com/authorvictoriawilder
tiktok.com/@authorvictoriawilder
facebook.com/victoriawilderauthor
bookbub.com/authors/victoria-wilder
threads.net/@authorvictoriawilder